Available in
from Mills

It had been a very long time since Meredith West had been so intensely aware of a man.

She held no illusions about her desirability as a woman. She'd always been a bodyguard first, a woman second, more in touch with her abilities to exist in a man's world than in her feminine one.

She got up from the table. Now that Chase had done what she'd wanted him to do in looking through the files, she felt the need to escape. The kitchen felt too small, his presence too big.

He rose and moved to stand within inches of her. His clean, masculine scent once again infused her head, making her half-dizzy.

She stared at him, wondering if she'd ever breathe normally again. Meredith had spent most of her life wishing she were a boy – but at this moment she was intensely grateful that she was a woman.

CHRISTMAS CONFESSIONS

If he just did his job right, he'd be home for the holidays.

Jack caught his reflection in the window. His five-o'clock shadow was working overtime. He leaned in closer, inhaling the lemony scent of her hair. He shifted his stance, sliding his grip from the back of her chair to her arm.

Jack hadn't been with a woman in a while, and Abby was wreaking havoc on his senses.

Too much time together in small spaces over long hours could do that to any two people. But Jack was a man of conviction. A man of control. And he wasn't about to let lust get in the way of focus or justice. Not now.

Not ever.

First published in Great Britain 2009
Harlequin Mills & Boon Limited,
Eton House, 18-24 Paradise Road, Richmond, Surrey TW9 1SR

Safety in Numbers © Carla Bracale 2007
Christmas Confessions © Kathleen Long 2008

ISBN: 978 0 263 87338 2

46-1109

Harlequin Mills & Boon policy is to use papers that are natural, renewable and recyclable products and made from wood grown in sustainable forests. The logging and manufacturing processes conform to the legal environmental regulations of the country of origin.

Printed and bound in Spain
by Litografia Rosés S.A., Barcelona

SAFETY IN NUMBERS
BY
CARLA CASSIDY

CHRISTMAS CONFESSIONS
BY
KATHLEEN LONG

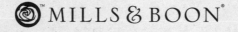

MILLS & BOON

SAFTEY IN NUMBERS

BY
CARLA CASSIDY

Carla Cassidy is an award-winning author who has written over fifty novels. In 1995, she won Best Silhouette Romance and in 1998 she also won a Career Achievement Award for Best Innovative Series, both awarded by *Romantic Times BOOKreviews*.

To Rhonda, my other daughter who drives me crazy!

Prologue

He stood beneath the awning of Marsh's Hardware Store and watched the tall, dark-haired woman as she crossed the street. A rush of adrenaline filled him as he noted the long-legged, loose-hipped walk more appropriate for a runway in Paris than for crossing a dusty street in Cotter Creek, Oklahoma.

She looked more like her mother every day. He closed his eyes for a moment, remembering the beautiful Elizabeth West. She'd been like nothing this little nowhere town had ever seen. She'd bewitched him, haunted his days and nights until he knew if he didn't have her he'd go insane.

Narrowing his gaze he watched Elizabeth's daughter until she disappeared through the café doors. He drew a deep, shallow breath, fighting the surge of adrenaline that coursed through him.

It was as if fate was giving him a second chance. If he could possess Elizabeth's daughter it would be almost like having Elizabeth. The thought sent a shiver of sweet anticipation through him.

Yes, fate was giving him another chance, and this time he wouldn't screw it up. It had ended badly with Elizabeth. He'd lost his temper and she'd wound up dead.

He'd do things differently this time. He'd get her to want him and he'd try, he'd really, really try not to lose his temper.

Chapter 1

She felt it again, that creepy-crawly feeling at the nape of her neck, like somebody was staring at her. Meredith West sat up straighter in the booth and glanced around the café as a chill walked up her spine.

It was the usual lunch crowd, locals seated at booths and tables sharing conversation along with the Sunny Side Up Café fare. Nobody suspicious lurked in the corners to give her the odd feeling.

"What's wrong?" Savannah Clarion asked.

Meredith flushed, feeling ridiculous but unable to dismiss the sense of unease that had struck her at odd times of the day and night for the past couple of weeks. "Nothing," she replied. "I guess I've just been a little on edge lately." There was no way she could explain to anyone the feeling she had of impending doom, of her life exploding out of control.

"Gee, I wonder why?" Savannah smiled wryly, the gesture causing her freckles to dance impishly across her nose. "It wouldn't have anything to do with the fact that we've just uncovered a huge ugly conspiracy right here in Cotter Creek, would it?"

As usual, Savannah didn't wait for a reply, but continued, "Everyone is more than a little on edge lately. I can't wait until those FBI agents wipe these dusty streets with the bad guys' behinds."

Meredith laughed and smiled at the red-haired woman across from her. How nice it was that her brother Joshua had fallen in love with Savannah, who was Meredith's best friend.

The strange sensation that had momentarily gripped Meredith eased somewhat. She picked up a fry and dragged it through a pool of ketchup, then popped it into her mouth and chewed thoughtfully.

Maybe it was all the craziness in the town that had her feeling so off center. It had only been a couple of weeks since Savannah had almost been killed after discovering that somebody was working with a corporation to buy up as much of Cotter Creek, Oklahoma, land as possible.

The MoTwin Corporation had conspired to obtain the land to create a community of luxury condominiums and town houses. With the help of Joshua, Savannah had uncovered a plot that involved the murders of half a dozen local ranchers.

The investigation was being taken out of the hands of local law enforcement and the FBI was now conducting the case.

Meredith frowned. "I can't believe they only sent two agents."

Savannah shrugged. "I don't care how many there are as long as they get the job done."

Meredith smiled. "Have you seen them yet? They're sure not going for subtlety with their suits and ties. They look as much out of place as a palm tree would look growing out of our stables."

Savannah leaned back in the booth and eyed Meredith. "I see you've been cutting your hair again."

Meredith raised a hand to her bangs and touched them self-consciously. "I just did a little trim."

Savannah laughed. "What did you use? A buzz saw?"

"There are times I don't find you half as amusing as you find yourself."

Savannah laughed again, then sobered. "I don't know why you don't take time to go to the Curl Palace and get one of the ladies to give you a real haircut and style."

Meredith stabbed another fry into her ketchup. "And why would I do that? I've got no reason to fancy myself up."

"If you'd fancy yourself up just a little you'd have all the single men in Cotter Creek vying for your attention."

"Half the men in town grew up thinking of me

as a little sister, the other half were scared to death
of my brothers. I don't want their attention. Just
because you're madly in love with Joshua doesn't
mean it's your job to see that I find a man. All I need
right now is work."

"Joshua has been complaining about how slow
things are at Wild West Protective Services right
now," Savannah said.

Meredith nodded. "Things have definitely been
slow. It's been over a month since I've had an assignment."

Wild West Protective Services was the family-
owned business that provided bodyguard and protection services around the country. Meredith
worked for the business along with her five brothers.

"I'm not used to so much downtime. It makes me
nervous," she said.

And maybe that was what was causing her feeling
of unease, she thought. Too much downtime. Or
perhaps her disquiet was because of the dreams she'd
been having lately, dreams of her dead mother.

She glanced around the café once again, then
focused back on Savannah. "I'm thinking about
asking Sheriff Ramsey to reopen the investigation
into my mother's murder," she said.

Savannah stared at her in surprise. "Talk about a
cold case. It's been what...twenty years?"

"Twenty-five. I was three years old when she
was murdered." Meredith shoved her plate aside,
her appetite gone. "I've been having dreams about

her." She frowned thoughtfully. "It's like she can't rest in peace until I find out who killed her."

"After all this time I'd think the odds were pretty poor that you'd discover who was responsible." Savannah eyed her friend worriedly. "You're right, you have too much time on your hands at the moment."

Meredith flashed a quick smile. "Maybe, but I am going to talk about it with Sheriff Ramsey."

Savannah's gaze shot over Meredith's shoulder. "You won't believe the hunk that just walked in the front door."

"Does Joshua know you talk about other men like that?"

Savannah raised a copper-colored eyebrow. "Honey, I love your brother, but I know a hunk when I see one." Her eyes widened. "And this one is coming our way."

The words were barely out of her mouth before he appeared at the side of their booth. In her first glance, Meredith registered several things. He was a tall drink of water, topped by sandy-colored hair, with ice-blue eyes that pierced rather than gazed.

Even though he was blond and blue-eyed there was nothing of a pretty boy about him. His face was lean, all angles that combined to give him a slightly dangerous aura. A faint white scar bisected one of his eyebrows. His presence seemed to fill the room with a pulsating energy.

"Meredith West?"

She jumped in surprise at his deep, smooth voice. "Yes? I'm Meredith."

"My name is Chase McCall. I'm a friend of your brother Dalton. He sent me over here to find you and ask if you'd be kind enough to take my mother and me to the ranch. This is my mother, Kathy."

It was only then that Meredith realized he wasn't alone. Next to him stood a short, white-haired woman with blue eyes and a sweet smile. "Hello, dear. It's a pleasure to meet you," she said. Despite the snowy hair on her head, there was a youthful sparkle in her eyes.

Meredith vaguely remembered Dalton mentioning something about friends coming to town, but at the time he'd mentioned it she hadn't paid much attention.

"And I'm Savannah Clarion," Savannah said. "Is it business or pleasure that brings you to Cotter Creek?"

Meredith wasn't surprised by Savannah's question. As Cotter Creek's star newspaper reporter, she had a healthy curiosity about everyone.

"Strictly pleasure," Kathy McCall replied, her eyes twinkling with good humor. "We decided to take a little trip together, you know mother/son bonding time, and Chase had heard so many things from Dalton about the charming Cotter Creek. So, here we are."

A flash of impatience shot across Chase's features. "We've had a long bus ride to get here and we'd really like to get settled in."

"You came by bus?" Meredith looked at him in surprise. Neither of them had any luggage.

"Somebody thought it would be a great idea," he said tersely.

Kathy's smile made her look like a good-humored cherub. "It was lovely to see the scenery without worrying about Chase getting a speeding ticket or two."

"Where's your luggage?" Meredith asked. She'd been in the bodyguard business too long to simply trust the word of two strangers who had appeared at her booth in the local café.

"We left it over at the office with Dalton," Chase replied.

Meredith stood and grabbed her coat and purse from the booth. As she did she couldn't help but notice that Chase's gaze swept the length of her, then he glanced away, as if dismissing her as not worthy of his attention.

She'd known the man less than three minutes and already something about him made her want to grind her teeth. She fumbled with her wallet for money to pay her lunch tab.

"Don't worry about it," Savannah said. "I'll get it this time. You can get it next time."

Meredith flashed her friend a grateful smile, then straightened and looked at Chase.

"Shall we?"

As she exited the café she was acutely conscious of the man following her. Handsome men weren't anything new to Meredith. She'd been raised with five brothers who most women considered unusually attractive. But in that first instance of laying eyes on Chase McCall, uncharacteristic butterflies had flitted erratically in her stomach. Meredith wasn't used to butterflies.

Kathy fell into step beside her as they walked toward the Wild West Protective Services office just down the street. "We thought we'd be staying with Dalton, but he said we'd be much more comfortable at the ranch," she said.

Meredith thought of her brother's one-bedroom apartment in town. "Dalton's place is pretty small and not real welcoming to guests. The ranch is much better," she agreed, although she wasn't at all sure she liked the idea of sharing her home space with the tall, silent man who walked just behind them. "We're used to company at the ranch."

As they entered the Wild West Protective Services office, Dalton stood from the desk. "Ah good, I see you found her," he said to Chase.

"Your description made it easy," Chase replied, a whisper of amusement evident in his voice.

Meredith turned to look at her brother. "And just what kind of description did you tell him?"

Dalton's cheeks reddened slightly as a sheepish grin stole over his lips. "It doesn't matter now," Chase replied smoothly. "We found you and that's all that's important." He picked up the two suitcases by the door and looked at her expectantly. For somebody who was on vacation he didn't look particularly eager to have a good time.

"Unfortunately I'm expecting a phone call that I need to take, otherwise I'd drive you to the ranch myself. But Meredith will get you settled in, then I'll see you this evening at dinnertime." Dalton smiled at her. "Take good care of them, sis."

She smiled at Dalton, but as her gaze fell on Chase McCall, the strange feeling of disquiet swept through her once again, making her uncomfortable and, oddly, just a little bit afraid.

Chase McCall sat in the back seat of the four-door sedan, leaving the two women in the front to chat. As Meredith drove she talked to Kathy about the town and the unusual cold snap of weather and the family ranch.

"You're here just in time for the Fall Festival," she said. "There's a parade on Saturday afternoon, then a big dance Saturday night."

He stared out the window at the passing scenery, wishing he were anywhere else. He couldn't think of anyone who needed a vacation more than he did, but this wasn't a vacation and he was here under false pretenses.

He glanced up and in the rearview mirror he caught Meredith West gazing at him. As he met her gaze, she quickly looked away and he looked back out the side window.

She'd been a surprise. Dalton had talked a little about his sister. In the days that Dalton and Chase had spent together, Dalton had talked about all of his family. He'd told Chase that his sister was tough, committed to her work as a bodyguard and preferred the company of her horse to most people.

But there was a wealth of things he hadn't mentioned about Meredith. Dalton hadn't told him she had eyes the color of an early-summer lawn or that her legs were long and lean beneath her tight jeans. He hadn't mentioned that her hair was dark mahogany or that her skin was flawless.

In that first moment of seeing her, a quick electric shock had sizzled through him; a shock of physical attraction he hadn't felt for a very long time.

It reminded him just how long it had been since he'd held a woman in his arms, felt sweet satisfied sighs against the crook of his neck.

He suddenly realized the women had gone silent and Kathy had turned her head to look at him expectantly. "Did I miss something?" he asked.

Kathy looked at Meredith and smiled. "You'll have to excuse my son. He sometimes forgets his social skills. Meredith asked you what you did for a living, dear."

Again those green eyes flashed in the mirror. Not warm and welcoming, but rather cool and wary. "I'm a Kansas City cop." It was the first of many lies he'd probably tell over the next couple of days.

"And is that where you met my brother? In Kansas City?" she asked. The eyes disappeared from the mirror once again.

"Yeah, he was working the Milton case last year

and we coordinated with him. Dalton and I struck up a friendship. We've stayed in touch through e-mail since then."

"When Chase decided to take his vacation time and mentioned he was coming out here, I just insisted he bring me along," Kathy said. "He stays so busy we rarely have quality time together."

"Our place is just ahead," Meredith said as she turned off the road and down a lane. Chase once again looked out the window with interest. He knew the West family was one of the largest landowners in the county.

He'd researched their entire clan before taking the assignment. Red West, the patriarch, had come from California to Cotter Creek as a young man and had begun his business, Wild West Protective Services. The business had grown along with his family.

He and his wife had six children before Elizabeth West was murdered. Since her death, Red had worked to establish Wild West Protective Services as one of the most reputable bodyguard agencies in the country.

On the surface the family looked for the most part like the American dream. But a couple of anonymous tips phoned into the FBI office said otherwise. His job was to dig beneath the surface and find any darkness that might be hidden, a darkness that might have led somebody in the West family to sell out an entire town.

"Here we are," Meredith said as she pulled to a

halt in front of a large, sprawling ranch house. It was impressive, the big house with its wraparound porch. As far as the eye could see were outbuildings and pastureland.

As they got out of the car and Chase got the suitcases out of the trunk, a tall man appeared on the front porch, a smile of welcome on his face. By the time they reached the porch another man had joined him. The short, gray-haired man had blue eyes that held a touch of wariness. "Welcome," the tall man said and held out a hand to Chase. "I'm Red West."

Introductions were made all the way around. The short older man was introduced as Smokey Johnson, head cook and bottle washer for the clan.

As Chase followed him through the front door, he had a feeling that Smokey Johnson was a man who might not be easily fooled. He and Kathy would have to be careful around the old man. But Chase didn't expect any of the West family to be fooled easily.

"Oh my, this is just lovely," Kathy exclaimed as they entered the living room. "I hope we aren't putting you out."

"Nonsense, nothing we like better than company," Red assured her. "Meredith, why don't we get them settled in their rooms, then we'll have Smokey rustle up some refreshments. It's a long bus ride from Kansas City to here."

"That sounds wonderful," Kathy said.

"We'll put Kathy in the guest room and Chase can go into Tanner's old room," Red said.

For the first time since they'd stepped into the house, Chase focused on Meredith. She had the face of a beauty queen, but if her hair were any indication of the local stylist's expertise then he wouldn't be visiting any of the town's barbers. Although a luxurious black, her bangs fell unevenly across her forehead and the left side of the shoulder-length locks was definitely shorter than the right side.

There wasn't an ounce of makeup on her face, that he could see, and she was dressed in a pair of jeans and an oversize man's flannel shirt. Once again a small ball of unexpected tension twisted in his gut.

Her gaze met his and her cheeks pinkened slightly. "If you'll follow me, I'll show you to your rooms," she said.

She led Kathy to a room decorated in cheerful yellow with an adjoining bath. Chase set Kathy's suitcase on the bed, then followed Meredith down the hall. Even though the flannel shirt struck her below the hips, it didn't hide the sensual sway of her walk.

The bedroom she led him to was smaller than Kathy's and had obviously been occupied by a male. The bed was a heavy mahogany covered in a navy spread. A chest of drawers stood against one wall. "Tanner? Which one is that?" he asked as he set his suitcase down.

"Tanner is my oldest brother," she said.

"The one who married a princess."

"That's right. Anna." Her chin rose a touch and she met his gaze. "Tell me, what description did my brother give of me that made me so easy to find in the café?"

"He said to look for the gorgeous, sexy woman who looked like she'd had a close encounter with a Weed Eater." He gazed pointedly at her uneven hair.

She raised a hand self-consciously, but before she touched her hair, she dropped her arm and narrowed her eyes, obviously not pleased as she edged toward the door.

"The bathroom is just down the hall on the left. Feel free to head to the kitchen after you get settled in." She slid out of the room as if she couldn't escape him fast enough.

He pulled his suitcase onto the bed and opened it. He'd improvised a bit on what Dalton had said. Dalton had called his sister neither gorgeous nor sexy.

As he hung some of his clothing in the closet, he wondered how difficult it had been for Meredith West to be raised in a house filled with men. By the look of her she certainly didn't seem to be in touch with her femininity. Not that it mattered to him. Not that he cared.

He wasn't here to care about anyone. He was here to do a job. It was bad enough he was here to betray a friend's trust; the only thing that could make it worse was if he also seduced his friend's sister.

Chapter 2

There was no way Dalton would have described her as gorgeous or sexy, although he certainly would have told Chase she looked like a woman who'd gotten too close to a Weed Eater.

Meredith thought about that all through dinner that night. Dalton had arrived at the ranch to share the meal and visit with his friends. Meredith had eaten quickly, then excused herself and retreated to the stables until bedtime.

Now, the faint gray of predawn painted the sky as she crept from her bedroom and down the hallway to the bathroom. As she showered and dressed for the day, her thoughts lingered on Chase McCall.

Gorgeous and sexy. He had to say that. Had he

been making fun of her? Nobody had ever used those terms to describe her.

She didn't like him and she wasn't sure why. He'd been pleasant enough at dinner the night before, entertaining them with cop stories and talking about the good times he and Dalton had shared while they'd worked on the same case.

But there was an edge to him, a whisper of something slightly dangerous in his eyes, an arrogant tilt to his head. She stood in front of the mirror and brushed her shoulder-length hair, then frowned.

Maybe Savannah was right. She needed to get into the Curl Palace and get one of the ladies to trim her hair the right way.

Fighting her impulse to pick up a pair of scissors and try to straighten out the mess, she reached for her toothbrush instead. She always cut her hair when she was stressed, and there was no denying that she'd been stressed lately.

She'd go to the Curl Palace this morning, then head over to Sheriff Ramsey's office to see if she could get her hands on the files of the investigation into her mother's murder.

She had a feeling Ramsey wouldn't be particularly pleased by her request. "As if we don't have enough going on around here," she could imagine him saying.

She finished brushing her teeth, then gave her hair a final finger comb. Her decision to get her hair professionally cut and styled had absolutely nothing to do with Chase McCall, she told herself. She would have done it whether the handsome man had come to town or not.

Leaving the bathroom, she was glad that Tanner's bedroom door remained closed. It was early enough that she didn't expect anyone to be up except Smokey, who would be in the kitchen working on breakfast.

Instead of heading into the kitchen, she walked to the front door and slipped outside to the porch. She moved directly to the railing and leaned against it, staring out at the land that stretched for miles all around.

This was her favorite time of day, when the sun was just starting to peek over the horizon and birds sang from the trees. Scents of hay and grass and cattle wafted on the air, as familiar to her as her own reflection in a mirror.

She loved the ranch, but there were times when she longed for the excitement of the city, the anonymity of a place where she wasn't one of those West kids, but rather simply Meredith West.

She drew deep breaths, filling herself up with the smells of home, then turned to go back inside. She jumped, startled as she saw the old man seated in the wicker rocking chair.

"Smokey! Jeez, you scared me half to death. What are you doing out here?" Even in the dim light she could see the frown that tugged his grizzled eyebrows together in an uneven unibrow.

"That woman is in my kitchen."

"Kathy? What's she doing?"

"Cooking." The word spat from him as if he found it distasteful on his tongue.

A small burst of laughter welled up inside Meredith, but she quickly swallowed it. As far as Smokey was concerned invasion of his kitchen was grounds for execution. "Think I'll go get a cup of coffee and check things out," she said.

Smokey merely grunted in response.

Meredith found the attractive white-haired woman in the kitchen cutting up fruit. "Ah, another early riser," she said in greeting to Meredith.

"You're supposed to be on vacation," Meredith said as she poured herself a cup of coffee, then perched at the island where Kathy worked.

"There's nothing I love more than cooking, especially for other people, but I rarely get a chance." She smiled at Meredith. "I told Smokey that I'd take over this morning and give him a little vacation. Besides, I'm not sure he was feeling well this morning. He looked positively gray when he left the kitchen."

"He's just not used to somebody else taking over his duties," Meredith replied.

Kathy smiled once again, a hint of steel in her baby blues. "Well, he'll just have to get used to it. I intend to pull my own weight around here and at my age about the only thing I am good for is cooking."

It was going to be an interesting couple of days, Meredith mused. At that moment Chase entered the kitchen clad in a pair of jeans and a navy knit shirt that clung to his broad shoulders and flat stomach. The sight of him filled her with an inexplicable tension.

"Good morning," he said as he walked to the countertop where the coffeemaker sat.

"'Morning," Meredith replied. "I hope you slept well."

"I always do." He carried his cup and sat on the stool next to Meredith, bringing with him the faint scent of shaving cream, minty soap and a woodsy cologne. The tension inside her coiled a little tighter. "What about you? How did you sleep?"

It was a simple question, but something about the look in his eyes made her feel like he was prying into intimate territory. "I always sleep well, too," she replied.

He took a sip of his coffee, then looked at her curiously. "Dalton mentioned last night that we've come to town at a time when things are pretty unsettled," he said.

"Very unsettled," she agreed, relaxing a bit as the subject changed.

"Tell me about it."

"It's complicated, but a couple of weeks ago we discovered that a corporation called MoTwin has been buying up property in the area."

"That doesn't sound unusual. Corporations seem to be buying up property everywhere in the United States," Kathy observed.

"Yes, but in this case, the land they were buying

was from ranchers who had died, ranchers who had been murdered."

"Oh, my," Kathy exclaimed, then picked up her knife to continue cutting up a kiwi.

"The deaths were made to look like accidents, so it took a while for anyone to realize what was going on," Meredith continued. "The latest death was a real estate agent who had written up the property contracts on the land in question. She was murdered. A couple of FBI agents are here now working the case. We know somebody in town has to be behind the scheme, somebody local has orchestrated the deaths and that's who we want."

"This MoTwin, what do you know about it?" Chase asked.

"Not much." Meredith took a sip of her coffee, then continued, "The address on all the paperwork is nothing more than an empty storefront location in Boston. Two men are listed as partners, Joe Black and Harold Willington, but as far as I know nobody has been able to find them or dig up any information on them. We know that the land was apparently being bought up for a community of luxury condos and town houses."

She took another sip of her coffee and fought off a chill at the thought that it could be a friend or a neighbor who was responsible for the deaths in the area.

"Hopefully the FBI will find out who here in town is responsible and they'll lock them up and throw away the key," she exclaimed. "In any case, it shouldn't interfere with your visit here. By the way, how long are you intending on staying?"

Chase's gaze was lazy and his blue eyes sparked with humor. "Trying to get rid of us already?"

"Of course not," she replied hurriedly. "I was just curious." Curious as to how long she'd have to put up with the strange feeling he evoked inside her.

"We aren't sure," Chase replied. "I have quite a bit of vacation time built up so we're kind of open-ended at the moment."

Kathy glanced at the clock on the wall. "I'd better get back to work if I'm going to have breakfast ready at a reasonable time. Why don't you two shoo and let me do my thing."

Meredith drained her coffee cup, placed it in the dishwasher, then started out of the kitchen. "Where are you headed?" Chase asked.

"To the stables," she replied. "I usually go out there every morning and most evenings to say hello to the horses."

"Mind if I tag along?"

Yes, I do. You make me nervous and I don't know why. She didn't say that, but instead shook her head. She grabbed a jacket from a hook next to the back door, and once she stepped off the porch, Chase fell in beside her.

"Dalton told me you're quite a horseback rider," he said as they crossed the thick, browning lawn toward the stables.

At five-ten there were few men who dwarfed Meredith, but Chase did. He made her feel small and oddly vulnerable. "Do you ride?" she asked.

"Motorcycles, not horses."

"Then you don't know what you're missing," she replied, her steps long and brisk. They walked for a few minutes in silence.

"Quite a spread you have here," he said. "Did this MoTwin Corporation contact you all about selling out? You said the deaths that occurred were made to look like accidents. Anything odd happen to your father?"

She stopped in her tracks and turned to face him with narrowed eyes. "For somebody just visiting the area you have a lot of questions."

"I'm a cop. Curiosity comes natural to me."

She gazed at him for a long moment, taking in the handsome chiseled features, the spark of the early-morning sun on his hair and the guileless blue of his eyes. "Then to answer your question, no. Nobody has contacted my father about selling because they probably know that won't ever happen. And no, nothing strange or suspicious has happened to my father.

"One thing all those dead ranchers had in common was either no children or family to take over their ranches, or kin that weren't interested in ranching. My father has five sons and me. Killing him wouldn't get anyone any closer to owning this place."

He frowned thoughtfully. "But, I would think if

this corporation planned a community of condos and town houses, they'd want this land." He cast a gaze around. "It looks pretty prime to me."

"I don't know what the intentions of MoTwin were where our land was concerned. I can't begin to guess what was in those men's heads."

They reached the stables and walked inside, where the horses in the various stalls greeted their presence with snickers and soft whinnies.

As she walked toward where her horse, Spooky, was stalled, she paused at each of the other stalls to pet a nose or scratch an ear. She tried to ignore Chase's nearness, but it was darned near impossible.

The man seemed to fill the stable interior with an unsettling presence that even the horses felt. They sidestepped and pawed the ground with an unusual restlessness, as if catching the scent of a predator in the air.

"Tell me about your other brothers," he said as she greeted her black mare with a soft whisper. "Your father mentioned they'd all be here for dinner tonight. I'd like to know a little about them before then. Dalton has mentioned them in the past, but never went into specific details."

"Tanner's the oldest. He's thirty-five and as you know married to Anna. Zack is thirty-one and married to Kate. He's running for Sheriff. Clay is thirty and just married Libby, who also has a little girl named Gracie. Then there's Joshua. He's the baby at twenty-five and he's dating my best friend, Savannah. You met her yesterday at the café."

He nodded, his eyes dark and enigmatic. "Do you all still work for the family business?"

"We did, but things are changing. Tanner was actively running things before he met and married Anna. They're now building a house and he's involved in that and not working so much right now. As I mentioned, Zack wants to be sheriff and it looks like he's going to get his wish. The man who's working as sheriff right now has plans to retire."

She scratched Spooky behind the ears, finding it much easier to focus on the horse's loving, brown eyes than Chase's cold blue ones.

"Joshua still works for the business and so do I, but for the last couple of months things have been rather slow." She gave the horse a final pat on the neck. "We should probably head back to the house for breakfast."

"So, what do you do in your spare time?" he asked as they made their way to the house.

"I occasionally do some volunteer work, but most of the time I keep busy around here. Running a ranch the size of ours requires lots of work."

"Dalton mentioned to me last night that you don't date. Why not?"

She stopped walking and held his gaze. "First of all, my brothers don't know everything that goes on in my life. Just because they don't know what I'm doing doesn't mean I'm not doing it. And secondly, it's really none of your business."

She didn't wait for his reply, but instead hurried toward the house, needing some space from the man, his endless questions and the hot lick of desire just looking at him stirred inside her.

It was just after ten when Chase sat in the passenger seat of Meredith's car. She'd mentioned at breakfast that she was heading into town to run some errands and he'd asked if he could hitch a ride with her. He could tell the idea didn't thrill her, but she was too polite to tell him no.

He'd told her that while she ran her errands or whatever, he'd hang out at the Wild West Protective Services office with Dalton.

He'd known most of the information she'd told him in the stables before he'd even asked the questions, but he'd hoped she'd give him something that would either exonerate or condemn somebody guilty.

The Wests might never have made the FBI radar if it hadn't been for a couple of anonymous tips that had come in pointing a finger at the family. He had no idea if the tips were valid or not. It was his and Kathy's assignment to find out.

"You asked me about my family earlier," she said, breaking the uncomfortable silence that had existed between them since they'd gotten into the car. "Tell me about yours."

As always, when Chase thought of what little family he'd had, a knot of tension twisted in his chest.

He reached up and touched the slightly raised scar that slashed through his eyebrow, then dropped his hand.

"There's not much to tell. It's just my mother and me. My father died a couple of years ago. He was a miserable man who gambled away his money, then drank and got mean."

It was a partial truth. His mother had died when he was five and his violent, drunken father had raised him until Chase turned sixteen and left home. Whenever Chase thought of his family he got a sick feeling in the pit of his stomach. God save him from people who professed to love him.

"I'm sorry," she said. "But your mother seems very nice."

He grinned. "Kat…Mom is a jewel. She left my father when I was ten and we have a great relationship." This was the cover story they'd concocted, a blend of half lies and half truths. Kathy was a jewel, not as a mother but as a partner.

"She stepped into dangerous territory this morning."

Chase looked at her curiously. "What do you mean?"

"She took over Smokey's kitchen."

"That's bad?"

She smiled and in the genuine warmth of the gesture she was so stunning that the blood in Chase's veins heated. "That's grounds for a firing squad. Smokey has always been fiercely territorial about his kitchen."

"What's his story? He's not part of the family, right?" Although Chase had no idea what financial benefit Smokey Johnson might get from conspiring with MoTwin, he knew that not all motives revolved around money.

"He's family. He might as well have been born a West," Meredith replied. "He worked as the ranch manager for years, then took a nasty spill from a horse and crushed his leg. He was still healing from that when my mother was murdered."

"That must have been tough on everyone." He watched the play of emotions that crossed her features, a flash of pain, a twist of anger, then finally the smooth transition into a weary acceptance. She'd be an easy mark at cards. She didn't have much of a poker face.

"From what I understand, my father was devastated. He and my mother had one of those loves that you only read about in novels. They were best friends and soul mates and Dad crawled deep into his grief. Smokey stepped in to help with all of us kids and he never left. He's a combination of a drill sergeant and a beloved uncle."

She pulled into a parking space in front of the Wild West Protective Services office. She shut off the car engine and unbuckled her seat belt. "Why don't I meet you back here around noon and we'll head back to the ranch."

"Why don't we meet back here at noon and I'll buy us lunch at the café?"

She looked at him in surprise. "Why would you want to do that?"

"Why wouldn't I?" he countered. "It's not every day I get the opportunity to buy lunch for a pretty lady." He watched her, fascinated by the pink blush that swept into her cheeks.

"I guess it would be all right to have lunch before we head back," she replied.

They got out of her car and she murmured goodbye, then headed across the street. "What are you doing, Chase," he muttered to himself as he watched her walk away.

Once again, she was dressed in an old flannel shirt and a pair of worn jeans. She intrigued him. She acted and dressed like a woman who didn't much care about a man's attention, and yet the blush that had colored her cheeks had spoken otherwise.

She was unlike any woman he'd ever been around before. Most of the women he dated were girly girls, high-maintenance savvy singles who cared even less about a committed relationship than he did. Meredith West blushed like a woman who wasn't accustomed to compliments or attention.

He watched until she disappeared into a store-front, then he turned and went into the Wild West Protective Services office.

"I don't care how difficult the client is," Dalton said into the phone receiver as he raised a hand in greeting to Chase. "You do what you have to do to make this right. You know how to do your job, just do it and try not to make people angry." He hung up the phone with a groan. "I think sometimes it's easier to have a boss than to be one."

Chase sat in one of the chairs in front of the desk and grinned at his friend. "As one who has a boss instead of being one, I'd argue the fact with you."

Dalton laughed and leaned forward in his chair. "How about one night you and I make plans to shoot some pool and drink a few beers?"

"Sounds good to me," Chase agreed. Maybe knocking back a few brews would get thoughts of Meredith West out of his head.

The two men visited for a few minutes, then Dalton got another phone call and Chase left the office to wander the sidewalks and see what kind of vibes he picked up.

Being around Dalton was almost as difficult as being with Meredith. The deception of his friend didn't sit well. But Chase had a job to do and work had always been the one thing he could depend on, the only thing he clung to.

Cotter Creek was a pleasant little town with side-walks and shade trees running the length of Main Street. Benches every twenty feet or so welcomed people to sit a spell.

An old man sat on the bench outside the barber-shop, his weatherworn face showing no emotion as Chase sat on the opposite end of the bench.

"Nice day," Chase said.

"Seen better," the old man replied.

"My name's Chase, I'm here in town visiting the West family."

"Too many strangers popping up here in Cotter Creek for my comfort and I'm Sam Rhenquist."

Chase leaned back against the bench. "Nice town."

"Used to be. Lately everybody's been looking cross-eyed at each other, wondering who might be guilty of some things that have happened around here." Rhenquist eyed him with a touch of suspicion and clamped his mouth closed, as if irritated that he'd said too much.

For the next few minutes Chase tried some small talk, but the old man was having nothing to do with it. Finally Chase rose, said goodbye and headed down the sidewalk with no particular destination in mind.

He knew the best place to pick up information would be the café or wherever Dalton intended to take him for the night of beer and pool. People talked when they ate, and people really talked when they drank. No telling what little tidbit he'd be able to pick up that might help the investigation.

Eventually he wanted to touch base with Bill Wallace and Roger Tompkins, the two agents who were actively working the case here in town. He wanted to know who they had in their radar and what they might have discovered in the brief time they'd been in town.

It didn't take him long to walk the length of the businesses on Main Street, then he crossed the street and headed back the way he'd come on the opposite side of the street. As he walked, his mind whirled.

He'd already learned two important things since arriving in town. The first was that Meredith West was sharp and he'd have to be more subtle with his questions than he'd been when they'd gone to the stables that morning.

The second was that for some crazy reason he was intensely attracted to the tall, dark-haired woman. If he allowed that attraction to get out of hand, he'd risk complicating his job here.

He'd share a simple lunch with her, then head out to the ranch and hope that Kathy had managed to glean some sort of helpful information about the rest of the West family.

He made it back to Meredith's car and leaned against the driver's side to wait for Meredith to return from whatever she was doing. It was damned inconvenient not to have a car at his disposal.

It had been Kathy's idea to ride the bus into town. She'd thought being at the mercy of the West family for transportation would afford them more time to chat with the various members of the clan.

He should have put his foot down and told her it was a dumb idea, but he found it difficult to argue with Kathy about anything. Those twinkling blue eyes and sweet smile of hers hid a stubborn streak that always surprised him.

He straightened as he saw Meredith in the distance coming toward him. As she drew closer, he realized she looked different…softer…more feminine. It took him a minute to realize it was her hair.

Where before it had hung without rhyme, without reason in various lengths, it now feathered around her face, emphasizing the classic beauty of her features. She carried with her a large file folder bound with several rubber bands.

"Wow," he said when she was close enough to hear him.

Her cheeks reddened slightly and she reached up to self-consciously touch a strand of her hair. "It's just a haircut," she said with a touch of belligerence.

"No, it's more than that. It's a total transformation," he replied.

"It's not a big deal," she replied, obviously not wanting him to make it a big deal. "You ready for lunch?"

He nodded. "What have you got there?"

"Just some paperwork I want to read." She opened the car door, set the papers on the seat, then locked the doors and gestured toward the café. "Shall we?"

The Sunny Side Up Café was in full swing serving a surprisingly large lunch crowd. They found an empty booth toward the back and settled in, but not before Meredith was greeted by half a dozen people.

She'd been attractive before, but with the new hairstyle Chase was having trouble keeping his gaze from her. "Is the food good here?" he asked as he opened a menu and forced himself to look at it. But it couldn't hold his attention the way she did.

"Excellent," she replied. She looked ill at ease, her gaze darting around the room then back at her menu.

"Is everything all right?"

Her bright green eyes met his gaze in surprise. "Yes, everything is fine." Once again she made a quick sweep of the room with her gaze.

"So, tell me about your work," Chase said after the waitress had departed with their orders. "It must be fascinating to be a bodyguard."

"It has its moments," she replied, then frowned. "Although lately there haven't been as many moments as I'd like."

"What do you mean?"

She picked up her napkin and placed it in her lap. "Business has been slow. None of us are working as much as we like."

The conversation halted momentarily as the waitress appeared to serve their drinks. "You mentioned that before. What's made things slow down?" Chase asked when they were once again alone.

"Who knows? I've talked about it some with Tanner, my oldest brother, and even he isn't sure what's caused the slow down. I guess people not needing bodyguard services doesn't necessarily translate to lower crime rates in the city. You must stay very busy."

Chase grinned ruefully. "Definitely. In the war on crime, the bad guys still seem to have the upper hand."

Her gaze held his for a long moment. "Speaking of crime, did Dalton tell you that our mother was murdered years ago?"

She had the kind of eyes that could swallow a man whole and make him forget his surroundings. At the moment they radiated a soft vulnerability, a wistful need he immediately wanted to fulfill, no matter what it entailed.

It was he who broke the eye contact, disconcerted by his own reaction. "Yeah, Dalton told me about it."

"Those papers I left in the car are copies of the reports concerning her murder. It was never solved and lately I've been thinking about it, about her a lot."

There was an unspoken question in her gaze as he looked at her once again. "I thought maybe by looking at the files I might see something that was missed in the initial investigation. I'm not telling my father or my brothers that I'm looking into Mom's death. I don't want to upset anyone." She paused a moment, then continued, "How long have you been a homicide cop?"

He suddenly knew what she wanted from him. "You want me to take a look at those files?"

She flashed him a grateful smile. "Would you mind? Maybe you'll see something important, something that I'm not trained to look for."

"Sure, I don't mind." He'd take a look at the files. It was the least he could do.

A few minutes later, the waitress delivered their food and Chase's mind worked to process his thoughts and impressions. And the one thing that kept coming back into his mind was the fact that business was slow at Wild West Protective Services.

Somebody in Cotter Creek had worked with the men at MoTwin to identify the weak in town, the ranchers without family, the men who could easily be killed and their deaths look like accidents. Money had certainly changed hands…a lot of money. Had Meredith or one of her brothers panicked about the financial status of Wild West Protective Services and made a deal with the devil?

Yes, he'd look at the file concerning her mother's murder and hope that in the end he didn't take another family member away from her.

Chapter 3

Dinner was chaotic. It always was when the entire West family broke bread together. Meredith let the conversation swirl around her, grateful that for the moment nobody was focused on her.

She'd had enough attention when each of her brothers had arrived at the ranch. They'd teased her unmercifully about her new haircut until her father had insisted they stop picking on her.

Red West had gazed at her for a long moment, a softness in his eyes. "You look exactly like your mother did when I fell in love with her," he'd said, then hugged her. "She would have been so proud of you."

His words had merely renewed her desire to get to the bottom of the crime that had stolen her mother. She and Chase had agreed to go over the file that evening, after her family had left and her father went to bed.

She cast a surreptitious glance across the table at Chase, who was in the middle of a conversation with Zack. There was no denying the fact that she was attracted to the Kansas City cop.

It had been over a year since Meredith had enjoyed any kind of relationship with a man. At that time she'd been working in Florida and had fallen into a relationship with a local man. It had lasted over two months, until her job in Florida had ended.

Todd Green had been a terrific guy and she'd hoped when it was time for her to return to Oklahoma that he'd beg her not to go, that he'd tell her he couldn't live without her.

But he hadn't. Instead he'd told her he'd had a lot of fun with her, but when he finally decided to settle down for a long-term committed relationship it would be with somebody softer, somebody less capable…a real woman who needed him.

She'd been devastated. Not so much because she'd been head over heels in love with Todd, but rather because his hurtful words had pierced through to a well of doubt and insecurities she'd secretly harbored.

How could she know what it meant to be a real woman when there had been no woman in her life? She'd learned martial arts and self-defense like her brothers. She'd been taught how to shoot a gun and how to assess a situation for danger. But nobody had taught her how to be a *real* woman.

Since Todd there had been nobody else. Until Chase McCall with his piercing blue eyes that for some reason made her feel oddly lacking whenever he gazed at her.

The talk at the table turned to the Fall Festival dance in three days. "The whole town shows up for the dance," Tanner said. "Except Meredith, she always heads home before the band starts to play."

"We've all decided she must have two left feet," Zack added with a teasing grin. His wife, Kate, elbowed him in his side.

Despite the teasing, there was no denying the sense of unity at the table, the fierce loyalty and love they all felt for each other was on display, no matter who the guests of the house might be at the time.

Chase gazed at Meredith from across the table. "Surely this time you'll stay. If fact, I insist you save me a dance or two just to prove to your brothers that you don't have two left feet."

The idea of being held in his arms even for the length of a song caused a stir of warmth to seep through her blood. She wanted to protest, to tell him that she never went to the local dances, but try as she might, the protest refused to rise to her lips and she found herself nodding her assent.

Chase and his mother had only been in town for three days, but each day had increased the annoying tension in Meredith. She'd tried to keep her distance from him, but it was difficult in the confines of the house.

After dinner there was another hour of small talk, then everyone began to leave. "Meredith, will you walk me to my car?" Dalton asked.

She looked at him in surprise. "All right," she replied. Together brother and sister left the house and stepped outside into the chilly night air. Darkness had fallen and the only light was the faint glow of the moon drifting down from the cloudless sky.

"I assume you wanted to talk to me alone?" Meredith said as they crossed the expanse of yard to where Dalton had parked his car.

"I've got a favor to ask you," Dalton replied. "About the dance on Saturday night. Even though you said you'd be there at the dinner table, I thought you might sneak out early. I know dances aren't your thing, but could you hang around and entertain Chase and his mother for me?"

Meredith had already decided to skip the evening festivities despite the fact that she'd said she would save a dance or two for Chase. Her experiences at the occasional town dances had never been pleasant ones.

"Why do I have to babysit your guests?" she asked, a touch of irritation deepening her tone.

Dalton grinned, leaned over and kissed her lightly on the forehead. "Because you're the best sister in the whole world and I have a date with Melanie Brooks for the dance."

She wanted to decline, she *so* didn't want to do

this, and yet Dalton had never asked her for anything. She also knew he'd spent the past month working up his nerve to ask pretty Melanie out on a date. "All right. I said I'd go, so I'll go and make nice to your friend and his mother."

"You're the best."

"That's what you guys always tell me when you've managed to talk me into doing something I don't want to do."

Dalton laughed and got into his car. She watched as he drove down the lane, his headlights eventually swallowed up by the darkness of the night.

She wrapped her arms around herself and remained standing in place for a long moment. She frowned as she thought about the dance and rubbed her hands along the soft flannel of her shirt.

She didn't even have anything to wear. Her closet was filled with jeans and shirts, and the only dress she owned was the bridesmaid dress she'd worn to Clay and Libby's wedding. It was floor length and far too fussy for a town dance.

Maybe she'd talk to Libby tomorrow about borrowing a dress for the night. The two women were about the same size, and Libby had a closet full of clothes she'd brought with her when she'd moved from California to make a life with Clay.

A night breeze blew a burst of chilly air through the nearby trees. Dying leaves swished against one another and a chill that had nothing to do with the night air swept up her spine. Once again she felt that creepy feeling, like somebody was watching her, like she wasn't quite alone in the night.

She told herself she was being foolish, but turned on her heels and hurried back into the house. She went into the kitchen to see if there was anything she could help Smokey with, but Kathy stood at the sink next to him chatting as she dried the dishes he washed. Smokey wore a long-suffering expression, as if her chatter was about to drive him insane.

Meredith's father, Red, was in the living room seated in his favorite chair and Chase was nowhere to be found. She sat on the sofa and smiled at her dad.

"I love family meals," he said. "I love having the family all together."

"It was nice," she agreed. As usual when speaking to her father she made her voice louder than usual. Although Red refused to admit any problem, all of his kids knew he was growing deaf. "It won't be long before the family gets bigger. Anna is pregnant and I have a feeling if Kate has her way she won't be far behind her."

Red's eyes took on a faraway cast. "Grandchildren are a blessing. I just wish—" He broke off and smiled at Meredith. "Well, you know what I wish."

She nodded. He wished Meredith's mother were here to share it all with him. He wished his wife were by his side in the autumn of their lives. Meredith thought of the file that was in the top drawer of her dresser in her bedroom.

She couldn't give her mother back to her father,

but maybe after all these years she could finally give him some closure. She could give him the name of Elizabeth's murderer.

Minutes later Kathy and Smokey came out of the kitchen and the four of them visited for another half hour or so. Chase came into the living room from his bedroom just about the same time Red decided to retire for the night.

By ten o'clock everyone had gone to his or her room except Chase and Meredith. "Is now a good time to go through that file?" he asked her.

"It's a perfect time. I'll just go get it." As she left the living room, she drew deep breaths, wondering what it was about Chase McCall's presence that made her feel as if she never got quite enough oxygen.

She retrieved the file from the dresser drawer, then returned to the living room. "Why don't we go into the kitchen where we can spread it out on the table?" she suggested.

He nodded and together they went into the kitchen and sat at the round oak table. Meredith placed her hand on the top of the file, for a moment feeling as if she were about to open Pandora's box.

Inside the folder was the last evidence of a life interrupted, the pieces of an investigation that had yielded no results, leaving a man and six children to wonder who had committed such outrage and left behind such devastation.

"You sure you want to do this?" Chase's voice

was soft, but his gaze was sharp and penetrating, as if he were attempting to look directly into her soul.

"No, I'm not at all sure I want to do this," she replied honestly. "But, I feel like I *have* to." She looked at the folder beneath her hand. "I feel like she wants me to do this, she needs me to do this." She laughed and looked at him once again. "I know it sounds crazy."

"No, it doesn't," he replied. "I know all about needing answers, but you realize it's possible we won't get the answers you want from that file."

"I know. I'm just looking for a lead, something that was perhaps overlooked when the initial investigation took place."

He pulled the folder from beneath her hand and opened it. He quickly withdrew three photographs and flipped them face down on the table just out of her reach. "There's no reason for you to see those," he said. There was a toughness in his tone that forbade her to argue with him.

She didn't want to argue. She didn't want to see crime-scene photos of her mother's broken body. She had a faint memory of her mother's smiling face, and she wanted nothing to displace her single visual memory of the woman who had given her life.

For the next hour they pored over the papers and while she read lab reports and crime-scene analyses she tried not to notice the evocative scent of Chase, the heat of his body so close to hers.

It had been a very long time since she'd been so

intensely aware of a man and aware of her own desire for a man. She held no illusions about her desirability as a woman. She'd always been a bodyguard first, a woman second, more in touch with her abilities to exist in a man's world than in her own femininity.

But as she sat next to Chase, she wished she knew more about womanly wiles, about how to flirt and how to let a man know she was interested in him.

She instantly chided herself. She knew nothing about Chase McCall, about what kind of man he was, what was important to him. She knew nothing about him except the fact that one glance of his eyes and everything tightened inside her, one brush of his hand against hers and the defenses she kept wrapped around herself threatened to shatter.

With a sigh of irritation at her own wayward thoughts, she consciously focused on the paper in her hand.

"Was it your mother's usual habit to go grocery shopping on a Friday night?" Chase asked.

"I don't know. Unfortunately, I don't know a lot about my mother."

His eyes held curiosity. "You never asked your father or any of your brothers about her?"

She leaned back in the chair and frowned thoughtfully. "Over the years I'd asked some simple questions. I wanted to know what kind of woman she was, what she liked and didn't like. But I never asked anything that might stir up Dad's grief all over again."

Chase nodded. "I'd be interested to know if your mother was a creature of habit or if the shopping trip that night was just a spur-of-the-moment thing."

"Maybe I should write down some of the questions." She got up from the table and went to the desk in the corner of the kitchen to get pen and paper. "Tanner would be the one for me to talk to. He was ten when Mom died and he still has a lot of memories of her."

It was a relief to have just that momentary distance from him, from his pleasant scent that seemed to fill her head. When she returned to the table, she noticed that the photos he'd placed on the side had been moved, letting her know that while she'd hunted for paper and pen, he'd looked at those photos.

He leaned back in the chair and frowned thoughtfully. "The investigation looks tight. The officials did everything that should have been done," he said. "Unfortunately they didn't have a lot to go on. There were no witnesses and not much evidence to examine. But it looks like they spoke to your mother's friends and acquaintances to see if there was anyone giving her problems or somebody she'd made angry." He shrugged. "It doesn't look like they missed anything."

Meredith sighed in frustration. She'd hoped he'd find something, anything that might provide a lead to the killer.

She stared toward the window where the black of night reflected her image back to her. "I think she was killed by somebody who knew her, somebody here in town. For a week after she was buried, a bouquet of daisies was placed on her grave. Daisies were my mother's favorite flowers and nobody from the family was responsible for putting them there. A bouquet of daisies is still put on her grave every year on the anniversary of her death."

"Has that been investigated?" He leaned forward, as if she'd captured his attention. His blond hair gleamed in the artificial light and she wondered if it was as soft as it looked.

She nodded. "Clyde Walker was the sheriff at the time of her death and he tried to solve the mystery of the daisies. According to Tanner what he discovered was that an FTD order was placed and paid for in cash from Oklahoma City directing the flowers be placed on the grave for that week. The florist here had no idea who had ordered them. Sheriff Ramsey has tried to get to the bottom of the yearly bouquets, but he hasn't learned anything new."

"I agree with you, I think she was killed by somebody she knew, by somebody she trusted."

"Why do you think that?" Meredith asked.

"The evidence, such as it is, supports it. I'm assuming that stretch of road between here and town is dark and probably not well traveled."

"That's right."

"There was no evidence in those reports that your mother had any kind of car trouble that night, yet she pulled over to the side of the road and got out of her car to meet her murderer. That's not consistent with a stranger kill. And there's something else…" He frowned, his gaze assessing, as if gauging how strong she was, how much she could hear.

She raised her chin and held his gaze. "Tell me. What else?"

He rubbed a hand across his lower jaw where she could see the faint stubble of a five-o'clock shadow. "According to the crime-scene report, there was evidence of a struggle and yet from the photo I saw that was taken when your mother was found, her clothing was almost artfully arranged in place. If I had to guess, whoever killed your mother had some sort of feelings for her."

He leaned forward and gathered the papers together and shoved them back into the folder, then looked at her once again. "Is it possible your mother was seeing somebody?"

"You mean like an affair? Absolutely not," she said forcefully. "Everyone who knew my parents talk about how devoted they were to each other. All of the women who knew my mother said she adored my father."

She didn't even want to think that the fairy-tale love her parents had shared wasn't true, that her mother had wandered outside her marriage vows. "Mom was a budding actress in Hollywood when she met Dad. She was just beginning to enjoy success and attention. She left her career behind to move here with him and have a family."

He tapped a finger on the file. "I don't see how I can help you on this," he said. "It looks like everything was done at the time to try to find the murderer. It's a cold case with no new evidence to explore."

"That's what I was afraid of," she replied. "I really appreciate your thoughts on this."

"No problem." He grinned, a slow, sexy gesture that caused her breath to momentarily catch in her chest. "Now, tell me, why don't you go to the town dances?"

She got up from the table. Now that he'd done what she'd wanted him to do in looking through the files, she felt the need to escape. The kitchen felt too small, his very presence far too big.

He rose from the table and moved to stand within inches of her. His clean, masculine scent once again infused her head, making her half-dizzy. "I thought all women loved dances," he said, his breath warm on her face.

"I went to a few but I got tired of standing around waiting for somebody to ask me to dance." *Step back,* her mind commanded, but it was as if her legs had gone numb.

"I find that hard to believe," he said, his gaze focused on her mouth. She fought the impulse to lick her lips, afraid he might see it as an open invitation, even more afraid she would mean it as an invitation.

"It's true," she said, the words seeming to come

from far away. "I don't know if the men in this town are more afraid of my brothers or because I carry a gun."

He touched her then, a mere brush of her hair away from her face. As his fingertips skimmed the side of her cheek, a coil of heat unfurled in the pit of her stomach.

"I've met all your brothers and I don't find them scary at all. And I carry a gun, too, so that definitely doesn't bother me. But, let me tell you what does bother me." His eyes were no longer cold and assessing, but rather warm and inviting. "It bothers me that since the moment I laid eyes on you I've wondered what your mouth would feel like under mine."

Her breath caught painfully tight in her throat. "Do you intend to keep on wondering or do you intend to find out?" Her heart crashed inside her chest.

How had they gotten from talking about a murder to contemplating a kiss? She didn't know and she didn't care. All she wanted at the moment was for him to kiss her…hard and deeply.

"I definitely intend to find out," he said as he wrapped her in his strong arms and pulled her tight against him. His mouth took hers, his lips possessing, demanding.

She opened her mouth to him, wanting the touch of his tongue against hers, the shattering heat of full possession. She raised her arms around his neck and placed her fingers where the bottom of his thick, silky hair met his shirt collar. Soft. The blond hair was definitely soft.

The kiss seemed to last forever, but it wasn't long enough for her. It was he who finally broke the kiss and stepped back from her, his eyes gleaming with wicked intensity.

"If you dance even half as well as you kiss, then we should have a great time on Saturday night." He walked over to the table and picked up the file folder. "Sweet dreams, Meredith," he said, then left the kitchen.

She stared after him, wondering if she'd ever breathe normally again. Meredith had spent most of her life competing with her brothers, but at this moment she was intensely grateful that she was a woman.

He'd seen the cars come and go at the West ranch from his hiding place in the stand of trees. The entire family had gathered. But he wasn't interested in any of the others...just *her*...just Elizabeth.

No, not Elizabeth, he told himself. Elizabeth was gone. Dead. But Meredith was wonderfully alive and having her would be like having Elizabeth.

It had only been in the last month or so that he'd realized that Meredith was the spitting image of the woman he'd loved, the woman he'd been obsessed with.

Before the last month, Meredith had been out of town a lot and he'd rarely run into her. Then one day he'd seen her walking on the sidewalk downtown, and he'd been electrified by the sight. It was as if Elizabeth walked again, breathed again.

He'd been unable to get Meredith out of his mind. She was so beautiful. He could almost feel the silk of her dark hair between his fingers. He wanted to drown in the green depths of her eyes. Just looking at her made it hard to breathe. She possessed his every thought.

He had to have her. His need soared through him, filling him with both a euphoric high and an edge of apprehension. He had to have her. He would have her, but this time he'd do things differently. This time he'd try not to kill her.

Chapter 4

The scents of popcorn, cotton candy and autumn rode the air as Chase got out of Red West's car. It had already been a full day with pie-eating, cattle-judging and jelly-tasting contests.

A carnival had taken up residency in the parking lot in front of the community center. Multicolored lights flickered on the Ferris wheel as the delighted screams of the riders competed with the raucous laughter coming from the Tilt-A-Whirl.

Soon the carnival would shut down and the night would belong to the adults of Cotter Creek. "It's a beautiful night," Kathy said as she and Smokey, Red and Chase walked toward the community building where the dance would be taking place.

It was a perfect autumn night. A full moon hung in a cloudless sky and it was unusually warm for early October.

"Mark my words, there will be mischief tonight," Smokey said gruffly as he looked up in the sky. "Add full-moon madness with a live band and liquor and there's sure to be trouble."

Maybe a little prefull-moon madness was what Chase had suffered two nights ago when he'd kissed Meredith. He hadn't begun the night with any intention of kissing her, but at the time of the kiss, he'd felt as if he *needed* to kiss her.

Even now, just the thought of the taste of her soft lips beneath his had the effect of heating his blood. He didn't like it. He didn't like it one bit. That kiss had shaken him up far more than he liked to admit.

Since the night of the kiss, he'd tried to keep his distance from Meredith, both mental and physical. Red had taken him into town each morning, and he'd caught a ride back to the ranch with Dalton in the evenings.

He'd spent a lot of time in the café, talking to the locals, trying to get a handle on the crimes that had brought him to Cotter Creek.

But he'd found the locals reluctant to talk to strangers. He was obviously viewed as an outsider in the small tight-knit community. The only person who seemed to talk fairly freely was old man Sam Rhenquist who stationed himself every morning on the bench outside the barbershop. Although initially the old man had been fairly closemouthed, the more time Chase spent seated on the bench with Sam, the more the man seemed inclined to talk.

Chase and Dalton had spent the night before slugging back beers and shooting pool at the local bar. Every minute he spent with his friend produced a sick guilt inside him as he thought of how he was deceiving him. But the tips pointing a finger at the Wests couldn't be ignored.

That morning he'd touched base with Agents Tompkins and Wallace to see what progress they'd made during their time in Cotter Creek. They were in the middle of investigating Sheila Wadsworth's life. Sheila Wadsworth was the real estate agent who had been responsible for the sales of the property to the MoTwin Corporation.

She'd been murdered, but the agents were hoping that in the reams of paperwork she'd left behind, they might find the identity of the local man or men behind the scheme. Unfortunately, they had little to report so far.

"I thought Meredith was coming with us tonight," Kathy said, the question pulling Chase out of his thoughts.

"She went over to Libby and Clay's and told me she'd meet us here later," Red replied.

As they entered the community building, a band was warming up on the stage and a group of young men stood nearby, most of them looking as if they'd already gotten their noses in the sauce. They snickered and elbowed one another as they eyed the women who crossed their path.

Red, Smokey and Kathy sat at one of the tables that ringed the dance floor while Chase spied Dalton across the room and excused himself to join his friend.

"If I didn't know better, I'd swear you were nothing but an Oklahoma cowboy," Dalton said with a grin.

Chase fingered the pearl buttons on his western-style black shirt. "Mom bought this for me this afternoon and insisted I wear it tonight."

"I'd expect you to have a black hat hanging on the wall and a black horse waiting for you in the parking lot."

Chase grinned. "Only it would be a white hat and a white horse. Have you forgotten that I'm one of the good guys?"

Dalton laughed and clapped him on the back, and once again a wave of guilt shot through Chase. He hoped he could complete this assignment and get back to Kansas City and Dalton would never know about his role in investigating the West family.

"I thought you had a date tonight," Chase said.

"I do. I've got to go pick her up in half an hour. In the meantime, how about I buy you a beer?" Dalton gestured toward the cash bar in one corner.

"You know me, I never turn down a beer."

The two men got their drinks, then joined the rest of the family at the table where Smokey and Kathy were arguing about what ingredients made the best coleslaw dressing.

Chase had learned quickly that Smokey Johnson was a stubborn, opinionated old cuss, but as he watched Kathy hold her own, he suspected the old man had met his match. He'd never seen his partner look quite so animated.

She had dressed up for the evening, wearing a blue dress that sharpened the blue of her eyes, and a touch of blush colored her cheeks. She looked like a small-town woman eager for a night of fun rather than the seasoned FBI agent she was.

People continued to arrive, everyone looking as if they'd donned their Sunday best for the dance. He wasn't surprised to see Bill Wallace and Roger Tompkins arrive. He didn't acknowledge the fellow FBI agents' presence in any way.

The band began to play and within minutes the dance floor was filled with twirling couples. "I think it would be nice if you asked me to dance," Kathy said to Smokey.

He looked at her as if she'd lost her mind. "Dancing is for kids."

She smiled and stood, her hand extended to him. "You're only as young as you feel, and right now I feel like a kid."

"But I've got a bum leg," Smokey protested.

"And I have arthritis. I figure we can lean against each other and make it around the dance floor."

Smokey looked helplessly around the table, as if

seeking some kind of support. Red offered a benign smile and Dalton merely shrugged his shoulders.

"You might as well go ahead," Chase said. "When she gets her mind made up about something, she doesn't take no for an answer."

With a frown that would have daunted most women, Smokey rose to his feet and took Kathy's hand. She was really working it, Chase thought. It wouldn't be long before Smokey Johnson didn't have a thought in his head that Kathy didn't know about. If he had anything to do with the death of the ranchers and the land scheme, Kathy would ferret it out.

Before the dance had ended, Zack and his wife, Kate, and Tanner and his wife, Anna, arrived and joined them all at the table.

Chase was beginning to wonder if perhaps Meredith wasn't coming, that maybe his indifference to her the past couple of days had made her change her mind. That was fine with him. He didn't like the hunger she stirred in him.

He saw Sam Rhenquist across the room and walked over to speak to the old man. "Hello, Sam."

"Chase." He nodded his head.

"How you doing this evening?"

"Same as I do every evening. My bones ache, I worry about world peace and heart palpitations and wonder if I'll wake up in the morning."

"I have a feeling you have lots of mornings left," Chase replied. "Good turnout for tonight."

"Nothing this town likes better than a party, especially after all that's happened the last couple of months."

Chase looked at him with speculation. "I figure a man who parks himself on Main Street for most of the day hears things, maybe sees things that others don't hear or see. What do you know about what's been going on?"

Sam looked at him for a long moment, his brown eyes wary. "I reckon I know that the last person who opened her mouth to talk about what was going on here in town wound up dead." He didn't wait for Chase to respond but instead walked off in the direction of the cash bar.

Meredith stood just outside the door to the community center, trying to get up her nerve to go inside. She hadn't been to a town dance in several years, but that wasn't what made her nerves dance in her stomach like overactive jumping beans.

Never had she dressed the way she looked this evening. Never had she put on makeup the way she had tonight. She had no idea what had gotten into her when she'd chosen to borrow the emerald-green dress from Libby.

Okay, she had a little bit of an idea. She suspected it had been irritation with Chase McCall that had prompted her to pick a dress that showed more cleavage than she'd ever displayed and hugged curves she hadn't even known she possessed.

As she thought of Chase, a new flash of irritation

swept through her. The man had kissed her, then ditched her. He'd seemed to go out of his way over the past two days to avoid her, and that had fed every single insecurity she had as a woman.

Tonight, for the first time in her life, she'd wanted to look like a woman. She smoothed the silky green material over her waist, then drew a deep breath and stepped into the crowded community center. She was going to try her best to act like a woman.

It didn't take her long to find the table her family had commandeered. As she approached, she was aware of several of the men eyeing her up and down and equally aware of the scowls that suddenly decorated her brothers' faces.

"Did you forget to put on the rest of that dress?" Zack asked darkly when she reached the table.

Kate elbowed him hard in the ribs. "Shush up," she demanded, then smiled at Meredith. "You look absolutely stunning."

Tanner frowned. "Any of those drunken cowboys make a move toward you, then I'll be spending the night kicking some cowboy butt."

Meredith sighed and sat next to Anna, Tanner's wife. "This is why I never come to these things. There's nothing worse for a woman's social life than overprotective brothers. Where's Smokey?"

Anna pointed to the dance floor where Smokey and Kathy were dancing. "Aren't they cute?" Anna said. "This is their third dance."

Meredith nodded, shocked at the smile that

curved Smokey's mouth upward. She wasn't sure she could remember the last time Smokey had smiled so much.

Everyone was accounted for except Dalton and Chase, not that she cared where Chase might be.

She'd only been seated for a few minutes when Buck Harmon walked over to her. "Evening, Meredith." He nodded to everyone else at the table, his gaze darting first left, then right with obvious nervousness. "I was wondering if you'd like to dance with me."

At forty years old Buck was a divorced man. He was nice, but with his long, pointed nose and small eyes he'd always reminded Meredith of a ferret.

"I'd love to dance," she replied and stood.

"Just don't hold her too close," Zack warned, and Buck's face changed to the color of a ripened tomato.

"'Course not," he replied.

Meredith shot her brother a dirty look, then allowed herself to be led onto the dance floor.

"You look real pretty tonight," Buck said as he held her at a respectable distance from him. "I don't believe I've ever seen you look so pretty."

"Thanks," she replied.

"I'm cutting in." The deep familiar voice came from behind Meredith. Buck instantly dropped his hand from her waist and stepped back as Chase dismissed him as if he were nothing but an irritating fly.

He took her hand and pulled her into his embrace with a possessiveness that renewed her irritation with him. It didn't help that he looked positively amazing in his black shirt and tight jeans.

"What makes you think I wanted you to cut in?" she asked peevishly.

He smiled, but the gesture didn't quite reach the depths of his eyes. "Because you had the look of a deer in the headlights. That guy wasn't your type at all."

"And you are?" He smelled wonderful, a hint of shaving cream and woodsy cologne. An utterly male scent that seemed to envelop her.

"I am for the length of this dance." He pulled her closer, so close her nose came precariously close to his shoulder. "Was it your intention to start a riot tonight?"

She leaned back and looked at him once again. "What are you talking about?"

"I'm talking about that dress." His eyes now held a hint of emotion, something dangerous and simmering just beneath the surface that caused her heart to beat erratically.

"What's wrong with my dress?"

This time there was no mistaking the spark that lit his eyes. "Absolutely nothing." Once again he pulled her closer. "You've got every man in this room wanting you and every woman in the room hating you." His voice warmed the air near her ear.

A breathless wonder filled her. Was being a desirable woman really as simple as putting on a formfitting dress and a little bit of makeup? Was this all that it would have taken to make Todd happy?

Somehow she didn't think so. Besides, the wonder was short-lived as she thought of how Chase had avoided her after kissing her.

"I've never much cared what people thought of me," she replied with a touch of coolness to her tone.

"Does that include me?" he asked.

"You're at the top of my I-don't-care list."

He laughed, as if he didn't believe her, as if he could feel the throb of her heartbeat against his muscled chest. *It's true,* she told herself. *I don't care anything about Chase McCall. He'll only be in my life for the length of his vacation, then he and his mother will be gone.*

But as his muscled thigh pressed against hers and his hand tightened around her back, she found it hard to convince herself that he didn't affect her on any level.

He danced well. He was a strong lead and managed to make her feel graceful as he moved her around the dance floor.

"You're angry with me," he said.

"Why on earth would I be angry with you?" she countered.

"Maybe because I haven't spent any time with you the past couple of days. Maybe because I kissed you and have barely talked to you since then. Or maybe because I haven't kissed you again." His eyes sparked with a touch of humor.

"Get over yourself," she scoffed. "What are you doing, Chase, looking for some excitement by playing head games with me? Bored with your vacation? Might I suggest you enter a local bull-riding contest to alleviate any boredom you might be suffering."

He laughed again, then sobered. "I'm not trying to play head games with you." His gaze intensified. "I'll admit that I'm very attracted to you and there's nothing I'd like more than to act on that physical attraction, but I'm not looking for any kind of relationship so I figured it was best if I backed away."

"And what makes you think I'm interested in any kind of relationship except a physical one?" she asked, surprised at how his blatant confession of wanting her thrilled her.

He looked at her in surprise. "Because every woman I've ever known wants more than just a couple of rolls in the hay from a man."

"I've been told on more than one occasion that I'm not like most women," she replied. At that moment the music ended and she stepped out of his embrace. "Thanks for the dance, cowboy. The next move is up to you." With these bold words she turned and walked away.

She went directly toward the ladies' room, unable to believe her own audacity. She'd practically given him an open invitation to seduce her. What on earth had gotten into her?

As she stood at one of the sinks and dabbed her warm cheeks with a damp paper towel, she realized exactly what had gotten into her. Loneliness.

Other than Savannah, Meredith had no close friends. Savannah was warm and funny and great to spend time with, but she wasn't a significant other. She wasn't what Meredith was lonely for…a man.

The brief relationship she'd had with Todd seemed like another lifetime ago and in the short time that she'd been with Todd she'd discovered that she liked sex. Of course, at the time she was having sex with Todd she'd believed they were building toward an *I do*. Instead he'd been working up his nerve to tell her *No thanks*.

At least if she decided to have a physical relationship with Chase she'd have no illusions of how it would end. It would end with him going back to Kansas City and her no worse for the experience. Her loneliness would be alleviated for a short time, and that in itself was appealing.

She tossed the towel into the nearby trashcan and left the restroom. As she walked out, she was immediately greeted by Doug Landers, a man who'd been a classmate all through school.

"Meredith," he said and slung an arm around her shoulder. He smelled like too little deodorant and too much whiskey. "Darling, who knew that beneath those ugly shirts and jeans you wear was the body of a goddess?"

"Let me go, Doug. You're drunk," she exclaimed.

"I'm not too drunk to appreciate a fine piece of ass when I see it," he replied.

She tried to move away from him, but he tightened his arm around her. She was vaguely aware of Chase coming out of the men's room. As he saw her, his pleasant expression transformed into something dark and dangerous.

"Doug, I'm warning you, let me go," she exclaimed.

The drunken cowboy laughed, his breath potent enough to stop a raging bull in its tracks. "I'm not letting you go until I get a little kiss."

Meredith acted purely on instinct. In one smooth move she grabbed his arm from her shoulder, whirled out of his embrace and yanked his arm up behind his back.

He yelped in pain. "Let me go, you bitch," he exclaimed.

She gave his arm a final yank upward, then released him and pushed him away. As he stumbled off, she saw the stunned surprise on Chase's face and she felt slightly sick to her stomach.

She had a feeling this was exactly what Todd had been talking about, her inability to allow a man to help her, her lack of helplessness and charming softness that every woman was supposed to embody.

Suddenly tired, all she wanted to do was go home. It depressed her, the fact that she knew how to be a great bodyguard but didn't know anything about being a woman.

"I'd ask if you were okay, but it's obvious you can take care of yourself," Chase said as he approached.

"Growing up with all my brothers, I had to learn

a little self-defense," she said as they walked in the direction of the table. To heck with her promise to Dalton to babysit his friend, she thought crossly. "I think I'm going to head home. I've had enough Fall Festival for one year."

"But I've only gotten to dance with you once," he said. "Are you sure you're okay?" he asked, a touch of concern darkening his eyes.

"I'm fine. Just tired." They reached the table and she said her goodbye to her family, then grabbed her purse and headed for the nearest exit.

As she wove through the people to reach the door, she was aware of Doug's malevolent glare following her progress. He was obviously angry with her, but he'd probably get over it when he sobered up.

She hadn't realized how noisy it was inside until she stepped out the door and into the still night. The unusually warm air wrapped around her, banishing the last of Chase's scent that had lingered in her head.

Maybe a brief, hot affair was exactly what she needed. No expectations. No disappointments. Just a momentary respite from her loneliness.

Pulling her keys from her purse, she realized she couldn't wait to get out of the dress, couldn't wait to wash the makeup off her face. She'd tried to be something she wasn't this evening, and she wouldn't make that mistake again.

Eventually she might find a man who cared about her, who could fall in love with her as she was, and if that didn't happen, then she would live her life alone.

As she approached her car she frowned, noticing something white sticking out from under the driver's windshield wiper. When she got closer she saw it was a piece of paper folded several times. She plucked it out and opened it.

"I've been waiting for you for a very, very long time. You are my destiny."

The words were printed in block letters and the note wasn't signed. She unlocked her car door and slid behind the steering wheel, the note clutched in her hand.

The creepy feeling returned, raising the hair on the nape of her neck, dancing goose bumps along her arms. A secret admirer?

Maybe some women would be thrilled by the very idea. Meredith wasn't. She didn't like secrets. She looked around the parking lot, seeking the source of the note. But while the lot was crowded with cars and trucks, she saw nobody standing in the shadows, nobody crouched down next to a car.

She tucked the note into her purse, started her car engine, then on instinct did something she'd never done before in Cotter Creek. She locked her car doors,

Chapter 5

Chase awakened late the next morning with the hangover from hell. A long hot shower eased most of his misery, and by the time he left his room he suffered only an irritating headache that he hoped a gallon of coffee would banish.

He rarely drank too much. He had far too many memories of his old man, drunk and mean, and a deep-seated fear that at any minute he might become the same kind of man.

But last night after Meredith had left the dance, he'd drunk to forget how good she'd felt in his arms. He'd drunk to erase the feel of her long, slender legs against his, the press of her breasts against his chest and the challenge in her eyes when she'd told him that the next move was up to him.

He'd just come down the hall and into the living room when he heard a knock on the front door. Seeing nobody else around he walked to the front door. A young man stood on the porch clutching a long, white florist box.

"I have a delivery for Meredith West," he said.

"I'll take it." Chase took the box, gave the kid a tip, then closed the door and went to hunt down Meredith. It was obvious somebody had sent Meredith flowers. It surprised him how much he didn't like the idea. However, it didn't surprise him that she'd managed to garner some man's attention the night before.

She'd looked hot, and the fact that she'd seemed unaware of just how good she looked had made her even hotter. Holding her in his arms had been an exquisite form of torture. Flirting with her had been stimulating, but nothing had prepared him for her giving him the go-ahead for a lusty, no-commitment-necessary relationship.

It had been the burn of desire deep in his gut that he'd tried to anesthetize after she'd left the dance. But no amount of beer had been able to vanquish the simmering heat she'd stirred in him.

He found her in the kitchen with Smokey and Kathy. The three of them were seated at the table, drinking coffee and chatting about the dance the night before.

"These are for you," he said as he entered the kitchen. This morning there was no red lipstick decorating her full, sensual lips, no mascara to darken her long, dark eyelashes. She didn't appear to have on a stitch of makeup, but she had a face that didn't need artificial enhancements.

Once again she was clad in a red flannel shirt and jeans, but he couldn't help but remember the creamy skin beneath the shirt, the full breasts the material couldn't quite hide.

Her eyes widened with a flare of pleasure as he set the box in front of her on the table. "For me?" she said in obvious surprise. She smiled, a gorgeous upturn of lips that renewed the burn in his stomach. He realized she might think the flowers had come from him.

"They were delivered just a minute ago," he said. The pleasure in her eyes dimmed a tad, and he suddenly wished he'd bought the flowers for her.

"Open it up," Kathy said with excitement. "Let's see what you've got."

Chase poured himself a cup of coffee, then joined them at the table as Meredith pulled off the top of the box to reveal a dozen long-stem, deep-coral-colored roses.

"Oh my, those are lovely," Kathy exclaimed. "Smokey, why don't you get her a vase?"

As Smokey got up from the table, Red came in the back door. "Who got the roses?"

"I did," Meredith replied.

"Who sent them?" He walked over to the sink to wash his hands.

Meredith frowned. "I don't know. There doesn't seem to be a card."

Red dried his hands on a towel, then joined them at the table. "Coral roses. That color means desire. I'd say you have an amorous new suitor."

Chase didn't like the sound of that, and from the expression on Meredith's face she wasn't overly thrilled. "I'd like to know who the suitor is. I don't like mysteries." She carried the box of roses to the counter where Smokey had filled a large crystal vase with water.

He watched as she arranged the roses, sticking them helter-skelter into the vase. Kathy jumped up from the table. "Here, honey, let me help you with that."

When the two rejoined everyone at the table, the talk once again turned to the dance the night before and the crime investigation taking place by the two FBI agents.

"I heard they were interested in Sheila Wadsworth's husband. You know he wasn't from around here," Red said. "I'd like to think that whoever is behind all this is somebody who isn't a neighbor or friend."

Chase tried to stay focused on the conversation, but a part of his brain was trying to figure out who might have sent the roses to Meredith.

"Whoever is behind it should have their hearts

torn out," Smokey said, his grizzled brows tugged together in a frown.

"My fear is that before this is all said and done, it's going to tear this town apart. Everyone is suspecting somebody else and those suspicions are going to hurt friendships," Red said.

Chase took a sip of his coffee, then said, "While I've been spending time in town, I've heard a few people who think you or one of your sons might be behind this land scheme."

"That's crazy," Meredith exclaimed.

Red laughed. "That doesn't surprise me." He leaned back in his chair. "Funny thing about being successful, seems along with the money and such, you manage to gain more enemies."

"There's a few in town who would love to see the West family fall," Smokey said. "Jealous, that's all they are, just pure jealous."

"Besides, what would I have to gain by being the mastermind of such a thing?" Red continued, "I've got enough money to keep my children and their children living in comfort for the rest of their lives. I own more land now than I'll ever know what to do with. I figure when you're investigating a crime the best way to solve it is to look for motive. Neither my children nor I have a good motive."

Chase took another sip of his coffee. He believed Red West. He'd only been in the bosom of the West family for less than a week, but he had found them all to be men of integrity.

He had a gut feeling that the tips that had been phoned in pointing a finger at the West family had been an attempt to lead the FBI on a wild-goose chase.

When they'd finished coffee and everyone had taken off in different directions, Chase waylaid Kathy and pulled her into his bedroom.

"My gut tells me we're wasting our time here," he said.

"I'm certainly not prepared to make that same assessment," she replied with a hint of stubbornness he recognized all too well. "I think it would be a big mistake to pull out of here too early."

Chase wasn't sure, but for some reason he felt like it was time to go, that they could be used better somewhere else, on another assignment. He had the distinct feeling that if they stuck around too much longer, things were going to get complicated between him and Meredith.

The adage of familiarity breeding contempt wasn't working for him. Each moment he spent near Meredith stoked the flames in his stomach a little hotter. "Kathy, the only thing we're gaining from sticking around here is that you're getting more recipes from that cranky old man," he said with a touch of irritation.

"Don't be disrespectful," Kathy exclaimed. "That cranky old man stepped in to fill a void formed from grief. He's done nothing but give to this family at the expense of him having his own life."

Chase stepped back, surprised by Kathy's quick

defense of the crotchety cook. Pink leaped to her cheeks. "All I'm saying is that we're in a perfect position as guests of the Wests to not only investigate them but to also hear local gossip and keep an eye on other townspeople," she said.

He suspected her interest in remaining here wasn't all about the job, but he didn't call her on it. "Okay," he relented. "We stick around another week or so and see what we can come up with."

She nodded and left his room. Chase walked over to the bedroom window and stared outside. What Red West said made sense. The Wests owned more land than they needed and had an incredibly successful business. Why would any of them want to become involved in some murderous land scheme?

Although prosecution of any crime didn't require the authorities to prove motive, Chase believed too that to solve a crime one had to look at motive. And as far as he was concerned, the Wests had none.

Sam Rhenquist knew more than he was saying about what was going on. The old man sat on that bench on Main Street day after day, watching and listening to the people who passed by. He knew more than he was telling, but he was afraid of the consequences should he talk. Chase wanted to make him talk.

And who in the hell had sent those roses to Meredith?

He heard the door across the hallway close, then

soft footsteps leading away. Meredith. He turned away from the window and left his bedroom, knowing he was walking in her wake by the faint scent of her perfume that lingered in the air.

He found her in the living room talking to her father. "I was just telling Dad that I'm headed into town. I have a lunch date with Savannah," she said.

"Mind if I catch a ride?" he asked.

"Suit yourself," she replied with a terse tone. She looked at him with a cool distance that made him wonder what was going on in her gorgeous head.

As he followed her to her car, he thought once again about the roses she'd received that morning and the look of both surprise and sheer pleasure that had lit her eyes.

It had been obvious that she wasn't accustomed to getting flowers. It irritated him that there was a small part of him that wished he'd sent them, that he'd been the one who had brought that smile of pleasure to her face.

"You have any idea who sent you the roses?" he asked when they were in her car and headed into town.

"Not a clue," she replied with a dark frown.

"Kind of romantic, huh," he said.

"Kind of creepy, if you ask me. If somebody feels desire for me, I prefer to know their name."

"Allow me to introduce myself," he said half teasing.

She didn't reply, but a faint pink stained her cheeks. They rode the rest of the way in silence. He tried several times to begin a conversation but she didn't respond and he finally gave up.

Just like a woman to get all moody and the man not to know what he'd done, he thought. Maybe it was a good thing that she seemed irritated with him. He had a feeling Kathy was getting far too close to Smokey Johnson. His partner was allowing her heart to get all twisted up, and as far as Chase was concerned that was always a mistake.

Chase didn't have a heart to get involved with anyone. A father who had professed to love him had beaten the heart right out of him. His biggest, deepest fear was that if he allowed himself to love somebody he'd turn out just like his old man and would eventually beat the heart right out of her.

Meredith and Chase parted ways in front of the hardware store. "If you want a ride back to the ranch, I'll be leaving around two," she said. She half hoped he'd find another way back to the ranch.

She needed to think. She needed to think about the note that had been left on her car the night before and the roses that had arrived that morning.

And she needed to think about Chase McCall and the bits and pieces of conversation she'd overhead him having with his mother.

Checking her watch, she realized it was too early to go to the newspaper office to meet Savannah. She had half an hour to kill before she was to meet her friend at eleven. She thought about heading to the

Wild West Protective Services office, but suspected that's where Chase had been headed. And what she needed at the moment was as much distance as possible from him.

Instead she crossed the street toward the direction of the floral shop, thinking that just maybe she could learn the identity of her secret admirer.

Cotter Creek Floral Creations was owned and operated by Mary Lou Banfield, a woman who had been one of Meredith's mother's closest friends.

A tiny bell tinkled cheerfully as Meredith entered the shop. The cloying scent of a variety of flowers hung in the air, each one fighting for dominance.

Mary Lou greeted her with a warm, friendly smile. "I wondered how long it would take this morning before I'd see you in here. The minute Joe carried those roses out of here for delivery, I knew sooner or later you'd show up."

"There was no card with the roses," Meredith said as she walked over to the counter where Mary Lou was making an arrangement of multicolored carnations and greenery.

"Whoever sent them didn't want you to know. It was a cash order written up and left in my mail slot this morning. The order was specific, a dozen orange roses sent to you, no card. I didn't have orange, but figured coral was close enough. Whoever ordered them overpaid by five dollars."

This information certainly did nothing to alleviate the unease that had gripped Meredith since the moment she'd opened the box of roses. "You still have the note that came with the money?" she asked.

Mary Lou nodded and opened the cash register. "Like I said, I figured you'd be in so I didn't throw it away."

Meredith took the piece of paper from her and read it. It was written in block letters just like the note she'd received beneath her windshield wiper the night before. It simply said, "Deliver to Meredith West one dozen long-stem orange roses." It was written on plain white bonded paper.

"I'd say you've got yourself a secret beau," Mary Lou exclaimed.

"I don't like secrets," Meredith replied. "I figure a real man doesn't stand behind anonymity."

Mary Lou smiled and picked up a bright-red carnation. "Your mother would have been so proud of you. You're just like her, strong and forthright. She was delighted you know, when you came along. Oh, she loved her boys but she desperately wanted a daughter. When you were born she told me that she'd just given birth to a person she hoped would become her very best friend."

A lump of emotion crawled into Meredith's throat as she realized again all she had lost when somebody had taken her mother's life. She swallowed hard against the lump. "Mary Lou, you probably knew my mother better than anyone in town. Do you think it was possible she was having an affair at the time of her death?"

"Who on earth have you been talking to that would put such nonsense in your head?" Mary Lou asked scornfully. "Elizabeth loved your daddy with every fiber of her being. She'd no more have an affair than she would have flown to the moon."

Even though Meredith hadn't seriously contemplated the affair angle, Mary Lou's staunch support of her mother was comforting. "I've been thinking about her a lot lately," Meredith said.

Mary Lou reached out and covered Meredith's hand with hers. "I miss her, too. She was a wonderful friend."

Meredith nodded, then withdrew her hand. "I've got to get out of here. I'm meeting Savannah for lunch."

"When are her and Joshua gonna tie the knot?"

"I don't know, they haven't set a date."

Mary Lou grinned. "It seems like every other month or so there's another West wedding to attend."

"You don't have to worry about me following in my brothers' footsteps. I can't even get a man who might be interested in me to sign a card."

"Maybe he's just shy. I'm sure when the time is right your secret admirer will reveal himself to you."

"I suppose," she replied, then with a goodbye she left the florist shop and headed toward the newspaper office to meet Savannah.

So, somebody shy had left her a note and sent her roses. There was no reason for her to feel anxious about it. Like Mary Lou had said, surely *eventually* he'd reveal himself to her.

Raymond Buchannan, the owner of the *Cotter Creek Chronicles* frowned as she walked into the office. "One hour, that's what Savannah's lunch break is supposed to be. Last time you two put your heads together over at the café she was an hour late back from lunch."

"I'll make sure that doesn't happen again," Meredith exclaimed. "I know how busy she is with all the news stories that are breaking minute by minute in this one-horse town."

Raymond's scowl deepened. He obviously had recognized her sarcasm. Savannah danced out of her office. "Right on time. I'll be back later, Mr. Buchannan," she said airily as she pulled Meredith out the front door.

"I don't know how you put up with him," Meredith said when the two hit the sidewalk. "He's so cranky."

Savannah linked arms with her. "I'll let you in on a little secret. I'm not going to have to put up with him too much longer."

Meredith stopped in her tracks and stared at her friend. "Don't tell me you're quitting your job. You love being a reporter."

"Of course I'm not quitting." Savannah pulled her into motion again. "But he's only going to be my boss until we can draw up the contracts."

Once again Meredith halted and looked at Savannah in surprise. "He's selling the paper to you?"

Savannah's freckled face wreathed into a smile. "Isn't it great? He's retiring and leaving town. We came to an agreement last night, and we're meeting with a lawyer tomorrow afternoon."

"Raymond has been talking about retiring for years, but nobody took him seriously," Meredith replied.

"I know. I was stunned when he approached me and told me it was time, that he was ready to pack his bags and let go of the paper."

"What does Joshua think about all this?"

"He thinks I'm crazy to want all the work and responsibility, but he's being totally supportive. I sometimes feel like I'm the luckiest woman in the world to have him."

The two entered the café and found a booth in the back. "Now, tell me what's new with you," Savannah said once the waitress had departed with their orders. "How's that hunky houseguest of yours? I've got to tell you, you two looked like you were going to combust last night on the dance floor."

Meredith suddenly remembered the conversation she'd overheard before she'd left the house. "I'm not sure I trust my hunky houseguest."

"From the way he looked at you last night, I wouldn't trust him, either. That man had lust in his heart."

"I'm not talking about that," Meredith said, although a tiny rivulet of heat swept over her as she thought about the way Chase's eyes had simmered as he'd held her in his arms. She'd never known blue eyes could look so…so…hot.

She grabbed a napkin and twisted it with her fingers. "I think he's not just here for a little friendly visit with Dalton."

Savannah frowned. "What do you mean?"

"I overhead a little of a conversation between him and Kathy this morning. First of all, he called her Kathy. Don't you find it odd for a man to call his mother by her first name?"

Savannah shrugged. "Not really. I mean, I call my mother The Monster."

"That's different," Meredith replied. "From everything you told me about your mother, she deserves to be called The Monster. But it's more than that. I could have sworn I heard Chase say something about being here on assignment."

Savannah frowned once again. "Isn't he a Kansas City cop? What kind of an assignment would bring him here?"

"I don't know. But I'm going to find out."

"How are you going to do that?"

Meredith took a sip of her water. "I'm going to ask him."

Savannah narrowed her eyes and studied Meredith intently. "Are you sure you aren't just looking for a reason to push him away?"

Meredith opened her mouth to vehemently protest, but instead closed it again. Was that what she was doing? She couldn't be absolutely certain she'd overheard correctly. Was she unconsciously looking for a reason to put distance between herself and Chase?

"I don't know," she finally admitted. "He scares me a little bit. He has a way of looking at me that makes me feel both wonderful and afraid."

Savannah nodded. "I know exactly what you're talking about. I feel the same way with Joshua."

"It's not the same," Meredith scoffed. "I'm not about to fall in love with Chase McCall." At that moment the waitress arrived with their orders.

Thankfully, the conversation as they ate revolved around the newspaper and Raymond Buchannan's decision to sell the paper to Savannah.

By the time they'd finished eating and Savannah had to get back to work, Meredith had managed to put thoughts of Chase on the back burner.

She didn't tell Savannah about the note and the roses. In fact, she hadn't told anyone about the note she'd found. She certainly didn't want to tell any of her family members, and Savannah would make a big deal out of it.

Savannah was the kind of woman who would think it was all wonderfully romantic. There was no way Meredith could explain to anyone the strange feeling of disquiet the note evoked in her.

It was almost two when Meredith returned to her car.

There was no sign of Chase, but there was a piece of paper placed beneath the driver's windshield wiper. Her fingers trembled as she plucked it out and opened it.

"You will be mine forever."

She crunched up the note into her fist as her gaze shot around the street. There were people everywhere, hurrying down the sidewalks to their destinations, sweeping off the sidewalks in front of their places of business. But nobody paid any attention to her. Nobody appeared to be watching her.

She didn't know how long she stood there with the note clutched tightly in her grip. This didn't feel like a secret admirer. It felt darker, more dangerous.

It felt like stalking, like a sick obsession.

He watched from the storefront as she got into her car and drove away. He closed his eyes, for a moment overwhelmed with need. Elizabeth. His heart cried out the name.

The afternoon sunshine had caressed her dark hair, and he wanted it to be his hands tangling in the rich strands. He'd been too far away to see her facial expression when she'd read the note, but he could imagine the sparkle of her eyes, the sweet anticipation that had flooded through her.

Soon, he thought. It was a promise to her. Soon. It was a promise to himself.

Chapter 6

She waited until quarter after two, and when Chase didn't show up, she left and headed back to the ranch. As she drove she tried to figure out who might be leaving the notes, who might have sent the roses.

Was it possible that Buck Harmon was responsible? He was the only man other than Chase who had asked her to dance. Had that brief moment in Buck's arms stirred something in the man?

Maybe she was overreacting to the whole situation. Maybe she should just sit back and enjoy the fact that she'd captured the interest of someone.

Like Mary Lou had said, when the time was right the man would identify himself. In the meantime there was no point in stewing about it.

As she thought of the florist she couldn't help but think about her mother. She liked to believe that if Elizabeth had lived she and Meredith would have been best friends.

By the time she pulled up at the house, she was hungry for a connection, any connection with her mother. If Elizabeth had lived, would she have taught Meredith the nuances of being a woman? A real woman?

She found her father where he usually was, out in his garden pulling weeds. He straightened as he saw her, a flash of pain creasing his features. The arthritis that had finally forced him to give up working for the family business seemed to grow more pronounced everyday. "Hey, girl. I thought you were in town."

"I just got back." She sat on a nearby stone bench and watched him once again begin to pull the weeds threatening to choke his fall-colored mums. "I've been thinking a lot lately about Mom."

Red smiled. "I think about her every single day." He brushed off his hands and joined Meredith on the bench. He smelled of earth and sunshine and that indefinable scent of Dad.

"I wish I could have known her. It's not everyone who can boast that her mother was a Hollywood starlet at one time."

Red laughed, a wistful sound of distant memories. "She was beautiful and she was a wonderful actress. She was on her way to stardom, and I couldn't believe it when she made the choice to give all that up to marry me and move out here in the middle of nowhere."

For a long moment he stared off into the distance, and Meredith knew he was remembering the woman he'd married, the woman he'd loved. He sighed, then looked back at Meredith. "You know there are boxes of your mom's Hollywood memorabilia in the old shed in the pasture."

"Really?" This was the first she'd ever heard of any boxes.

Red nodded. "Your mom packed that stuff out there and said those boxes were like her own personal time capsules. Maybe it's time you looked in them."

"I'd like that," she replied.

He stood. "I'll just go get the key to the shed."

Minutes later Meredith took off down the pasture lane. Once again it was an unusually warm day for October, but even the bright sun couldn't heat the cold places that the appearance of that second note had left inside her.

As she walked, her head swirled with disturbing thoughts. She apparently had a stalker, she had a houseguest who might not be who or what he claimed to be, and she had the haunting mystery of her mother's murder all battling for dominance.

The large shed was in the middle of nowhere with nothing but pasture around and in the distance groves of trees and other outbuildings. An overhang shielded bales of hay that were stored there and the other part of the shed was a typical locked storage area.

She unlocked the door and pushed it open, allowing the bright sunshine to add to the light coming in through a small window. Dust motes flew in the air, and she didn't even want to think about what spiders and bugs might be occupants.

The inside was stuffed with outcast furniture, old lamp fixtures and boxes. She moved around a sofa she never remembered seeing in the house and to a stack of boxes that were neatly labeled on the sides. She read the labels until she came to one that said Elizabeth.

With an effort, she pulled the box out from beneath several others, then carried it to the sofa. She sat down next to the box and opened the lid.

Playbills, old photographs and reviews greeted her, along with a swell of emotion for what might have been, what should have been. She should have had her mother in her life to guide her, to teach her, to love her.

How she wished she could find the sick bastard who had stolen that from her when he'd strangled the life out of her mother. What had Elizabeth West done to deserve being choked to death and left by the side of her car on a deserted road?

She picked up an old photograph and stared at the image. It was like looking into a mirror. She touched her mother's smile with the tip of her finger, and tears burned at her eyes.

She'd always thought it was impossible to mourn for something you'd never had, but she realized now that wasn't true. She mourned the mother she'd never had, mourned the girl talk and the hugs and kisses. In Meredith's world of five brothers, a father and Smokey, there had never been a soft place to fall. Her mother would have been that place, if she'd lived.

"Meredith."

The deep voice startled a cry from her, and she jumped up from the sofa, ready to defend herself from some unknown threat. She relaxed as she saw Chase standing in the doorway.

"What are you doing out here?" she asked. She sank back on the sofa as her heart resumed a more natural rhythm. She hadn't realized how on edge she'd been until he'd startled her.

"Your dad said you were out here going through some things of your mother's. I thought maybe if you were looking for clues you might need an extra pair of eyes." He walked over to the sofa and sat next to her.

"I'm pretty sure I won't find any clues out here to who might have murdered her. These boxes mostly contain things of my mother's from her days in Hollywood." She wished he hadn't sat so close to her, for his nearness created a tiny ball of tension in the pit of her stomach.

"What have you got there?" He pointed to the picture she held in her hand.

She held it out to him. "A picture of my mom."

"Wow, the resemblance is amazing." He looked from the picture to her, his gaze assessing. "Your hair is a little bit lighter and your face is a bit longer, but the differences are so subtle."

Meredith took the picture back from him and once again traced the smile with her fingertip. "I've read a few of the reviews of some of her work as an actress. She was as talented as she was pretty."

"Maybe you need to let it go," he said softly. She looked at him in surprise. "Maybe you need to let her go. Even if you solve her murder, it won't bring her back."

"I know that," she replied. She set the picture aside and sighed. "You don't know what it's like to grow up without a mother."

His eyes darkened, holding secrets. "I know what it's like to feel alone," he countered. "I know what it's like to feel isolated. Even though I had Kat…Mom, my childhood wasn't exactly a bag of chips."

She didn't miss his tongue bobble when he'd mentioned his mother, and it brought back the conversation she'd overheard that morning along with an edge of suspicion. "Who are you and what are you really doing here?"

His eyes narrowed slightly. "What do you mean?"

She stood, her gaze searching his features. "I think you know exactly what I mean. You aren't here on vacation, are you? There's something more. You and Kathy didn't just suddenly get a hankering to visit Dalton here in Cotter Creek. Tell me what you're really doing here."

He held her gaze for a long moment, a muscle ticking in his lower jaw. He finally broke the gaze and swiped a hand through his hair. "We're here on an investigation."

"An investigation?" She returned to the sofa and once again sat. "An investigation into what?"

"Into your family. We're looking into a couple of tips we got that somebody in your family is behind the land scheme and the death of those ranchers."

She stared at him in disbelief. She knew she should probably be angry, but she wasn't. She was somewhat relieved that her suspicions about him had proven correct. "So, you're what? FBI?" He nodded. "And Kathy?"

"Is my partner."

She sat back and tried to digest what she had just learned. "Does Dalton know?"

"No. Nobody knows except the two agents in town and now you. What gave us away?"

"I overheard some of a conversation you had with Kathy this morning," she replied. "I didn't mean to eavesdrop."

"But you did," he said flatly. "I don't suppose you'd consider keeping the information to yourself?"

"You know you're wasting your time. Nobody in my family would ever have anything to do with this," she said. "That's not the kind of people we are."

"We've pretty much come to that conclusion," he

replied. He reached and grabbed her hand in his, his gaze intent. "I'm asking you not to tell anyone about who we are and what we're doing here. We have a perfect cover as your guests to investigate people in this town."

She didn't like the way his hand felt holding hers, so warm and inviting. His scent filled the shed, a wonderful smell of male and wind and that woodsy cologne.

She pulled her hand from his. "I'll keep your secret for now," she agreed. "And I want you to investigate my family inside and out. I don't want there to be any doubt as to our innocence."

"Okay." He looked relieved.

"What's happening with the investigation? Any suspects?"

"Agents Wallace and Tompkins are still sifting through Sheila Wadsworth's papers and personal items, looking for a clue that might point a finger at somebody."

"So, basically, nothing is happening," she replied.

He frowned. "I think Sam Rhenquist knows something, but I can't get him to tell whatever it is he knows."

"That man gives *cranky* a new meaning."

"Yeah, well I tried to get him to talk to me this afternoon, but he was having nothing to do with it. Did you find out who sent you the roses?" he asked in an obvious attempt to change the subject.

"No. I went to the florist shop but didn't get any

answers. The order for the roses was left in the mail slot along with cash."

"You think maybe they were from that cowboy who tried to maul you outside the bathroom? Maybe some kind of apology for his behavior?"

She laughed and shook her head. "Doug is the kind of man who thinks it's funny to pass gas in church, he certainly doesn't have the class to send roses in apology for anything."

"You certainly put him in his place. That was a smooth move you did on him." There was a hint of admiration in his voice.

"I told you last night that you don't grow up with five brothers without learning the basics of self-defense, and in any case in my line of work I have to know how to take care of myself." And maybe that was the problem with her. Maybe that was why Todd hadn't wanted her, because she wasn't needy like a real woman should be.

"If I kissed you right now would you use some of that self-defense to fend me off?" he asked.

Her heartbeat stuttered. The last time he'd kissed her he'd taken her breath away, stirred a desire in her she'd never felt before. "I guess you won't know until you try. I did tell you last night at the dance that the next move was up to you."

His eyes fired with a familiar spark that lit something hot and hungry inside her. With a studied determination he stood and reached out to take her hand. He pulled her up off the sofa and into his arms.

She didn't even think about protesting. She'd wanted him to kiss her every moment of every day since he'd last kissed her. "You drove me crazy in that little green dress last night at the dance," he said as his arms tightened around her. "But you drive me just as crazy in your flannel shirt and jeans."

There was nothing else he could have said that would have effectively melted her as these words did. "Do you intend to just stand there, or do you intend to do something about it?" she asked.

"Oh, I definitely intend to do something about it." His mouth took hers in a kiss that demanded surrender, that took no prisoners.

And she surrendered. She opened her mouth to him as her knees weakened and she melted against the hard length of his body. His tongue rimmed her lower lip, then plunged inside to battle with her own.

Meredith wrapped her arms around his neck, wanting to feel the silk of his gorgeous blond hair, needing to mold herself to him.

There was no slow build. As he deepened the kiss, there was nothing but hot hunger ripping through her.

His hands moved up and down her back, heating her skin through the shirt's fabric, deepening the hunger in her for more—more intimacy, more tactile pleasure, more Chase.

She'd set the rules when she'd told him she wasn't interested in anything but a physical relationship with him. And that was still true, now more than ever.

He was an FBI agent, here for the moment but before long he'd be gone back to Kansas City and out of her life. She had no illusions, no expectations. All she knew was that she wanted this man right now.

He broke the kiss only long enough to move his mouth from her lips to her neck where he nipped and nibbled as if he couldn't get enough of the taste of her.

She gasped as his hands gripped her buttocks and pulled them against him. He was aroused, and the feel of his hardness thrilled her. She ran her hands up beneath his shirt, loving the feel of his warm skin over taut muscles. Her fingers encountered several ridges of skin, the telling feel of scars, and vaguely she wondered about them, but had no ability to process any rational thought.

He in turn moved his hands beneath her shirt, the heat of his hands warming her back, then making her gasp once again as he moved them around her body to cup her breasts. Once again his mouth took possession of hers and she was no longer capable of conscious thought.

His thumbs rubbed across the tips of her breasts, warming despite the barrier of her bra. Her nipples tightened and hardened as if to greet the touch.

She ground her hips against his, needy as she'd never been. As her fingers began to fumble at the buttons on his shirt, he caught her wrists in his hands and stepped back.

His ragged breathing filled the silence of the shed. "Not like this," he said when he finally found his voice. "I want you more than I've ever wanted a woman in my life, but not here in this dusty shed." He dropped her wrists and took another step backward. "I want you in a bed, Meredith. I want you naked between the sheets."

She didn't say a word, wasn't sure at the moment that she was capable of speech. Desire pooled like hot liquid in the pit of her stomach, and her limbs felt heavy with it.

He raked a hand though his hair, then looked at his wristwatch. "Dalton is picking me up in half an hour. I don't want this between you and me to be a fast, frantic groping in an old shed. If you want me like I want you, then come to my room tonight." He took a step toward the door and smiled. "I guess that means the next move is up to you."

He didn't wait for her reply but turned and exited the shed. Meredith stared after him. She wasn't sure what scared her more, the mysterious notes and the idea of an obsessed mystery man or Chase McCall, who she suspected had the power to shake up her life like it had never been shaken before.

Chase had no idea if Meredith would come to his room or not. He now sat on the edge of his bed clad only in a pair of boxers. It was almost eleven, and the rest of the occupants of the house had retired over an hour before.

If she didn't come to the room, then he had a feeling an ice-cold shower was in his very near future, for just thinking about making love to her had him painfully tense.

He'd spent the evening with Dalton, eating dinner in the café then heading to the bar to shoot some pool and enjoy a few beers. As usual he'd kept his eyes and ears open in hopes of seeing or hearing something that might point a finger of blame to the guilty party.

Agents Wallace and Tompkins had come in just as Dalton and Chase were getting ready to leave. The two men looked tired and nodded curtly to both Dalton and Chase before settling at a table and ordering drinks.

"I don't envy them their jobs," Dalton had said as they'd left the bar. Once again guilt had gnawed at Chase as he thought of how he'd deceived his friend.

He'd been concerned when he'd told Meredith the truth about himself. He hadn't known how she might react. He'd been pleased that she didn't intend to tell the rest of her family members that he was a viper among them. And he wasn't surprised by her easy belief in the integrity of her family members.

Stretching out on the bed, he thought about the Wests. In the times he'd seen them all together, the warmth and strength of the connection between them all had been undeniable.

Family. There had been a time in his distant past when he'd been hungry for family, for a loving connection to somebody, anybody besides the father who had twisted him inside and out.

Over the years he'd stuffed that need deep inside where it couldn't be trampled by false expectations or disappointments. Work had taken the place of family, work had filled the needs he might have once allowed himself. But being around the Wests stirred that old hunger to belong, to be loved.

He froze as a soft knock fell on his bedroom door. All thought of family fell away as he opened the door to see Meredith standing there. He pulled her into his room and closed the door, electrified by her very presence.

Instead of jeans and a shirt, she wore a navy-blue knee-length nightshirt. She smelled of night-blooming jasmine, and her eyes shone with both excitement and a hesitant self-consciousness.

He didn't say a word, but instead pulled her into his arms and lowered his mouth to hers, taking up where they had left off that afternoon in the shed.

The skin-to-skin contact of their bare legs, and the feel of her braless breasts against his chest sizzled desire through his veins. He couldn't remember ever wanting a woman as much as he wanted her. He wanted her naked and gasping beneath him, wanted her mewling with pleasure as she cried out his name.

He reached down and grabbed the bottom of her nightshirt and broke the kiss only long enough to pull the material up and over her head. He threw it to the floor as his gaze hungrily took in the sight of her, clad only in a pair of tiny navy panties.

She was beautiful, her body sleek and toned and her eyes holding the same hunger that burned inside him. She stepped out of her panties, and he tore off his boxers, then they tumbled to the bed as their mouths met again.

His hands cupped her breasts, thumbs playing over the hardened nipples. It was only when he replaced his thumbs with his mouth that she uttered her first sound, a low, deep moan that seemed to come from the very depths of her.

As he laved her breasts with his mouth, her hands danced up and down his back, kneading and softly scratching until he was half-mindless with pleasure.

He skimmed his hands down the flat of her abdomen, her skin silky and soft. As his hands moved farther down she tensed against him, as if anticipating the intimacy to come.

But he wanted her to have complete pleasure before he took his own. As far as he was concerned, there was nothing as stimulating as giving his partner her release.

He found the soft folds of her center. She was already moist and ready for him. As he caressed, she thrust her hips upward.

Her eyelids were half-mast and her eyes glittered as she wrapped her fingers around the length of him. He almost lost it then, almost gave in to his need to take her fast and hard. But he closed his eyes and fought for control.

The only sound in the room was their ragged

breathing, but as she stiffened against his fingers, she buried her face in his chest, shuddered and released a long, deep moan.

Before her shudders had completely passed, he rolled over, grabbed the foil package off the night-stand and opened it with trembling hands. Within seconds he had positioned himself between her thighs and slid into her.

She surrounded him, with her evocative scent, with her tight heat. He knew no matter how much he wanted to make this last, it wouldn't. It couldn't. She felt too good for him to maintain any kind of control.

He stroked into her fast…faster, and she met him thrust for thrust until he knew she was once again on the verge of release, until she cried out his name. It was only then that he allowed himself his own release.

Afterward he rolled over to the side of her, his heartbeat still crashing with speed. She lay on her back, her hair in wild disarray, her own chest rising and falling at an abnormal rate. He got up and quietly left the room to go to the bathroom in the hallway.

When he returned to his room she hadn't moved but she looked at him, her gaze slightly challeng-ing. "I'm not a slut. I don't fall into bed with every man who comes into town."

"The thought didn't even enter my mind," he replied as he got back into bed.

"It's been over a year since I've been with any man," she said.

"It's been almost that long since I've been with

a woman," he replied. For several moments they lay side by side, not speaking.

When his heartbeat had slowed and drowsy contentment swept over him, he reached for her and pulled her into his arms. She relaxed against him, her head on his chest and one leg sprawled over his.

He breathed in the scent of her as he swept a hand through her thick, dark hair. "I love the way you smell," he said softly.

"I love the way you feel," she said, her voice almost a purr. Her hand moved up his chest, stopping as it encountered one of his scars. "How did you get this?" She raised her head and looked at him.

"I had a broken bottle thrown at me."

"Were you involved in a barroom brawl?"

He fought the emotion that crawled up the back of his throat. "No barroom, just our kitchen. I'd forgotten to take out the trash and my father lost his temper."

Her fingers were soft as silk against his skin. "Your father did this to you?" Her gaze held a slight touch of horror.

Chase refused to let the baggage of his past destroy the fragile happiness he felt at this moment. "I told you my old man wasn't exactly Father of the Year." He took her hand in his and raised it to his lips. "And the last thing I want to talk about right now is him. He's dead and the past is gone."

"Except the scars," she replied.

"And they don't even hurt."

She laid her head back on his chest, and once

again his fingers danced through her hair. She'd been a good lover. For some reason he hadn't expected her to be so giving and so incredibly passionate.

It was nice that they were both on the same page, that he could enjoy this, enjoy her without worrying about what she might expect from him. No emotional entanglements, that was his creed, his motto for living.

Once again she raised her head and looked at him, her green eyes giving nothing away, not allowing him anywhere inside her head. "How long are you planning on being here?"

"I'm not sure. If it were up to me I'd say it's time to pack our bags. I don't believe any of your family members are involved in the crimes we're investigating."

"Why? Because we're all so charming?"

"There is that," he said with a smile. "But there's also the fact that we've run background checks on all of you and investigated your personal finances, your family business and everything else that might point to criminal activities."

"I should be outraged," she replied. "But right now I don't have the energy."

"Look at it this way, the suspect pool is considerably smaller if we remove all the Wests from the list."

She laughed, a low sexy sound. "I have a feeling that you could talk your way out of any difficult situation."

He grinned at her. "Why aren't you married?" he

asked. "You're gorgeous and bright. Even if you aren't particularly interested in being married, why don't you have a boyfriend? Why has it been a year since you've been with anyone?"

The sparkle in her eyes dimmed. "I did have a man I was seeing for a while, although not here in town. I was in Florida on assignment and met Todd. We dated for almost three months, then my assignment ended, and that ended our relationship."

He had a feeling there was more to the story than what she'd told him. But he didn't want to know about her heartaches. He didn't want that kind of emotional intimacy with anyone.

"What about you? Any near misses when it comes to matrimony?" she asked.

"Not even close," he replied. "I make sure the women I date understand that I'm not interested in marriage or long-term commitments of any kind." He recognized that his words were not only the truth, but also meant as a reminder to her.

"Not the marrying kind, huh. Neither am I," she said. She stifled a yawn. "And now it's time for me to sneak back to my own room."

For just a brief moment he wanted to tighten his arms around her and keep her from leaving. It might have been nice to wake up to the morning dawn with Meredith in his arms.

The quicksilver desire for that irritated him, and he immediately released her. "Good night," he said before she'd even placed her feet on the floor.

He watched as she got up, her sleek body
tempting him for another go round. Thankfully it
took her only a minute to pull the nightshirt over her
head and step into the bikini panties.

"Good night, Chase," she said softly, then disappeared out of the room.

He immediately turned off the bedside lamp and
shoved away that momentary whim of holding her
through the night. He'd just closed his eyes when
she screamed.

Chapter 7

The scream clawed up her throat and released itself, piercing the silence of the night as she saw the face pressed against her bedroom window. The face was there only a moment, then gone.

Chase burst into her room, a gun in his hand and his eyes narrowed with dangerous intent. "What's wrong?" Urgency deepened his voice.

Meredith pointed at her window. "Somebody was there…looking in. There was a face." She shuddered, fear whipping through her like a bitter winter wind.

At that moment Kathy and Smokey both appeared, Smokey holding a shotgun and Kathy clutching a small revolver. "What's going on?"

Kathy asked. With her free hand she clutched her robe more tightly around her.

"For God's sake put that pea shooter away before you hurt somebody," Smokey exclaimed to Kathy, obviously surprised that she had a gun. He turned his attention to Meredith. "What's wrong?"

Once again Meredith explained that she'd seen somebody at the window. "I'll go check it out," Smokey said.

"I'll come with you," Chase said.

As the two men left the room, Kathy placed an arm around Meredith. "Come on, honey, let's go wait in the kitchen."

Kathy dropped the revolver into the deep pocket of her robe as she and Meredith left the bedroom and walked down the hallway to the kitchen.

It was just a Peeping Tom, Meredith told herself. There was no reason to feel such fear. She was over-reacting and yet no amount of rationalization seemed to be able to banish the fear that chilled her to the bone and twisted her stomach into knots.

Kathy pointed her toward a kitchen chair, then set about making them each a cup of tea. Meredith sank down at the table, grateful for the solid chair beneath her as her legs trembled uncontrollably.

"Did you recognize the person?" Kathy asked as she placed tea bags into the two cups.

Meredith shook her head. "It all happened so fast. I couldn't tell you whether it was a familiar face or not, whether it was blue eyes or brown that

I saw peering in." She wrapped her arms around herself in an attempt to get warm. "I should have paid more attention, but I was so shocked, then I screamed and the face disappeared."

How long had the person been there? Had he watched her change from her clothes into her night-shirt? Had he watched her rub the scented cream on her body in preparation of going to Chase's room? The very thought made her ill. Her skin wanted to crawl right off her body.

Kathy added boiling water from the microwave to the cups, then set one of them in front of Meredith. "Drink up. There's nothing better than hot tea to take the chill out of you."

Meredith dunked her tea bag several times, then placed it on the saucer and added a spoonful of sugar to the cup. She wrapped her hands around it, welcoming the warmth. "I know I'm overreacting, but I feel so creeped out."

"That's not overreaction. That's normal," Kathy replied. "Somebody violated your personal space. Chase insisted a couple years ago that I get a gun and learn how to use it. There are too many creeps in the world these days."

Meredith took a sip of the hot tea, the liquid effectively warming the cold knot in her stomach. "I wish I hadn't screamed. I should have pretended I didn't see him then left the room and run outside to confront him."

Kathy reached out and patted one of Meredith's

hands. "Don't beat yourself up. You reacted on instinct. Maybe it's your secret admirer."

"If you're trying to make me feel better it isn't working," Meredith said dryly.

"I'm not trying to make you feel better. It just makes sense that maybe the person who sent you the roses was the person who peeked in your window."

"What kind of a man does things like that?" Meredith asked. It was a rhetorical question.

At that moment Chase and Smokey came into the kitchen. "Whoever it was, is gone now," Chase said. He'd managed to pull on a pair of jeans but was bare-chested. In the light of the kitchen the scars on his chest stood out.

"We checked all around the house and the immediate area surrounding it," Smokey said. "Who knows in what direction he ran when you screamed. It was probably just some kid looking for a cheap thrill."

Meredith knew he said these words to reassure her and she smiled at him. "Go back to bed, Smokey. I'm sorry for getting you up."

"From now on pull your shades at night," he said. "No sense in giving anyone a free peep show." With these words he ambled out of the kitchen.

Kathy got up from her chair. "I'm heading back to bed, too. When you get to be my age, you need all the beauty sleep you can get." She paused at the doorway. "Are you sure you're okay?"

Meredith nodded. "I'm fine. Thanks, Kathy."

Chase remained standing next to the counter after

Kathy left. "Are you really okay?" he asked. "Do you want to call Sheriff Ramsey and make a report?"

"No, there's not much he can do about it. Besides, these days he's got more important crimes to worry about than some pervert looking into my window. And yes, I'm really okay." She took another sip of her tea. The chill that had gripped her had finally passed. "Go to bed, Chase. I'm fine. I'm just going to finish my tea, then I'm going to bed."

"Are you sure?"

"I'm positive," she replied. Despite the fact that she'd just had a scare, she felt the need to be alone, to try to process everything the night had brought.

"You know where I am if you need me," he said, then left the kitchen.

The idea of going back to his bed and curling up in his arms for the remainder of the night was appealing. Too appealing.

She'd already been shaken up when she'd left his bedroom in the first place. Making love to Chase had been more wonderful than she'd expected. It hadn't just been the passion and intensity coming from him that had shocked her, but it had also been his unexpected tenderness.

That tenderness had found its way into a part of Meredith's heart that had never been touched before. It had frightened her almost as much as the face at the window.

She couldn't allow herself to get involved with Chase on an emotional level. She knew that could only lead to heartbreak. He'd made it very clear that he wasn't looking for any kind of real relationship.

She was nothing more than an appealing convenience, a break in his routine, and that was fine with her. She told herself she had no desire for anything long-term, either. She'd hoped for something like that once, with Todd, and that had ended with nothing but heartache. She didn't hope anymore.

Aware of the kitchen windows being open to anyone's gaze, she quickly finished her tea, carried the cup to the sink, then shut off the light and returned to her bedroom.

Once there the first thing she did was pull the shades on all the windows, making it impossible for anyone to peek in. She tried to visualize that face in her mind, to make sense of it, identify it. But all she got was a blur.

As she got into bed, she realized she hadn't told anyone about the notes she'd received. She wasn't sure what could be served by telling somebody about the notes now. There was certainly no way to discern who might have penned them simply by looking at the block letters.

She had little doubt that whoever had written the love notes had also sent the flowers and peeped into her window. Maybe what she needed to do was hang out more in town and see if she got any creepy vibes from anybody.

Creepy vibes. That's what she'd been feeling for the last month. Until she'd gotten the first note, she'd thought she was just imagining somebody watching her. Now she knew there was a reason for those vibes. Somebody was watching her... wanting her. All she had to do was figure out who and why he didn't just come forward and just ask her for a date.

A secret admirer. It was the stuff that romantic comedy movies were made of, the stuff of young girls' fantasies. But Meredith wasn't a young girl and her life wasn't a movie set.

She forced her eyes closed, seeking sleep to take the disturbing thoughts out of her head. Maybe tomorrow an assignment would come in that would take her away from Cotter Creek and her secret admirer.

She was surprised to see the light of dawn against the drawn window shades when she opened her eyes. She rolled over on her side and gazed at her alarm clock. Just after six. She'd slept through the night without dreams.

Though it had been a late night, she felt rested and ready to take on whatever the day might bring. She showered and dressed in her usual jeans and long-sleeved shirt, then pulled on a lightweight jacket and headed for the kitchen where Smokey and Kathy were already up and drinking coffee.

For a moment they didn't see her standing in the kitchen doorway, and she noticed how they leaned toward each other as they spoke, how there was a quiet intimacy between them that spoke of something more than houseguest and cook.

She had never known Smokey to show any kind of interest in any woman. His life had always been the West family, but there was something in the way he looked at Kathy that made Meredith realize Smokey might want something more from his life.

Her impulse was to warn him that Kathy was an FBI agent and would leave town at the same time Chase left. Guard your heart, she wanted to say to the man who'd helped raise her. Instead she said good morning and stepped into the kitchen.

"Meredith, how are you feeling this morning?" Kathy asked. "Did you sleep all right?"

"Like a baby," she replied. She got herself a cup of coffee, then joined them at the table. "Where's Dad?"

"He got up a little while ago and decided to take an early-morning ride around the property," Smokey said.

"Did we wake him last night with our little excitement," she asked.

Smokey grinned. "You know your dad, even though he won't admit it he's about half-deaf. He didn't hear anything last night."

"Good. I don't want him upset by any of it. I'm sure whoever was looking in the window last night didn't mean any harm." She took a drink of her coffee, then forced a smile to her lips. "I think what I have is a very shy admirer, and hopefully in the next day or two he'll get up his nerve to approach me in a more traditional manner."

"Anymore window peeping and I'm going to kick somebody's butt," Smokey said with his usual gruff flare.

They small talked for a little while longer, then Meredith got up and put her cup in the sink. "I'm going to go say hello to the horses, then take a walk out to the shed in the pasture."

"What in the hell are you going to do out there?" Smokey asked.

"I've been going through some of the boxes that Mom had packed out there."

"Why?" Smokey looked at her as if she'd lost her mind.

"If Meredith has a need to go through her mother's things, then there's nothing wrong with that," Kathy exclaimed. "Believe it or not, Smokey Johnson, some people are sentimental."

Meredith left them arguing about the merits of being sentimental. She walked out the back door, surprised that despite the early hour the sun was already warming the air.

They'd probably pay for these unusually nice days with tons of snow in another month or two. Although she'd played off the peeper from the night before with Smokey and Kathy, her 9 mm was tucked into her waistband beneath the jacket. She wouldn't be unprepared should he decide to show himself.

Again she told herself that she was probably

overreacting, but the idea of being out on the ranch alone and vulnerable was definitely not appealing.

Her boots whispered through the brown grass as she headed toward the stables where she spent several minutes with the horses.

As she left the stables, her gaze shot around the area, looking for what, she didn't know. There were plenty of places to hide on the property if somebody wanted to. Stands of trees were in every direction. Outbuildings dotted the landscape, making perfect places for somebody to hide behind.

"Stop it," she muttered with irritation. She refused to let the benign events of the past couple of days freak her out. There was no real reason to believe that any of it was a threat of harm.

The shed loomed in the distance, and she wondered what had drawn her back here again this morning. Maybe a dream she hadn't remembered? Or maybe it had been that in making love with Chase she'd felt a fierce desire to connect with the mother she'd never known, a mother she'd love to ask about men and love and life.

You don't miss what you never have. That's what people always said, but she mourned the mother she'd never had.

She unlocked the shed door and stepped inside. The box she'd looked in the day before was still on the old sofa. But there were several other boxes marked with Elizabeth's name.

She put away the one she'd already looked

through, grabbed another one and returned to the sofa where she sat and opened the box.

Once again she found old copies of reviews and playbills and photos. There were fan letters, too. She read each item with interest, lost for a few moments in another life, another time.

The box also contained several of Tanner's report cards from first and second grade, a construction-paper Valentine that read "To Mommy from Zack" and a variety of other items. Because of the mix of family items and Hollywood memorabilia, it was obvious to Meredith this box had been packed away long after her mother had moved to Cotter Creek.

Elizabeth West had given up so much to come here with her husband. She'd left behind a life of luxury and a budding career that most women would have envied.

Once again Meredith stared at a photo of her mother and wondered, *Will that kind of love ever find me?* Would she ever love somebody enough to leave her family, her life here in Cotter Creek?

Unbidden a vision of Chase entered her mind. It would be easy to let him into her heart just a little bit. Seeing the scars on his body had touched a soft core inside her, knowing that they had come from his father had appalled her.

She tried to imagine the little boy he'd been, a boy who had a father who abused him. Even though Meredith had grown up without the benefit of her mother, she'd had the love of both her father and Smokey.

Still, it would be foolish to let Chase into her heart in any small way. That path led to heartache, and she wasn't masochistic enough to want to consciously walk there.

She was about to put all the items back into the box when she realized there were several yellowing folded pieces of paper still in the bottom. She pulled out the first and carefully opened it. Her heart leaped into her throat.

"I've been waiting for you for a very, very long time. You are my destiny."

She stared at the note, and her fingers began to tremble. It was the same. The words and the block lettering were the very same as the notes that had been left on her car windshield.

Scarcely breathing, she set the note aside and reached for another of the papers. The second piece of paper made her heart race so fast she feared she was going to be sick.

"You will be mine forever."

The familiar words shot a trembling through her body. The same. These notes were identical to the ones she had received.

There was one piece of paper left in the box and she stared at it for a long moment, afraid to open it, afraid of what it might say. And yet there was a perverse curiosity that needed to be fed, an overwhelming need to know what might come next.

She picked up the piece of paper. The yellow, brittle paper felt evil in her fingers. She opened it and stared at the block letters.

"It's time."

Horror edged through her as her brain made the logical connection. Somebody had been stalking her mother, and her mother had wound up murdered. That same somebody was stalking Meredith.

Blinded by fear, she whirled around and screamed as her shoulders were grabbed by firm big hands.

Chapter 8

"Whoa," Chase exclaimed as he found himself suddenly looking at the business end of a 9 mm gun. "A little jumpy, are we?"

"What are you doing out here sneaking up on me? I could have shot you." Her voice trembled as she lowered the gun.

"I came out here to tell you if you didn't get back to the house you'd miss breakfast." He frowned, noticing her face was bleached of color. "Are you all right?"

"No. No, I'm not." Her green eyes held fear that forced a flurry of adrenaline through him.

"What's wrong, Meredith?" Her utter stillness

and blanched features caused a rising tension in him. Something had happened, something bad.

"I think my secret admirer is the man who murdered my mother."

She couldn't have surprised him more if she'd told him that she had been impregnated by a marauding alien. "What are you talking about?"

She tucked the gun in the back of her jeans, then grabbed his hand and led him to the sofa. Her ice-cold hand trembled in his. "I was going through a box of my mother's things and I found these." She handed him three pieces of old, yellowed paper.

He read each one, then looked back at her. "Rather troubling, but what does this have to do with you?"

"I got notes." She sank to the sofa and buried her face in her hands.

"You got notes?" He waited for her to continue.

"Just like these. Oh God, he killed my mother and now he wants me."

"Meredith, what are you talking about? What notes did you get? When?" He felt as if he had entered a movie halfway through and now had to play catch-up. Chase didn't like to play catch-up. "Meredith, answer me," he said impatiently.

He set the papers on the arm of the sofa, then sat next to her and pulled her hands away from her face. "What notes?"

As he stared at her she visibly pulled herself together. She straightened her back and some of the color returned to her cheeks. "I got the first one the night of the Fall Festival dance. When I went to my car to go home it was stuck beneath the windshield. 'I've been waiting for you for a very, very long time. You are my destiny.' That's what it said."

He still held on to her hands. It was like holding two ice cubes. "And the next note?"

"I got it yesterday when I was in town. It was on my windshield when I got ready to come home. It said 'You will be mine,' just like the notes that I found in the box. They were written in the same kind of block lettering as the ones I found in my mother's box." Her eyes were dark with a simmering fear. "I haven't gotten the third note yet."

"Why haven't you told me about the notes before now?" He rubbed her hands, trying to warm them up.

She caught her bottom lip with her teeth, for a moment looking more vulnerable than he'd ever seen her. "I thought they were love notes from a secret admirer. I was embarrassed by them. I thought they were a little bit weird, but nothing to be worried about."

"We still don't know that they're anything to worry about," he said. He wanted to take the fear out of her eyes. He needed to reassure her despite the cold, hard knot of apprehension that lay heavy in his chest. "We don't know exactly when your mother got those notes or that they were written by her killer. We don't want to jump to conclusions before we have any facts."

Some of the sharp edge of fear left her eyes but

no warmth crept back into her hands. "You'll probably think I'm crazy, but I've felt it. For the last month I've felt it getting closer to me."

"What? Felt what?"

She licked her lips, as if they were painfully dry. "Evil." The word whispered from her as if forced out against her will.

Meredith West was not a woman given to dramatics. In the brief time he'd known her, she wasn't given to histrionics or exaggeration. The knot in his chest grew a little bigger.

"Come on, let's get out of here." He released her hands and stood. "I think you should go talk to the sheriff. Do you still have the notes you got?"

She nodded and also stood. "They're in a drawer in my bedroom."

He grabbed the notes from the arm of the sofa. "Then we'll take them and these and let the sheriff know what's going on."

"He won't be able to do anything," she said, her voice sounding stronger than it had before. She locked up the shed and they began the walk back to the ranch house.

"That may be true, but it doesn't hurt to have it on record," he replied.

"I don't want anyone to know about this." She shot him a quick glance. "I don't want to worry my father and I sure don't want to stir up my brothers." A hint of stubbornness crept into her voice. "This is my business and I'll handle it."

"There might come a time when you have to tell them," he replied.

"When that time comes I'll deal with it."

"I'll ride into town with you to see the sheriff," he said.

He thought she might protest, but instead she flashed him a look of gratitude. "I would appreciate it."

"Why don't we head into town now and I'll buy you breakfast at the café after we talk to Sheriff Ramsey."

"That sounds like a deal," she replied.

They walked for a few minutes in silence. Although Chase had tried his best to waylay her fears, to convince her that just because she'd gotten the same notes as her mother that didn't mean the same fate awaited her.

Still, even as he'd told her that, told himself that, he couldn't help but wonder what might happen if and when she got the third note.

"It's time."

He didn't know what those words meant, but he had a sick feeling that it wasn't good.

Even though Meredith appreciated how Chase had tried to alleviate her fears, his rational words had done little to do the trick.

When they got back to the house, she asked her father when the boxes had been packed away in the shed. He told her that her mother had packed and sent them to the shed two days before her death.

This information only intensified the bad feeling she had of impending doom. Now, driving into town with Chase in the passenger seat, she mentally repeated all the things Chase had said to her.

There was no reason to believe that the notes had anything to do with her mother's death—except she believed they did. There was no way to know exactly when her mother might have received the notes in relationship to her murder. And yet Meredith felt the connection in her very bones, in her very soul.

Evidence didn't always matter. Sometimes you had to go with your gut instinct, and Meredith's gut instinct was screaming that her mother's murderer now had her in his sights.

"You know it won't help going to Sheriff Ramsey," she said, needing conversation to halt the thoughts whirling around in her head. "There's not much he's going to be able to do about this."

"I know, but I still think it's a good idea to make a report. Besides, who knows what he might be able to find out." He was silent for a moment then continued, "You know, maybe your mother had a secret admirer. Maybe it's the same person as your secret admirer, but that doesn't mean he's a killer."

She flashed him a quick glance. "Do you really believe that?"

"I'm not sure what to believe at this point," he admitted. "But I think it would be a mistake to jump to any conclusions. Right now all we know for sure is that it looks like a person who wrote notes to your mother is also writing notes to you."

She parked her car in front of the sheriff's office and grabbed the two plastic bags on the seat between them. One contained the notes she had found in her mother's box. The other contained the ones she'd received. "Let's get this over with," she said and got out of the car.

Molly Richmond, the dispatcher and receptionist, greeted them and told them Sheriff Ramsey was in his office. She led them down the hallway to his inner sanctum.

He rose in surprise as Meredith and Chase walked in. "Meredith…Mr. McCall, what brings you here?" He gestured them into the two chairs in front of his desk and shut the back door that he'd apparently had open to allow in some fresh air.

Chase remained silent as Meredith explained to Sheriff Ramsey about the notes she'd received, the roses and the notes she'd found in the box of her mother's things.

When she'd finished, the sheriff leaned back in his chair, a deep frown cutting across his broad forehead. "I'll send those notes to the lab in Oklahoma City and see if they can pull anything off them."

"My fingerprints will be all over them," she said.

"And so will mine." Chase grimaced, as if irritated with himself for touching the notes.

"Then we'll see if the lab can get anyone else's

off them, although I've got to tell you I don't have much hope. If what you think is true, if the person who wrote those notes is the same person who killed your mom, then he's been smart enough to have eluded everyone for twenty-five years. I figure he's smart enough not to leave behind any fingerprints."

"Of course, there's no way of knowing if the person who wrote these notes is the same person who might have killed Elizabeth," Chase said. "We just thought it was important to make a report of what we found and about the notes Meredith has been receiving."

"Absolutely," Sheriff Ramsey agreed. He looked at Meredith for a long moment, his expression soft. "I was the one who found your mom that night. I was a young deputy and I saw her car off at the side of the road and went to investigate."

All his features tightened and he shook his head. "I'll never forget it. There were sacks of groceries in the back of the car, and she was laid out on the ground like she was sleeping." He shook his head again as if to rid his brain of a bad memory. "We investigated her death vigorously at the time." He looked at Chase. "Did she show you the file?"

"Yeah, I looked it over. It looked to me like you all did everything possible to investigate the crime."

"We did. The town was in an uproar. She was well liked and it was such a tragedy." He looked down at the top of his desk for a minute, then looked back at Meredith. "It's possible whoever wrote those notes means no harm at all, but my recommendation to you is for you to be aware of your surroundings and just be careful."

Meredith nodded, oddly disappointed. She wasn't sure what she had expected. Perhaps she'd hoped that Sheriff Ramsey would look at the handwritten notes and exclaim that he knew who had written them. Of course that was crazy because the block letters could have been written by anybody.

"Well, that was a wasted effort," she said a few minutes later as they left the office.

"Not necessarily," Chase replied. "Who knows what Ramsey might stumble on, now that he knows what's going on and about the notes."

She started toward her car, but he grabbed her by the elbow. "Oh no, we aren't going back to the ranch yet," he said. "I already missed one breakfast, and part of the deal was that we'd stop in at the sheriff's office, then have breakfast at the café."

She'd thought she just wanted to go home, but maybe the clatter of noise and friendly conversation in the café would take her mind off things.

"Breakfast sounds good," she agreed.

As they headed across the street toward the café she once again felt as if somebody was watching her. The morning sun cast shadows between buildings and in the overhangs of storefronts, and she wondered if somebody was hiding in one of those shadows watching her progress, wanting her for some sick reason.

She was grateful to get inside the café where the morning crowd was noisy and there were no shadows. She and Chase grabbed a booth toward the back, both of them moving to slide into the booth so they faced the door.

He pointed her to the opposite side, as if he understood her need to face out and watch for danger. "I'm on duty. You sit and relax."

Relax. Would she ever be relaxed again? At the moment every muscle in her body ached with stress, every nerve ending felt as if it was exposed.

"Talk to me, Chase," she said after the waitress had taken their orders and they each had a cup of coffee in front of them.

"What do you want to talk about?"

"Anything. Everything," she exclaimed with a hint of desperation. "I just want you to take my mind off all of this."

His eyes glimmered with a touch of humor. "We could talk about sex. It's been my experience that when it's on my mind, I find it hard to think about much of anything else."

She laughed, surprised that she was still capable of amusement. "You're such a man," she replied.

He grinned. "I'll take that as a compliment."

"You can also take it that I don't want to talk about sex," she replied. She wished he'd never mentioned it, because now her head filled with memories of making love with him. "Tell me about your life in Kansas City."

"There's not a lot to tell," he replied. "I live in a ranch house that I bought two years ago, but I spend most of my time working. In the small amount of leisure time I have, I like to ride my bike and do yard work. It's a pretty normal life."

"What made you decide to become a cop?"

He leaned back in the booth, and his hand reached up to touch the faint white scar that bisected his eyebrow. "When I was sixteen I got up one morning and went to school as usual, but while I was at school I remembered that it was my dad's payday."

He paused and took a drink of his coffee, and any hint of a smile that had been on his face was gone. His eyes took on a darker hue and she knew his memories were bad ones.

"Paydays weren't good?" she asked.

"They were hell. It was my dad's usual habit on paydays to stop after work at one of the local casinos. He'd drink and gamble away most of the check, then come home in the foulest mood imaginable."

"And you were his favorite scapegoat."

He smiled then, a tight expression that did nothing to lighten the darkness of his eyes. "You've got it. Anyway, the longer I thought about it that particular day, the sicker I got. I was tired, sick and tired of him and my life. I skipped the rest of the school day and went home. I packed a bag, took whatever cash I could find around the house, then split for good. I wasn't going to take one more beating. I wasn't going to listen to one more of his drunken apologies or empty promises."

"Where did you go?" She realized she wanted to know everything about him. She knew where he liked to be touched when making love, she knew that a kiss in the hollow of his throat made him groan.

But she wanted to know what kind of man he was, what choices he'd had to make in his life that had formed Chase McCall.

"My dad and I lived in St. Louis and all I knew was that I needed to get out of there. I wanted to go somewhere where he'd never find me and wouldn't be able to force me to come back home. I had enough money for a bus ticket to Kansas City and that's where I went."

Meredith tried to imagine what it had been like for a sixteen-year-old to strike out on his own for a different city, a life alone. "You must have been terrified."

This time his smile did reach his eyes. "Nah, I was too stupid to be terrified. Anything had to be better than the life I'd been living, even life on the streets."

The conversation halted as the waitress appeared with their orders. When she left again Chase continued. "Anyway, I lived on the streets for about two months, sleeping under highway overpasses, eating whatever I could scrounge. I met a lot of people, sad homeless men without hope, drug addicts without a future. I realized that if I didn't do something positive with my life I was going to end up either dead or in jail. I got a job sweeping floors and stocking for a man who ran a little food mart. He let me sleep on a cot in the storeroom and I got my GED. Student loans and financial aid helped me get a bachelor's degree, then I was accepted into the police academy and the rest is history."

"What happened to your father? Did you ever see him again?"

"Two years ago I got word that he was ill so I went back to St. Louis to see him. He was still angry with me for abandoning him. He told me all he'd ever done was love me and I'd run out on him." Chase shook his head and emitted a humorless laugh. "He'd either rewritten history or didn't even remember the abuse. Anyway, he died not long after."

"That's sad," she said. She wanted to reach out and touch his hand. She wanted to pull him into her arms and somehow comfort the child he had been.

He shrugged. "It's the past. They say what doesn't kill you makes you strong."

She wondered if perhaps he hadn't been made too strong? He seemed to be a man who needed nobody. He'd made it clear he wasn't willing to invite anyone into his life, into his heart for any extended period of time. Not that she cared. Not that she wanted to be in his life, she told herself.

"Now are you ready to talk about sex?" he asked, the twinkle back in his eyes.

She laughed and sat back in the booth and wondered when she'd begun to like this man. Certainly she had wanted him, but the warmth that flooded through her now had nothing to do with physical desire.

It had everything to do with the fact that she liked being with him, she liked the way his brain worked and the unexpected humor that transformed his features from something slightly dangerous to something decidedly wonderful.

"Thank you," she said. She pushed away her empty plate.

"For what?"

"For making me forget for a few minutes. For letting me enjoy my breakfast without thinking about anything but you."

"Then we're even because I haven't been able to think of anything but you since last night."

She felt as if the confines of the café got smaller as his gaze lingered on her lips. "You're a dangerous man, Chase McCall," she said softly.

He laughed, low and deep, the sound rumbling inside her. "You ready to get out of here?" he asked.

She nodded and together they got up from the booth. It was only as they arrived at her car and she'd checked the windshield for a note that she realized it was now a waiting game.

Sooner or later she knew she'd get a third note. "It's time." She had no idea what those two words meant, but she definitely had a feeling it wasn't good.

Chapter 9

Chase sat on the bench next to Sam Rhenquist and pulled the collar of his jacket up around his neck. Over the past two days the warm weather had fled and cold Northern air had swooped south to settle in.

"You sit out here all year long?" Chase asked the old man.

"Unless it's raining," Sam replied. "I dozed off one day last year during a snowfall. Didn't wake up until old Mrs. Johnson came by and thought I was dead. She screamed so loud it about broke my eardrums."

Chase smiled and stole a glance at his watch. Meredith was having lunch with Savannah, and he'd ridden into town with her. In fact, over the past two days he'd been right at her side unless she was inside the house.

"She won't be out for another hour or so," Sam said, apparently noticing the glance at the watch. "When those two women get to gabbing it's always a two-hour lunch."

"Are you married, Sam?"

"Was married for forty-two years. Abby passed away on a warm summer night. She rubbed my back until I fell asleep, then died peaceful without making a sound."

"Must be tough to find yourself alone after all those years," Chase said.

Sam smiled. "I hear her voice in my head all the time. I never think about her being gone. She's with me all the time." He pointed across the street to an old woman with a cane heading into the Curl Palace. "That's old Mrs. Crondale. She lost her husband two years ago and her grief has made her one of the most miserable, bitter women in town. She gets her hair done once a week then heads to the café to get a cup of soup and under-tips the waitress."

Once again Chase was struck by how much the old man knew about the comings and goings of the people. "Sam, I'm going ask you straight out. You know something about the deaths of those ranchers?"

Sam gazed across the street, his weatherworn face not changing expression. "I know a lot of things about most of the people of Cotter Creek, some things I'm sure they'd rather nobody else knew. But I don't know who killed those men."

"You're a smart man, Sam. Surely you've got some idea," Chase pressed.

Sam turned back and looked Chase square in the eyes. "I'm smart enough to know better than to talk to a man who isn't what he's pretending to be."

Surprise jolted through Chase. "What are you talking about?"

Sam gave him a look of disgust. "You aren't here for a little vacation. When folks get a chance to go on vacation they sure as hell don't choose to come to Cotter Creek. Besides, you got a look about you that tells me you're here for another reason."

Chase was silent for a long moment, considering his options. "I trust you, Sam. I trust you to be a man who can keep his mouth shut when it's important. I'm FBI."

Sam nodded. "I figured as much." He sat forward and reached for a cup of coffee on the ground next to the bench. The drink was in a to-go cup from the café.

Chase hoped like hell that he hadn't made a mistake in confiding in Sam. It wasn't exactly a great thing to be undercover and then tell people about it. But his instincts told him he could trust the old man.

"I saw Sheila meet with a stranger one night," Sam said. He took a sip of his coffee, then continued. "It was right about the time that the Nesmith place was sold. I figure the man I saw her with was this Joe Black that everyone is talking about, the man who owns MoTwin."

Chase nodded. "We know Black came into town several times over the course of the last year to sign contracts on behalf of the MoTwin Corporation."

"What I never understood was what business he might have over at the newspaper office."

Every nerve in Chase's body electrified. "You saw Joe Black go to the newspaper office?"

Sam nodded. "After hours. Ray Buchannan met him at the door and they were inside together for about an hour."

"Have you told anyone else about this?" Chase's mind whirled. He knew from Meredith that Raymond Buchannan had just made Savannah an offer on the paper. He had plans to get out of town. Now his retirement plans took on a different perspective.

"I didn't know who to tell," Sam said. "Didn't know who to trust and I damn sure didn't want to be seen consorting with those suited fools you all sent to town."

"Thank you for trusting me." Chase knew he needed to call the two agents as soon as possible and give them this lead. Hopefully it would result in the end of this assignment and he could leave Cotter Creek far behind.

Or could he? Even though every day he felt the need to leave, he knew he couldn't walk away knowing that Meredith might be in danger. There had been no more flower deliveries, no more notes, but Chase felt as if they were in a holding pattern and waiting to see what happened next.

He glanced over to where her car was parked. There was no way she'd get a note on her windshield today without him seeing who put it there.

Maybe there won't be another note, he thought. Maybe whoever had sent them was finished, momentarily obsessed with Meredith as they might have been with her mother. Obsession was rarely good. And no matter how he tried to twist his mind to convince himself there was no danger, he wasn't quite successful.

At that moment Meredith and Savannah walked out of the café. Meredith's gaze found him, and the smile that lit her features caused a flutter of crazy regret in his gut.

If the lead that Sam had just given him led to solving the land-scheme crimes, then Chase's work here would be done. What shocked him was the realization that he wasn't ready to say goodbye to Meredith.

He stood to wait for her as she said goodbye to Savannah, who then disappeared into the newspaper office. As Meredith walked toward him, the familiar heat of a simmering desire stoked through him. It had been with him for the past two days as he'd scarcely let her out of his sight.

The problem was he didn't know whether to act on it or ignore it. She was getting to him in ways no woman had ever gotten to him before. Even though he'd known her less than two full weeks, he felt as if he'd known her for half a lifetime. He was comfortable in her presence. Aside from the desire he felt for her, he liked the way she thought, admired her and enjoyed the sound of her laughter.

He wanted to run from her because she stirred in him a hunger for something more than he'd had in his life. She drew him to her, and he felt the need to fight like hell to keep some sort of distance.

Kathy certainly hadn't been overthrilled at the news that he'd told Meredith who they really were and exactly why they were here. "Too close," she'd warned him. "You're getting too close."

"Hi," Meredith said as she stopped in front of him. "Good afternoon, Mr. Rhenquist."

"What's good about it?" he asked with his usual scowl.

She smiled, obviously not bothered by his attitude. "What's good about it? I just had a wonderful lunch with my best friend. Even though the wind is cold, the sun is shining and today's meat loaf at the café was the best I've ever tasted."

"You better not let Smokey hear you say that," Rhenquist replied. "That man takes great pride in his cooking skills."

"You're right," she said with a laugh. "The meat loaf will be our little secret." She looked at Chase. "You ready?"

He nodded and with a goodbye to Sam, he and Meredith headed for her car. It was obvious her lunch with Savannah had been pleasant. Her mood was light, and he felt his mood responding likewise.

"It must have been a good lunch," he said as they got into the car. "You look like you had a good time."

She started the engine, a smile curving her lush lips. "I always have a good time with Savannah. She's so bright and funny." A faint frown creased her forehead. "You know she had terrible parents, too. Her mother basically told her she was ugly and no man would ever fall in love with her, and her dad simply ignored her."

"That's too bad," he said, as always finding it hard to concentrate on anything but the scent of her, which always reminded him of their night together.

"She and Joshua met when they were both investigating the death of Charlie Summit. He was an old man who lived on the edge of town, and he was killed for his land." She flashed him a quick glance. "But you probably know about that."

"I do." Before his arrival in Cotter Creek, Chase had read all the files concerning all the deaths.

"Anyway, the big news is not only did Savannah sign the papers to make the newspaper hers, but she and Joshua set a date for their wedding. Isn't that terrific?"

"It's great. My big news is that Sam told me that Joe Black had business with Raymond Buchannan late one night after newspaper hours."

She looked at him with surprise, then quickly focused her attention back on the road. "Wow. So, you think maybe Buchannan is behind it all?"

"I'm not sure what to think, but he definitely just rose to the top of the suspect list as far as I'm concerned. In fact, when I get back to the ranch I need to call Wallace and Tompkins and let them know what Sam told me."

She shook her head, the dark strands beckoning him to touch them. "Raymond Buchannan. I just can't believe it. He's been a lifelong resident here. Why on earth would he betray his town, his friends and neighbors?"

"Whoever orchestrated this stood to gain tons of money," he replied. "Love or money, those seem to be at the crux of almost every crime committed."

For a few minutes they rode in silence. Chase stared out the window, fighting the wealth of need that pressed inside him. The need to hold her in his arms once again, the need to taste her mouth one more time.

"You don't have to do this you know," she finally said.

"Do what?" He looked at her curiously.

"You don't have to go everywhere with me. You don't have to be with me every minute that I'm away from the house. I know how to take care of myself. I'm a professional bodyguard."

He looked at her, taking in the soft curve of her jaw, the long lashes that framed her impossibly green eyes. "It's my professional opinion that the bodyguard needs a bodyguard."

She flashed those gorgeous eyes his direction once again. "I think maybe we're both overreacting to the notes. I mean, yes, it's creepy that somebody wrote notes to my mother and apparently is now writing them to me. But that doesn't mean it was the person who killed her."

"I'm aware of that," he replied. "But I'm also aware that we can't know right now that the note writer wasn't responsible for your mother's death. I'd feel better if we could learn the identity of the person who wrote those notes. It's possible he's nothing more than a harmless eccentric who had a crush on your mother years ago and now has a crush on you."

"That would mean he's probably old," she replied. She flashed him a smile that didn't quite lift the shadows from her eyes. "If he's old, then I could probably take him in a brawl."

"There's no guarantee he's that old," Chase replied. "Maybe he was just a teenager when he got a crush on your mother. That would mean he might be as young as forty."

"Buck Harmon's age," she replied thoughtfully.

"Or a dozen other men in town."

She pulled her car up in front of the house and turned off the engine. "For the last month or so I've had the feeling of somebody watching me." She turned in the seat to look at him. "You know that prickly sensation you get on the back of your neck when you feel like you're being watched."

"But you haven't seen anyone suspicious? Don't have a clue who might be watching you?"

She shook her head. "Believe me, if I did I'd

confront them." She paused a moment, her expression thoughtful. "So, if this lead about Raymond Buchannan pans out, then you'll probably be leaving soon."

"We'll see how things play out," he replied. He got out of the car then, needing distance, fighting the ever-present desire for something he couldn't quite define, something that scared the hell out of him.

He managed to keep his distance from her for the remainder of the day. He made the phone call to Agent Wallace, then spent the afternoon chatting with Red about ranch life, his children and the family business.

Even while he talked to Red, he was always conscious of where Meredith was in the house. It was as if he had a built-in radar where she was concerned. She spent most of the afternoon in the kitchen with Smokey and Kathy, then went to her room.

He didn't see her again until dinner. Tanner and Anna arrived to share the meal, Anna glowing with happiness as she stroked the bulge of her pregnant stomach.

As they ate, Smokey and Kathy argued about the right way to make brisket, Tanner and Anna talked about their plans for their growing family and Chase found himself unable to take his attention off Meredith.

Instead of her usual jeans and flannel shirt, she'd changed for dinner into a pair of slim black slacks and a deep-burgundy blouse that did amazing things to her creamy complexion. She made it damn hard for him to concentrate on the meal.

It was after supper and after Tanner and Anna had left when Meredith said she was headed out to the barn to check on the horses.

Chase grabbed his jacket and fell into step with her. "I doubt I need bodyguard protection in my own stables," she said as they walked toward the wooden structure in the distance. "Besides, I have my gun." She moved the side of her jacket to show the weapon stuffed into her waistband.

"Armed women always turn me on," he said teasingly.

"I think probably breathing women turn you on," she retorted with a laugh.

"That's not true," he protested. "You make me sound like a helpless womanizer and I'm not."

"I know you aren't. I was just teasing." She fell silent as they reached the stables.

He sat on a bale of hay and watched as she went from stall to stall. She seemed softer here, oddly vulnerable as she greeted the horses with a whispered voice and a stroke on the head. He could almost see the tension rolling off her shoulders, disappearing from her facial features.

It was as if the world shrank to nothing bigger than the interior of the stable with the scent of hay and horse and leather, and he knew by her posture and her facial expression that this had always been a safe place for her.

When she was finished telling each of the animals good-night, she joined him on the bale of hay, as if reluctant to go directly back to the house.

Instantly he was aware of her scent, that arousing smell of jasmine. "You like it out here, don't you."

She smiled. "This was always my place. You can't imagine how difficult it was to grow up with five brothers who loved nothing better in the world than to torment and tease me. This was always where I'd run if I needed to cry or I needed to cuss."

He laughed and tried to imagine her as a child. "But surely you had girlfriends who you could talk to, bond with."

Her smile turned rueful. "That's the other problem with having five gorgeous brothers. Most of the girls who wanted to be my best friend really just wanted to hang out here and be around my brothers."

"It sounds lonely."

She frowned thoughtfully, then turned to look at him. "I know you've said you have no intention of getting married or anything like that, but don't you ever get lonely, Chase?"

He wanted to answer her with a resounding no, but the very question itself illuminated the loneliness he'd struggled with for a very long time. And it irritated him, that somehow in the past two weeks at the West ranch, she'd made him feel that loneliness again.

"Never," he replied curtly. He stood. "We should probably get back to the house. It's getting dark."

He didn't look at her, was afraid that if he did she might see the lie in his eyes, might know the depth of loneliness that had always been with him.

Chapter 10

That night Meredith lay in bed fighting against a restlessness she'd never known before, and she suspected the restlessness had a name and its name was Chase.

It had been days since he'd touched her, since he'd kissed her, and there was a burn of want in the pit of her stomach. There was no denying the tension that existed between them every moment that they were together. But he'd made no move to act on it.

And that's good, she told herself as she rolled over on her back and stared up at the ceiling where the moonlight danced with faint silver hues. It was good because she was falling in love with Chase McCall.

She hadn't planned it; she didn't even want it, but there it was. He'd gotten to her with his sharp blue eyes and edge of arrogant confidence. He'd touched her with his easy laughter and sexy flirting. But more than anything, he'd crawled directly into her heart when she'd seen a flash of his wounded soul.

She wasn't a rescuer, knew that there was no way to take away the pain of his past. But, God help her, she wished she could be part of his future.

It wouldn't be long before he and Kathy would pack their bags and leave Cotter Creek behind. Meredith had a feeling Smokey would miss Kathy desperately. She'd never seen him so animated, so ready with a smile as he was when Kathy was around.

There would be hearts needing healing when they left. And they would heal…eventually. She squeezed her eyes closed, willing away thoughts of Chase.

Instead she focused on the question of who might be her secret admirer. He could be as young as forty or as old as her father. That certainly didn't lessen the list of potential suspects, rather it pointed a finger to almost any man in Cotter Creek.

The notes held the quality of obsession rather than love. If she were to guess, the person had been obsessed with her mother, and because Meredith was the spitting image of her mother, she'd now garnered the attention of the same person.

So what did he want from her? Why hadn't he made himself known yet? Was it possible that he'd identified himself to her mother, and Elizabeth had rebuffed him? Had that been the end of it, or was he the man who had flagged Elizabeth down on the side of the road and strangled the life out of her?

Meredith wasn't even sure if her fear was warranted. But warranted or not, she couldn't help the cold chill that gripped her heart each time she thought of those notes. She couldn't help the instincts that screamed that something bad was going to happen.

A soft knock fell on her door. She reached out to turn on the nightstand lamp, then slid out of bed and to her bedroom door. She opened it an inch to see Chase.

"I lied," he said softly. "I do get lonely. I'm lonely right now."

She knew she had two choices. She could either open the door all the way and let him in or she could tell him to go back to bed and shut the door.

If she let him in, there was no question that they would make love again. There was no question that her feelings for him would only intensify. But if she sent him back to his room she had a feeling she would regret it for the rest of her life.

She opened the door wider and once he was in her room she closed it behind him. He stood for a long moment, his gaze searching hers as if seeking the answer to a question he hadn't voiced.

Taking his hand, she led him to her bed. He laid the condom he'd brought with him on the nightstand, then took off his boxers and slid beneath her sheets.

He was going to break her heart, this man with passion in his eyes. He was going to break her heart and there was nothing she could do about it.

With a sense of both resignation and sweet anticipation, she pulled off her nightgown and joined him in the bed. He reached for her and she went willingly into his arms even knowing that there was a piece of her heart she would never be able to claim back from him.

His kiss was achingly tender, his lips soft against hers. It was impossible for her to think when she was in his arms, impossible to do anything but feel.

He seemed to be in no hurry but rather moved with a languid sensuality, as if he recognized they had all the hours of the long night ahead of them.

As he caressed her breasts first with his hands, then with his mouth, unexpected tears pressed hot at her eyes. This would be the last time she'd feel his touch, taste his mouth. As much as she cared about him, she wouldn't, couldn't do this again.

This knowledge made each kiss, every touch more intense and tinged with a bittersweet element. They didn't say a word, but no words were necessary as the kisses grew deeper and the caresses hotter and more intimate.

He knew just where to touch and kiss her to evoke the most intense response…her inner thigh, the skin just behind her ear, the back of her knees.

And she responded in kind, finding the places on

his body that produced a deep moan and tightened all his muscles and made him hoarsely whisper her name.

When they were both gasping and aching with need, it was she who put the condom on him, she who urged him to move over her and take her.

She wanted to be lost in him, and as he stroked deeply into her she *was* lost. She gave him every-thing—her passion, her tenderness and her heart. And at least while they made love she felt as if she had his in return.

Afterward she expected him to get up and creep back to his own room, but he didn't. He went to the bathroom, then returned and got back beneath her sheets.

The lamp that she had turned on when she'd heard the knock on her door had remained on during their lovemaking. He now reached over her to turn it off, then gathered her into his arms.

His heartbeat was strong and steady against hers and she nuzzled her head into his shoulder, wishing for things that would never be, wanting something different than she knew the future contained.

But she couldn't change anything that might come. All she could do was grasp with both hands the moment happening right now.

"I spent a lot of years being lonely," he said softly as one of his hands stroked the length of her hair. "I sometimes think I invented lonely."

His words pierced through her, and once again she wished she could go back in time and fix the pain and isolation he'd felt as a child. As the only girl in the West family, she'd certainly at times felt isolated and alone, but she'd always known that she had a houseful of people who loved her, people who would never really hurt her.

"Was there nobody you could talk to? Nobody to tell about your dad's abusiveness?"

He sighed. "Looking back now there were probably people I could have told. Maybe a teacher or a neighbor. But at the time it never occurred to me. And even if it had, I think I would have been too afraid to tell. Besides, as crazy as it sounds, there was a part of me that was fiercely protective of my dad."

She knew he'd gifted her with a piece of himself that he'd probably never shared before and she was honored by that.

"Anyway," he continued. "I learned to live with the loneliness. It's been a part of my life for so long I'm not sure I'd feel right without it."

She tightened her arms around him, wanting to memorize the feel of his body next to hers, the scent of his skin that filled her head. She closed her eyes as she matched her breathing to his.

For the first time in her life she felt as if she belonged where she was, in Chase McCall's arms. And all too quickly he'd be out of her life.

He leaned against the side of the house, fighting the rage that swept through him. His tight chest made it hard to breathe, and he fisted his hands into balls at his side.

He'd come here hoping to get a glimpse of Meredith, just a quick peek of her to feed him, to sustain him until he could make her his forever. Her shades had been drawn but one of them wasn't completely down and gave him a tiny peephole into her room.

He'd looked in and had been shocked as he saw Meredith and Chase McCall moving intimately together beneath the sheets on the bed.

He now squeezed his eyes tightly closed as if he could banish the image.

It was his fault...Chase McCall. He'd seduced her, just like Red West had seduced the sweet Elizabeth so many years ago.

He'd pay. Chase McCall would pay. There was no way anyone was getting in the way this time, especially not some big-city boy with his sweet-talk and charm.

He stole away from the house the way he had come, melting into the shadows of the night.

Chase awoke with the dawn, for a moment disoriented as he gazed at his surroundings. Then he remembered he was in Meredith's room. He turned his head to see her curled up on her side facing him, her features relaxed with sleep.

He watched her for a long moment, taking in the strong features that worked together to create beauty. He'd told her more than he'd ever told anyone about himself and his past. Something about her had encouraged trust and confidence.

It was time to leave, time to escape before she got any further into his heart. She drew him toward her with the promise of no more loneliness, with the promise of happiness. But he was scared of that, afraid that eventually that happiness would shatter and he would show himself to be nothing more than his father's son.

He crept out of bed, careful not to wake her, and stole out of the room. As he stepped into the hallway he was shocked to see Kathy, clad only in a long nightgown, sneaking down the hall toward her bedroom. For a moment they stood and stared at each other, then she quickly disappeared into her room.

So, it's like that, Chase thought as he got dressed a few minutes later. He had no doubt that his partner had spent the night in Smokey's room. It would appear that neither of them had been able to withstand the charm of certain members of the West family.

They were all at breakfast when Clay came in and joined them for coffee. "Where's Libby and Gracie?" Meredith asked her brother.

"They had an appointment over at the Curl Palace for hair cut and styles and manicures and pedicures. I figured I'd come and hang out here with dad while my two girls are doing their girl thing."

"I'm glad," Red said with a smile at his son. "I always like it when you boys come to visit."

"What's everyone's plans for the day?" Clay asked and looked around the table.

"Smokey and I are going into town to buy some groceries," Kathy said while Chase looked at Meredith expectantly. Whatever she had planned he wouldn't be far away. He'd told her the truth when he'd said that the bodyguard needed a bodyguard.

"I thought I might do a little riding after breakfast," she said.

"Riding?" Chase frowned. "I hope you're talking about riding in your car."

A faint whisper of a smile curved her lips. "No, I'm talking about getting on my horse. I haven't taken Spooky out for over a week. She needs a good ride. Besides, I figured it was time you got on the back of a good horse."

"Do you ride, Chase?" Clay asked.

"Never in my life," he replied.

"There's almost nothing better than being on the back of a horse on a fall morning," Red said. "Meredith's a fine horsewoman. She'll get you set up and you'll never forget the experience."

"That's what I'm afraid of," he said dryly.

As they finished breakfast, Clay told them about a new advertising campaign his stepdaughter, Gracie, had been offered. "It's a new line of kids' clothes. They're using her for the print ads and then in November we're flying to New York to do a television commercial."

Chase knew that Clay had gone to California to

work as a bodyguard for eight-year-old Gracie who was a successful child star. In the process of caring for the child, he'd fallen in love with Gracie's mother, Libby.

"We're being very selective of what we let her do, but she wanted to do this, and both Libby and I like the people involved," Clay continued.

The conversation remained pleasant for the rest of the meal. When they were finished eating, and Smokey and Kathy were clearing the dishes, Meredith shot him a quick smile. "Go on, cowboy, get a jacket and then it's time to introduce you to a horse."

After he went to his room and she went to hers, they met in the hallway, both wearing jackets for the brisk morning air.

"I can't believe you're going to do this to me," he said as they left the house and headed in the direction of the stables.

"Oh, stop whining, Mr. FBI Agent," she chided teasingly. "If you ride motorcycles, then a horse should be a piece of cake."

"A motorcycle does what you tell it to do because it doesn't have a brain. A horse is more unpredictable." He grinned at her, noting how the morning sunshine sparkled in her hair. "I'll tell you what, you ever come to Kansas City I'll get you on a motorcycle and see how comfortable you feel."

Her smile faltered just a tad. "I may come to Kansas City someday. As much as I love it here I don't see my future here forever."

Her words surprised him. "Really? Why?"

"For a while now I've had a desire to get away from Cotter Creek, find my own place in a city where nobody knows my family."

"What would you do?" He'd never thought that Meredith would have any desire to leave this quaint town or her family.

"I don't know, maybe join a police department or go into private investigation or maybe do something altogether different."

"You know if you ever come to Kansas City and want to apply at the police department I could put in a good word for you."

"Thanks, I appreciate it." She opened the stable door, and they walked in to see a young man brushing down one of the horses. "Good morning, Brian," she greeted.

"Morning." He smiled pleasantly.

"You want to saddle up Sugarpie while I get Spooky?"

"No problem." He led the horse he'd been brushing back into a stall, then disappeared into another stall.

"I'm going to ride a horse named Sugarpie?" Chase followed behind her as she walked toward her own horse. "My masculinity balks at the very thought."

She laughed. "Would you rather I put you on a horse named Thunder or Lightning?"

He pretended to consider it. "Nah, I guess Sugarpie is a good choice for a first ride."

He watched as she got to work saddling up Spooky. They hadn't spoken about last night, but when she'd seen him this morning there had been a secretive smile on her lips and in her eyes that had made him want to take her into his arms once again.

She was the strongest woman he'd ever known, not just in a physical sense, for he'd seen at the dance that she could take care of herself. But she radiated a quiet strength of character that he found incredibly appealing, a strength of character he thought every previous woman in his life had lacked.

She didn't need him. She would be fine when he left. At least that's what he told himself. But there were moments when he saw such vulnerability in her eyes, moments when he thought he saw love for him in those green depths.

He didn't want her to love him. He didn't want to leave here knowing he left behind pain. She'd told him she had no interest in anything long-term, in anything permanent, but something about the way she looked at him, the way she touched him denied her words.

"All set," Brian said as he led a huge chestnut mare toward Chase.

"Perfect timing," Meredith replied, her horse saddled and ready to ride, as well. She led both horses out of the stable and into the corral. "The only thing you have to remember is tug left to go left, tug right to go right and pull up on the reins to stop." She flashed him a reassuring smile. "You won't have any problems. Sugarpie is always willing to please."

He watched her mount her black horse and he couldn't help but admire how good she looked, confident and relaxed, but almost regal.

Although Chase had never been on the back of a horse in his life, he had seen enough western movies to know how to get on one. He placed a foot in the stirrup and swung himself up and into the saddle. "Piece of cake," he said.

"You look good in the saddle, cowboy," she replied, then took off.

Chase nudged his horse in the ribs with his heels and Sugarpie responded, following Meredith at an easy pace. It took him a couple of minutes to adjust to the rhythm and sway, but by the time they hit open pasture he felt as if he was getting the hang of the motion of the animal beneath him.

Red was right. There was nothing quite as magnificent as riding a horse with the brisk morning air whipping through your hair and filling your lungs with the scents of earth and sunshine and horse. Add to that the pleasure of watching Meredith, with her hair tossing and her eyes shining and Chase was a happy man.

The horse seemed to know the usual path that a morning run took and Chase had to do little but hang on as they began to gallop. It was as exhilarating as a motorcycle run and when Meredith finally reined in to slow her horse, he was almost sorry to do the same.

"Not bad for a novice," she said as they came to a halt.

He leaned over and patted Sugarpie's neck. "Thanks. You were right. This is terrific."

"You look like a natural."

"It's a piece of cake."

"Oh, yeah?" Her eyes lit with a hint of challenge. "Then I'll race you to those trees." She pointed in the distance to a thick grove of autumn-colored trees. She took off, Spooky's hooves thundering against the ground.

He laughed and watched her go. He wasn't a fool. He wasn't about to match his horse-riding skills against a woman who'd practically been born on a horse.

He was still laughing when the crack of gunfire split the air. Almost simultaneously he felt a piercing burn in his left side. The pain blackened his sight and he was vaguely aware of casting sideways before the ground rose up and smacked him in the face.

Chapter 11

"Chase!" The scream ripped from Meredith as she reached for her gun, jumped off her horse and hit the ground. She pointed her gun in the direction where she thought the shot had come from but saw no movement in the trees, couldn't find a target to defend them against.

Her heart thundered in her chest with sickening speed as she crawled on all fours across the ground toward Chase. As she reached him he rolled onto his stomach, his gun also out and pointed in the same direction as hers.

"I'm okay," he told her, but she saw the grimace of pain and the sweat that beaded his brow. Fear stole through her.

"Are you hit?" she asked. "Where? Where are you hurt?"

"My left side." His hand holding the gun trembled just a bit, and her fear for him intensified.

"We've got to get you back to the house. Spooky... home!" she shouted. "Home, Spooky."

The horse whinnied as if in response to the command and took off running in the direction they'd come. Sugarpie raced after, leaving Chase and Meredith alone.

"Are you sure that was a good idea?" he asked.

"Hopefully somebody will see them coming home without us and will know we're in trouble." She had scarcely taken her gaze off the stand of trees. "I don't see anyone."

"That doesn't mean nobody is there."

She was heartened by the fact that his voice was still strong, that he didn't appear to be losing consciousness. "Why would somebody want to shoot you? I thought I was the one who might be in danger."

"If I find out one of your overly protective brothers did this, I'm going to be pissed," he said.

She knew it was an attempt at humor, but she couldn't find anything humorous about any of this.

"Maybe somebody found out I'm FBI and think I'm too close to finding out about who is behind the land scheme," he said.

She didn't know how long they remained there, guns pointed, before she heard the familiar sound of a pickup approaching in the distance.

Clay's truck kicked up dust as it sped toward them. Clay drove, Kathy rode shotgun, and Smokey sat in the back, rifle ready. The truck came to a halt a few feet from where they lay and Clay got out.

"What happened?" He reached for Meredith, but she waved him away.

"Help Chase. He's been shot. It came from the trees." She pointed to the grove, and both Smokey and Kathy aimed their weapons in that direction as Clay helped Chase up off the ground.

Meredith cried out as she saw the blood that stained his side. "Get him in the back. We need to go directly to the hospital," she exclaimed.

Clay put him into the pickup, and Meredith and Smokey got in next to him. Within minutes they were out of the pasture and on the road to the hospital.

"Can you tell how bad it is?" Meredith asked. She tried to fight the terror that shivered through her as she saw how pale he was, how much pain he seemed to be in.

He forced a thin smile to his lips. "It hurts like hell, but my heart is still beating and my lungs are still breathing, so I'm guessing it's not life threatening."

Unless he bled to death before they got him to the hospital, or unless some organ had been pierced they weren't aware of. Her head filled with all kinds of terrible things.

Chase reached for her hand and squeezed it. "Don't look so scared. I'm tough. It takes more than a bullet to bring me to my knees."

"I'd just like to know what bastard did this," Smokey said, his expression grim.

"That makes two of us," Chase replied. He closed his eyes, his face more pale by the minute.

When they reached the hospital, two orderlies whisked Chase away, and Meredith sank into a chair in the waiting room, fighting back tears. Kathy sat next to her and took her hand.

"He's tough," she said. "And he was still conscious when we got here. That's a good sign."

Meredith nodded. "We need to call the sheriff. We have to report this."

"Is it possible it was just some sort of freak hunting accident?" Kathy asked. "Maybe somebody target shooting and didn't realize you were in the pasture?"

Meredith frowned thoughtfully. "I suppose anything is possible. Chase thought maybe somebody knows he's FBI and thinks he's getting too close to naming a guilty party." She rubbed her forehead where a headache threatened to split her skin. "Maybe Sam Rhenquist told somebody about Chase." She kept her voice low so that Clay and Smokey couldn't hear their conversation.

"As soon as I know Chase is all right I'll have a little chat with Sam," Kathy said, a steel in her tone that Meredith had never heard before. Meredith had a feeling there were many layers to the cherub-faced, blue-eyed woman seated next to her.

"And I'm going to call Sheriff Ramsey now. I want him here." Meredith took her cell phone and left the waiting room. She stepped outside the small hospital entrance and punched in the number for the sheriff's office. Molly Richmond, the dispatcher answered.

"Molly, this is Meredith West. Is the sheriff in?" Meredith asked.

"He left a while ago. If I was to guess, he was probably heading out for lunch then was going to sit on Highway 10. You know he loves handing out those speeding tickets."

"Can you contact him and tell him to come to the hospital as soon as possible?"

"I should be able to raise him on the radio."

Meredith hung up and for a moment remained standing in the brilliant noon sun. The world she knew had suddenly become a dangerous place. She'd always believed that her home and the surrounding land were a safe haven where nothing bad could happen. Now that sense of security was gone.

The moment that she'd seen Chase slide off his horse and hit the ground, the full extent of her love for him had exploded in her heart.

She'd allowed him in where no man had ever been before and knew when he left Cutter Creek she would never quite be the same again.

She hurried back inside to wait for news of his condition and to wait for the arrival of Sheriff Ramsey. It took two hours before Dr. Carson came out to talk to them.

"The bullet went right through his side. The entrance and exit were both clean and it hit nothing vital, although it did bust a rib. He lost some blood and I'd like to keep him overnight. But, he was damned lucky."

"Can I see him?" Meredith asked.

Dr. Carson hesitated a moment then nodded. "Room 110. He's got some pain medication in him but he's doing just fine."

Meredith turned to her family. "You all might as well go on home. Let Dad know everything is okay."

Clay, Smokey and Kathy left, and Meredith hurried down the hallway, eager to see for herself that he was really okay.

The curtains in room 110 were drawn to guard against the bright sunshine, but a dim light was on above the bed. Chase's eyes were closed, and Meredith crept silently to the chair next to the bed and sank down.

"I don't think I'll be riding a horse again anytime soon," he said without opening his eyes.

"How did you know it was me?"

"I smell your perfume." He opened his eyes. and to Meredith's surprise she began to cry.

She hadn't been aware that she was going to; the tears just brimmed over and a deep sob tore from her. The emotion that she'd kept in check from the moment he'd fallen off his horse until now could no longer be suppressed.

"Hey, don't cry. I'm okay," he said.

"I know, but I can't help it." The words came out between sobs. "I was so scared for you."

There was no way she could explain the horror that had gone through her when she'd heard that shot, then had seen him slide off the back of Sugarpie and hit the ground.

She scrubbed the tears off her cheeks with the backs of her hands and drew a deep breath to get herself under control. "I'm sorry," she exclaimed. "I didn't mean to do that."

He smiled. "Don't apologize. I'm sorry I scared you."

"Maybe my bodyguard needs his own bodyguard," she said.

The smile fell from his face. "I'd like to meet the guy who pulled that trigger."

"I called Sheriff Ramsey. He should be here soon, and maybe he'll be able to get to the bottom of it," she replied.

Chase nodded and closed his eyes, and Meredith knew he'd fallen asleep. She remained in the chair, watching over him. She found herself wondering who had watched over him when he'd been little and had been sick? Who had nursed him through the childhood illnesses? The father who had beaten him?

It wasn't pity that stirred in her breast, just a sadness. Even though she hadn't had her mother, she'd had Smokey and Red to nurse her, to stroke her forehead and fix her special treats. She'd been a lucky woman and she hadn't realized just how lucky she'd been until this moment.

Maybe it was time to do as Chase had said, to let

her mother go. She was tilting at windmills, thinking that she could solve a crime that none of the investigating officers had been able to solve at the time it occurred.

Chase was right. Solving the crime wouldn't bring her mother back. Solving the crime wouldn't fill the hole that Elizabeth West's death had left behind. It was time to let it go and get on with her life.

She didn't know how long she sat there watching Chase sleep before Sheriff Ramsey arrived. She stepped out into the hall to talk to him and explain what had happened.

"And you think the shooter was in the trees?" Ramsey asked.

"That's where the shot came from."

"Did Dr. Carson dig out a bullet? If I have a bullet I'll know what kind of gun it came from."

Meredith shook her head. "The bullet made a clean exit."

At that moment Chase called her name, and both Meredith and Sheriff Ramsey went into his room where Ramsey questioned him further.

"I'll need somebody to take me out there and show me exactly where it happened," Sheriff Ramsey said. "Maybe we can find a shell casing or something that the shooter left behind."

"I'll be out of here tomorrow. We'll do it then," Chase said. "I don't want Meredith out there at all."

She started to protest, but then decided not to

argue with a man who'd just been shot and was on pain meds.

Ramsey nodded. "I'll ask some questions around town. It's possible some damn fool was either doing a little target shooting or hunting and didn't realize there were people in the pasture."

He closed his small notebook where he had been taking notes, then tucked it into his breast pocket. "You need a ride home?" he asked Meredith.

"No, thanks. I don't know when I'll be going, and when I do I'll just call somebody at the house to come and get me." She wasn't ready to leave Chase.

"Then I guess I'm finished here. I'll call you if I find out anything." With those words Sheriff Ramsey left.

"I'm not going to hold my breath for a phone call," Chase said once he had gone.

"Kathy said she was going to talk to Rhenquist and see if he told anybody that you were FBI. Maybe she can find out something that will point a finger to a shooter."

"If Kathy finds out who did this before I do, then I pity the guy. If she doesn't kill him outright, she'll make him wish he were dead," he replied, his voice slurring with the edges of impending sleep.

The day passed with Chase sleeping, then awakening to talk for a few minutes with her, then him falling asleep once again.

The nurse came in at regular intervals to take his vitals and administer medication. The phone rang occasionally as members of her family called to see how he was doing.

Night was falling when he encouraged her to go home. "There's nothing you can do here," he said. "I'd feel better if I knew you were at the ranch, sleeping in your own bed instead of here."

"Are you sure? I don't mind staying," she said.

"Please, go," he said gently. "I'll sleep the night through and I'd have more peaceful sleep if I knew you were at the ranch where you belong."

"Okay," she replied. "I'll call and get somebody to pick me up." She made the phone call to the ranch and got her dad, who told her somebody would be there to pick her up in the next twenty minutes or so.

Meredith remained in the room for another ten minutes, then said her goodbye and stepped outside the hospital's main entrance to wait for her ride.

She tried not to think about how tragic this day might have been. She tried to keep her mind off the idea that if the path of that bullet had been an inch or two different, she'd be visiting Chase's body in the morgue rather than in the hospital.

The cool night air seemed to seep beneath her jacket to chill her heart. She wrapped her arms around herself as if to defend against the cold that she knew had little to do with the weather.

A familiar truck pulled into view, although Smokey wasn't behind the wheel. Kathy pulled the truck up to the curb and Meredith got into the passenger side.

"Smokey wanted to come and get you," she said once Meredith was settled in. "I don't know if any of you have noticed it or not, but that damn fool has no business behind a steering wheel after dark."

Meredith smiled. "Believe me, we've noticed, but Smokey is nothing if not bullheaded."

"How's Chase?" she asked as she pulled away from the curb.

"All right. He's been pretty doped up for most of the day, but he seems to be doing fine."

"He's tough," Kathy said. "But sometimes I'm not sure he's as tough as he'd like everyone to think he is."

"Kind of like Smokey," Meredith observed.

Kathy smiled, and in that smile Meredith saw Kathy's affection for Smokey. "Can I tell you a little secret, Meredith?"

"Sure."

"I've spent my whole life focused on the job. I never met a man who I thought I could tolerate for any length of time so I never married, never had children and focused only on work."

She paused a long moment and Meredith waited for her to continue, knowing instinctively that the information Kathy wanted to impart had little to do with her work obsession.

"Then I come out here and meet Smokey Johnson, a cranky old man who thinks he makes better coleslaw than me, and for the first time in my life I feel like a schoolgirl."

"You're in love with Smokey?" Although Meredith had seen the growing relationship between Smokey and Kathy, she'd suspected that Kathy was just playing a role.

"Crazy, huh. The tough-as-nails FBI broad brought to her knees by a cowboy with a bum leg and an attitude as big as Oklahoma." She shook her head and released a small laugh. "And the wonder of it all is that Smokey says he's crazy about me."

"So what happens now for the two of you?" Meredith asked. "It won't be long before the crime that brought you here will be solved."

Kathy nodded. "I'm expecting the case to break wide open in the next day or two. After that I'm returning to Kansas City and retiring, then I'm coming back here and living out the rest of my life with Smokey."

"Kathy, I'm so happy for you and Smokey." Happy tears misted Meredith's vision. "Smokey sacrificed the good years of his life to step in and take care of us."

"Don't let him hear you say that," Kathy replied. "As far as he's concerned sacrifice had nothing to do with it. He loved you all. You were the children he never had. You filled his life with love."

At least somebody was going to get a happy ending, Meredith thought. For she knew in her heart there was no happy ending for her and Chase.

Chase shifted positions on the chair on the porch, wincing as his side throbbed with a dull ache. It had been three days since he'd been released from the hospital.

Thankfully there had been no sign of infection in the wounds, and that morning at an appointment with Dr. Carson, the doctor had been pleased with how quickly Chase was healing.

It wasn't quickly enough for him. He didn't like feeling like an invalid, hated that everyone was waiting on him hand and foot.

The sheriff had been unable to find out who had shot him. Chase hadn't expected any different. He knew how difficult it was to investigate a random shot by an unknown assailant, especially when the shooting occurred in the middle of a pasture. A sweep of the wooded area where the shot had come from had yielded nothing, and unless somebody came forward and confessed, the odds were slim to none that Chase would ever know who was responsible.

Kathy had spoken to Rhenquist, who had been mightily offended that anyone thought he'd broken Chase's confidence. He'd insisted that he'd told nobody about the real reason Chase was in town.

It was now just after ten in the morning. He'd sneaked out here on the porch to have a moment to himself. Meredith had been like a shadow since he'd been home from the hospital. Nurse Nightingale had nothing on Meredith West.

He'd said he was going to his room to lie down. Then while nobody was looking he'd come out here to the porch to sit and think with nobody hovering over him.

Actually, he'd found the hovering rather nice. He knew his convalescence would have been much different in Kansas City. There would have been nobody checking on him, nobody making sure he was okay, because he had never allowed anyone into his life.

And that's the way I like it, he told himself, although he had to confess that having the West family closing ranks around him and taking care of him had been nice.

He sat up straighter as he saw a car coming in the distance, dust rising up in its wake. As it drew closer he recognized it as belonging to Savannah Clarion.

She parked and stepped out of the car, her red hair appearing to catch fire as it sparked in the sunshine. "Hey Chase, how are you feeling?" She danced up the stairs and plopped into the chair next to him.

"Stiff and sore and maybe just a little bit cranky," he admitted.

"Men don't deal with any kind of illness well," she said. "Joshua is the worst. When he isn't feeling well he gives *cranky* a new meaning." Chase smiled. "Where's Meredith?" she asked.

"Inside. I sneaked out here to have a few minutes to myself."

"I'm going to go get her. She's going to want to hear what I have to tell you all." Savannah jumped out of the chair and disappeared into the house. A few minutes later she and Meredith came out on the porch.

"I thought you were in your room resting," Meredith said to him. "Do you need anything?"

"Yeah, I need Nurse Nancy to be off duty," he replied with a grin.

She returned his smile, obviously not offended by his words. She looked at Savannah. "So what's this news you're bursting to tell us?"

Savannah's eyes gleamed brightly. "Raymond Buchannan has been arrested and word around town is that he's at the sheriff's office with those two FBI agents, spilling his guts."

Chase wasn't surprised. From the minute Sam had told him that he'd seen Buchannan with Black, he'd known the newspaper man had something to do with the evil going on in Cotter Creek. "Have you heard who else might be involved?"

Savannah shook her head. "He was only arrested about an hour ago and so far no word is leaking out about who else might be guilty. I can't believe that man fooled me. No wonder he discouraged me from investigating the deaths in the area. He was responsible for them." Her outrage was evident in her voice.

"So it's just a matter of hours and it will all be over," Meredith said. There was something in her tone that kept Chase from looking at her, a hint of wistfulness that pierced through him and made him not want to see the expression on her face.

Just a matter of hours and it would all be over. The bad guys would be identified and arrested and Chase and Kathy's work here would be done. He'd say goodbye to the family who had embraced him and goodbye to the woman who had touched him as none ever had.

He had no other choice. As much as Meredith drew him, as much as he wanted her every minute of every day, he refused to consider anything other than telling her goodbye. He would never put anyone in the position to discover that he was his father's son. Especially not a woman he might love.

"Oh, I almost forgot." Savannah pulled an envelope out of her purse and handed it to Meredith.

"What's this?" she asked curiously.

"Beats me. It was left in the mail drop at the paper with your name on it."

Meredith opened the envelope and took out the single sheet of paper that was inside.

"What does it say?" Chase asked, although he was afraid he knew.

She looked at him, and in the shadows of her eyes he knew. "It says, 'It's time'."

Chapter 12

Meredith stared at the note in her hand. In the past four days since Chase had gotten shot she'd forgotten about the notes. Her entire focus had been Chase's health. But now the mystery of the notes and the strange, ominous feeling they brought came crashing down around her.

"It's time? Time for what?" Savannah asked curiously.

"I wish I knew," Meredith replied. "I've been getting some weird notes. I think they're from my secret admirer." She kept her voice light, as if there was nothing to be concerned about. She didn't want Savannah to know the depth of her worry.

"Maybe it means it's finally time for her secret admirer to make himself known," Chase said.

"How exciting. You'd better call me the minute you find out who it is," Savannah exclaimed. "And now I've got to get out of here. I need to get back to town in case the big news breaks."

They said their goodbyes, and Meredith watched as her friend got into her car and headed back toward town. When Savannah's car was out of sight, she sat in the chair next to Chase.

For a long moment neither of them spoke. She set the note on the floor next to her chair, not wanting to hold it in her hand another minute.

"You know, it's possible that's all it means," she finally said. She looked at him and could tell by his frown that he wasn't sure what to believe. "In any case, this is almost over for you. I guess you'll be packing up and heading back to Kansas City."

She hoped her voice didn't betray the rich emotion that filled her as she thought of him leaving. She didn't want him to know how deeply she cared, how much she'd ache when he was gone.

She'd told him she was only interested in a hot affair, no strings attached, and that's the way it had to be. Even if he wanted it otherwise, she knew that in the end she could never be what any man wanted forever in his life.

"Maybe I should hang around for a while," he said. "At least until you know the identity of this secret admirer."

"That's not necessary," she replied with forced lightness. "The more I think about it the more I think it's possible it's Buck Harmon. I think it's possible he might have even had a crush on my mother years ago. He's about the right age, and his ex-wife even looked a bit like Mom." She was rambling and wasn't sure whether she was trying to alleviate his concerns or her own.

"I still don't like the idea of leaving here and not knowing for sure if you're in any danger," he replied.

"Chase, my family members work as bodyguards. I'm probably safer than anyone else in the county." She was suddenly eager for him to go, not wanting to be around him another day, not wanting to fall any deeper in love with him than she already was.

"You haven't even told your family about the notes," he replied.

"If it will make you feel better, I will."

"When?"

She sighed. "Before you leave."

His eyes were enigmatic as he gazed at her. "We'll see what tomorrow brings," he finally said.

It was Clay who delivered the news the next morning that Raymond Buchannan had sung his heart out and named Mayor George Sharp as the brains behind the land scheme. The ambitious mayor had arranged the accidents that had occurred to the rancher and had murdered Sheila Wadsworth and who knew how many others.

They were all seated at breakfast when he came in with the story. "I always knew he was ambitious," Smokey exclaimed as if the news didn't surprise him at all.

"Apparently he was all set to be king of the condos," Clay said as he and Libby sat at the table and Gracie crawled up into Red's lap.

"Grandpa, Mr. Mayor might be king of the condos, but Daddy says Mommy is queen of the shoes," she exclaimed.

Libby laughed. "Clay doesn't understand a woman's need for more than two pairs of shoes. Tell him, Meredith, explain to him that shoes are important to a woman's mental health."

"I'm the wrong person to ask," Meredith replied. "I'm afraid I'm a dismal excuse of a woman who owns only three pairs. Sunday best, everyday and mucking boots."

Gracie crawled out of Red's lap and walked over to lean against Meredith's side. "Aunt Meredith, you come shopping with me and mommy and we'll buy you fairy-princess shoes."

Meredith laughed and gave the little girl a hug. "Don't you have to be a fairy princess to wear princess shoes?"

Gracie touched a strand of Meredith's dark hair. "You're as pretty as a fairy princess."

Meredith felt a blush sweep over her face. "And you, little one, are too sweet not to tickle." Meredith gave her tummy a tickle.

With a delighted laugh Gracie sprinted away and crawled into her mother's lap. As the conversation continued, Meredith watched Libby stroking her daughter's hair, saw the way Gracie seemed to melt into her mother with absolute trust and love.

Meredith had never thought much about having children until Gracie had joined the family. Seeing the relationship Libby had with her daughter stirred a new wistfulness in Meredith.

She'd probably never know the joys of mother-hood. She glanced over at Chase, who looked better, healthier this morning than he had in the past couple of days. She'd love to have his baby, but she would never bring a child into the world without both parents being involved with each other and with the baby.

"I guess this means you'll be heading back to Kansas City," Red said to Chase. "Your work here is done." He smiled at Chase's surprised expression. "I knew you were FBI and working the case from the second day of your arrival. I'm no fool. I like to know the people who come into my house so I did a little checking."

"Does Dalton know?" Chase asked.

"All the boys know."

"Why didn't somebody say something?" Chase looked around the table.

"We respected your job and what you were trying to do," Clay replied.

Chase looked down at his plate for a long

moment, then looked at Red. "I'm sorry for the deception. It didn't sit right with me, but I had a job to do."

"No reason to apologize," Smokey replied. "I knew that woman wasn't an ordinary one the first time I saw her whip out her pistol." He smiled at Kathy. "But I don't give a damn if she's FBI or not. I still make better coleslaw than her." Everyone laughed.

It was evening when Meredith and Chase sat on the front porch watching the sun go down. "Your family humbles me," he said. "I've never felt so accepted by anyone."

A lump formed in her throat. "They know a good man when they meet one."

"I spoke with Agents Wallace and Tompkins a little while ago," he said. "They're confident that Raymond Buchannan and George Sharp were the only men in town working the deal. They also told me that Joe Black was arrested this morning at one of his properties in Aspen, Colorado. They're anticipating picking up Harold Willington in the next day or two."

"So the bad guys go to jail and all is well in Cotter Creek, Oklahoma," she replied. "When are you heading back to Kansas City?"

"I told you earlier I'm not sure I'm leaving right away," he said.

"You have to," she said, and turned in her chair to look at him. "Please, you have to leave now." His blue eyes radiated surprise as he studied her features intently. She looked away from him and stared out in the distance. "You have to go, Chase, because I can't stand it if you stick around too much longer."

Looking back at him again, she fought the wealth of emotion that pressed tightly against her chest. She got up out of the chair and walked to the porch railing so her back was to him.

"I know I told you that I was fine with just a hot physical relationship, but I didn't expect to fall in love with you. It's not your fault. You made it clear that you aren't looking for love, for commitment, and in any case I know I'm not the kind of woman men want to marry."

"What are you talking about?"

She heard him rise from his chair and felt his nearness just behind her. Tears burned at her eyes but she willed them away, refusing to allow him to see her cry.

"Meredith, what do you mean you aren't the kind of woman men marry?"

She turned to look at him, loving the lean angles of his face, the rakish scar that cut through his eyebrow and the sensual lips that were at the moment thinned and pressed tightly together. "That's what the last man I dated told me. He said I was a great girl, but when he decided to marry, it would be to a real woman, somebody soft and needy."

She shrugged. "I'm a bodyguard. I don't know much about being a woman. I only own three pairs of shoes."

"The man you were dating was obviously a fool,"

he exclaimed. "Just because you're strong and capable doesn't mean you don't know how to be a woman."

His gaze was warm and the curve of his lips were soft. "Meredith, you're sexy and incredibly feminine and more of a woman that anyone I've ever met. It would be easy for any man to fall in love with you and look forward to spending the rest of his life with you."

Her vision blurred slightly as the tears she'd tried to force back once again burned, then filled her eyes. "If what you say is true, then why didn't you fall in love with me? Why aren't you looking forward to spending the rest of your life with me?"

His eyebrows tugged together in a frown. "It's complicated."

"Yeah, right." She turned back around as tears fell onto her cheeks.

"Meredith." He grabbed her arm and forcefully turned her to face him once again. "Don't you get it? It's not about you. It's about me. Any man would be damned lucky to have you in their life. But I decided a long time ago that I wouldn't put any women at risk." He reached up and rubbed his thumb against her cheek. "Especially not you."

"At risk? What are you talking about?" She searched his features.

He dropped his hand and stepped back from her. "You know my history. You know what kind of man my father was. His blood runs inside my veins. He was my role model for too many years."

She stared at him in surprise. "And you're afraid you'll be like him?" He didn't reply, but his jaw tightened and his eyes grew darker. "When was the last time you hit somebody? When was the last time you were abusive?"

"That doesn't matter. What does matter is that I love you too much to take a chance." There was implacability in his voice.

Joy battled with despair at his words. He loved her. He loved her and he wasn't going to do anything about it. Tears once again misted her vision as despair won out. And on the heels of that despair was a hint of anger.

"You love me so much that you aren't going to reach out for happiness? You're going to turn your back on me and my love?" The anger inside her grew. "Then your father wins. He's managed to totally destroy your life."

"It's important to me that I don't destroy yours," he replied.

She needed to get away from him. The tears that she'd tried so desperately to contain needed to be released and she refused to allow them more freedom in front of him. "You lied to me, Chase. You told me that the scars your father left behind didn't even hurt anymore. But that was a lie. They must hurt like hell for you to choose to live your life alone."

She didn't wait for his reply, but instead turned and ran inside the house, needing the privacy of her room to cry, wanting the seclusion of her space to grieve for what might have been.

Sleep didn't come easily to Chase that night, and he got out of bed late the next morning with the self-loathing of a man who'd kicked a puppy in a temper fit and now regretted his actions.

But it wasn't regret that weighed heavy in his heart. He told himself that turning his back on Meredith was the right thing to do. She would eventually find another man who would love the woman she was and she would build a life with him that would banish him from her memory.

That's what he wanted for her. Happiness and love. He just knew she couldn't have that with him. Today would be his last day here. He was well enough to travel, and it was time to get out of Dodge.

Before he left he'd make sure Meredith told her family about the notes she'd been receiving and he'd get a personal assurance from each of her brothers that they would watch over her, make sure she remained safe.

He was still stunned over the fact that Kathy intended to return to Kansas City, retire, then come back out here to be with Smokey. He hadn't tried to talk her out of it when she'd told him. He'd seen the light of happiness in her eyes and knew that for the first time in her life she was following her heart.

By the time he washed and dressed, it was after ten-thirty. Breakfast had passed, but he found

Smokey and Kathy sitting at the kitchen table lingering over coffee.

"There's our lazy man," Kathy said as he walked into the kitchen.

"I can't believe I slept so late," Chase replied. He walked over to the cabinet, withdrew a cup and poured himself coffee.

"Want me to rustle you up some eggs?" Smokey asked.

"No, thanks, this will be just fine." Chase joined them at the table and took a sip of the hot strong brew.

"We were just sitting here talking about Raymond Buchannan and George Sharp," Kathy said. "I spoke with Agent Tompkins this morning and he said both men confessed to everything."

"I never trusted Mayor Sharp, but I would never have suspected that Raymond Buchannan would have been involved in anything like this," Smokey said.

"Love or money, those are the motives for most crimes," Kathy said.

"In this case love of money," Smokey replied.

"Where's Meredith?" Chase asked.

"She left about twenty minutes ago to go into town," Kathy replied.

"By herself?" Chase frowned.

Smokey released a gruff laugh. "Last time I looked she was a grown woman."

"I think she was meeting Savannah." Kathy paused and took a sip of her coffee. "She probably wants to hear all the gossip about what's happened over the past twenty-four hours."

Although there was no reason for it, Chase had a bad feeling. "I think I'll give her a quick call," he said, and excused himself from the table.

He went back to his bedroom and grabbed his cell phone, then punched in the number for hers. She answered on the second ring.

"I don't like you wandering around all on your own," he said without preamble.

"I'll be fine." Her voice held a distance that ripped through him.

"I still don't like it."

Her sigh was audible. "I'm not a fool, Chase. I don't intend to stop for anyone or anything along the side of a deserted road. I'll be around people. Believe me, I'll be fine. I'm meeting Savannah for lunch, then I'm coming back home. I should be back around two or two-thirty, long before dark."

"When you get home we need to have a talk with your family. You need to tell them about the notes before I leave here in the morning."

"No problem," she replied, then before he could say anything else she disconnected.

He closed his phone and tossed it on the bed, the feeling of disquiet growing inside him. He had a feeling he wouldn't feel good until Meredith was back at the ranch safe and sound.

Chapter 13

Meredith tossed the cell phone to the car seat next to her. She'd awakened that morning with a fierce restlessness that urged her to get out and away from the ranch, out and away from Chase.

After their conversation the night before, she'd spent the remainder of the evening in her bedroom. There was nothing more to say to him, and just the thought of looking at him had caused a stab of pain to bolt through her.

Before meeting Savannah for lunch, she intended to go to the Wild West Protective Services office and beg Dalton to find her a job, something that would take her far away from Cotter Creek, something that would take her mind off Chase McCall.

She'd told Chase the truth. She intended to be careful, to make sure she was surrounded by people throughout the day. "It's time." She clenched her fingers more tightly around the steering wheel as she thought of the note Savannah had delivered to her the night before.

"It's time." What did it mean? There was no question that the two words portended something happening. But what? Maybe after lunch she'd stop into Sheriff Ramsey's office and find out if the reports had come back from the lab on the other notes.

She told herself that surely nothing bad could happen to her on such a gorgeous autumn day. As she drove toward town she noticed how the sun dappled light through the vivid red and yellow leaves on the trees. It wouldn't be long before the leaves would fall to the ground and winter would move in with its icy grasp.

Rolling down her window she allowed the sweet scents of fall to fill the car, hoping to banish the smell of Chase that seemed to linger in her head.

He'd be gone tomorrow. Kathy had told her that morning that they planned to catch the bus back to Kansas City the next day.

She told herself she couldn't wait for him to be gone, that she was sick of his presence and tired of looking at him. But her heart knew the truth. Telling him goodbye would be the single most difficult thing she'd ever done in her life.

Pulling into a parking space in front of the Wild

West Protective Services office, she consciously willed away thoughts of Chase McCall. She had to stop thinking about him. She had to stop mourning for what might have been, for what would never be.

Dalton was behind the front desk, tossing balled-up paper into the waste-can basketball-style. "You look productive," she said dryly.

"Two points," he exclaimed as the paper hit the rim, then fell into the can. "Boredom is a terrible thing. What are you doing here?"

She sat in the chair opposite the desk. "Boredom is a terrible thing," she echoed. "I need to work. Please find me a job."

"I didn't realize you were wanting to go out. Something came in last night but I sent Joshua this morning."

"Where?"

"Oklahoma City. It's just for a day or two. Senator Abraham's son is attending a concert, and the senator wanted us to send somebody to go with him and make sure he stays out of trouble."

"Doesn't he already have bodyguards?" Meredith asked curiously.

"Yeah, but the senator wanted an outsider to keep an eye on things. Anyway, that's all I had, and now it's gone." He smiled sympathetically. "Maybe something else will come up in the next day or two."

"I hope so. If it does, I'll take it." She tried to keep the desperation out of her voice. "I never asked you, how did your date go with Melinda?"

Dalton sighed. "That woman could talk the ears off a mule and, to be perfectly honest, I found her boring. It took me months to get up my nerve to ask her out, then the date was excruciating. Thankfully she felt the same way. We agreed to be friends." He grinned at her. "It's just you and me, kid. We're the last of the Wests to find love."

She'd found it. Oh, how she'd found it, but it apparently wasn't meant to be. "As far as I'm concerned, love is vastly overrated," she replied.

"Spoken like a true cynic," he replied with a laugh. "So, what are your plans for today?"

"Lunch with Savannah."

Dalton winced. "Don't mention my name to her. She wasn't thrilled that I talked Joshua into taking the job."

"Ah, she'll be all right. She knows how important this kind of work is to Joshua." She stood and looked at her watch. "And speaking of Savannah, I'd better get out of here. I'm supposed to meet her at the café in ten minutes."

"See you later, sis." Dalton balled up another piece of paper, apparently intent on returning to his one-man trash can hoops.

Even though Savannah was rarely on time, Meredith headed for the café. She waved to Sam, who sat in his usual spot on the bench outside the barbershop, then went into the café where a lunch crowd had begun to arrive.

She found an empty booth, slid in and told the

waitress she was waiting for a friend. As she waited for Savannah she caught snippets of conversations going on at other tables. The topic of the day was definitely the arrest of Mayor Sharp and Raymond Buchannan.

She'd always hoped somewhere in the back of her mind that it would be discovered that the person or persons responsible for so many deaths would turn out to have no ties to Cotter Creek.

It was hard to digest that the men responsible had been born and raised right here and had betrayed the entire town with their evil intentions. She was glad it was over, glad that the town could now begin the healing process.

It was exactly quarter after eleven when Savannah flew through the café door and beelined to Meredith's booth. As her friend slid in across from her, Meredith saw the lines of exhaustion that rode her features.

"Remind me again of why I wanted to be a newspaper mogul," she said as she motioned to the waitress. "I was up all night getting a special edition of the paper ready."

"I hear you're single for the next couple of days," Meredith said.

"It's probably a good thing Joshua's gone because I won't have time for anything but the paper for the next two days. By the time he gets back from his assignment, the worst of the furor will be over."

Their conversation halted as the waitress arrived

to take their orders. After she left, Savannah chatted about the stress of being the new owner of the *Cotter Creek Chronicles* and the biggest news break the town had seen in years, but it was obvious she loved her new position.

"Now, tell me what's going on with you. What's wrong?" Savannah asked abruptly.

Meredith leaned back against the booth. "What makes you think anything is wrong?"

Savannah leaned forward, her gaze holding Meredith's intently. "I can see it in your eyes. Something has happened."

Unexpected tears sprang to Meredith's eyes and she hastily wiped at them. "I feel like such a fool." She stared down at the top of the table. "I made the terrible mistake of falling in love."

"With Chase." It wasn't a question but rather a statement of fact.

She looked up at Savannah. "Is it that obvious?"

Savannah smiled. "Only every minute the two of you are together. He looks at you the same way you look at him. So what's the problem?"

"The problem is he isn't in the market for a relationship with anyone. The problem is he has no desire to take things any further with me." Meredith sighed unhappily.

"Men never think they want a long-term relationship. It's up to you to convince Chase that he can't live without you."

Meredith shook her head. "You know the old

saying, 'You can lead a horse to water, but you can't make him drink.' He's leaving tomorrow to go back to Kansas City and I'll go back to my usual life."

Usual life. She wasn't even sure what that was anymore. At that moment Buck Harmon entered the café. As his gaze fell on her, he jerked his cowboy hat off his head.

He hurried over to their booth, a shy smile stretching his thin lips. "Savannah." He nodded his head with a fast bob, then turned his attention to Meredith. "You look nice today," he said. "I was sorry we didn't get to finish our dance at the Fall Festival." He worried the brim of his hat between his fingers.

"Buck, you didn't by any chance send me flowers the morning after the dance, did you?" she asked.

"No. Why? Should I have?" He looked at her in surprise.

Meredith studied his features carefully. He was over the age of forty. He obviously liked her. Although he professed not to have sent the roses, she wasn't sure if she believed him or not. "I got some flowers that morning but there was no card. I've been trying to figure out who was nice enough to send them to me."

"If they made you happy then I'm sorry it wasn't me," he replied.

At that moment the waitress arrived to deliver their orders and Buck moved away from their booth and took a stool at the counter.

"He's definitely working up his nerve to ask you out," Savannah said when the waitress had left. "But he's way too old for you. You're twenty-eight and he's on the wrong side of forty."

"I'm not exactly in the mood to go out on a date with anyone right now," Meredith replied. Was Buck Harmon just a shy man trying to get up the nerve to ask her out or was he her secret admirer?

"It's time". Never had two simple words brought with them such a feeling of quiet alarm. Never had two words evoked such a feeling of impending doom.

As she and Savannah ate lunch, she was grateful that the conversation moved away from Chase and love. Savannah talked about the challenges ahead of her in running the only newspaper in town.

"I'm going to be so involved with the daily operation that I need to hire a couple of reporters to do the actual stories. You don't have a secret burning to be a reporter, do you?" Savannah asked.

Meredith laughed. "No way. Besides, I'm not sure I'm going to stick around here for long."

"What are you talking about?"

"Savannah, I know how much you love it here, that when you came here from Scottsdale you felt as if this town was finally home for you. But it's different for me. I have a need to head to a bigger city, someplace where I won't be one of the West kids but just Meredith. I really don't expect you to understand."

Savannah drizzled ketchup across a pile of fries. "Where would you go?"

"Not far. I'd never want to be so far away that I couldn't come home pretty regularly to see everyone. Maybe Tulsa or Oklahoma City."

"Or Kansas City?" Savannah arched a copper-colored brow.

"No, not Kansas City," Meredith replied firmly. There was no way she could be in the same city as Chase and not feel his presence. There was no way she wanted serendipity to work so that she ran into him in a grocery store or at a shopping mall.

They chatted until they were finished eating, then Savannah looked at her watch and frowned. "I hate to eat and run, but I've got tons of work waiting for me at the office." She opened her purse to get out her half of the bill.

"Don't worry about it," Meredith said. "It's on me today."

Savannah paused a moment, her expression somber. "If you do move away you know I'll miss you dreadfully."

"You'll be too busy to miss me," Meredith replied with a forced lightness. "Go on, get out of here."

"Call me," Savannah said, then she whirled around and walked toward the exit.

Meredith watched as her friend left the café. If she did decide to move she would definitely miss Savannah. The two women had bonded from the first moment they'd met.

She turned her gaze toward the counter. Buck was gone. Even though he seemed like a nice enough man, she was glad he had already left. Something about him just gave her the creeps.

"It's time." How she wished she could get those two words out of her head. Tonight she'd tell her family about the notes. She knew Chase wouldn't leave unless he knew safety measures were in place for her.

She hated telling them about the notes she'd found in the shed. She knew it would reopen wounds, bring back the grief of her mother's death to them all.

She had hoped that she and Chase would be able to get to the bottom of it without involving any of her family members, but it appeared that wasn't going to happen.

After paying for the meal, she left the café and headed for the sheriff's office. She needed to find out if Ramsey had gotten any reports back from the lab about the notes she'd received. She realized it was probably a useless trip, that if he had learned anything, he would have already told them.

But she wasn't ready to return to the ranch where Chase would be. She couldn't look at him, couldn't talk to him without it hurting.

Entering the sheriff's office she was surprised to see nobody at the front desk. Usually Molly Richmond would be there taking phone calls and manning the small reception area.

Maybe she took a late lunch, Meredith thought. "Hello?" she called.

The door to Ramsey's office opened and the

sheriff looked at her in surprise. "Meredith, what are you doing here?" He motioned her in and to the chair in front of his desk.

"I came by to see if any of those lab reports had come back yet from Oklahoma City?"

Ramsey didn't take a seat behind his desk, but rather leaned against it. "Sorry to say nothing has come back. You've got to understand that those notes wouldn't be a top priority in the lab. Why? Has something else happened?"

"I got another note."

He frowned, his salt-and-pepper eyebrows drawing downward. "What did it say?"

"'It's time.' That's what it said."

"And just what in the hell is that supposed to mean?" he asked.

She shrugged. "Your guess is as good as mine."

"Did you bring the note with you?"

"No, it's at the ranch." She cursed herself for not bringing it to him. "I'll try to get back into town tomorrow and bring it to you." She stood, her business here done. "You'll let me know if you hear anything?"

"Of course," he replied.

With a murmured goodbye Meredith turned to exit the office. But before she could reach the door an electric jolt struck her from behind.

She had no time to wonder what had happened. It was like a bolt of lightning had slashed down from the sky and she was nothing more than a lightning rod.

The current sizzled through her and she immediately lost control of her arms and her legs. She felt herself falling but was unable to do anything to stop the fall. Her head banged against the floor and darkness descended.

At three o'clock Chase sat on the front porch staring down the road and looking for Meredith's car. She'd said she'd be home around two or two-thirty, and he was trying not to read anything into the fact that she was thirty minutes late.

She was having lunch with Savannah and he knew how those two loved to talk. She was probably just running late. Didn't women always run late? Besides, she was in downtown Cotter Creek in the middle of a sun-filled day. What could possibly happen to her there?

He turned as he heard the front door open and smiled at Kathy. She eased into the chair next to him, and for a moment neither of them said a word.

"You ready to leave all this?" she finally asked.

"Yeah. It's time to get back to the city," he replied.

"Are you ready to leave her?"

He didn't have to ask who Kathy was talking about. He released a long sigh. "I have to be ready."

"Are you sure you're doing the right thing? She's a fine woman."

"The finest I've ever met, but don't try to make me feel bad about the decision I've made where Meredith is concerned. I know what I'm doing and I'm doing what's best for her."

"God help every woman who has a man doing what's best for her," Kathy replied dryly.

Chase remained silent. He wasn't going to fight with Kathy about Meredith. What surprised him was that he hadn't expected to hurt while he was doing what was best for Meredith.

Before meeting her, he had thought he didn't have a heart, or at least knew that his heart was so heavily armored he hadn't worried about pain. But if there was one thing he'd learned over the past couple of weeks, it was that he did have a heart and at the moment it ached like hell. But he was determined to do the right thing, and the right thing was to walk away from Meredith.

"Regrets are a terrible thing when you get to be my age," Kathy said. "I don't regret the things I did, but I do regret the things I didn't do…like get married and have a family." She held Chase's gaze. "Don't make the same mistakes I did, Chase. Don't think that work can ever fill the hole that love should fill."

"Are you through?" he asked with more than a touch of irritation.

"I'm through."

He looked at his watch. Quarter after three. Where in the hell was Meredith? "Meredith said she'd be home around two or two-thirty," he said. "I wonder what's taking her so long?"

"If you're going to let her go, then leave her alone," Kathy exclaimed. "She was having lunch with Savannah. She's a big girl and doesn't need you to set a curfew for her. Besides, maybe she's in no hurry to come back here and spend time with you." She got up and went back inside the house.

He stared off in the distance, slowly digesting Kathy's words. Why would she want to come home and see him? He'd made it quite clear to her the night before that he intended to break her heart.

She'd told him she loved him, and there had been a moment when hope had shone from her eyes. And he'd taken that hope and crashed it to the ground. No wonder she wasn't eager to come back here and face him again.

He was probably worrying for nothing. Still, he couldn't quite shrug off the simmering concern he felt. "It's time." How he wished he knew what those words implied. Was it a threat of something bad or the promise of something good?

He knew that Meredith hadn't wanted to open a can of worms by telling her father about the notes, and yet at this very moment he realized how foolish they'd both been not to talk to Red, not to ask him about the identical notes they'd discovered in the shed.

She'd managed to lull him into keeping the secret and suddenly that felt like the wrong thing to do. With this thought in mind, he left the porch and went searching for Red.

He found him in the study, seated at the large mahogany desk. "Am I interrupting?" he asked from the doorway.

"Not at all. I'm just paying bills. A little interruption would be welcome." Red motioned him to the chair in front of the desk. "I have to admit the house is going to feel empty with you and Kathy gone."

"I have a feeling it won't be long till Kathy will be back here," Chase replied.

Red smiled. "I'm glad. Smokey has been a good friend, like a brother to me, and there's nothing I'd like to see more than him happy."

"I have something rather sensitive to discuss with you," Chase said, his mind formulating where to begin. "Meredith found some strange notes in the shed in the boxes of your wife's things."

Red frowned. "Strange notes?"

Chase nodded. "There were three of them. One said something like 'You're my destiny.' Another said 'You will be mine,' and the last one said 'It's time.' You know anything about them?"

"Not those specifically, but it wasn't unusual for Elizabeth to occasionally get those kinds of notes, especially in the first year or so that we moved out here. Some of the California paparazzi got hold of the story that she was abandoning her Hollywood dreams for love and came out here and took pictures. After they appeared in a couple of the tabloids, she got a ton of mail, both good and bad."

"So you'd have no idea when exactly she might have received those particular notes?"

"Don't have a clue. Why is it important?"

"Meredith has been getting the same notes. They

appear to be written by the same person. We think that same person sent her the roses."

Red sat up straighter in his chair and frowned thoughtfully. "I don't quite know what to make of it. Do you?"

Chase shook his head. "All I know is I don't like it."

"Why hasn't Meredith come to us about this? Why hasn't she told me or her brothers?"

"I think at first she was embarrassed. She thought it was just somebody who was too shy to approach her and she was afraid of being teased."

Red sighed. "Her brothers have always teased her unmercifully, but it's only because they care about her." He leaned back in the big, overstuffed leather desk chair and stared at a place just over Chase's shoulder. He sighed again, then directed his gaze back to Chase. "Do you think she's in danger?"

"I think it's possible," he replied.

"Where is she now?" Red asked.

"She went into town to have lunch with Savannah. She should be getting back anytime now." Chase looked at his watch. It was just after three-thirty. She wasn't so late that he should feel panicked, and yet the first stir of panic whispered in his ear.

"I was wondering if you'd mind if I borrowed your car. I thought maybe I'd take a drive into town," Chase said.

"You think she's in trouble now?" Red asked.

Chase weighed his options. He knew Red wasn't in the best of health. He also knew he had absolutely no reason to believe Meredith was in trouble except his gut instinct, and that instinct had been wrong before. "Nah, I just need to pick up a few things before Kathy and I head back to Kansas City tomorrow."

Minutes later as he drove away from the ranch he told himself he was overreacting to Meredith being late. It wasn't as if she were hours late back to the ranch. And it was possible she was intentionally staying away because she wanted to spend as little time with him as possible.

Still, all the rationalization in the world couldn't dissipate the knot of tension in his chest. He drove slowly, checking along the sides of the road for her car, grateful that he didn't see it.

As he approached the place where Elizabeth West had been found strangled to death next to her car, he hoped and prayed that the man responsible for that crime didn't now have Meredith in his sight.

It was quarter after four when he drove down Main Street and breathed a sigh of relief as he saw Meredith's car parked in front of the café.

He parked next to her car and as he got out he scanned the streets, surprised to see that Sam Rhenquist wasn't seated on the bench in front of the barbershop as he usually was. He hoped the old man wasn't sick.

Dismissing Sam from his mind, he stepped into

the café and looked around, seeking Meredith and Savannah. They were nowhere inside.

Maybe they'd gone to the newspaper office after lunch, he told himself. There was no reason to get excited just because they weren't still in the café.

He tried to quiet the whisper of panic inside him as he strode down the sidewalk toward the newspaper office. He was being ridiculous. There was absolutely no evidence that the notes were written by anyone who meant Meredith harm.

When he stepped into the newspaper office, Savannah was seated at the front desk and talking on the telephone. She held up a finger to indicate she'd be with him momentarily.

She finished the call. "Hi, Chase. Have you come to give me a tidbit of inside investigation gossip for the paper?"

"Actually, I'm looking for Meredith, but it's obvious she isn't here."

"We had lunch earlier, but we parted ways about an hour ago," Savannah replied.

"Did she mention that she had errands to run or something in particular to do? Her car is still parked in front of the café."

"She didn't mention anything, but if her car's still there then she's got to be around town somewhere," Savannah replied. At that moment the phone rang, and with a murmur of apology Savannah answered.

Chase gave her a wave, then left the newspaper office and gazed first up the street, then down.

Meredith wasn't the type of woman to spend an afternoon shopping at the few dress shops Cotter Creek had to offer.

So, where might she have gone? His gaze fell on the Curl Palace and he wondered if she might have gone in to get a hair trim. Although it seemed unlikely, he hurried down the sidewalk toward the beauty salon.

A glance inside let him know Meredith wasn't there. He stepped back out on the sidewalk, the panic that had been just a whisper before now screaming inside his head.

Chapter 14

Pain crashed through Meredith, pulling her from the darkness and into some semblance of consciousness. The back of her head felt as if it had exploded outward, and every muscle in her body hurt.

Tentatively she opened her eyes, shocked that the profound darkness didn't go away but rather lingered. It was then that she became aware of the vibration coming from beneath her and the feeling of motion.

Disoriented, she flung her hands out and tried to straighten her legs, but with a shock realized exactly where she was…in the trunk of a car.

What car? Sweet Jesus, the pain in her head made it almost impossible to think. And she had to think. She had to figure out why she was in a car trunk and how she had gotten here.

Her hand automatically went to her waist for her gun, but it was gone. She had to figure out what was happening, but it was impossible to focus on anything other than the desire not to throw up. Her head pounded and the motion of the car combined with the fumes of exhaust threatened to make her sick.

Fear added to her illness, a rich raw fear that clawed at her, that forced any thought she might have out of her head. She gave in to the fear, screaming at the top of her lungs as she kicked with all her might against the sides of the trunk.

It was only exhaustion that eventually forced her to stop. She panted to catch her breath…and remembered. She remembered lunch with Savannah. She envisioned watching Savannah leave the café. She'd remained behind and finished a cup of coffee, then had left and gone to see Sheriff Ramsey.

She'd talked to the sheriff about the notes and asked if lab reports had come back, then she'd turned to leave. And nothing. Sheriff Ramsey? Was she in the trunk of his car? But why? What on earth was going on?

Her brain began to work overtime. Sheriff Ramsey was the first person to the scene when her mother had been murdered. Or had he been there all along? Had he been the one who had strangled her, then pretended to find her car and investigate the murder?

Oh, God. Oh, God. She tried to draw deep breaths

to still the rising hysteria inside her. She was in trouble and nobody knew it. Nobody knew where she was. Nobody suspected the good sheriff was a murderer.

Where was he taking her? She had no idea how long she'd been in the truck, how long they'd been driving. She had no idea how long she'd been unconscious, how many hours had passed since she'd entered the sheriff's office.

She had to think, not about what was happening, but rather about how to get herself out of this mess. Ramsey was soft and older than her. It was possible she might be able to kick him and run if the car ever stopped. The only way she'd have a chance to escape was if he opened the trunk.

She knew the moment they left paved road and turned onto a gravel road. The gravel crunched beneath the tires, and his speed slowed. She remained lying in a fetal position, gathering her strength so she could take advantage of any opportunity for escape.

Chase. Her heart cried his name. Did he realize she was missing? She'd told him that she'd be back at the ranch around two or two-thirty. Had enough time passed that he knew she was in trouble?

She tensed as the car slowed to a mere crawl, then stopped. The engine shut off and her heart raced with terror. Rolling over on her back, she pulled her legs up, preparing to kick the first body part that came into view when he opened the trunk. Kick and run, her brain commanded. She couldn't think of Chase. She couldn't think of her mother. All she needed to focus on was kick and run.

Her heartbeat was the only thing she could hear, booming in her head. She tried to keep her breathing deep and regular as she prepared for the fight of her life.

The driver door opened, then slammed shut. She heard his heavy footsteps on the gravel as he approached the trunk. Despite the pounding of her head and the ache of every muscle in her body, she stayed focused on the trunk lid. Kick and run.

The trunk opened but before she could strike out she was hit with a stun gun. As electricity jolted through her she was helpless, a mass of uncontrollable muscles. Unable to move, she watched in horror as Sheriff Ramsey leaned over her and placed a sweet-smelling rag over her nose and mouth. Darkness crashed around her.

Consciousness returned in bits and pieces. She became aware of the fact that she was in a bed. Fresh-scented sheets covered the soft mattress beneath her, and for a moment she thought she was in her own bed, safe at the ranch.

Then she remembered. The trunk…Sheriff Ramsey. Her eyes snapped open and she found herself in a small bedroom. The walls were covered with photos and posters, and an open closet contained gowns and dresses that were vaguely familiar.

But it was the photos that held her attention.

Photos of her mother. The room wasn't a bedroom, rather it was a shrine to Elizabeth West.

She sat up and took a moment to look around, noting that the window the room boasted was boarded up and the door a jail cell door complete with steel bars.

She flung her legs over the side of the bed and stood on trembling legs. There was a doorway to her right with no door and a peek inside showed her that it was a bathroom. Everything in there was sturdy plastic and there was no mirror on the wall, nothing that could be used as a weapon or to aid her escape.

Everywhere she looked a picture of her mother returned her gaze. There were publicity shots, newspaper clippings and snapshots. In some of the snapshots it was obvious her mother hadn't known that her picture was being taken, in others she smiled into the camera with the ease of a woman accustomed to being photographed.

One photo in particular stunned Meredith. In it were three people, her mother, her father and a much younger Jim Ramsey. It had obviously been taken on a movie set. So, Jim had known her mother in Hollywood. She digested this information with a sinking horror.

It seemed obvious now that he must have followed her from California to Cotter Creek. He'd bided his time, wanting her, obsessing about her, then one night on a deserted stretch of road he'd killed her.

"Ah, I see you're awake."

She whirled around to see him standing on the other side of the steel bars. Jim Ramsey, the man who had sworn to uphold the laws of the county, the man who had murdered her mother. She said nothing.

"I'm sorry I had to be so rough with you, but things are going to be fine now." He smiled and in the light of his eyes she saw his madness. "I'm going to have to leave for a little while, but it would be nice if while I'm gone you freshened up a bit and changed into that blue dress." He pointed toward the closet area. "Remember you wore that in *Paris Nights*. That was my favorite of your movies. You were stunning in that dress."

The lines of reality had blurred for Jim Ramsey. As he stared at her, she knew he was seeing another woman in another time. "I'm not Elizabeth, I'm Meredith," she exclaimed. "Let me out of here and we'll forget all about this." It was a lie, but she needed to jar him back to reality. "Sheriff Ramsey, you need to let me go now. Elizabeth is dead and this isn't going to bring her back."

He slammed his hands against the bars, his face contorted with a sudden rage. "Shut up. You need to shut up. I've waited so long for this. You're mine. You were always supposed to be mine. I'll be back later and I want you in that blue dress."

He turned and disappeared from the doorway. A chill of horror washed over her. She was the prisoner of a man obsessed with her mother, the man she knew had killed her mother. And nobody knew where she was.

By the time five o'clock arrived, Chase knew something was terribly wrong. He first went to the sheriff's office where he was told that Ramsey was out in the field, then he went to Wild West Protective Services and told Dalton to rally the family.

Within twenty minutes Tanner, Zack, Clay and Red had joined Dalton and Chase in the office. The men wore grim expressions as Chase explained what had been going on and his concerns for Meredith's safety.

They agreed to meet back at the office in twenty minutes, then split up to check each and every store in the two-block area for signs of her.

As Chase headed for the north end of town, he tried to stop the raw emotion that threatened to consume him. He recognized it as fear, something he hadn't felt for a very long time.

He hadn't felt this kind of fear since he'd been a child and had sat in school knowing he had to go home to his father. He hadn't felt this kind of terror since the night his mother had died and he'd known that any goodness that had existed in his world had died with her. But this time his fear wasn't for himself, but rather for the woman he loved.

Even though he'd had every intention of walking away from Meredith, he wanted her alive and well when he left her. He hadn't realized how intricately his heart had wound with hers until this moment, when he sensed danger closing in around them as dark as the night falling all too quickly.

Where are you, Meredith? The evening shadows were getting darker, thicker and he had the feeling that if they didn't find her before night fell completely, they might never find her.

He raced from store to store, his heartbeat gaining speed with each step. How did a woman simply disappear? "It's time". The words echoed in his head like the notes of a dreadful song. "It's time." What in the hell did they mean?

They had all gathered back at the Wild West Protective Services office when Sheriff Ramsey walked in. As quickly as possible they told him what was going on. By that time Smokey, Kathy and Savannah had joined the search party.

"I've tried to call her cell phone a dozen times in the last hour, but she's not answering," Chase said, the sense of panic a living, breathing entity inside him.

"Is it possible she left town with somebody?" Sheriff Ramsey asked. "Maybe she met a man and they drove somewhere for dinner?"

"Not possible," Chase replied flatly. "She's in trouble and it has something to do with those notes she got."

"Maybe we should search one more time," Ramsey said. "It's possible you just missed her in one of the stores."

They agreed to spread out once again, this time

knocking on doors to the houses along Main Street to see if anyone had any information about Meredith's whereabouts.

It was only as Chase passed the barbershop and noticed once again that Sam Rhenquist wasn't in his usual place that his absence suddenly took on an ominous aura.

The man never missed a day of bench sitting, but he'd been absent from the bench the whole time Chase had been in town. He spied Dalton across the street and hurried toward him.

"You know where Rhenquist lives?" he asked.

"Sure." Dalton pointed to the barbershop. "He lives in the apartment on the second floor. Why?"

Chase didn't reply, but instead hurried across the street toward the barbershop. His gut instinct told him that Sam Rhenquist was no more a kidnapper or murderer than Chase was a Buddhist monk. He also knew he couldn't ignore an anomaly and Sam Rhenquist not seated in his usual spot was definitely an anomaly.

On the side of the building that housed the barbershop was a set of stairs that led up to the second floor. Chase took the steps two at a time, his side aching painfully and reminding him that he still wasn't up to par.

Still he didn't allow the pain to slow him. When he reached the door he pounded on it with his fist. He was vaguely aware of Dalton and Clay at the bottom of the stairs, watching with fierce intensity.

When there was no immediate reply, he pounded again, this time hearing Sam's voice. "All right, all right. I'm coming. Don't break down the damn door."

The minute he opened the door Chase realized why he hadn't been sitting on his bench. Sam looked sick as a dog. He was clad in a ratty bathrobe and looked weak as a kitten.

"Chase," he said in surprise. "Don't come any closer, boy. I've got a bug or something. I've been puking my guts up for the last couple of hours."

Chase could smell the faint scent of vomit and knew the old man was telling him the truth. "Sam, we can't find Meredith West. Have you seen her today?"

Sam frowned and clutched his robe more tightly around his thin body. "I saw her earlier. She and Savannah ate at the café, then afterward Meredith went into the sheriff's office."

Chase frowned. Ramsey hadn't said anything about seeing Meredith earlier. "Did you see her leave there?"

Sam shook his head. "It was about forty-five minutes after she went inside that I started feeling poorly and decided to come up here. Before I left the bench I didn't see her come out of the office."

What would Meredith had done in the sheriff's office for forty-five minutes? Nothing that he could think of. "Thanks, Sam."

Sheriff Ramsey? Was it possible he knew something about her disappearance? Was it possible he was responsible? A new burst of adrenaline accompanied Chase down the stairs. "Where's Ramsey?" he asked Dalton and Clay.

"I'm not sure," Dalton said. "I guess he's searching like everyone else. Why?"

"We need to find him," Chase said and strode off in the direction of the sheriff's office. Ramsey, who was first on the scene when Elizabeth West had been murdered. Ramsey, who would have helped conduct the investigation that had yielded nothing useful. Chase's head reeled with horrible suppositions.

"Chase, what's going on?" Dalton and Clay hurried to catch up with him.

Chase stopped and turned to gaze at the two men. "I think the good sheriff knows where your sister is. I also think he just might be the man who murdered your mother."

Chapter 15

"There has to be a way out," Meredith said with frustration. She'd spent every minute since Ramsey had left trying desperately to rip the boards off the window, but they were immovable. She now stood in the center of the room and looked around.

She had no idea when Ramsey might return, no idea what might happen when he did. One thing was certain, she sure as hell wasn't going to play into his fantasy by putting on one of her mother's old costumes.

There was no point in trying to get through the door. Ramsey must have plundered the city funds to buy the steel door that belonged in a prison or a jail.

She sank down on the edge of the bed and closed

her eyes, trying to figure out how she was going to get out of this mess.

She couldn't count on anyone riding to her rescue. All the time that she and Clay had discussed the murder of her mother and the notes, the sheriff would have been the last person they would have suspected.

She had the horrifying feeling that she was on her own, that if she were going to survive this it would be by being smarter and faster than the portly, crazy Jim Ramsey.

Maybe it would be smarter to play into his fantasy. Although she had no doubt in her mind that he had strangled her mother, it was also obvious that he wanted Elizabeth, needed Elizabeth. And maybe if Meredith pretended to be Elizabeth she could convince him to let her out of this cell.

She walked over to the closet where the glittery blue dress hung. *Paris Nights* had been the movie that had put Elizabeth's name on the lips of the movers and shakers of Hollywood. It had been the last movie she'd made before leaving it all behind to marry Red and move to Cotter Creek.

"Mom," she whispered as she stroked her hand down the sequin-laden fabric.

She'd never know her mother's soft touch, never have the special heart-to-heart talks that mothers and daughters shared. She'd believed that the lack of her mother in her life had somehow made her less of a woman, but Chase had taught her differently.

Closing her eyes, she remembered the desire that

had lit his eyes when he looked at her. He'd told her she was a strong and sexy woman…a *real* woman. And she believed him. Todd had been an ass, and she had been a fool to believe what he'd told her. She'd seen the truth in Chase's eyes and she embraced it into her heart, into her soul.

She pulled the dress off the hanger and laid it on the bed, then quickly pulled off her flannel shirt and jeans and pulled the dress on.

It fit as if made for her, and for a moment she felt as if her mother's arms enfolded her. The fear that had been with her since the moment she'd first regained consciousness in the trunk of the car eased.

She walked over to the wall and studied one of the photos. It was a head shot of Elizabeth. She studied each and every detail.

Her mother wore her hair parted on the left side. Meredith had always worn her hair parted down the middle. In the bathroom she found a plastic brush and comb and despite lacking a mirror, she carefully parted her hair on the left and brushed it around her shoulders.

She had a feeling if she did have a mirror she'd be stunned by her likeness to the woman who had given her birth. She knew she was playing an extremely dangerous game, but she was out of any other options.

Trembling with dread, the fear once again rising up inside her, she sat on the edge of the bed to wait for Ramsey to return.

* * *

"We can't find him anywhere," Zack announced when they were all once again gathered in the Wild West Protective Services office. "His patrol car is gone, too."

"Why would Sheriff Ramsey have anything to do with Meredith's disappearance?" Tanner asked.

"I just remembered something," Clay said. "When I was on assignment in California, Gracie's agent gave me a picture that showed Mom and Dad and Jim Ramsey."

"That's right," Red said. "Jim was a friend of ours back in Hollywood. Like me, he worked as a stunt man on lots of the movies. We all worked on several movies together." Red's face paled as his gaze met Chase's. "You think Ramsey wrote those notes to Elizabeth? You think he's the man who killed her?"

"Circumstantial evidence points that way," Chase replied. The knot in his stomach twisted so tight he had trouble catching his breath. "Anyone know where Ramsey lives?"

"He's got a little place on the west side of town. Follow me." There was fire in Smokey's eyes as he headed toward his truck. The rest of them all scrambled toward their own vehicles.

Chase and Red got into Red's car, Chase behind the steering wheel. "I helped that man get settled here in town," Red said, his vast torment evident in his voice. "He called me from California and told me he wanted to get out of the business, and I encouraged him to come here to Cotter Creek and settle in."

"Don't beat yourself up. If Ramsey wanted to be near Elizabeth you couldn't have stopped him from coming here," Chase replied.

"She would have pulled her car to the side of the road for the sheriff. Elizabeth would have felt safe stopping for him." Red released a deep sigh. "If he's hurt Meredith, I'll kill him," he said fervently. "And if I find out he is the man responsible for Elizabeth's death I'll kill him again."

Chase didn't reply, but when he thought of Meredith hurt or worse, the same killing rage filled him that he knew Red was feeling.

His hopes rose when they pulled in front of a small ranch house and the patrol car was parked out front. Lights were visible beneath the closed shades.

Everyone got out of their vehicles with the silence of thieves. "Clay, Tanner and Red, you all go around the back of the house. Zack and Smokey and I will check out the front. Kathy, call Agents Tompkins and Wallace and tell them to stand by, we might need their help." Chase kept his voice low. He didn't want Ramsey to have any warning. He pulled his gun and released the safety. "Nobody do anything until I give the word."

There was no way of knowing if Meredith was dead or alive, but he didn't want to storm the place and force Ramsey to do anything drastic.

He crept to the front window, cursing the fact that the shades were pulled tight, making it impossible to see inside. There was also no way of knowing in what room Meredith might be. He'd wanted Tompkins and Wallace here in case there was a hostage situation. Ramsey wouldn't trust his own safety to any of the West family or him, but he might trust it to FBI agents who had no ties to the town or the family.

He stepped up on the porch, careful to not make a sound, then pressed his ear against the door. *Just let me hear her voice,* he prayed. *Just let me hear her voice so I know she's all right.* But there was no sound emanating from inside the house.

The man had been sworn to serve and protect, but if what they believed were true, that oath had been twisted into something ugly, something that had allowed him to kill one woman and kidnap another.

Chase couldn't pretend to understand the forces that drove a man to commit such acts. He couldn't get into the head of a man who could kill a woman he professed to love.

Meredith. His heart screamed her name as his hand reached for the doorknob. It twisted beneath his grasp. His heart pounded like it had never done before, a racing beat that beaded sweat on his brow.

He drew a deep breath and motioned with his head for the others to move closer, then with a yell he opened the door and burst inside.

The sound of a back door splintering in its frame

accompanied him inside. With his gun leveled
before him he cleared the living room. Smokey
headed for the kitchen and Zack followed Chase
down the hallway.

"Meredith!" Chase shouted her name as he
cleared the first bedroom in the hallway.

"Kitchen clear," Clay called.

Chase ran to the next room, aware of a sticky
warmth on his side. He'd reopened his wound, but
he couldn't think about that now. All he could think
about was Meredith and the fact that she was
nowhere in the house.

"You look lovely."

Meredith shot off the bed at the sound of Jim's
voice. He stood just outside the doorway, his gaze
warm and loving. She wanted to throw up. Her skin
crawled as if his sick gaze physically touched her.

"You told me to put on the blue dress," she said,
trying to keep her revulsion from her voice. "I want
to please you if I can."

He closed his eyes, as if finding her words too
exquisite to believe. "I thought I'd lost you," he
said, his voice soft and barely audible. He opened
his eyes and stared at her with hunger. "I thought
I'd lost you that night on the road. You remember,
don't you?" There was a fervent light in his eyes.

"The night when I was coming home from the
grocery store. The night you stopped me along the
side of the road," she said.

He nodded. "I'd sent you those notes. I thought you understood. I fell in love with you the first day that I met you. We were meant to be together, but then Red stepped in and you got confused. I tried to forget you. I tried to let it be, but you haunted me. That's why I moved out here. You're why I took this job."

"But it didn't work," she said softly. "I didn't understand what you wanted, what you needed." She had no idea if she was playing this right or not, but she wanted to keep him talking on the off chance that somebody might come to help.

"I didn't blame you. I knew Red had seduced you. He'd blinded you to my love, to how happy I could make you. I was a patient man. I waited while you had all your babies. I was patient, but I knew eventually I'd get a chance to make you see that you belonged to me."

"And that chance came that night along the side of the road." She wanted to weep as she thought of her mother pulling over to meet her killer.

He nodded. "I put my lights on and you pulled right over. You looked so pretty that night." He gazed just past her, as if reliving that fateful moment in his mind. "You were wearing a skirt and a green sweater that perfectly matched your eyes. You got out of the car and asked if you'd done something wrong."

"And that's when you told me how you felt about me," Meredith said.

"I thought you'd understand, that I was your destiny, that I was the man you were supposed to be with forever, but you didn't understand." It was obvious he was getting agitated. He began to pace in front of the doorway, his hand touching the butt of his gun.

Meredith's heart jumped into her throat. Had she played the game too hard? Had she pushed him into remembering something that might cause her harm?

He stopped pacing and stared at her with accusation. "You laughed at me. You laughed and said I was being foolish, that you were Red's destiny and you would be with him through eternity. I just wanted you to shut up. I didn't want to hear it so I grabbed you and you screamed. Why did you scream?" His face grew red as he grabbed hold of the bars. "Why in the hell did you scream?"

She didn't answer, but rather remained perfectly still, afraid that by doing anything, by saying anything she'd push him over the edge.

He raked a hand through his thinning gray hair and drew a deep, audible breath. "Fate has given me a second chance. You're here with me now and I'm never going to let you go. You are my destiny."

She decided to risk it. She moved closer to the bars. "Jim, why don't you open the door so we can talk face-to-face instead of with these bars between us." If she could just get him to open the door she'd at least have a fighting chance.

A shrewd light shone from his eyes. "Do you think I'm a fool? I know it's going to take time for you to fully understand that we belong together. I have all the time in the world. Nobody will ever find us here. Eventually I'll open the door, but we have years together."

With these words he turned and left, leaving behind a cold wind of desolation blowing through her. She returned to the bed and sat, fighting a feeling of hopelessness, of helplessness.

We have years together.

She tried to imagine being here in this room for one year…two years…ten years. She'd go mad. Eventually she'd break. Somehow, someway she had to get out of here.

A deep sob welled up inside her and tears seeped down her cheeks. At that moment all hell broke loose. She jumped off the bed as it sounded as if the house was coming down.

She heard a shout. A wonderfully familiar voice. "Chase! I'm in here!" She ran to the bars and clung to them, trying to see what was happening.

A shot rang out followed by a deep silence. Her heart seemed to stop beating. Then Chase was in front of her, fumbling with a set of keys to unlock the door. As the door opened she fell into his arms, sobbing his name over and over again.

It took her a moment to realize he was crying, too. He clung to her so tightly she could scarcely breathe. "Thank God," he murmured. "Thank God you're all right."

"How did you find me?" she asked as she molded herself to him.

"It's a long story." He kissed her lips, her cheeks and her forehead, then finally released her. "Come on, let's get you the hell out of here." He took her by the hand, turned to leave and fell unconscious to the floor.

Meredith sat in the chair next to the hospital bed where Chase lay asleep. She no longer wore the blue dress but rather had on her comfortable pair of jeans and one of her flannel shirts.

It had been three hours ago that Chase and her brothers had stormed the fishing cabin where Sheriff Ramsey had taken her.

She'd gotten the story in bits and pieces on the way to the hospital, how they had frantically searched the town. How they had finally realized Ramsey might be responsible. After going to his house and not finding her there, they had checked property records and discovered that Ramsey owned the cabin forty miles outside of Cotter Creek.

Ramsey would live to spend the rest of his life in prison. It had been Red who had shot him in the leg and Chase who had tackled him to the floor, further ripping his wound in the process. After twenty-five years the mystery of her mother's murder was finally solved.

"You looked unbelievable in that blue dress, but flannel suits you better."

She leaned forward as his eyes opened and he smiled at her. "Chase." His name trembled out of her as she reached for his hand.

His smile faded and his gaze held hers intently as his fingers squeezed hers. "Did he hurt you, Meredith?"

"No, no, he didn't hurt me. He didn't touch me at all," she assured him.

He closed his eyes for a moment, relief relaxing his features. "I was so afraid we wouldn't find you." He looked at her again. "I was so afraid we'd be too late."

"He thought I was my mother. He thought he was getting a second chance to spend eternity with her. He was sick, he thought he was in love with her, but what he felt had nothing to do with love."

He closed his eyes again and was silent for so long she thought he'd fallen asleep. His hand still held hers, and the warmth of his touch wound a band of heat around her heart.

He'd saved her life. He was her hero. But more, he was the man who had made her believe in herself as a woman. He was who she wanted to spend the rest of her life with, the man she loved as she knew she'd love no other. And all too soon he was going to walk out of her life without a backward glance.

He looked at her then, as if he had picked up her thoughts out of the air. His gorgeous blue eyes stared at her for a long moment. "I thought I'd lost you. Those were the longest hours in my life, when I couldn't find you."

"I was afraid nobody would ever find me again," she said.

"For a smart man, Ramsey was stupid. That

cabin was in his name. He should have known eventually we'd find it."

"I think he had every intention of acting normal, returning each day to Cotter Creek and playing sheriff until his retirement. He never intended for any suspicion to fall on him."

"Thank God for Sam Rhenquist," Chase said. "Thank God he's as nosy as a bad neighbor and saw you go into the sheriff's office but never saw you leave."

"And thank goodness you're going to live to fight another day," she replied. She moved to pull her hand from his, finding even that simple connection too painful to endure, but he tightened his grip and held fast.

"I've been thinking. I learned about abusive love from my dad. Now I've learned about obsessive love from Ramsey. I'm thinking maybe it's time I let myself know about good, healthy love."

She stared at him wordlessly, her heart stepping up its rhythm. She wasn't sure exactly what he meant and she was so afraid of jumping to conclusions.

"You were right when you told me I'm not my father. As filled with rage as I was when we burst through the door to Ramsey's cabin, I didn't kill him. When I wrestled him to the floor to get his gun away from him, I didn't beat him to death. I don't remember ever in my life being as angry as I was then. In the important things, I'm not my father's son."

"So now that you realize that, do you intend to

do anything about it?" Her heart thundered in her chest as she waited for his reply.

He smiled then, that gorgeous sexy grin that made her want to laugh and weep at the same time. "I definitely intend to do something about it. There's this woman I'm in love with. She's bright, she's beautiful and she's more of a real woman than any I've ever met. I'm hoping she'd consider marrying me and going to Kansas City with me."

For a moment her heart was so full she couldn't speak. She finally found her voice and smiled. "I can be packed and ready to go in fifteen minutes. After all, I only have some jeans and flannel shirts and three pairs of shoes to pack."

He pulled her up from her chair then, up and into the hospital bed next to him. "You wouldn't mind leaving your family to come with me? We could visit as often as you want. I'd never want to keep you from your family."

She pressed a finger to his lips. "My mother left behind everything she knew to come here with my father. I like to think that if she hadn't been killed they would have lived out their dream, a life filled with love and passion and family. I want all that with you, Chase. I want to show you how good love can be, I want you to finally know the joy of love, real love."

He leaned forward and captured her mouth with his in a tender kiss. She was careful not to get too close to him to hurt him, aware that he was healing from the exertion that had opened up his wound again.

Still even a soft, sweet kiss from him had the ability to make her toes tingle, to flutter warmth into her heart. It was she who ended the kiss, not wanting to get anything started that they couldn't finish.

He grinned at her, that familiar sexy smile that thrilled her. "Can we talk about sex now?"

She laughed. "You have a hole in your side, you're in a hospital bed and you want to talk about sex? You're such a man, Chase."

Love poured from his eyes. "And you're quite a woman, Meredith West. My woman."

Her heart swelled with happiness, and she knew that somewhere Elizabeth West was smiling because she knew her only daughter had found the special kind of love that lasted a lifetime.

* * * * *

CHRISTMAS
CONFESSIONS

BY
KATHLEEN LONG

After a career spent spinning words for clients ranging from corporate CEOs to talking fruits and vegetables, **Kathleen Long** now finds great joy spinning a world of fictional characters, places and plots. A RIO and Gayle Wilson Award of Excellence winner, and a National Readers' Choice, Booksellers' Best and Holt Medallion nominee, her greatest reward can be found in the letters and e-mails she receives from her readers. Nothing makes her happier than knowing one of her stories has provided a few hours of escape and enjoyment, offering a chance to forget about life for a little while. Please visit her at www.kathleenlong.com or drop her a line at PO Box 3864, Cherry Hill, NJ 08034, USA.

For Writers At Play with love and thanks for
your friendship, encouragement, cheers and
commiserations. Unconditional love with an endless
supply of laughter. What more could a girl ask for?
This one's for you.

Chapter One

Unknown number.

Detective Jack Grant frowned at his phone's caller ID and swore softly. He put down his case notes and took the call.

"If you're about to read from a script, you can save your breath by hanging up," Jack growled into the receiver, his throat tight and dry from too many hours without sleep or food.

He glanced at the clock over his kitchen table. Eight-fifteen in the morning. He'd been working nonstop since he got home from the precinct the night before.

The caller hesitated before speaking, and for a split second Jack thought he might get lucky and avoid conversation completely. He thought wrong.

"I wondered if you'd seen the latest blog at Don't Say a Word?"

Don't Say a Word? The name rang a bell, but Jack couldn't pry a connection loose from the jumble of facts and evidence his current case had planted in his mind.

"The confession site?" the caller continued.

The caller's voice indicated he was male, older, and either a heavy smoker or someone with a serious bronchial condition.

"Buddy," Jack said, "I think you've got the wrong number."

The caller began to cough—a sputtering, choking sound that made Jack feel as though he was violating the man's privacy by listening.

He thought about asking if the man was all right, but that would indicate concern on his part, and concern was something Jack offered to no one, not if he could avoid it. Concern indicated vulnerability, and vulnerability indicated weakness.

Jack hated weakness.

He held the phone away from his ear until the sound of coughing subsided.

"It's about Melinda," the caller ground out as if struggling for air between choking spasms.

Melinda.

Jack had no doubt there were millions of Melindas in the world, but the combination of the caller's voice and the name Melinda shifted Jack's thoughts from the present to the past—eleven years past, to be exact.

"How have you been, Mr. Simmons?"

"Have you seen it?" the man asked, ignoring Jack's question.

Melinda Simmons had gone missing from a New Mexico university campus not long after Jack's sister, Emma, had vanished from a college fifty miles to the east.

Unlike Emma, Melinda's body had never been found.

Her case had joined a handful of others—unsolved, their connection suspected, but never proved. The man Jack had thought responsible for the rash of college coed abductions and murders had been a self-proclaimed photographer who'd been in possession of photos of Emma, as well as of Melinda and the others upon his arrest.

Boone Shaw had walked free after a trial that had blown up in the prosecution's face. The press had blamed the acquittal on a lack of evidence and an airtight alibi the defense attorney had presented immediately before closing arguments.

Life for Jack had tilted on its axis the day his sister's lifeless body had been found.

Life for the Simmons family hadn't fared much better.

Melinda Simmons's mother had succumbed to her lung cancer not long after the trial.

Her father, Herb, had dropped out of society instead of facing his daughter's tragic disappearance and presumed death alone.

Jack had figured him dead years ago. But here the man was on the other end of the phone, resurrected like the heartache Jack had denied since the day he'd buried Emma, since the day Boone Shaw had walked free.

"Are you near a computer?" Simmons asked.

"Give me a second." Jack settled in front of his PC, clicking the icon to gain Internet access.

He waited for the entry page to open, cursing the cable connection under his breath. He initiated a search for the Don't Say a Word Web site, then clicked onto the site via the list generated by the search engine.

As the site's entry page came into focus, Jack's chest tightened.

Apparently Herb Simmons wasn't the only family member back from the dead. Anyone looking at the modeling shot of Melinda would never guess the young woman had allegedly been strangled and left in the desert eleven years earlier.

"Is he back?" Herb Simmons asked, his voice faltering, his emotion palpable across the phone line.

Jack winced.

Damn Boone Shaw for causing so many families so much pain.

"Could be," Jack answered as he skimmed the site for an indication of just who was responsible for posting the girl's photograph.

Jack remembered now where he'd heard the confession site's name. The Web site and its cofounders had been profiled a few weeks back in *People* magazine.

The site promised an anonymous means for the public to air their most personal secrets, the thought being that confession was good for the soul.

According to the feature story, the public visited the site in droves, their morbid curiosity no doubt driving them to salivate over the suffering of others.

So much for keeping a secret.

Broken promises. Broken marriages. Broken dreams.

As if any of the bull the confessor spouted was true.

Each Saturday the site's blog featured a sampling of handmade postcards received during the previous week.

Today was Thursday. That meant the posted blog had gone up five days ago, and apparently the selected "confession" had been strong enough to carry the site alone.

The faded black-and-white modeling shot of Melanie Simmons filled the majority of the visible page, and included only a one-line caption.

I didn't mean to kill her.

Jack raked a hand through his close-cropped hair and winced. "Sonofa—"

"I thought you'd want to know."

"You thought right."

"Don't let him get away this time." Simmons's tone dropped soft, yet suddenly clear.

"I didn't let him—"

But the line had gone dead in Jack's ear.

"—get away the first time," Jack said for the benefit of no one but himself.

He'd always thought that if he uttered the statement often enough, one day he'd believe the Shaw acquittal to be no fault of his own.

That theory hadn't paid off yet.

Jack might have been a rookie detective at the time, and the powers that be might have kept him as far away from the actual casework as they could, but still, the thought that he might have done something—anything—differently haunted his every moment.

He'd failed to keep his baby sister safe, and he'd failed ever since to find a way to bring her killer to justice.

Jack woke each morning, wondering how he might have saved Emma from the monster that had taken her life. He went to bed each night determined to find a way to make Boone Shaw pay for what Jack knew he did.

He'd never doubted the man's guilt. He never would. And he'd never stop trying to bring the brutal killer to justice, not while there was a breath of life left inside him.

Jack dropped the now silent phone to his lap and pulled his chair close to his desk, studying the blog entry—the reproduced photo postcard, the card's typewritten message, and the weekly editorial.

Apparently the site owner responsible for writing the weekly comments had deemed the postcard a crank.

Jack scrubbed a hand across his tired face and laughed.

What an idiot.

Had the woman even thought to touch base with the local police or the FBI?

No matter. Abby Conroy had just given Jack the first new lead he'd had in years. Maybe he'd have to say thanks…in person.

Jack's gaze shifted from the monitor screen to the calendar tacked haphazardly to the wall. Nine days until Christmas.

The calendar illustration consisted of a holiday wreath draped over a cactus, no doubt someone in the Southwest's idea of holiday cheer.

But the timing of the Don't Say a Word posting gnawed at Jack.

Melinda, Emma and the other coeds had vanished during a ten-day period leading up to Christmas.

Had Boone Shaw decided to resurrect his own special brand of holiday cheer? And if so, why now? Why wait eleven years?

Granted, the man's trial had dragged out over the course of two years, but after Shaw had gone free, he'd never so much as been pulled over for a speeding ticket again.

And Jack would know. He'd kept tabs on the man's every move.

As crazy as the thought of Shaw sending a postcard to a secret confession site seemed, Jack had seen far stranger things during his years on the force.

He'd seen killers tire with getting away with their own crimes. He'd seen men who might never have been caught, commit purposeful acts to gain notoriety.

Who was to say something—or someone—hadn't motivated Shaw to come forward now?

Jack rocked back in his chair, lifting the hand-carved front legs from the floor as the possibilities wound through his brain.

Truth was he wouldn't sleep again until he'd held that postcard in his own hand.

He blew out a slow breath.

Christmas.

On the East Coast.

In the cold.

He supposed there were worse things in life. Hell, he knew there were.

He pulled up the Weather Channel Web site and keyed in the zip code for the Don't Say a Word post office box. Then Jack leaned even closer to the monitor and studied the forecast.

Cold, cold and more *cold*.

Jack hated the cold.

Almost as much as he hated Christmas.

"Ho, ho, ho," he muttered as he dialed his chief's home number.

The senior officer answered on the second ring, and Jack didn't waste a moment on niceties, clicking back to the image of Melinda Simmons's smiling, alive face as he spoke.

"I'm going to need some time off."

ABBY CONROY COVERED the ground between her post office box and the Don't Say a Word office in record time. The morning air was cold and raw, teasing at the possibility of a white Christmas the region hadn't seen in years.

"Good morning, Mrs. Hanover," she called out to an elderly woman walking a pair of toy poodles, each dressed in full holiday outerwear complete with tiny Santa hats and jingle bell collars.

Now there was something worthy of confession.

Abby stifled a laugh and pulled the collar of her wool pea coat tighter around her neck.

The local retail merchants' association had gone all-out this year in an effort to draw tourists into the Trolley Square section of town from the nearby attractions such as Winterthur, Brandywine Art Museum and Montchanin.

Thanks to their hard work, the Christmas holiday proclaimed its approach from every available storefront, lamppost and street sign.

Good thing Abby loved the holidays—or should she say, *had* loved the holidays.

This Christmas marked an anniversary she'd just as soon forget, but knew she never would.

Abby shoved the depressing thought far into the recesses of her mind and glanced at the stack of postcards in her hands.

She'd started the Don't Say a Word online secret confession site just shy of a year earlier, and as the site's anniversary approached, so had the number of "secrets" shared anonymously by the public each week.

Sure, the profile in *People* magazine hadn't hurt. Sadly, it had also drawn the phonies and the cranks out of the woodwork.

Whereas Don't Say a Word had started small and had grown via word of mouth, helping those who truly needed to share something from their past in order to ease their souls, the recent media attention had drawn confessions above and beyond anything Abby had ever imagined, including last week's.

She tightened her grip on the mail as she pictured the card featured in this week's blog. Typically she chose three or four for the blog, but last week she'd chosen only one.

I didn't mean to kill her.

Anger raised the small hairs at the back of her neck. She'd shown the card to a local police detective before she'd published the photograph—an older black-and-white shot of a young woman sporting a ponytail and huge grin.

Even the officer had shared her first reaction. Someone wanted his or her fifteen minutes of fame and had decided to take the sensational route to get there.

Well, perhaps Abby had made a mistake by giving the so-called confession space on the very public blog, but she'd wanted to call attention to the sender's callousness.

The site and service were for people who spoke from

the heart, not for someone who found sending a card like last week's feature amusing.

She'd been a bit harsh in her blog, but so what? There were thousands of people out there with secrets, secrets that needed to be told in order to ease the keeper's heart and mind. Abby wasn't about to tolerate anyone's sick humor at the expense of her site or her readers.

Her business partner, Robert Walker, had wanted her to toss the card in the trash, but she hadn't been able to. Matter of fact, instead of archiving the card in the office files after she'd written her blog, she'd tucked it into her briefcase, where it still sat as a reminder of her commitment to preserve her site's integrity.

Abby crossed a side street then hopped up onto the sidewalk running alongside her office building. The heels of her well-loved boots clicked against the cobblestone walkway as she headed for the entrance.

She glanced again at the stack of cards in her hand, but instead of flipping through them, she tucked them into her coat pocket. The cold had found its way beneath the heavy wool and under her skin. The only thing she cared about right now was finding the biggest, hottest, strongest cup of coffee she could.

"Good morning, Natalie," she called out to the receptionist as she entered the building.

The young woman looked up with a grin, her blunt-cut hair swinging against her slender neck. "Cold enough for you?"

Abby faked a shudder as she headed for the office kitchen.

Theirs was a shared space. One receptionist and administrative assistant for several tenants, allowing each company to share basic expenses with several other start-ups. Perfect for the work she did.

A few moments later, she headed toward her office space, steaming cup of coffee in hand, just as she liked it, heavy on the cream, no sugar.

She reached into her pocket to pull out the mail, but stopped in her tracks when she realized someone had reached the office ahead of her.

A broad-shouldered man stood talking to Robert. Based on the look on Robert's face, the call was anything but social. Robert's typically laughing eyes were serious and intent, focused on the other man's every word.

As she approached, Robert ran a hand over his close-cropped blond hair and frowned. When he caught sight of Abby he nodded in her direction.

The visitor turned to face her and Abby blinked, stunned momentarily by the intensity of the man's gaze. She'd never quite understood the term dark and smoldering until that moment. No matter, she wasn't about to let the man intimidate her, and certainly not because of his looks.

"Abby—" Robert tipped his chin toward the visitor "—this is Jack Grant, a detective from Phoenix, Arizona."

Detective?

She'd heard stories from other Web site owners such as herself about law enforcement trying to gain access to information on certain postcard senders, but Abby had made a promise to her blog visitors. A secret was a secret. Let the police do their own detective work.

"Detective," she said as she lowered the coffee to her desk and reached to shake the man's hand. "Welcome to Delaware."

He said nothing as he gave her hand a quick shake, all business and confident as could be. The contact sent a tremor through her system.

Attraction? Apprehension?

Abby shook off the thought and shrugged out of her coat, then reached again for her coffee.

"Coffee?" she asked the man.

He shook his head, his gaze never leaving hers.

She fought the urge to swallow, not wanting to provide the man with any clue as to how much he'd unnerved her simply by his appearance.

"I wanted to speak to you about your blog," he said, his voice a deep rumble of raw masculinity.

"Detective Grant claims he knows the woman from last week's blog." Robert thinned his lips as he finished the sentence.

Abby could read Robert's mind. He'd told her to toss the card in the trash, and when she'd chosen instead to feature the photograph and the caption, he'd been angry with her.

Robert and she had been friends since elementary school and they rarely argued. She supposed there was a first for everything.

"A friend of yours, Detective Grant?" she asked.

He pursed his lips, studying her, his brown eyes going even darker than they'd been a split second earlier. Then the detective shook his head.

"I never had the pleasure of meeting the young lady."

"No?" Abby took another sip of coffee, trying to guess exactly why the detective had made the trip to Delaware from Arizona. "Old case?"

Grant nodded. "Old case."

Robert dropped into a chair and ran his fingers through his hair. "I told you to throw it out."

"I wanted to make a point," Abby said, her voice climbing.

"I'm glad you didn't throw it out." The detective spoke slowly, without emotion. "Matter of fact, I'd like to see it."

Robert pushed away from his desk. "We keep every card archived. I'll get the most recent box."

Abby shook her head. "I never put it in the file."

Robert turned to face her, a frown creasing his forehead. "Why not?"

She shrugged as she reached for her bag. "I don't know."

Abby pulled the card from an inside pocket and handed it to Detective Grant.

He touched the card as if it were a living, breathing thing as he studied the front, the back, the label, the print of the message.

"Anonymous," he muttered beneath his breath.

"No postmark," Abby added. "I'm still trying to figure that one out."

"I don't suppose the idea of contacting the authorities ever crossed your mind?"

The detective's dark gaze lifted to hers, and for a brief moment Abby saw far more than an officer of the law out to solve a cold case. She saw the heat of emotion, the hint of…what?

The dark gaze shuttered and dropped before she had a chance to study the detective further.

Abby pulled herself taller. "As a matter of fact, I took the card to the local police, who said there's no indication this woman is a victim of a violent crime."

"And they knew this how?"

Abby opened her mouth to speak, then realized the detective was right. A chill slid down her spine.

"You're here because you think differently?"

He nodded as he pulled a folder from his briefcase.

Abby held her breath as Jack Grant carefully extracted a single photograph from the thick file. A black-and-white portrait of a young, dark-haired woman.

The shot might be different, but the subject was the same. The girl from Abby's anonymous postcard.

"Her name was Melinda Simmons." The detective placed the photograph on Abby's desk and slid it toward her.

Her name *was* Melinda Simmons.

The implication of the detective's phrasing sent Abby's insides tumbling end over end.

"Was?" she asked.

"Missing and presumed dead," he answered.

Abby thought about the card and its one-line message. *I didn't mean to kill her.*

"You're going to tell me you honestly believe a murderer sent us that card?" Her heart rapped so loudly against her rib cage she was sure the detective could hear the sound, yet she concentrated on maintaining her composure.

"Someone did. And I want to know who and why."

"Maybe you sent the card, Detective." Abby knew she was out of line, but the detective's holier-than-thou attitude had gotten under her skin. "How do we know you didn't decide to get creative in drawing attention to one of your cold cases?"

Jack Grant smiled, the expression even more unnerving than his scowl. "You can think whatever you want, Ms. Conroy, as long as I have your word you'll notify me when another card arrives."

Abby blinked. "Another card?"

Detective Grant nodded, handing her a business card before he zipped up his leather jacket. "If this is the guy I think it is, he likes Christmas, and he likes attention. And apparently he's picked you as his target for this year's holiday cheer."

Abby took the card, staring down at the contact information, complete with cell number. "How long will you be in town?"

"Long as it takes." Grant moved quickly back toward the lobby.

"What if he doesn't send a second card?" Abby winced at her suddenly tight voice.

"He will." Detective Grant gave a curt wave over his shoulder. "He will."

Chapter Two

Abby slowed as she rounded the corner in front of her townhouse. Dwayne Franklin stood stringing tiny white Christmas lights along the hedges that framed her front window.

"Oh, Dwayne. I told you we could skip that this year. It's too much work."

Her next-door neighbor pivoted at the sound of her voice, moving so sharply he lost his balance and stumbled, catching himself against the window frame.

Abby reached for his arm and he straightened, anchoring his hands on her elbows and squeezing tight. Too tight.

She swallowed down the nervousness her neighbor inspired, knowing she was being ridiculous.

He was as harmless as a fly. A man who'd been down on his luck for as long as she could remember, and a man who'd been a good neighbor to her for as long as she'd lived on the quiet city street.

"How about some coffee?" she asked.

"I'll be right in after I finish," he said with a smile.

Abby stepped back and admired his work. The twinkling strands did wonders for the front of her house. But then, Dwayne kept up her property as if it were his own—cutting her small patch of lawn in the summer, weeding her garden in the spring, and now stringing holiday lights before Christmas.

"I'll leave the door unlocked," Abby called as she headed around the side of the house toward the entrance to her townhouse.

"You have to admit there's nothing like holiday cheer."

Dwayne's words did nothing to warm her, instead reigniting the chill she'd felt ever since Detective Jack Grant's visit.

Holiday cheer.

The detective had seemed sure whoever had sent the Melinda Simmons postcard would strike again.

That holiday cheer, Abby could do without.

The temperature inside her living room seemed overly warm as Abby stepped indoors. She adjusted the thermostat, shrugged off her coat and tossed it over the arm of the overstuffed chair that had once been her grandmother's. She'd love nothing more than to pour herself a cup of coffee and curl up with a good book, but Dwayne would no doubt dawdle and Abby would end up cooking them both dinner.

Oh, well, she thought as she headed toward the kitchen. There was no harm in letting the man spend time at her house.

He was lonely, and he'd proved to be a good neighbor time and time again. Plus, she had nowhere better to be.

Abby worried occasionally that Dwayne wanted something more in terms of a relationship, but he'd never so much as tried to kiss her. She probably had nothing to worry about. Matter of fact, she ought to check her ego.

A framed photograph captured her gaze as she flipped on the kitchen light, and she plucked the picture from the counter.

In it, she and two friends stood in front of a series of

paintings. Abby's first gallery show. At the time, Abby's specialty had been landscapes, her work recreating what she considered the most beautiful canvas of all—nature. But in the years since, Abby had found her time spent creating murals to be more lucrative. Enough so that she could afford to run the confession site on the side.

She refocused on the photo, the faces. Gina and Vicki had been by her side during every moment of her career, just as they'd been by her side during every moment of her life from first grade forward.

Until last year.

Until Christmas Eve when Abby had let a call from Vicki go unanswered and she and Gina had found Vicki's body the next morning.

Suicide by hanging.

Her heart squeezed at the memory, the image burned into her mind's eye as if she stood there now, filled with horror and disbelief. Filled with shame and guilt that she might have been able to stop her friend from doing the unthinkable if she'd only answered the damn phone.

She'd vowed to never again make that same mistake. And then she'd founded Don't Say a Word.

"All done."

Dwayne's voice startled her, and Abby dropped the frame. The glass and pewter hit the granite countertop with a crash, and a wicked crack shattered the glass, sending shards skittering across the counter.

Dwayne was at her side in an instant, taking her hands in his, checking her fingers for any sign of blood.

He held her hands until Abby felt the urge to squirm. "I'm okay." She wiggled her fingers free from his grip, swallowing down the memories of the past. "Just careless…and tired." She waved a hand dismissively. "Let me clean this up and I'll make that coffee."

Dwayne shook his head, staring at her with such intent she felt he could see into her thoughts.

"I'll take care of this." He spoke without emotion as he reached to moisten a paper towel, then set to work capturing each shard of glass.

As Abby measured the coffee grounds by sight and set up mugs and cream for two, her neighbor diligently worked behind her, carefully erasing every last trace of her clumsiness.

Then he stood and watched her work, his eyes staring into the back of her head.

She fought the urge to tell him to go sit in the living room.

He was harmless, lonely, and she'd had a long day.

Nothing more, she told herself. Nothing more.

But she couldn't shake the sense of dread that had enveloped her every sense since Detective Grant had left the office.

He'd called her a target for the postcard sender's holiday cheer.

A target.

Abby couldn't help but wonder who it was that had put Don't Say a Word in his crosshairs.

She'd researched the old case thoroughly after Grant walked out of the office. She'd studied every piece of information she could find, including biographical data on Boone Shaw and information on each of the victims— including Grant's younger sister, Emma.

No wonder the detective wore such a scowl. If Abby understood one thing, it was how the pain of losing a loved one never left you. So much for the adage about how time heals all wounds.

No wonder the detective had made the cross-country trip as soon as he'd seen the blog.

And no wonder he was focused on the question that now haunted Abby's mind.

Had Boone Shaw chosen *Don't Say a Word* to bring attention to his crimes? Why?

And if somehow the sender wasn't Shaw, who was it?

Abby's stomach caught and twisted as the next question slid through her mind.

When would the next card arrive?

JACK PAID THE pizza delivery kid, then flipped the dead bolt back across the hotel door.

He opened the cardboard box and pulled one slice free from the pie, sinking his teeth into the dough and cheese.

Cold.

The pizza was cold.

Just like Delaware. Just like this room. Just like this case.

He was kidding himself if he thought one anonymous postcard was going to break the old murder case wide open, let alone an anonymous postcard bearing no postmark.

That particular piece of the mystery had been nagging at Jack all day.

In addition, he'd made some calls on his way back to the hotel. His source in Montana had said Boone Shaw fell off the radar several weeks back.

The man could be anywhere.

Grant muttered a few unkind thoughts aloud, then tossed the pizza box onto the bed.

He'd stopped at the local police department to let them know he was in town and working unofficially. While they'd been more than polite, they'd offered no help, no resources.

He couldn't blame them. Surely they had more important things to worry about than a postcard featuring the photo of a young woman missing and presumed dead eleven years earlier.

He'd also met with the officer who had checked out the card on Abby's behalf. Detective Timothy Hayés.

Jack couldn't blame the man for thinking the card a hoax.

The card itself was nondescript—available at any office supply store. The same could be said for the white label, and the message had been printed on what could be one of a thousand different laser printers.

Simply put, the card offered nothing distinctive. Nothing out of the ordinary. Nothing except the image of Melinda Simmons, a young girl the rest of the world had forgotten years ago.

The photograph itself was the only unique aspect of the card, and without further cause, no crime lab was about to waste precious time on an analysis of paper, age and adhesive.

The thought of tracing fingerprints was a joke. What better way to wipe out any prints than by sending a postcard through the United States mail?

Yet, how had the sender managed to avoid the card receiving a postmark? Luck? Not likely.

Had the card been hand-delivered? If so, whoever was responsible might be close. Too close.

Jack took another bite of cold pizza and groaned before he tossed the rest of the slice back into the box.

He slid the copies of his old case notes from his bag, spreading the contents across the hotel room's desk.

Five faces stared back at him from the case photos. Five victims, all struck down within a ten-day period years earlier. There had been no known victims since, so why had Boone broken his silence? Why now?

Jack studied the photos taken of young, vital women— Emma included—during happier times. Each shot had been provided by a grieving relative—a relative who had trusted Jack and the investigative team to bring their daughter's killer to justice.

Jack pulled the mug shots of Boone Shaw free from the file and stared down into the man's dead eyes. Shaw had been a big man, strong, yet fairly nondescript as far as physical features went.

Even eleven years ago, he'd been all but bald, and his round face had offered no unique features or scars. His manner of dress had blended seamlessly into the New Mexico culture.

For all intents and purposes, Shaw had been exactly what he claimed to be—a photographer out to build a business as he helped young wannabe models get their starts.

Jack knew better. He *knew* it, felt it, believed it.

Boone Shaw had been as guilty as they came.

Yet, when push came to shove, the lack of DNA evidence and Shaw's airtight alibi had been enough to let the accused walk.

Jack had waited every year, every month, every day since the trial ended for the chance to go after Shaw again. The Melinda Simmons card might not be much, but Jack planned to work it for everything he could.

Jack flashed back on the image of Abby Conroy.

The woman looked more like a waif than the co-owner of the thriving Internet site. Short and slender, she'd sported a navy knit cap, pulled low on her forehead, the pale blond fringe of her bangs peeking from just below the hat's ribbed edge.

Her long hair had been tucked behind her ears, and her nose, reddened by the cold, had matched the bright circles of determined color that had fired in her cheeks as she defended her actions.

A real spitfire.

Yet her ice blue eyes had remained as chilly as the temperature outside, faltering only when she realized Jack was telling the truth.

She'd been carrying around the photo of a dead girl, and she'd done exactly what the killer had wanted by publishing his message.

Even so, the woman had made it clear her first priority was the integrity of her site and the anonymity of the site's supporters, but she'd no doubt change her tune as soon as another card arrived.

And it would arrive.

Jack hadn't been so sure about anything since the day he'd first looked into Boone Shaw's eyes and known the man had killed Emma.

Abby Conroy might think her precious blog site innocent in the sins of the past, but as long as she encouraged confessions, she sure as hell wasn't innocent in the sins of the present.

And Jack had no qualms about blowing Abby Conroy and Don't Say a Word sky-high.

He'd vowed long ago to do whatever it took to bring Emma's killer to justice.

Now all Jack had to do was sit back…and wait.

ABBY RETURNED TO the broken photo frame after Dwayne left.

For once, her neighbor hadn't lingered. Matter of fact, Abby was used to the man being quiet, but tonight he'd been more distant than ever. If Abby hadn't known better, she'd swear there'd been something he wanted to tell her, a secret he wanted to share.

Abby knew Dwayne regularly read the blog. He'd told her so on various occasions over the past year—while they shared a glass of iced tea after he'd worked in her yard, or on the occasional evening she offered him a quick sandwich when he'd bring over her mail.

He'd never told her much about his life, his work, his past. Perhaps that was better.

The man was a loner in the true sense of the word, and yet he'd befriended Abby. He looked out for her, kept an eye on her property, trusted her.

He even went so far as to take Abby's personal mail from the small box by her front door if she worked too late. He had a fear of the mail sitting out all day.

Perhaps he'd once been the victim of identity theft—who knew—but on the occasions Dwayne did take in her mail, Abby would thank him for his kindness and write off the odd practice as a quirk of a lonely mind.

The fact Abby hadn't put a stop to the practice drove Robert and Gina insane, but Abby knew Dwayne was only trying to be neighborly.

Both Robert and Gina felt Dwayne's overfamiliarity was just that. Overfamiliar. Robert had gone so far as to say Dwayne's behavior bordered on stalking, but Abby didn't agree.

Dwayne was lonely and more than a little paranoid. End of story. And as far as Abby knew, none of the other neighbors gave Dwayne the time of day.

Well, she, for one, wasn't about to ignore him.

Abby dropped her gaze to the scarred picture of herself with Gina and Vicki. Just look where ignoring a friend had gotten her once before.

Vicki's death was the reason Abby spent so much time with each postcard she received. She tried to put herself in the sender's position, tried to imagine the anguish, the guilt, the relief each felt at finally coming clean.

She was no therapist, nor did she profess to be one, but she could offer space. Space to come clean. Space to confess. Space to shed the burden of a secret's weight carried for too long.

Abby understood the pain of holding a secret inside, she understood how the truth could slowly eat away at you, uncoiling like a snake.

She'd never told a soul—not even Robert or Gina—about the call she'd ignored from Vicki.

Perhaps someday she'd send herself a postcard.

She laughed at the irony, glad she could laugh at something today.

A mental image of Detective Jack Grant flashed through her mind and her belly tightened. The man's intensity was breathtaking, albeit foreboding. If he hadn't scowled so intently the entire time he'd been at the office, she might be tempted to call him handsome. But she wasn't about to make that leap, not anytime soon.

She thought again about the case information she'd uncovered on the New Mexico murders.

Seemed Detective Grant had left out a bit of information himself. So much for full disclosure.

No matter. Abby recognized his type.

He'd tell her what she needed to know, when he thought she needed to know it. He probably believed he was protecting her by sparing her the gory details—like the killer's signature.

She shuddered at the thought.

Abby had been too harsh with the detective, too defensive about her work and the site, and she knew it.

The detective had called briefly later in the day, asking to go through the archives in order to check each postcard for any sign the sender had reached out before.

Abby thought the exercise would be nothing but wasted time, but if that's what Jack Grant wanted to do, that's what she'd help him do.

And then it hit her.

Postcards.

She'd never so much as flipped through the contents of the post office box that morning. She'd been so taken aback by the detective's visit and the harsh reality of his disclosure she'd forgotten about today's mail.

Abby retraced her steps to the living room and dipped her hand inside the large pocket of her coat. Today's stack of cards hadn't been quite as cumbersome as those in recent weeks. Perhaps the onslaught of submissions that had followed the *People* magazine article was finally tapering off.

Maybe now business would return to usual.

She checked the thought immediately. Business as usual did not include an apparent murder confession.

Abby sank into her favorite chair and flipped through the cards one by one, reading each message before she studied the accompanying graphic.

I never told my father I loved him.

Abby's heart ached as she studied the apparently scanned image of a scribbled crayon drawing of a house and tree on the reverse side of the card.

I cheated on my bar exam.

The submission featured a store-bought, glossy image of a lush tropical resort.

Apparently this particular confessor didn't suffer remorse. Abby laughed and moved on.

She shouldn't have ignored me.

Simple black type on a white label.

No postmark.

Abby choked on her laughter.

She dropped the card into her lap and reached for her gloves. She pulled them from her coat pocket and slipped them over her fingers before she reached for the card again, this time turning the simple card over.

Surely she was overreacting.

This card couldn't be the same, couldn't be another confession, another photograph of some poor girl who'd thought she had a shot at a modeling career and ended up dead.

Abby held her breath, gripping only the edges of the card as she turned it over.

A beautiful young woman looked back from the black-and-white shot. She smiled, and yet her eyes hinted at something other than joy. In them, Abby saw nervousness...and fear. Had she known she was in danger at the moment this shot was taken?

The coffee Abby had shared with Dwayne churned in her stomach as she turned back to the message, reading it again.

She shouldn't have ignored me.

Dread gripped her by the throat and squeezed even as the bright white lights twinkled through her sheer curtains from the bushes outside—an ironic juxtaposition of holiday present and past.

Abby carefully placed the card on an end table and reached into her coat pocket again, this time in search of Detective Grant's business card.

Her own words echoed in her brain.

What if he doesn't send a second card?

She'd been so sure of herself, even after the detective's explanation of the case and the killer's cruelty.

Detective Grant had been equally sure, and he'd been correct in his prediction.

He will. He will.

Little did the detective know the second card had been in her coat pocket even as he'd spoken.

Abby dropped her focus to Jack Grant's business card and studied his cell phone number.

The man had traveled all the way from Arizona to Delaware to chase a single lead. She had to admire him for that.

Then Abby took a deep breath, reached for her phone and dialed.

Chapter Three

Jack pulled his rental car to a stop in front of the quaint townhouse. Small white lights twinkled from the short hedge lining the home's oversized windows.

Figured Abby Conroy would have holiday lights.

Based on the tone of her voice when she called, Jack's earlier visit had served to snap her out of any holiday cheer she'd been experiencing.

Jack unfolded himself from the car and headed toward the door. *Around the side,* she'd said.

Dark sidewalk. Isolated entrance.

The woman was nothing if not a picture of what *not to do* when devising personal security.

She'd provided him with her home address, but Jack had already been able to ascertain that information without so much as pulling a single departmental string.

He'd tracked her by working backward from her post-card confession site through the registration database and public contact information he'd pulled online.

If Boone Shaw—or anyone, for that matter—decided to target Abby Conroy, nothing about the woman's life would make finding her a challenge.

Now that Jack had had time to stew on the information

he'd received, he was certain Boone Shaw had gone underground for a reason.

Shaw had never vanished so thoroughly before, and even though he'd never been picked up on any sort of charge during the eleven years since the trial, he'd left a trail.

Until now.

Business dealings. A new photography studio. Credit card and mortgage debt.

The man had led a normal life, a full life, a life he didn't deserve.

A calm sureness slid through Jack's system as he headed toward Abby Conroy's door.

There was always a chance Shaw wasn't the person physically sending the cards, but Jack had no doubt he was responsible. Somehow.

The man had killed Emma, just as he'd killed Melinda Simmons and the others.

Jack had seen it in Shaw's eyes the day they'd pulled the man into custody along with the piles of so-called modeling shots he'd accumulated during his time as a photographer.

The man had been guilty--a sexual predator with a camera. And his victims had been only too willing to pose, believing his promises of bright futures, bright lights, big dreams come true.

"Can I help you?" A thirtysomething man wearing only a pair of jeans, sneakers and gray sweatshirt stepped into Jack's path.

Jack's hand reached automatically for his weapon before he remembered he'd left his service revolver back in Arizona, part of the agreement he'd struck with his chief.

The weight of his backup weapon in his ankle holster provided comfort, but reaching for the gun didn't fall under the subtle category, nor was the move necessary.

The ghost of Boone Shaw had Jack jumping like a rookie.

Besides, the man before him was more than likely nothing but a neighbor, someone suspicious of a man approaching Abby Conroy's door.

Jack couldn't fault him for that, but he could ask questions.

Jack measured the man, from his feet to his face. "A bit cold to be outside without a coat, isn't it?"

"I spend a lot of time over here." The man's dark eyes shifted, their focus bouncing from side to side, never making direct eye contact. "With Abby," he added, as if use of her name would prove something to Jack, somehow put him in his place.

Jack extended his hand. "Detective Jack Grant. I'm here on official business."

The other man blinked, his expression morphing from aggressive to vacant. "Dwayne Franklin. Abby and I have a…relationship."

Jack doubted the validity of the man's statement based on his inability to make eye contact.

If anything, the man was a neighbor who thought he had a relationship with Abby Conroy—yet another security issue Jack planned to talk to the woman about.

Jack flashed his shield, and the man uttered a quick good-night as he headed toward the house next door.

Abby pulled the door open, having apparently heard voices.

"Detective Grant?"

"You might as well start calling me Jack." He jerked a thumb toward the neighbor's house. "Does your neighbor make a practice of lurking outside your house?"

A crease formed between Abby's brows and Jack noted her coloring seemed paler than it had been that morning. "Dwayne?"

Jack nodded.

"He hung the lights for me earlier. He was probably checking his work."

Jack gave another sharp nod, saying nothing. Let the woman believe what she wanted to believe. As far as Jack was concerned, her neighbor's actions were a bit too over-protective.

Jack had always been a master at assessing people and their situations, and this situation was no different.

Abby Conroy apparently trusted everyone, her postcard confessors and loitering neighbor included.

Jack trusted no one.

Any work they did together ought to prove interesting, if nothing else.

He chuckled under his breath, quickly catching himself and smoothing his features. He couldn't remember the last time he'd found anything humorous. But if he was forced to work alongside Ms. Conroy in order to flesh out this lead, he might as well enjoy himself.

"Something funny, Detective Grant?"

Confusion flashed in the woman's pale eyes, yet it was a second emotion lurking there that sobered Jack, an emotion visibly battling for position.

Fear.

Maybe Abby Conroy wasn't as naive as Jack had thought.

He shook his head. "I meant no disrespect, but you and I need to talk about protecting yourself."

He patted the door frame as he pushed the door shut behind them. The flimsy door boasted nothing more than a keyed lock.

He tapped the knob. "There's this new gadget called a dead bolt. You might want to check it out."

But his warning fell on apparently deaf ears. Abby showed no sign of having heard a word he'd said.

She hadn't explained the reason for her call, and Jack

hadn't pressed her. He'd hoped she wanted to talk to him about a change of heart regarding the archived postcards.

But as Abby pointed to a stack of postcards sitting on an end table, then reached for one in particular, Jack's stomach caught.

"He's sent another, hasn't he?"

She handled the card by the edges, handing it to Jack even as she spoke, not answering his question, but rather reciting the card's message from memory.

"She shouldn't have ignored me." Abby's voice dropped low, shaken.

Jack forced himself to look away from her face, to shove aside the ridiculous urge to reach for her, to promise her he wouldn't let the man responsible for sending the postcards touch her.

He forced himself instead to reach for the card, to study the message.

The sender had once again used a nondescript white mailing label, printed in what appeared to be laser printer ink. The label had been adhered to the back of a plain white postcard.

Nondescript. Untraceable.

Again.

But there was nothing nondescript about the photograph glued to the opposite side.

Jack turned the card over in his hand and swore beneath his breath at the sight of the face captured in the black-and-white print.

His features fell slack, slipping like the strength in his body.

Abby placed one slender hand on his arm. "Detective? Are you all right?"

Her words reached him through a fog of semiawareness. The face on the photograph fully captured his focus, his senses, and yet he'd never seen this particular photograph before.

Never before.

Jack set down the card long enough to reach for his briefcase, extracting a small evidence bag. He slid the postcard inside, carefully touching only the edges even though he knew the card had been handled countless times during its journey through the mail.

"Detective?" Abby released his arm, but her tone grew stronger, more urgent. "Is she one of the five from New Mexico?"

Impressive. Abby Conroy had done her homework during the hours since he'd stepped into her life and world, something that didn't surprise Jack in the least.

He steeled himself then nodded, tucking the card away before he looked up. "Her name was Emma. She was nineteen when he killed her."

"Emma?"

Jack shoved down the tide of grief threatening to drown his senses.

"Emma Grant?" Abby asked softly.

Jack gave another nod, not trusting his voice at the moment and not wanting Abby to sense how much the card had rocked him.

The bastard had sent a picture of Emma. A picture Jack had never seen either in Emma's personal belongings or the photos taken from Boone Shaw during the original investigation.

"I'm so sorry, Detective."

"Are you ready to work with me now?" Jack purposely redirected the conversation, wanting Abby's cooperation, not her sympathy.

Abby's throat worked. "I'm sorry for how I acted earlier. I was being defensive and I was wrong."

Jack pointed to one of the living-room chairs, gesturing for Abby to sit. "Tell me what you found out since this morning, then I'll fill in the gaps."

As Abby recounted the news articles she'd uncovered online, Jack leaned his hip against a second chair, and wondered whose face Shaw would feature in his next message. And when?

No matter. Jack was here now. He had eleven more years of experience than he'd had the last time he'd gone up against Boone Shaw, and this time he was ready.

Jack planned to do exactly what Herb Simmons had asked him to do—whatever it took to make sure Shaw didn't get away again.

This time, Boone Shaw was going to pay for the lives he'd ended, the families he'd ripped apart and the heartache he'd inflicted.

This time, Boone Shaw was going away.

For good.

HE WONDERED HOW many people remembered the girl in the photograph—her blond hair bouncing around her shoulders in natural waves, her dark eyes bright and hopeful.

He remembered those eyes in death, still searching as if pleading for her life.

Her parents had died not long after she'd been found dead and battered, her body dumped in Valley Forge National Park. A freak accident in a snowstorm had taken their lives, if he remembered correctly.

His mind and sense of clarity might not be what they'd once been, but his sense of what drew people's attention hadn't faltered.

If he played this right, the Don't Say a Word site might prove to be the opportunity he'd been seeking for years.

One more anonymous card confessing a murder, one more innocent face, one more blog and the story would take on a life of its own.

And there was nothing he loved more than a story—a good story.

A new postcard would launch this particular story into the national focus, and he'd be right there to reap the benefits.

What would the media call the sender? The Christmas Killer? The Christmas Confessor?

He laughed, enjoying the moment.

The Christmas Confessor.

He liked it. He liked it a lot.

He carefully adhered the print to the postcard then affixed the one-line message to the back.

No one likes a show off.

What would Abby Conroy say about this card? Would she call him an opportunist?

Perhaps.

But then, she wouldn't be far from the truth, would she?

He thought about logging on to the Internet and visiting the confession site again to stare at the first card, to study the expression on Melinda Simmons's young features, but he forced himself to focus.

Forced himself to finish the task at hand.

He carefully tucked the postcard into his briefcase, careful not to leave any prints. Then he reached for his coat. After all, the night air outside had gone cold and raw and he had miles to go.

Miles to go.

Things to do.

And *confessions* to deliver.

Chapter Four

Abby started a second pot of coffee while Jack Grant worked in the office's shared conference room. She'd checked the schedule when she and Jack arrived late last night, and knew no one had the room booked for today. It was Saturday, after all.

"I need to raise a pertinent question," she said as she headed back into the room where stacks of postcards covered every available space.

Jack grunted, his version of a reply, Abby had quickly learned during the hours they'd been working side-by-side, studying postcard after postcard.

"It's Saturday. I need to post a new blog."

The detective's hand stilled on the card he'd been reading and he lifted his gaze to hers. "Any thoughts?"

Did she know what she wanted to say this week? Which secret confessions she wanted to feature?

She'd had three cards picked out and her thoughts ready to go, but that had been yesterday. Yesterday, before her sense of reality had been turned on its ear.

Today, she could think of only one message. One card.

She shouldn't have ignored me.

"I want to flush him out." She braced herself, expecting a harsh response from Jack.

Instead, the detective narrowed his eyes thoughtfully, reached for the outstretched coffee cup and took a long drink.

The man took his time before he answered, and Abby could almost hear the wheels turning in his brain. The depth of his concentration turned his caramel eyes chocolate and his sharp features smooth.

Abby swallowed down the sudden tightness in her throat at the precise moment the detective spoke.

"Do it."

Abby blinked, surprised by his lack of objection. "Really?"

He shrugged with his eyes. "That's the answer you wanted, correct?" Jack gestured to the piles of cards, the thousands they'd spent the night sorting.

Abby could follow his thoughts without him saying a word. They hadn't found another card like the first two, and out of thousands and thousands of postcards, they'd found only a handful of cards without a postmark.

What were the odds the two cards—the photos of Melinda Simmons and Emma Grant—both happened to slide through the United States Post Office machines unscathed? Fairly high, she'd imagine.

Somehow, whoever had sent those cards had gotten around the system, but how?

"He either hand-delivered the cards or slipped them into your post office box," Jack said matter-of-factly. "He's closer than you think, Ms. Conroy. The sooner we find him, the better."

Abby's belly tightened. "How close?"

The detective dropped his focus back to the pile of postcards sitting in front of him. "That's what I intend to find out."

A SHORT WHILE LATER, Jack shifted his focus from the remaining stacks of cards to Abby Conroy herself.

He watched her as she sorted through a stack, pulling at her lower lip with her top teeth as she concentrated. She tucked a wayward strand of long, sleek hair behind her ear then abruptly looked up at Jack, as if she'd sensed him watching.

Her eyebrows drew together. "Something I can do for you?"

Even as exhausted as he knew the woman must be, determination and stubbornness blazed in her expression. She was a spitfire, of that there was no doubt.

Jack shook his head, realizing he must be more tired than he realized. He'd allowed the woman to catch him openly staring at her.

Busted.

Then he asked the question he'd been pondering since he'd first set foot inside the Don't Say a Word office.

"I can't help but wonder why someone like you felt compelled to solicit all of—" he gestured to the thousands of cards on the table "—this. Don't you have demons of your own to contend with?"

Abby's throat worked as if he'd hit a nerve. "Maybe that's why I wanted to give others a vehicle, a safe and anonymous way to cleanse their conscience."

"Because you don't have a way?"

"Maybe I'm just a sympathetic person, Detective."

Detective.

He *had* hit a nerve.

Abby dropped her focus back to the stack of cards, effectively telling him to buzz off without saying so. What she couldn't realize was that her nonverbal response had set off the investigative portion of Jack's brain.

The woman had tapped into his curiosity as soon as they'd met, with her all-American looks and her stubborn demeanor, but now that Jack had stolen a glimpse through the crack in her protective wall, he wanted more. He wanted the full story.

"You're right, though," he said, never taking his focus from her, wanting to read her response.

"Right about the site?"

"Right about the cards."

That got her attention and she lifted her curious gaze, her eyes the color of a clear, winter sky.

"I think Melinda's card was the first. There's nothing here to suggest this guy's reached out to you before last week."

"But you think he'll reach out again?" She spoke slowly, using his terminology.

Jack nodded.

"I don't understand why." Her voice tightened. "Why Don't Say a Word? And what does he hope to gain?"

"That, Ms. Conroy, is the sixty-million-dollar question."

She disappeared after that, claiming the need to clear her head. Jack couldn't blame her.

They'd been working all night and the truth was, the cold, cruel world outside had marched right into her life the moment Jack had arrived on the scene and burst her crank-postcard-theory bubble.

He'd have been surprised if she didn't need space at some point.

As for Jack, he'd finished sorting postcards and didn't care if he never saw another so-called confession again in his life.

What he needed to do now was to get back to his hotel. He had calls to make and a former suspect to track down.

When footfalls sounded behind him, Jack never guessed anyone but Abby would be stepping into the conference room.

He rocked back in the chair without turning around. "I'm not finding anything."

But the voice that answered wasn't Abby's.

"What was it you were looking for?" Humor tangled with curiosity in Robert Walker's voice.

Jack straightened, pushing himself out of the chair to greet Abby's partner. "Surprised to see you here on a Saturday."

"I should probably say the same thing to you." Robert looked as impeccable today as he had the day before. He held a cup of designer coffee in one hand and a newspaper in the other. "I had some paperwork to get caught up on. End of the month bills, et cetera."

The other man's gaze skimmed Jack from head to toe. The look of disdain in Walker's eyes didn't go unnoticed. Quite frankly, Jack didn't give a damn. He knew he looked rough after traveling the day before and working through the postcards all night.

So be it. He'd rather worry about a case than his appearance any day. At this point in his career as a homicide detective, Jack had come to accept the fact that most days his appearance wasn't much better than that of some of his victims.

Walker, on the other hand, appeared to be a man who put a high price on fashion and first impressions.

"We were out of cream, so I ran next door." Abby's voice filtered into the room several moments before she appeared. "I don't know about you, but after last night, I'm not settling for black coffee."

One of Robert's pale brows arched in the moment before he shifted his attention to Abby.

"Robert." She stuttered to a stop in the doorway. "I didn't realize you were working today."

"Just came in." He smiled, tucking his newspaper under one arm to reach for the box of doughnuts Abby juggled along with two foam coffee cups.

"Thanks."

An odd sensation rankled inside Jack's gut as he

watched Abby shift her load, transferring the box to Robert. Her features softened, her eyes brightened, and if he weren't mistaken, she and Robert shared a lightning-fast look reminiscent of the way Jack had seen lovers do.

Were Abby Conroy and Robert Walker more than business partners? Jack had seen no sign of that possibility at Abby's apartment other than the occasional photograph. And she'd mentioned nothing of the sort, not that she would. The woman struck him as anything but someone who shared her thoughts easily. Ironic, considering she spent her days hoping the public would confess en masse.

"Something going on I should know about?" Robert asked, never taking his gaze from Abby.

She nodded, but it was Jack who spoke.

"There was another postcard in yesterday's mail."

Robert's brows drew together as he frowned.

"I forgot to sort the cards." Abby gave a quick shrug as she handed Jack his coffee then set her cup on the table. "I went by the post office box on my way in, but once I stumbled upon you and Detective Grant, I never took the mail out of my pocket. I remembered them last night after Dwayne left…"

Her voice trailed off noticeably toward the end of her sentence and Jack noted the angry look that flashed across Robert's face.

Apparently Abby's partner wasn't a Dwayne fan, either, although he said nothing in response to Abby's statement.

"Did you call the authorities?" Robert asked.

Jack nodded, pursing his lips. "I'm working with local police, keeping them abreast of any developments. And I dusted for prints myself."

"And?" Robert's features tensed.

"And they agree with me that as of right now we have nothing to go on except the fact both cards bore no useable prints and were prepared using materials that could have been acquired anywhere."

"What about the photographs?" Robert asked.

"My thought—" Jack pulled the second postcard from his case file "—is that the photos used to make the post-cards are scans of the originals."

"And you're some sort of photography expert?" Robert's brows lifted toward his too-neat hairline.

Jack shook his head, not even trying to hide his amuse-ment at Walker's arrogance. "And you are?"

Walker shrugged. "I used to dabble. May I take a look?"

Jack handed the photo to Robert, studying the man as he stared intently at both sides of the card.

"I think you're right. The quality isn't that of a true pho-tograph."

"More like a high-quality personal printer."

Robert nodded, continuing to scrutinize Emma's pho-tograph, his expression revealing not a clue as to what he was thinking. "Pretty girl."

"She was." Jack fought the urge to put his fist through a wall, something he had only done once in his life—the day Boone Shaw walked free.

"One of your victims?" Robert's expression brightened.

"Yes." Jack gave a sharp nod. "And she's my sister."

Robert let loose a long, low whistle. "My sympathies." He turned over the card to reread the message, drawing in a sharp breath as if the words meant more now that he knew the victim was a relative. "When?"

"Same week as Melinda Simmons. Christmas week, eleven years ago."

Robert handed the card back to Jack. "Why confess now? Why use our site?"

Jack tucked the card back into the file without looking at Emma's full-of-life eyes captured in the photograph.

How long had she lived after that moment? What hell had she suffered at the hands of her killer?

"I'd imagine he saw your *People* magazine feature and decided you were the surest means to an end."

"An end?"

"His fifteen minutes of fame." Jack gathered up his notes, tucking the folder and his papers back into his brief-case. "For some reason he's decided now's the time to get the credit he deserves."

"I'm not following you." Robert narrowed his eyes.

"You'd be surprised how many psychopaths reach a point where they want to be caught," Jack replied.

A shadow crossed Robert's face, an emotional response Jack couldn't quite read.

"Isn't that a bit clichéd?" Robert asked.

"Perhaps." Jack forced a polite smile. "But true. These killers work so hard not to get caught that there's no noto-riety for them. Sometimes they crack. They want the at-tention they feel they deserve."

"The credit?" Robert repeated, as if weighing the word.

Jack nodded.

"Why now?"

"Maybe he's sick or feels he's running out of time. Maybe he feels threatened by a new killer. Maybe he's simply bored with being anonymous."

"Amazing." Robert smiled, the move not reaching his unreadable eyes. "Good work, Detective." Then he turned, heading toward the door. "Speaking of work, I'd better get to mine."

With that, Robert was gone, leaving Jack and Abby to their roomful of postcards.

"Not a warm and fuzzy fellow?" Jack asked after Robert was out of earshot.

"He doesn't like the cards." Abby handed Jack a cup of

coffee. "He probably broke into a cold sweat just being near this many."

Jack frowned.

"Says they give him the creeps," Abby continued.

"So why does he do this?"

She screwed up her features as if the answer were a no-brainer. "He does it to help me."

Jack said nothing, knowing from years of interrogation that sometimes silence was the fastest way to discover additional information. Abby didn't disappoint.

"He handles the business aspect and the promotion. I handle the postcards and write the weekly blog."

"And this keeps you both busy full-time?"

She shook her head. "I paint. Landscapes mainly. Murals. Robert does freelance marketing. Speeches. Brochures. Advertising design. Things like that."

"So you both work here all day then work at home each night."

Abby nodded. "More or less. We rarely put in full days here. This—" she gestured to the office in front of and behind her "—allows us flexibility to do our own things."

"You working on a mural right now?" Jack asked the question knowing it seemed unrelated to the case at hand, but realizing you never knew where the facts of a case might lead you.

But Abby only shook her head. "Last thing anyone wants at Christmas time is a mural painter in their home or office."

Jack scanned the stacks of cards filling the room. "Any income from this?"

"Only from the advertising. It's enough to cover hosting and office expenses, but not much more. We really didn't start this for the money, so that aspect doesn't matter to either one of us."

"Any enemies?"

His question visibly startled Abby and she took a backward step. "Not that I know of."

Jack pushed away from the table. "Then we keep our eyes and ears open until we know for sure who's on your side and who isn't. And in the meantime, let's go write that blog of yours."

JACK STOOD OVER Abby's shoulder as she worked, later than usual in drafting her weekly blog.

Typically, she tried to have the site updated just after midnight each Friday night. Considering it was now after noon on Saturday, she was running seriously behind schedule.

Robert had stayed less than forty-five minutes before he'd claimed to have forgotten a social event scheduled for that afternoon. Abby knew him well enough to know he hadn't planned on having company here at the office. He'd probably packed up the bills to take home for processing.

As for the blog, Abby had tucked away the cards she'd planned to feature, working instead from only one.

The postcard and photo featuring Emma Grant.

The young woman's smiling face haunted Abby. She couldn't begin to imagine the kind of hurt the image had brought to life deep inside Jack.

For all of his hard-shelled bravado, the detective's eyes provided a window into the pain he'd locked inside. Abby didn't need to be a rocket scientist to spot his true emotions, and she grimaced on his behalf.

She hadn't known him long, but she'd seen enough to know Jack wouldn't be pleased by her observation. Some men prided themselves on being strong, resilient, alpha males. Jack Grant fell soundly into that camp—the camp that said real men didn't show their feelings.

But as her gaze dropped again to Emma's face, and Abby considered the magnitude of the loss Jack had suffered, she didn't see how he could feel nothing, yet nothing was all he projected.

A man would have to be a robot to keep that sort of heartache locked inside forever. Sooner or later, he'd snap. Either that, or he'd shut down completely. How else could a person survive?

Jack stood behind her as she worked, the heat of his body warming the back of her sweater.

Well, the man definitely was not a robot.

Abby had never written one of her blogs with someone breathing down her neck, but she understood why the detective watched her every move, studied her every word. He'd made a commitment to clear a case, to catch a killer, to ease the suffering of the families left behind.

He was here because he thought Abby could help him. Plain and simple. He was here to make sure she didn't misstep in their efforts to flush out the postcard's sender.

She might be used to working alone, but Jack's goal had become her goal, and she'd do whatever it took to help him in his cause.

"Am I distracting you?" Jack asked, as if reading Abby's thoughts.

He leaned so close his breath brushed the strands of the hair she'd twisted up into a clip so that she could concentrate. In fact, she'd thought about the detective's proximity long enough that she'd begun to imagine the feel of his breath against the bare expanse of her throat.

What would the touch of his hand be like should he shift his grasp from the back of the chair to her shoulder?

A shudder rippled through her, coiling her belly into a tight knot. Heat ignited, low and heavy at her core.

What on earth was wrong with her?

She'd had no sleep, true. Perhaps she could use that to explain the unwanted thoughts about Jack Grant…and his hand…and the heat he inspired.

Abby's face warmed, making her thankful Jack stood where he couldn't see her sudden flush of embarrassment.

"Abby?"

"Yes?"

"I asked if I was distracting you, but based on the fact you didn't hear me, I'd have to say no."

If only he knew the truth.

She shook her head. "No. You're not distracting me at all."

And then she forced her thoughts back to the screen and the words she'd written, her admonition of a killer out to leave his mark on the public psyche by sending handmade postcards confessing his former sins.

Yet as much as she tried to deny it, the distraction of Jack's presence hung in the back of Abby's mind, a tiny voice refusing to be silenced, refusing to be ignored— even though that's exactly what Abby intended to do.

TENSION VIBRATED OFF of Abby Conroy, pulsating in waves. Jack had shattered her illusions of the world and the innocence of her postcard confession site, he knew that. But he wasn't sorry.

He'd done what he'd had to do, and if he had to expose Abby to the harsh reality of the world in order to unearth Boone Shaw, he would.

He had a job to do, and a killer to track down and trap.

"You're sure you don't mind me reading over your shoulder?" he asked again.

The woman answered with only a sharp shake of her head.

Jack leaned in closer, inhaling the lemony scent of whatever products she'd used on her hair the day before.

Fresh. The woman smelled fresh, even after the long night they'd shared.

Her fingers flew across the keyboard as she typed. Long, slender fingers, sure in their purpose. She leaned forward slightly. Moving away from his nearness? Or lost in her concentration?

He'd guess the latter, though the increasing tension arcing between them had grown palpable.

Too much time together in small spaces over long hours could do that to any two people. He should know.

He thought back to the cases he'd worked over the years. The women he'd met. He'd allowed himself brief involvements, but nothing more. His work didn't allow room for distraction of an emotional nature.

Then Jack pulled his thoughts back to this moment, this woman, *this* case.

His gaze drifted from the blog's words to Abby's face, lit by the monitor screen, her eyes bright, animated, determined. Her chin jutted forward as if nothing scared her, as if nothing could touch her. The protectiveness simmering deep inside Jack edged aside to allow another emotion to spring to life, uncoiling and spreading. Admiration? Attraction?

He shifted his stance, sliding his grip from the back of her chair to the arm by her side.

Abby's body stiffened, then immediately relaxed. She was more affected by his presence than she'd admitted.

Something tightened deep in his center. A need he'd long denied, a craving he'd vowed to never honor again.

"You think this works?"

Abby's voice filtered into his brain, her soft tone adding to thoughts of the case, his past, and Abby, swirling and battling for position.

What would it be like to hear that soft voice under different circumstances? Whispered in his ear? Against his neck? Lips feathering the bare skin of his chest?

"Good job." Jack cleared his throat and pushed back from her chair, hoping Abby hadn't heard the raspy quality of his voice. "I'd better be heading back to my hotel. I've got some work to do."

Lord knew he needed something to redirect his brain from thoughts of Abby back to thoughts of the case. Plus, he imagined the woman would be ready to head home once the blog was posted. Neither of them had slept since the night before.

Jack's last mistake had been getting involved with an associate on a case, a young district attorney who'd turned out to be playing for both sides.

While he didn't expect Abby to do anything to jeopardize his search for Shaw, he couldn't deny his thoughts had begun to border on distraction.

Jack hadn't been with a woman in a long, long time, and Abby Conroy was wreaking havoc on his senses.

But Jack was a man of conviction. A man of control. And he wasn't about to let lust get in the way of focus or justice. Not now.

Not ever.

Chapter Five

Jack had been gone for less than an hour when Abby heard the bell at the front of building signal a new arrival.

Even though she'd been happy with her blog entry calling out the postcard sender, she hadn't yet hit the publish button on her management program.

The bell sounded again and Abby sucked in a breath, held it and keyed in the steps to update the blog.

Then she pushed out of her chair, filled with a sense of anticipation, not knowing what the future would bring. For the sake of Jack Grant and the other victims' families, she hoped the postcards and blogs would lead the authorities to the killer, this time bringing him to justice and the cold case to closure.

She squinted as she headed toward the reception area, not recognizing the man who stood on the other side of the glass door.

Well-dressed and polished, she'd guess him to be in his late thirties based on the tinges of silver at his temples. He smiled as she approached and Abby found herself reminded of her partner Robert's smile at times. Too perfect. Too practiced.

Robert had spent years being a misfit during their

younger days and had used his smile to project a confidence he never felt.

Abby couldn't help but wonder what this stranger's excuse was.

"Can I help you?" She asked the question without unlocking the door.

She considered the Trolley Square area to be safe, but after Jack's comment that the postcard sender could be close by, she wasn't about to open the door to a stranger. Not when she was here alone.

"May I come in?" The man pressed a business card to the glass door as he spoke.

Sam Devine. Associated Press.

It looked like the killer's fifteen minutes of fame had just begun.

Abby unlocked the door, yet stood in the opening, not letting Mr. Devine any further into the building than necessary.

"I hope you won't mind my less than gracious welcome." Abby crossed her arms, hoping to make her message crystal clear. "I'm about to lock up, Mr. Devine. We're not open for business today."

"Your photo in the *People* article didn't do you justice."

Just what she needed. Hollow flattery. Abby plastered on a smile she in no way felt. "Can I help you, Mr. Devine?"

"Please—" he held out his hand and Abby gave it a quick shake "—call me Sam."

"Can I help you, Sam?"

"I received a tip about a second postcard."

Abby's heart caught. "A second postcard?"

Unless this man had somehow pulled up the Don't Say a Word site as he rang the bell, he'd have no way of knowing about the second card. Not to mention the fact his comment suggested he understood the significance of the first card, the photo of Melinda Simmons. Perhaps he'd spoken with Jack or the local police.

"Have you spoken to the police?"

Confusion slid across the reporter's features. "My tip wasn't from the police. It was from the killer."

Perhaps Don't Say a Word hadn't been the sender's sole target after all.

"You know about the Grant photo?" she asked.

Devine's eyes narrowed as he shook his head. "The Bricken photo."

"Bricken?" Abby didn't recognize the name from the articles she'd found regarding the New Mexico murders.

Devine's gaze brightened. "You're saying you received a card after the Simmons photo?"

So Jack Grant hadn't been the only one to recognize Melinda Simmons. How could Abby have published the postcard and called it a crank without digging deeper?

"You're familiar with the New Mexico case?" she asked.

Devine nodded, his features intent. "I studied it during my coverage of the local Bricken murder."

"*Beverly* Bricken?" Abby suddenly recognized the name and remembered the case.

The young woman had been a University of Delaware coed with everything to live for until someone had taken away all of her hopes and dreams by brutally ending her life five years earlier. Her body had been found shortly before Christmas, dumped in Valley Forge National Park.

The similarities between the Bricken case and Jack's case hit Abby like a sucker punch.

"When did you receive the Emma Grant postcard?" Devine asked.

Abby realized she might as well tell him. The information was public knowledge as of a few minutes ago. "Yesterday."

"Another message?"

She nodded. "She shouldn't have ignored me."

"Sonofagun."

Abby swallowed down a sudden knot in her throat. "You're saying the killer contacted you about the Bricken case?"

"Beverly Bricken," he repeated, stepping closer to where Abby stood. She instinctively took a matching step backward.

"What kind of tip?"

"E-mail."

"Did you trace his return address?"

Devine shook his head. "I tried after it came through my contact screen on the AP site, but our IT guys say it's untraceable."

But Abby was savvy enough to know there had to be a way to trace the contact. Her pulse quickened.

Beverly Bricken.

"Were you very involved in the investigation?" she asked, her mind spinning.

"Made my career." Another too-perfect smile. "Hey, what about your new postcard. May I see it?"

Abby pushed away from the reception desk. "It's in police custody."

Devine's face fell. The reporter had no doubt smelled an exclusive, as he did with the possibility of a third card.

"So, no Bricken card yet?" he asked.

"Not yet." But if this man were telling the truth, Abby would be receiving the new photo soon, if she hadn't already. She needed to check the site's post office box and fast.

"Have you retracted your statement about the Melinda Simmons card?"

Her statement, calling the killer a crank.

Abby nodded.

"I'd like to pursue the story, help draw this man out and bring him to justice. Would you let me do that, Ms. Conroy?"

Devine stepped close, too close, and suddenly Abby felt pinned in, her gut screaming a warning.

Something about the man was off.

"Do you have any other identification, Mr. Devine?"

"Sam." He reached into the inside pocket of his overcoat and Abby's stomach tightened.

She'd been beyond foolish to unlock the door based solely on a business card. Devine was more than likely harmless, but Abby needed Jack here with her, if for no other reason than to make sure she did or said nothing to jeopardize his work.

Devine held out his driver's license. Maryland.

The name matched the business card, but fake identification was bought and sold every day, wasn't it?

"I have another meeting, Sam," she bluffed, "but if you'd leave your card with me, I'll call you later. We can schedule a time to meet. I'd like you to meet the detective on the case. He was involved in the original investigation."

"Beverly Bricken's?"

"No." Abby handed back his license. "The New Mexico cases."

Devine's features fell, his disappointment evident. "The killer reached out to me, Ms. Conroy. You can trust me."

Sam Devine's words stopped Abby in her tracks, sending ice sliding through her veins. She'd always thought people who felt the need to say you could trust them frequently were unworthy of any trust at all.

Devine appeared anxious to claim this story as his own. He'd said the Bricken case made his career. Just how far would he go to relive that success? Had he seen the first blog, recognized Melinda Simmons and seized the opportunity to create a local angle?

"I'm not sure I'm ready to speak to the media just yet." Abby stepped toward Devine, hoping he'd take the hint and back toward the door. He sidestepped around her instead, moving past the reception desk, leaning against a pile of work to be sorted and filed.

"I'm more of a media consultant these days."

Abby moved quickly, stepping into Devine's path before he could move deeper into the building. Her pulse hummed in her ears.

"To-may-to, to-mah-to." Abby did her best to project a sense of bravado she in no way felt, wanting to keep the tone amicable yet move Devine out of the building. She pointed toward the front door. "I'll call you later to set up a meeting."

"So, you're refusing to comment?"

Now the man was putting words into her mouth. "I never said that. I assure you I'll comment later."

Sam Devine's friendly expression turned dark, almost menacing, and Abby realized she had no idea of what Boone Shaw looked like.

None of the articles she'd found online had included the former suspect's photograph, and Detective Grant hadn't yet provided that information to her.

For all she knew, the man standing within striking distance could be a cold-blooded killer posing as a consultant to the Associated Press.

Her insides tilted sideways.

Abby brushed past the reporter, pushing open the door to speed his exit.

Devine hesitated at the door, one hand on the jamb, a primal hunger flashing in his eyes. "I'll expect your call, Ms. Conroy."

The unease in Abby's belly tightened down into a knot. Surely she was overreacting, but Jack Grant had already accused her of being careless when it came to security.

Now was as good a time as any to change her ways.

She locked the door as soon as Devine was on the other side of the glass, not caring whether or not she'd offended the man.

She waited until he'd vanished from her sight, walking down the sidewalk and around the corner.

Closer than you think. Jack's words echoed in her brain.

The hair at the nape of Abby's neck pricked to attention.

Had someone given Sam Devine a tip? Or had he made up the story hoping to create a story where there hadn't yet been one?

Yet, if a third card existed, Jack would want to know about it right away. Abby's mind swirled with possibilities and questions, and she realized she needed Jack.

And she needed him now.

She reached for the phone tucked under the reception counter, knocking the pile of Natalie's work askew. She pulled Jack's card from her pocket and dialed, stretching to straighten up the mess she'd just made.

Natalie would have her head. The receptionist might be a sweetheart, but she took issue with anyone using—or messing up—her workspace.

Jack answered just as Abby's brain realized what she'd stumbled upon.

A black-and-white print. Tucked into Natalie's files.

She could make out pale hair, the curve of a feminine cheek, a slender neck.

For a split second, Abby's mind shut down, refusing to process what she was seeing.

A third postcard.

In the exact location where Sam Devine had just stood.

JACK TOOK A long swallow of weak coffee, grimaced then adjusted the screen on his laptop. He'd used his Phoenix police department identification to log in to his favorite database as soon as he'd gotten back to his hotel room.

The gray sky outside was threatening snow and he'd been in no mood to get swept up in the crush of holiday shoppers swarming the mall next to his hotel. Nor had he been in the mood to take a drive in the nearby countryside to clear his head.

He'd been in the mood to find Boone Shaw and know exactly what the man was up to. But Boone Shaw was gone, falling off the radar screen more than a month earlier. The man had left the antique shop and photography studio he ran behind, taking only one thing—his camera.

Jack ran a search on Shaw's known credit cards and came up with nothing. Not a single hit during the past six weeks. The man was nothing if not smart, and if he had traveled from Montana to Delaware, he'd done so using cash. Anything else would have been flagged by the system.

Cash, on the other hand, would allow Shaw to become a ghost—untraceable in a society that had become a master of tracing the movements of its citizens.

Jack attempted another drink of the weak coffee, then pushed away from the desk, carrying the coffee cup toward the bathroom sink. He dumped the contents down the drain, then tossed the cup into the waste bin. He caught his reflection out of the corner of his eye and stopped cold.

His five o'clock shadow was apparently working overtime. Jack scrubbed a hand over his jaw, and cranked open the spigot. He'd learned a long time ago that a shower and shave did wonders for a man's thinking.

Ten minutes later, he stood in front of the same mirror,

towel anchored around his waist, beads of moisture glistening on his shoulders and chest.

And then it hit him. The certain something that had been nagging at him all day.

Robert Walker.

Jack didn't like the man, and he couldn't figure out why.

Was it because the man and Abby were so close they shared the same unspoken language? Did Jack envy Robert the relationship?

"Snap out of it," Jack said to his reflection.

Abby Conroy was a beautiful woman, and her secret confession site was most likely the key to finding Boone Shaw. Nothing more.

But Robert Walker. Something about the man ate at Jack, but what?

He had no reason to suspect him of anything other than being a know-it-all, but what could it hurt to have a bit more information?

Jack settled in front of the laptop once more, this time keying in Robert Walker's name. Jack pulled first the man's home address and driver's license information, then worked backward, accessing previous tax information, addresses and employer records.

Walker had spent his years in Delaware, at least since he'd graduated from the University of Delaware. He'd also devoted his career to the computer industry, so working on the Don't Say a Word site hadn't been a stretch.

He'd attended high school and grade school locally and by all appearances was a loyal native who had never done so much as miss a day of school. So why did he make the tiny alarm bells in Jack's brain clang to attention?

Simple.

Abby Conroy.

Much as Jack hated to admit it, the woman had thrown his typically astute judge of character off-kilter.

He was just about to give himself a sound mental thrashing when his cell rang.

He'd put a call in to a buddy who specialized in private investigation; with any luck at all, the guy had made contact with Boone Shaw's wife.

"Yeah." Jack spoke even as he did his best to shove all inappropriate thoughts of Abby Conroy out of his mind, yet it was Abby whose voice filtered across the line.

"I found another card."

He was on his feet, dropping the towel from his waist and pulling a clean pair of jeans from his bag before she could say another word. "You're still at the office?"

"Yes."

"Was it in the mail?"

Silence beat across the line.

"Abby?" Damn, but he should have never left her alone.

"Front desk."

How in the hell? He buttoned his jeans and dug around in his bag for a shirt. "The reception desk?" Jack balanced the phone on one side of his neck and then the other as he shrugged into a well-worn denim shirt, fastening the buttons as he searched for his shoes.

"Yes."

"Don't touch anything and lock those damned doors. I'm on my way."

"Jack?"

"Yeah." He grabbed his coat from the bed and headed for his hotel room's door.

"A reporter came to see me."

"And?"

"He said he'd received a tip."

A tip? "From where?"

"The killer."

Jack squeezed his eyes shut momentarily. If there was one thing he hated, it was the press.

"What was the reporter's name?"

"Sam Devine."

Jack made a mental note. He'd be calling Detective Tim Hayes the second he disconnected from Abby. "You found the new card after Devine left?"

Abby's sharp intake of air was all the answer Jack needed.

"I'll be there in ten minutes."

If he hurried, he could make it in five.

Chapter Six

Jack pounded on the locked glass door six minutes later. Without thinking, he grasped Abby's shoulders the moment she opened the door, meeting her frightened eyes and wanting to turn back time so that he could have been with her when she found the card.

"What does he look like?" she asked, her question pouring out in a monosyllabic slur of words.

"Who?"

"Shaw."

"Early fifties by now, bald, big and burly."

She blew out a sigh. "This wasn't him, then."

Jack furrowed his brow.

"The reporter," Abby explained. "Sam Devine. For one crazy moment, I thought he might be Shaw pretending to be a reporter." She shook her head. "You probably think I sound hysterical."

Abby turned to break away from him, but Jack tightened his hold on her shoulders, forcing her focus to his.

"I think you finally sound smart." Their gazes locked and held. "Boone Shaw is no one you want to mess around with, and neither is anyone who might be working with him."

Abby said nothing, but she also didn't move away. She

stood her ground, meeting Jack's stare. Her eyes searched his, until he broke contact, suddenly unable to stand close to the woman and think clearly at the same time.

"Tell me exactly what happened."

Abby recounted the exchange, ending with her discovery of the card during the moments she waited for Jack to answer the phone.

"Were you watching him the entire time?"

She nodded, her pale eyes huge with the shock of the day's events.

"Do you think he could have planted the card?" Jack asked.

"I would have seen him, but you have to admit the timing is a bit tough to overlook."

Jack couldn't agree more. "I already put in a call to Hayes."

He slipped on a pair of thin gloves as he spoke, preparing to lift the card from the stack of files. "He knows Devine, vouched for him actually, although he said the guy was more than a little obsessed with a local murder victim, Beverly Bricken."

Abby reached for Jack's arm, her touch heating the skin beneath his shirt. "Devine said that was who the third postcard would be based on his tip."

Jack frowned. Maybe Boone Shaw wasn't behind the postcards after all. Was it possible?

"Could she have been killed by the same guy?" Abby asked.

The question stopped Jack in his tracks. "If there were any similarities, the national database would have triggered a call to me."

His voice trailed off as he studied the young woman's image captured on the card. She was physically different from the New Mexico victims, as blonde as they'd been brunette. Her face was fuller, her makeup heavier, yet she'd been posed similarly, as if the shot had been intended for submission to a modeling agency.

"Would you recognize this Beverly Bricken?" he asked.

Abby's throat worked. "That's her."

"You're sure?"

"I'm an artist, Jack. I remember details."

He turned over the card and read aloud. "No one likes a show off."

When he looked up at Abby this time, the color had drained from her cheeks. The episode had shaken her badly and he needed to get her away from here.

He also needed to get in touch with Sam Devine. He had a few questions for the man.

Perhaps there was a way to kill two birds with one stone.

"Did he leave a contact number?"

"Devine?"

Jack nodded and Abby reached into her pocket, stepping toward Jack to hand over the card she'd extracted.

Jack kept his focus on Abby as she moved, measuring her body language and the set of her features.

Even though her coloring reflected her fragile state, she hadn't relaxed the proud set of her shoulders, nor had she surrendered the stubborn line of her jaw. Her eyes, however, reflected the slightest glimmer of fear.

Much as he wanted to erase that fear and the sense of vulnerability he'd put there with his harsh words about her safety, Jack had a killer to put away before the man began to do more than deliver postcards.

Priorities were priorities and right now Jack needed to know how much Sam Devine knew about Boone Shaw, Beverly Bricken and the postcard now resting on top of the receptionist's desk.

He also needed to know whether or not Devine had planted the newest postcard.

If not Devine, he didn't want to consider the fact the killer might have been as close to Abby as this reception desk.

"Has anyone else been here today since I left?"

Abby shook her head. "No one since Robert stopped by this morning."

Robert.

Jack flashed on the image of Abby's partner as he'd arrived earlier that day. Hell, the man could have hidden a fistful of postcards in the newspaper he'd carried.

The bottom line was that the third postcard had been hand-delivered. The question now was, by whom?

Jack studied Devine's business card then did his best to give Abby a reassuring smile.

"What do you say we see what your new friend Sam Devine is doing for dinner?"

SAM DEVINE EAGERLY agreed to meet Jack and Abby at the Concord Mall food court later that evening.

In the meantime, Jack followed Abby home and waited outside her apartment until her friend Gina arrived to keep her company. Based on Gina Grasso's take-no-prisoners appearance, Jack had the feeling Abby was in good hands for the time being.

Then Jack headed straight to the local precinct. Judging from the skeptical look on Tim Hayes's face, the man was as wary of Sam Devine's sudden appearance as Jack was.

"So you're saying he claims the sender sent him an e-mail?" Hayes asked.

"An untraceable e-mail through a contact form on the Associated Press Web site."

"And you believe that?"

"No."

Detective Tim Hayes squeezed his eyes shut momentarily and pinched the bridge of his nose. "I'll have my guys check that out."

It was obvious the man felt lousy, his voice scratchy and his eyes shot with red.

Jack apparently wasn't the only one who could live without experiencing a cold, white Christmas. Give him a cactus and a Santa cap any day and he'd be content. Actually, he could skip the Santa cap.

"You said you knew him?" Jack asked, leaning forward across the break room table.

Each man nursed a high-test cup of coffee. It was no wonder most officers' stomachs rotted out by the time they earned their pensions, if not sooner.

The two men had settled in the precinct's break room, blissfully quiet at this time on a late Saturday afternoon. The calm before the storm of a Saturday night, Jack imagined.

"I remember the name from the Bricken case." Hayes studied the postcard through clear plastic, grimacing. "If he's the guy I think he is, he was a pain in the ass. Always wanting the latest and greatest news on the case before we held press conferences. His coverage made him a local celebrity for a short time."

Hayes shook his head. "I'll be honest. I haven't heard his name or seen his byline in a long time. I'd forgotten the man existed."

Exactly the sort of reporter to seize the postcard scenario as an opportunity to create a renewed purpose... and fame.

"You think he made this himself?" Hayes asked, looking from the card to Jack then back to the card again.

"It's crossed my mind."

Hayes nodded. "That would be my first thought. Unless your killer spent some time in Delaware five years ago and we never matched up the pieces."

Jack shrugged, knowing Hayes's theory could be a possibility. "Were there other victims at the time?"

Hayes drew in a breath, coughed, then sat back against the metal chair, the legs of the chair scraping against the battered linoleum floor.

"Just the one. Beverly Bricken. She went missing the week before Christmas."

Jack recognized the frustration in the other man's grimace. Call it the curse of a homicide detective who cared, call it whatever you want.

Good detectives never forgot the cases they didn't clear or the families to whom they never gave closure.

And if they were good at what they did, some small part of their brain never stopped working the cold cases—Jack thought of Emma, laughing and alive—as much as they tried.

"Her body was found in Valley Forge Park three days later, by a family out for a walk. Dog was off the leash. He veered off the trail and never looked back once he got the scent."

"Cause of death?" Jack slid the stack of crime scene photos from in front of Hayes, turning them to face him.

"Ligature marks at the neck indicated strangulation," Hayes said flatly, without emotion. Another telltale sign of a homicide detective who had learned to shut down his own humanity in order to relate the cold, harsh facts of a case without losing his sanity.

"Same as my guy." Jack's hand settled on a photo of Beverly Bricken's face, still beautiful, even in death. "Sexual assault?"

Hayes nodded. "This was not a nice guy."

"None of them are."

"You had five dead in one spree?" Hayes asked, leaning forward again, the alert edge returning to his voice.

"Only four bodies." Jack flashed again on the day Shaw had walked free. He remembered the anguished faces of Mr. and Mrs. Simmons as they realized their daughter's killer had just gone free. "Melinda Simmons was never found."

"But you included her in the case?"

"Her photos were part of what we took from Shaw's studio. Her personal effects were found in the desert."

"Animals?" Hayes spoke the word softly for being such a big man.

"Coyotes more than likely." Jack narrowed his gaze. "They'd gotten to some of the other victims, as well, but we'd still been able to make IDs."

"But not with the Simmons girl?"

Jack shook his head, the uninvited memory of Herb Simmons's voice echoing in his brain.

Don't let him get away this time.

"So you had no way of knowing whether or not she was marked like your other victims?"

Marked.

Detective Hayes had done his homework.

A crude eye had been drawn onto each New Mexico victim's upper thigh by what investigators had theorized was some sort of branding tool, similar to those used by artisans to engrave leather.

They'd never matched the wounds to anything found in Boone Shaw's possession. Another piece that hadn't helped the prosecution's case.

"I see you know a bit about my case." Jack flipped to the next photo in the stack.

"It's not every day a detective from Arizona shows up

in Wilmington, Delaware, hoping to find his man for a series of murders in New Mexico."

But Jack barely heard Hayes's words. His focus had locked on the subject of the photo before him.

Beverly Bricken's body bore some sort of symbol on the flesh of her upper thigh, the spot identical to where the New Mexico victims had been marked.

Jack tapped the photograph. "Did you release this nationally?"

He'd flagged the interstate database to alert him if so much as one other murder or assault victim were branded by their attacker, as his victims had been.

He'd never had a hit that matched or came close. He'd also never heard of Beverly Bricken before today, yet there she was. Branded.

"We kept it quiet for a while," Hayes said. "Never let the media get a hold of it. When we did put it in the system, nothing came back."

"That doesn't make sense. Every single one of my cases is in there." Jack caught himself. "At least the four victims we were sure about." He looked more closely at the photo. "What is that?"

"Looks like her killer cut it into her skin," Hayes answered. "A pair of lips as best we can tell. Sick idea of a signature."

"Lips," Jack muttered. Then the ramification of the rest of Hayes's statement hit him. Jack set down the photo and winced. He'd been looking for other victims branded with an eye. Branded. If the Wilmington investigation had deemed their marking to be a pair of lips cut into the victim, no wonder the database had never connected the dots.

"Any chance that's burned into her skin?" Jack asked, angling the photo toward Hayes.

"Burned?"

"Branded into her flesh."

"Anything's possible," Hayes said flatly.

Jack pushed to his feet and scrubbed a hand across his face. "This guy's not wired like we're wired. He wants the control. What better way to communicate you're in charge than to brand your victims?"

"Like cattle."

"Like cattle," Jack repeated.

Hayes straightened from his chair and stepped into Jack's path. "You think this is your guy?"

Jack thought long and hard before he answered. Same MO. Similar signature. Young coed killed in the prime of her life, her body dumped in a nearby national park. "Too many similarities to ignore."

"Maybe my guy read about your case, decided to try it for himself. Maybe that explains the similarities."

Hayes had a point. "True. Or maybe my guy decided to mix it up a bit in a new location."

"After a six-year hiatus?" Hayes frowned.

"All depends on the trigger." Jack flipped through the file, not finding what he wanted. "What about trace evidence on the body? Hair? Fiber?"

"Nothing." Hayes shook his head. "A careful and cruel killer."

"Same here."

"If it's the same killer, why wait until the third card to reach out to Devine?" Hayes asked.

Jack pressed his lips together before he spoke. "Local case. Local contact. As long as whoever killed Bricken stuck around long enough, he'd have witnessed Devine's obsession with the case. Maybe he wasn't happy with the reaction he got from Abby.

"Or maybe Devine saw the connection none of us had

spotted before," Jack continued. "Maybe he saw the first postcard as his opportunity to resurrect the case."

"Or his career," Hayes added.

"No arguments there."

"What about your original suspect, Boone Shaw?"

"He fell off the radar screen several weeks back," Jack explained. "I've got someone working on finding his trail. I'll have him check out Shaw's whereabouts at the time Bricken was murdered. Make sure he didn't take any cross-country trips."

"In the meantime, we've got to figure out how deep Devine's involvement goes." Hayes lifted the encased postcard from the table. "I'll walk this to the lab myself."

"With any luck at all, we'll figure this mess out before our guy strikes again."

"As long as he sticks to postcards, we're all right." Hayes smiled grimly.

Hayes was right. One postcard might be the work of a man seeking public acknowledgment of his work. Two postcards was the work of a man who was either pissed off about Abby's first blog or who wanted broader media coverage.

Three cards, potentially linking cases years and miles apart, was a message from the killer that he'd shifted tacks once before, and was more than capable of doing so again.

Assuming, of course, that the third card came from the same source as the first two. An assumption Jack wasn't ready to make. On the other hand, he couldn't afford to dismiss the possibility.

Abby's beautiful face flashed through Jack's mind, his gut tightening with an unforgiving twist as he echoed the other detective's words. "Let's hope he sticks to postcards."

ABBY WILLED HER temples to stop pounding as she and Jack headed toward their meeting with Devine. It was bad enough that Gina had all but thrown herself at Jack the moment they'd met, but she'd also thrown herself at Dwayne…for far different reasons.

Abby's neighbor had handed over the mail he'd taken earlier that day from her private mailbox. Unfortunately, he'd done so in front of Gina, who had gone ballistic, accusing Dwayne of everything from mail theft to identity fraud to stalking.

Abby groaned at the memory then held her head.

"You all right?"

"Nothing a little food won't cure."

Food…and some answers.

According to what Jack had found out during his meeting with Detective Hayes, Devine had gone from hero to zero after the Beverly Bricken case grew cold.

Experience in the art world had taught Abby that some people would do most anything to return to the limelight once they'd had a taste of success in their chosen field.

She couldn't help but wonder whether or not Devine was one of those people, and if so, how far would he go to regain his public persona?

Would he plant evidence? Copycat a killer's postcard? Fabricate a phantom e-mail?

The local police, working with the Web master for the AP site, had confirmed Devine had not received the e-mail in question.

Abby couldn't wait to see how fast Devine's smile crumbled once Jack hit him with that fact.

"What's our objective here?" she asked.

An uncharacteristic grin pulled at the corner of Jack's mouth. Abby rankled. The man considered her nothing more than an amateur.

"Your objective is to sit quietly and let me work," he answered.

Abby shot a look out the passenger window then turned her now volatile combination of fear and impatience on Jack.

"Why am I going with you if you consider me such a liability?"

Jack's grin widened, warming the sharp lines of his profile. "My reasoning is simple." He smiled, enjoying whatever it was he was about to say. "I don't know what Devine looks like."

Abby laughed, the sound more a tired burst of air than anything else. "That's why I'm included?"

"Take it or leave it."

She had no intention of missing this meeting. "I'll take it."

Fifteen minutes later, she'd located Devine, sitting alone at a table intended for four. Devine, however, had removed one chair and shoved it alongside the next table over, as if he needed the assurance no surprise guest would sit in on their meeting.

"There." She pointed quickly, dropping her arm back to her side before she drew attention.

A matter of moments later, the necessary introductions had been made and Sam Devine had started talking.

Jack had dealt with a lot of reporters in his day, but he'd never encountered one so passionate about a case.

Excitement danced in Sam Devine's eyes. He wanted this too much.

More than a reporter out for a story.

More than a curious brain at work.

The Beverly Bricken case was personal for Sam Devine. The question was, why?

"Did you bring the postcards?" Excitement dripped from the reporter's words.

Jack shook his head and Devine's eager smile slipped.

The reporter reached up to brush a lock of hair from his forehead. A nervous tell, Jack decided. Something to take note of.

"I was looking forward to seeing them in person."

"And reliving your past success?" Jack asked.

Jack knew from talking to Hayes that Devine had been obsessed with the case. How far would he go now to solve it? Or to recreate his time in the spotlight?

"The Bricken case was a big part of my career, I'm not going to deny that. But the Christmas Confessor reached out to me and me alone. I deserve to be in the loop here."

"No, you don't," Jack said sharply.

"Why did you just call him the Christmas Confessor?" Abby asked, taking the words out of Jack's mouth.

Much as he agreed with her line of questioning, Jack shot Abby a warning glare and she fell silent once again.

Devine tipped his chin proudly. "Perfect timing, don't you think? Nothing the public loves more than the holidays and having a name for their serial killers."

No wonder this guy had fallen from grace.

"We don't know that this is a serial killer." Jack shook his head, enjoying the disappointment plastered across Devine's face. "For all we know, it's some kid sending in photos he found in a Dumpster somewhere."

Jack had learned long ago that some reporters were so hungry for a headline it made no difference who they trampled on their way to the top. "Someone who wants to spin the news, if you will," he continued.

Devine blanched and Jack knew he'd hit the mark. The reporter knew far more about the arrival of the third card than he was letting on.

Jack decided to cut to the chase.

"Did you plant the card in the Don't Say a Word office?"

Devine straightened defensively. "Detective, I am a

newsman, and a newsman does not fabricate a story. He reports the news."

"In an ideal world." Jack took a bite of the sandwich he'd snagged from one of the fast-food counters framing the seating area. He let Devine stew a bit while he chewed then swallowed. "In an ideal world, a reporter doesn't make up a bogus e-mail tip."

He studied Devine's shocked expression. The reporter had underestimated the speed with which the local police would blow his story sky-high.

"We know you lied." Jack pursed his lips and nodded. "There never was an e-mail."

"Perhaps I just know how to protect my source."

Jack arched a brow. "A murderer? You'd protect a murderer?"

Devine said nothing, although hot color blazed to life in his cheeks.

"In an ideal world," Jack continued. "A third murder victim's photograph—a murder never before connected to the other two—does not appear within minutes of a reporter's uninvited arrival, tucked between files on the very desk beside which that same reporter stood."

Devine remained silent, exactly the reaction Jack had anticipated.

Jack leaned back in his seat and blew out a sigh. "There's one other piece of this puzzle that confuses me, Mr. Devine. Maybe you can help me out here. Why do you suppose your *source* would wait until the third card to reach out?"

Devine blinked, pushing away his food tray. His complexion had gone splotchy beneath the unforgiving lighting inside the food court. "Maybe he felt he wasn't getting enough attention from Ms. Conroy's blog."

Much to Abby's credit, she said nothing, sitting back and soaking in every word, just as Jack had requested.

After the reporter declared Jack's investigational skills incompetent and stormed off, Jack turned to Abby, offering her one of his fries.

"What's your take?"

"He's lying." Abby's gaze widened before she bit into the fry. "Flat-out lying."

Jack turned to study Devine's hastily retreating figure. "There never was a tip."

"How do you explain the Bricken card?" Abby dropped her voice to a whisper.

"I think he pasted it together himself." Jack finished the last of his food and stuffed the leftover wrappers back into the restaurant bag. "He either wants the spotlight, or he wants to tie the two cases together."

"Maybe he wants both." Abby shrugged. "So where does that leave us?"

The fear Jack had spotted in Abby's expression earlier that day had eased a notch. Jack was glad, but he also didn't want her letting down her guard prematurely.

The real killer was out there somewhere, and until they found him, Jack couldn't risk leaving Abby alone again.

He pushed to his feet and held out a hand, savoring the touch of her slender fingers as she let him help her to her feet.

"It leaves me sleeping on your couch," Jack answered. "Until we know what in the hell is going on, I'm not leaving your side."

Chapter Seven

Abby was tired and chilled to the bone by the time she and Jack reached her apartment. The fresh wave of fear she'd experienced after finding the third card had eased, Jack's presence by her side infusing her with a sense of calm and security.

She'd noticed him stealing glances at her on the drive home and attributed the detective's attention to nothing more than the man doing his job—acting as protector.

Abby, however, found her head filled increasingly with thoughts of Jack Grant not purely as a detective, but also as a man.

He'd handled Sam Devine with such finesse he'd left Abby close to speechless, something not easy to do, if she admitted so herself.

On the drive back into town he'd called a private investigator named Max, asking the man to add a full background check for Sam Devine to his work, as well as checking Boone Shaw's whereabouts during the time Beverly Bricken had been murdered.

Jack had vowed to leave no stone unturned, and based on what Abby had seen, he was doing just that.

The curtains next door shifted as she and Jack covered the ground between Jack's car and the entry to her apartment. She almost lifted her hand to wave, when Jack gripped her elbow and hurried her along the sidewalk.

"He watches every move you make. You've got to stop encouraging him."

"He's harmless," she'd whispered, although a thread of anxiety wound its way through her at the intensity of Jack's words.

Now, a short while later, she found herself staring at the framed photo of Gina, Vicki and herself. It was Vicki's face in particular from which Abby couldn't wrench her focus.

She couldn't stop thinking about how Vicki's suicide had somehow set everything into motion. The birth of Don't Say a Word, the focus of a killer, postcards of young victims, their lives ended before they could begin.

Abby lost herself in her friend's image as if the truth lay hidden somewhere in the nuances of Vicki's features, clues left behind and captured on film.

She was being irrational, illogical, and she knew it. But she was tired and her sense of security and reality had been tilted on its axis.

Abby had surprised herself by letting Jack accompany her home. Normally, she rebelled against doing anything someone told her to do, but the shock of the past two days were enough to make even Abby realize she might not always know what was best.

If the detective thought she was safer with him inside her home, so be it.

Abby sat across from him now, watching the man stare down into a steaming mug of hot chocolate. The juxtaposition of floating mini marshmallows and the man's tough exterior were enough to make her wish *she* had a camera.

Her gaze flickered again to Vicki's framed image.

"Do you want to tell me about it?"

"About what?" Abby let the steaming cup of hot chocolate she held warm her hands. The heat helped take the edge off the chill Devine's visit and today's postcard discovery had imprinted on every inch of her body.

Jack merely widened his gaze, the look saying he'd caught her staring again at the picture—the shot of Abby, Gina and Vicki, happy and smiling.

Abby had thought the detective engrossed by his own thoughts, but apparently he'd been watching Abby the entire time.

The intimate nature of Jack's question surprised Abby more than seeing the detective drink hot chocolate ever could.

"Do you really want to know?" Abby spoke without lifting her gaze to Jack's, without risking the way her heart had begun to catch each time their eyes met.

Tired. She was tired. Her defenses were weak. She kept telling herself that she and Jack Grant had been tossed into surreal circumstances. Take away the risk and the danger, and the attraction she felt would undoubtedly evaporate. She was sure of it.

She avoided his eyes, just the same.

"When was it taken?" he asked.

"Robert took it a few years ago at the unveiling of one of my murals." She pointed at the frame. "That's Gina and our friend Vicki. We've known each other—" she caught herself "—knew each other, since first grade."

"The three musketeers," Jack said with a slight smile.

The move softened the hard lines of his face, crinkling the skin around his dark eyes. Abby couldn't help but wonder how long it had been since the man smiled fully with abandon. Even now he held back, as if he'd decided long ago to disallow himself happiness.

Abby understood the feeling, understood the pain. She

stared again at the photo, remembering the night, the laughter, the friendship.

"We were the four musketeers, actually," she explained. "With the exception of the year after Robert's father died, we've been together since grade school."

"Any romantic involvement there?" Jack asked.

Defensiveness rippled through Abby. "Why is it people find it so difficult to believe men and women can be friends?"

Her sharp tone wiped all traces of Jack's smile from his face.

He set down his cup and leaned forward, elbows on knees. "I want to know how Don't Say a Word helps. Why did your friend's death compel you to reach out in such a public way?"

So Jack Grant knew about Vicki. The realization shouldn't surprise Abby. The detective had surely done his research before he'd traveled east. Hell, anyone who'd read the *People* magazine article would know about Vicki.

Was it the article that had drawn the attention of whoever was sending the postcards?

Abby dropped her focus from Vicki's picture, unable to meet her late friend's laughing eyes. "I could have been a better friend, Detective. I could have listened more."

"And you think that would have saved her?"

His voice held a note Abby hadn't heard there before. Concern. Perhaps there was far more heart hidden beneath the man's brawny physique than she'd imagined.

"I think it could have," Abby answered. Yet even as she spoke the words, she felt small and naive.

Once Vicki had decided to take her life, chances were nothing Abby might have said or done would have dissuaded her. At least, that's what the so-called experts had told Abby in an effort to ease her anguish in the days after Vicki's senseless death.

"We never found a note," Abby continued. "That's always bothered me."

"You doubt her death was suicide?" Jack's voice tightened.

"No." Abby set down her cup of hot chocolate and met Jack's stare. The intensity of his dark eyes momentarily stole her breath. "It makes me sad that even in that moment, in the seconds before she ended her life, she felt she had no one to talk to, not even in a suicide note."

"So you decided to give the public a forum?"

"For confessions." Abby pulled up her knees and wrapped her arms around her legs, settling back into the chair.

"To help them or to ease your guilt?"

Jack's words hit Abby like a slap. "So much for you being nonjudgmental."

His lips lifted in another subtle smile. "Who ever said anything about being nonjudgmental?"

Abby pushed out of her chair, suddenly tired of Jack's company and ready to be alone. She'd changed her mind about tonight. "Maybe your staying here isn't such a great idea."

But Jack didn't move. In fact, he settled further into the sofa, smoothing the cushions and readjusting the throwback pillows.

"I'm not going back to my hotel tonight, and you're not staying here alone."

"Well, I don't remember issuing an invitation for you to stay in the first place."

"You didn't. I made the decision all on my own."

Abby moved toward the door. "I'm happy for you, Detective, but I don't need you here. I want to be alone."

"Until we know how the Beverly Bricken postcard got inside your office, I'm not going anywhere."

Inside your office.

Jack's words stung, breaking loose the flood of anxie
Abby had worked so carefully to keep at bay.

She swallowed, struggling to maintain composure when she was so tired she could barely stand.

"Fair enough." She pointed to the hall leading back to her bedroom. "There's a guest bath and a linen closet that way. I'm sure there are plenty of leftovers in the fridge if you get hungry."

"You're going to give in, just like that?"

Abby couldn't help but laugh. This guy was one serious piece of work. "Just like that," she answered. "It's been a long two days. Good night, Detective."

"Sleep tight, Abby."

That had been two hours ago, and now here she stood, watching Jack Grant sleep.

Sleep tight.

She'd been on her way to the kitchen to grab a cup of water when she'd stopped to study the man.

Jack slept soundly on the sofa, his hand draped across a sheaf of papers. Even in sleep, his features reflected the tension of the day, the magnitude of the unknown they were facing.

She reached for a fleece throw and pulled it up over his legs, not wanting to disturb him and yet longing to touch his cheek. She shoved the crazy thought from her brain. Obviously, she'd better get some sleep herself. She'd begun to lose control of what little rationality she had left.

Jack's words rang through her mind as she watched him sleep.

Inside your office.

A shudder raced across her shoulders and down her spine.

The third postcard hadn't just been mailed to the

s post office box, it had been placed inside her office. What next?

"You all right?" The rumble of Jack's tired voice jolted Abby from her thoughts. She hadn't realized he'd awakened; yet there he lay, watching her.

She nodded. "Just thirsty."

Jack narrowed his gaze and gave a quick shake of his head. "Thirsty doesn't put a look that worried on a face as beautiful as yours."

Now she was imagining things. There was no way Jack Grant had called her beautiful. Abby's traitorous stomach caught and twisted just the same.

"Abby?" Jack pulled himself to a sitting position and patted the sofa beside him.

"You were right," she said.

"I usually am."

"And humble." Abby warmed inside, enjoying their banter yet understanding the only reasons the mood had turned intimate was the late hour and their combined fatigue.

"I have a gift for reading people."

Abby wasn't about to argue—she'd seen him in action.

"So Don't Say a Word is more about your guilt than about helping others?"

She flinched, then moved to sit beside him on the sofa, keeping a respectable distance between them. "I wouldn't say that, though I do think it's helped the postcard confessors more than it's helped me."

He studied her, and she read his thoughts as if they were stamped on his forehead. Jack Grant saw right though her. His next statement confirmed the point.

"I've dealt with a lot of suicides during my time on the force. I know how difficult the situation can be for those left behind—"

"The situation?" His word choice left Abby cold.

"You probably think you neglected your friend in some way. You think you could have done more, listened more." He gave a slight lift and drop of his shoulders. "You think you should have seen her pain in time to stop her."

Abby had seen Vicki's pain, but she'd never guessed her oldest friend would take her life. How wrong she'd been.

And she wasn't about to tell Jack that not only had she stopped listening, she'd started avoiding, no doubt adding to Vicki's sense of despair.

"What about you? Do you think placing someone behind bars will help you put Emma's death behind you?"

He sank back against the sofa cushions, saying nothing for a moment. "It sounds straightforward when you say it like that, but I'll never put Emma's death behind me. I don't see how it's possible."

Abby glanced again at Vicki's framed image, the smooth glass obscuring details in the dim lighting. "I pick up the phone to call her at least once a day. I can't seem to make my subconscious realize she's gone."

She realized then that someone had replaced the broken glass. Gina, perhaps? She must have come back while Jack and Abby were with Devine.

"You didn't do anything wrong, Abby." Jack touched her knee lightly, sending a jolt of awareness through Abby's system.

He broke contact, but they remained where they were, both motionless.

"I won't let anything happen to you."

Jack's abrupt change of topic took Abby by surprise, but she realized in that moment that she trusted him, believed him, as if she'd known him for years.

The thought scared her to death. She hadn't trusted anyone in a very long time, and surely not with her life. Just the same, she realized she didn't want Jack to go back to his hotel in the morning. She wanted him by her side.

"I'd better get that water and let you get some sleep." She pushed to her feet and forced herself to look anywhere but into the detective's sleep-softened eyes.

Abby hugged herself, rubbing her upper arms as she turned once again for the kitchen.

The silhouette of something the size of a postcard, taped to the kitchen window, snapped her out of her protective cocoon in one fell swoop.

She leaned close to read the message on the card, flipping on the overhead kitchen light to better illuminate the simple black type.

It's time to stop living in the past.

Abby's blood ran cold.

"Jack."

He was at her side in a single beat of her heart, following the line of her gaze.

"Sonofa—" He spun away from her, racing for the front door. "Don't move."

Don't move. As if she could pull so much as a toe from the virtual concrete the postcard had set around her feet.

Jack reappeared outside, careful not to move too close to the window, yet scowling as he studied the image on the other side.

Another victim? Local? Or from New Mexico?

Based on the look on Jack's face, the photograph was of one of his victims. The anger flashing across his features went deep, too deep to have been a victim he didn't know.

He pulled his cell phone from his pocket and dialed, speaking quickly. Abby did her best to read his lips through the insulated glass, but failed miserably.

By the time he stepped back inside, the far-off wail of sirens could be heard, drawing steadily closer.

"Who did you call?" Abby asked the question without turning around, unable to rip her gaze from the postcard.

Jack's hands closed over her shoulders and squeezed, pulling her to him, her back to his chest. She longed to relax into his reassuring strength, longed to feel his arms reach around to hold her tight.

She longed to wake up tomorrow to find out tonight had been nothing more than a bad dream.

"Detective Hayes. Police are on their way."

The sirens outside intensified, closer now.

Abby asked the inevitable. "Who is it?"

"On the picture?"

She nodded.

Jack turned her to face him, shifting his hands to maintain contact, holding her as if he expected her to topple over at any moment. His expression had gone unreadable, a mixture of anger and determination and...*attraction?*

"Jack?"

His mouth opened and shut once before he answered.

"It's you, Abby. The picture on the card is you."

Chapter Eight

"We're not going to get too far with this one." Detective Tim Hayes jerked his thumb toward the yard where the investigative response team worked diligently looking for any incriminating evidence. So far, apparently, they'd found none.

The frozen earth was unforgiving this time of year, and the tape and postcard had yielded no obvious prints. Both had been sent back to the lab for further analysis.

"What about the card itself?" Jack asked, shoving his hands farther into his pockets, trying to ignore the sensation of bitter cold leaching through his skin and into his bones.

Lord, he hated the cold.

Why did people choose to live here?

Hayes blew into his hands, sending a fog of moisture into the night air. "This card has two key differences from the rest." Hayes ticked off the points on his fingers. "Number one, the subject of the photograph is still alive."

Beside Jack, Abby visibly shuddered regardless of the knit cap pulled low over her forehead and ears and the heavy wool coat into which she'd bundled.

Jack should have insisted she wait inside where it was warmer, where she couldn't overhear this conversation.

"Number two," Hayes continued, "This is no modeling shot. Whoever took this probably used that same window to watch and photograph your moves."

"Any idea of when this was taken," Jack asked, shifting his stance so that Abby would know the question was meant for her.

She nodded. "Last night. Right before I found the second card. I'd just been in my kitchen."

Last night.

So much had happened in the past two days. It was a wonder Abby was still on her feet, though based on the circles beneath her eyes and the exhausted tone of her voice, she wouldn't be on her feet for long.

Whoever had taken the photo must have been somewhere in this general area.

Jack glanced from Abby's kitchen window to the house next door where Dwayne Franklin unabashedly watched from a darkened window.

The angle looked right. For all they knew, Franklin had taken the shot, printed off the photograph and taped the postcard to Abby's window.

By now, news of the postcards had begun to spread. No major news stories had broken, but anyone familiar with Abby's blog knew there had been at least two cards.

What was to keep someone out for attention—like Franklin—from trying a little scare tactic of his own?

And if whoever had left the card hadn't been Franklin, chances were pretty damned good Franklin had seen the entire thing. Jack had yet to visit Abby's apartment that he hadn't spotted Franklin waiting and watching.

Regardless of the role Dwayne Franklin had played, whoever left this postcard had been too close to Abby.

Jack had to operate on the belief that the postcard was a legitimate threat from an as-yet-unseen foe.

What if Jack hadn't been here tonight?

Would whoever had left the card have stopped at the window? Or would he have left the postcard as a message once he'd abducted Abby?

What if the card had been left by Boone Shaw? What if all of Jack's ruminations about copycats and attention-seeking neighbors were bull?

He had to proceed as if the threat to Abby had just been kicked up to the next level. From this moment on, Jack stayed with Abby, and she with him. No matter what.

He waited for the police to finish taking statements and questioning neighbors before he made his next move. Gina had arrived to offer moral support and Abby had moved inside. The two women sat huddled together in the living room, nursing steaming mugs of tea. From what Jack had overheard, Robert was on his way over.

Surrounded by her friends, Abby would be safe.

Besides, Jack wasn't going far.

He passed Robert on the sidewalk headed toward Abby's door as Jack headed in the opposite direction. Abby's partner shot Jack a look so cold he felt his blood slow.

"Maybe she was right about you." Uncensored vehemence hung in Robert's voice. "Maybe you started all this to resurrect your case. Maybe you're simply using Abby and our site to fuel your work."

Jack read the look on the other man's face, a mix of anger and protectiveness. Was Robert Walker in love with Abby? Abby insisted the two were nothing more than friends, but perhaps she had no idea of the emotion she apparently inspired in her *friend*.

Jack bit down the annoyance simmering in his gut. He didn't like Robert, although he could say that about a lot of people he'd met over the years. But Jack's dislike for

Robert rose from something deeper, something instinctual, something he hadn't yet put his finger on.

"I have no intention or need to use Abby," Jack said flatly. "If you'll excuse me, I've got work to do."

Yet as Jack walked away, Robert's words took hold deep inside Jack's brain. Of course he was using Abby. He'd set out to do just that. He'd traveled to Delaware to do whatever it took to bring Emma's killer to justice. And he'd intended to destroy Don't Say a Word, if necessary.

Jack might not like Robert Walker, but the man was spot-on about Jack's intentions, much as Jack didn't appreciate the observation.

The curtain at the side window of the house next door swept shut, belying the presence of Dwayne Franklin, lurking at the window. Watching.

Dwayne Franklin studied every move Abby made. A classic stalker, or at least a stalker in the making.

Protectiveness welled inside Jack, and this time he did nothing to bury or deny the feeling. This time he let the emotion infuse him with determination.

He thought of the look of sheer horror on Abby's face when she'd discovered the card.

If Franklin were responsible for putting that fear in her eyes, Jack was sure as hell going to make sure the man never put that same look there again.

He climbed the duplex's front steps, noting the way the concrete had begun to crumble in several spots. For all of the attention Franklin allegedly paid to Abby's property, the same couldn't be said for the neglected shrubbery framing his home's entryway. Overgrown holly branches reached out, clawing at Jack's clothing and partially blocking the handrail.

Jack quickly stepped clear, hitting the front door with a sharp knock.

Footfalls sounded on the other side, and through the frosted glass he spotted a shadowy shape approaching, a shadowy shape consistent with Franklin's paunchy build.

Franklin snapped the door open barely six inches—enough to eyeball Jack, not an inch more.

"I already spoke to the real detectives."

Jack bit back the grin that threatened. If this lowlife thought he could put Jack in his place, he'd better think again.

"You remember my badge, correct?"

Franklin nodded.

"Maybe this time you'd like to see my gun?"

The other man blinked, his gaze narrowing.

"Open the door, Mr. Franklin. I'll take five minutes of your time, then I'll be on my way."

Franklin did as Jack requested, allowing Jack access to a wide, paneled foyer. The apartment door at the end of the hall sat partially open, consistent with the location of the window in which Jack had spotted Abby's neighbor surveying the scene.

"Why don't we step into your apartment?" Jack did his best to force a cordial tone.

"Why don't we skip that step?" Franklin replied.

Much as Jack wanted to get inside Franklin's space, he wasn't about to press the man. Not yet. He'd save intimidation for later. Now wasn't the time.

Besides, if Detective Hayes or one of his team had been inside Franklin's apartment, Jack would be privy to a full description of Franklin's living space.

"I know you've already spoken with the Wilmington detectives, but I wonder if you could answer a few questions for me?"

Franklin visibly stiffened. "I already told them I didn't see a thing."

Jack considered his next move, considered it carefully, deciding to go directly for the information he needed most.

"I saw you at that window—" Jack gestured toward the doorway to the man's apartment "—every single time I glanced at this house tonight. Are you going to tell me you didn't see what happened?"

"I was watching a movie." Franklin gave a dramatic shrug. "So sue me. No one pays me to play neighborhood watch."

"Then who did I see at the window?"

Another shrug. "I haven't the slightest idea."

A sour smell teased the edges of Jack's senses. Urine? Stale clothing? He couldn't place the odor, but he knew the smell originated from Dwayne's apartment. Heaven only knew what lay on the other side of the door.

Jack attempted a step in that direction, but Franklin moved to block him.

"No warrant, no search."

"Warrant? Search?" Jack chuckled. "Who said anything about a warrant or a search? This is a friendly visit to see if you saw the same man Abby saw at her window."

He watched his bluff hit its intended mark. Franklin frowned, then twisted up his features.

"I thought she found some sort of a card stuck to the window? I didn't hear that she saw anyone."

"To the best of my knowledge, the police haven't released specifics, so I'm not at liberty to discuss that."

"But you were inside her apartment when it happened, right?"

So Jack had been right. Dwayne Franklin hadn't missed a trick.

Jack nodded, watching a mix of anger and jealousy play across Franklin's face. "I thought maybe you'd seen the same man. I know how much you'd want to help her."

"I've never done anything but help Abby." Franklin's voice grew shrill, defensive. "I think you're trying to trick me. I'm not an idiot, Detective, and I didn't see a thing."

With that, Franklin turned and raced back to the sanctity of his apartment, slamming the door behind him.

Jack chuckled as he headed back toward the front steps. If Detective Hayes hadn't told Franklin about the postcard, Franklin had just tipped his hand. He also would have just explained how it was that he hadn't seen anyone at Abby's window.

Dwayne Franklin hadn't seen anyone leave the postcard, because he'd left the postcard himself.

Jack called Hayes's cell before he headed back into Abby's apartment, getting the answers he expected. Franklin had held off the detectives at the doorway, just as he'd done with Jack.

He'd also mentioned the postcard, although none of the responders had released that information.

Much as Jack wanted to point an accusatory finger, he couldn't. Not yet. Anyone watching the house closely enough could have spotted the postcard and recognized it for what it was, and Franklin sure as hell watched Abby's house closely.

The man was a threat to Abby whether she believed Jack or not. Her neighbor might not have anything to do with the case other than carrying out a poorly executed copycat effort aimed at gaining her attention, but he was a menace, just the same.

"You wouldn't be meddling in my case now, would you, Jack?" Hayes's voice pulled Jack's focus free of his myriad thoughts.

"Just being neighborly," Jack lied, glancing over his shoulder just as the curtain at Dwayne Franklin's side window swung shut.

"I DON'T CARE what you think." Robert drained the beer Abby had offered him, his cheeks flushed with color. "The guy doesn't care a thing about your safety. He cares about solving his case. End of story."

Abby's headache had built to a pulsating, pounding intensity that had taken on a life of its own.

As much as she appreciated his show of testosterone, she'd never known Robert to be anything but disagreeable when it came to welcoming new people into his trust. She was in no mood to discuss his current dislike of Jack Grant.

"I think you sound jealous." Gina pursed her lips and nodded. "Matter of fact, I know you sound jealous. Besides, Detective Grant was here with Abby when the card was left. I seriously doubt he tiptoed outside, stuck it to the window and tiptoed back in."

Annoyance flickered in Robert's gaze. As close as they were, he was sometimes irritated by Gina's less-than-tactful way of saying what she thought. "That's not what I'm suggesting."

Gina raised one dark brow in question.

"What I'm saying is that I don't trust him. I never said I thought he hand-delivered the cards."

"Then why don't you trust him?" Abby's voice visibly startled her two friends, as if they'd forgotten she were in the room. "He's here because he thinks the cards might lead him to his sister's killer." She kept her voice low and soft on purpose, hoping her tone might somehow diffuse the growing tension in the room "I can't fault him for that. Can you?"

Gina pursed her lips again, this time shaking her head. Robert glared at Abby, silent momentarily before he let loose.

"I can't believe how quickly you bought his line of bull." Robert's features tensed. "You believe the justice system set Boone Shaw free?" Robert jerked his thumb toward the outside. "Your detective probably tampered with evidence or screwed something up. You'll see. All this has less to do with catching a killer than it does with Jack Grant easing his guilty conscience."

Abby drew in a slow, steady breath, deciding it was better not to tell Robert she'd find almost as much sympathy for wanting to ease a guilty conscience as she did for wanting to solve the case.

"You need to spend less time dreaming up conspiracy theories, and more time getting some sleep." Gina patted Robert on the shoulder. "I mean, you do lean toward the miserable side, but you're way over the edge tonight."

Robert spun on her. "I suppose you're okay with whoever this madman is putting a postcard of Abby on her window? What happens when her detective isn't here? Who protects her then?"

"Seems to me that's all the more reason you'd like Jack," Abby said. "He promised me he's not going to leave me alone until this nightmare is over and done with."

Gina nodded. "That detective is a man you can trust."

Jack walked through the door before Robert had a chance to respond. Robert chose that moment to grab his coat, brush past the detective, and leave without saying another word.

"Something I said?" Jack scowled at the door as it slammed shut.

Abby forced a smile, when she felt like doing anything but. "He's upset about tonight, that's all."

"Lord, you find an excuse for everyone." Gina reached for her own coat and pushed to her feet.

"Where were you?" Abby asked Jack, choosing to ignore Gina's comment.

"Wanted to ask your neighbor a few questions."

"He had nothing to do with this." Anger and fatigue bristled the hairs at the base of Abby's neck.

Gina pointed at Abby. "Do not try to excuse Dwayne Franklin. That guy is up to no good." She shifted her focus to Jack. "Did she tell you he goes through her mail? It gives me the creeps. I saw him earlier tonight and told him to mind his own business and get a life."

"He's lonely and he looks out for me. He's harmless." But the sudden chill tap dancing down Abby's spine belied her words. "Did he tell you anything, Jack?"

Jack's stare locked on Abby's, making her insides squirm. "Enough for me to distrust him even more than I did before."

Gina crossed to the door with such sharp movements her blunt-cut dark hair swung against her face. As much as Abby loved and appreciated her friend, she'd had just about all of Gina's brassiness she could take for one night. What she needed now was quiet…and sleep.

Gina shrugged into her coat. Her features went serious as she turned to Abby then retraced her steps to give her a hug.

Abby would be lying if she didn't admit her friend's embrace was welcomed and needed.

"Call me," Gina whispered in her ear, as soft-spoken now as she'd been arrogant not a moment earlier. "I can be here in minutes. I'd still feel better if you'd come stay with me, but as long as you won't be alone, I'm okay with you staying here."

"She won't be alone." Jack's deep voice broke the close moment between the two lifelong friends.

"Don't forget to call me," Gina said as she backed toward the door.

'Gina." Abby moved quickly to follow her friend. "I forgot to thank you for the frame." Abby had completely forgotten about the repaired glass amidst the chaos of the night.

Amusement danced in Gina's dark look. "Frame?"

Abby pointed to the picture of the three friends, the once-broken glass now intact. "I broke the glass the other day when Dwayne was here. Did you fix it when you were here earlier?"

Gina pursed her lips, giving her head a slow shake. "It wasn't me. Maybe your little neighbor does more than watch your house while you're not here."

With her parting shot delivered, Gina slipped out the door and into the bitter night, leaving Abby and Jack alone.

Before Abby could thank Jack for everything he'd done, he spoke. "She's right, you know."

"About Dwayne?"

Jack moved two steps closer to where Abby stood, arms wrapped defensively around her waist. "Could be, but I was talking about staying here. You can't."

"And just where I am supposed to go in the middle of the night, Jack?"

"Let me take care of that."

Mind-numbing fatigue washed through her and Abby decided then and there that she didn't have another argument left in her just then, not for Robert, not for Gina and not for Jack.

"I need to sleep. I'll go wherever you want me to go in the morning, but for now, I need to sleep."

Before Jack could so much as say a word, Abby turned and headed for her bedroom. She opened the hall closet as she passed, pulling her overnight bag down from the top shelf.

She'd pack in the morning. She'd listen to Jack then.

But for now, she wanted nothing more than to pretend tonight had never happened, even though she knew the memory of her image on the postcard and the sender's eerie message would most likely haunt her every dream.

Chapter Nine

Abby unpacked her overnight bag, tucking her clothing into the drawers of a hand-painted period piece.

She'd been amazed when she'd woken up and read the bedside clock back at her apartment. Eleven-thirty. She couldn't remember the last time she'd slept so late. Of course, she also couldn't remember the last time she'd pulled an all-nighter or had her life turned so thoroughly on its ear.

She'd awakened to the smell of bacon, eggs and freshly brewed coffee, and as she'd watched Jack work in her kitchen as though he belonged there, something inside her had shifted. Something that she'd long denied. The part of her that wanted to be loved and that wanted to love in return.

But fantasies about a future with Jack Grant would be little more than the work of an overactive imagination. Yes, Abby had seen the undeniable attraction in his eyes when he looked at her. She was fairly sure she wasn't so far out of practice that she'd forgotten how to read the romantic signs. But Jack wasn't here for Abby. Jack was here for his sister, her memory and the memories of the other victims.

He was here to find the truth.

And as Abby watched him carefully prepare her breakfast she knew helping him had become her first priority.

Perhaps by helping Jack find justice for Emma and others, Abby would find a way to forgive herself for the role she'd played—or hadn't played—in Vicki's death.

"I'd like you to look at the case files, if you think you can handle it."

Jack's words and his accompanying knock at the door to the suite's bedroom jolted her from her memories of a few hours ago.

They'd eaten brunch, packed up enough clothing for Abby to stay away for a few days and then they'd checked Jack out of his hotel.

He'd driven to the Inn at Brandywine Valley, a one-of-a-kind resort that boasted several small suites, free-standing homes once used by workers operating the local gun powder production.

The inn's owners, Sharron and Harold Segroves, had welcomed Jack and Abby with open arms. They'd ushered the pair to their suite loaded down with fresh fruit, pastries and that morning's *Sunday News Journal.*

The suite itself was small, but lovely, appointed with antique furnishings and lush draperies reminiscent of a centuries-old wildflower garden.

"I want you to understand what Boone Shaw is capable of," Jack explained.

Abby slid the drawers of the antique bureau shut. "Do you still believe he's responsible?"

"I believe he's responsible for the New Mexico murders, yes. But I'm not sure he's responsible for the postcards or for Beverly Bricken's murder."

Abby stepped toward Jack, drawn to the unflinching strength reflected in his eyes. "Who then?"

"A student? An admirer? A stranger?" Jack shut his eyes and grimaced, a fleeting glimpse of the toll the investigation had taken on his spirit.

He straightened, locking stares with Abby and forcing a tight smile so quickly Abby wondered if she'd imagined the momentary display of emotion.

She moved so close she could smell the fresh scent of the soap he'd used in her shower that morning. She reached toward his face, but stopped herself short of touching his clean-shaven cheek.

His features remained impassive, unreadable. "You can't trust anyone, Abby. Not anymore."

"What about you, Jack?"

The tension between them grew palpable, but Jack didn't so much as blink. He also didn't answer her question, turning toward the living area and gesturing for her to join him at the small dining table.

"Your investigator hasn't found Shaw?"

A muscle in Jack's jaw tensed then released, then tensed again. "I plan to call him in a bit, but at last check, Boone Shaw's financial activity showed no movement, no deposits, no withdrawals, no charges."

"So he could be anywhere?"

"Or we could be chasing a ghost."

The word sent a shudder through Abby as she eyed the fat case folder Jack pulled from his briefcase.

"You don't think the card last night is the same guy, do you?" she asked.

Jack's gaze locked with hers, holding her captive with the intensity of his stare. "I think last night might very well have been the work of a copycat, but I won't risk your safety either way."

"You're saying I'm not in danger if it was a copycat?"

"You're safer if the copycat is only out for attention. I can't risk that he's not out to copy the original crimes. I also can't risk that my gut instinct is off for some reason and last night's card is legit."

Jack spoke surely and strongly, a man confiden.
thought and action, a man unfazed by the events of the pa.
two days.

"How often has your gut instinct been wrong?"

"Never." He dropped his focus back to the folder,
removing the contents and studying each piece of paper,
each photo as if he might see something he'd never seen
there before.

"Is that the original file?" Abby asked. "Or a copy?"

"Copy."

"They let you do that?"

"*They* don't have to know."

She stepped toward him, trying not to gawk at the crime
scene photos he'd pulled from the folder. As she neared,
Jack slid the photos beneath a sheet of bullet point notes,
hand-written, perhaps something he'd compiled over the
years.

"Are you protecting them? Or me?"

"Both." He looked up at her and frowned. "Do you
always ask so many questions?"

Abby ignored his question, settling into an empty chair
at the table. She sat without saying another word, watching
him move through the notes, through the transcripts of
what she imagined to be testimony, through the photos of
the missing and the dead.

Jack's hand stilled when he came across the crime scene
marked with a large number two. His sister Emma. Even
in death, she'd been a breathtaking young woman, taken
too soon from a life too short.

"You and me, we're not so different after all, are we?"
Abby asked.

Jack humored her with a reply. "How so?"

"We're haunted by what we might have done differently."

Something deep inside Jack's penetrating gaze shifted, and for a moment Abby glimpsed the raw grief he still held there. Then just as quickly, the look was gone, and Jack dropped his focus back to the file contents.

"I let go of the guilt a long time ago."

"Did you?"

He said nothing, instead tucking the notes and printouts and photos back into the folder.

"I see it in your eyes, Jack," Abby continued. She knew she was pushing her luck, pushing the man, but she couldn't help herself.

Something about Jack Grant made her want to help him, made her want to pull him into her arms and tell him he wasn't to blame for his sister's death.

A madman was to blame. A madman Jack had chased for eleven years, never once accepting the defeat he'd faced years ago as anything but temporary.

He closed the folder, returned it to his briefcase, then pushed to his feet. "This was a bad idea."

Abby stood, facing him head-on. "None of this is your fault."

"You," his voice dropped low, so distant it chilled Abby to the core, "don't know a thing about me or my faults. Let's keep it that way."

He turned to walk away, but Abby followed, reaching for his arm. "Let me get this straight. You can sit in my house lecturing me on letting go of my guilt, telling me I couldn't have done a thing to save Vicki, but I'm not allowed to say so much as boo to you about your sister's death?"

He pulled his arm free of her touch, leaving her fingers cold. "Sounds about right."

JACK SHUT THE bedroom door behind him and swore beneath his breath.

Damn Abby Conroy.

None of this is your fault.

For someone he'd expected to be a pushover, she proven to be anything but, and he admired her for the annoying trait. How could he not? But he wasn't about to sit across the table from her, holding hands and sharing psychobabble.

If she thought he was a man who wanted to get in touch with his feelings, she'd best think again.

The only thing Jack wanted to get in touch with was whoever had sent the cards, and he was growing more and more certain he was chasing more than one man.

He pulled out his cell and dialed Max in Montana.

Jack and Max had gone through the Academy together, and after a few years on the force, Max had decided the life of a private investigator suited him better than that of a police officer.

Max had apparently made a smart choice.

Jack had yet to hear of a case Max hadn't been able to unravel.

Jack could only hope this case wouldn't be the one to break Max's streak.

The private investigator answered on the first ring. "I was waiting for your call."

"You have something for me?"

Max blew out a whistle. "Matter of fact, I've got a whole lot of nothing for you."

"So why do you sound excited?"

"Because that nothing comes at the end of a trip east that ended not far from where you are now."

"Shaw's here?" Jack's pulse quickened. "You've got a location for me?"

If Max had found Boone Shaw, Jack's investigation had just taken a huge leap forward.

"Not a one," Max answered.

Jack let loose a string of expletives. "Are you playing with me, Max? Because things are escalating here and I don't have time for games."

"Apparently Shaw didn't have time for games, either. Told his wife he had to take care of business before it was too late."

Too late? "For what?"

"Dying." Silence beat across the line before Max explained. "Lung cancer. Stage four. He's probably only got weeks left to live."

"Sonofa—"

Someone that ill didn't strike Jack as a likely candidate for sending the cards or posing a threat to Abby, unless the man was trying to go out with a bang.

"Did the wife say what business it was Boone had to take care of?"

"She did." Another pause.

"And?" Impatience flared inside Jack, but he knew better than to push Max. The investigator enjoyed a dramatic delivery, always had.

"She said he wanted to clear his name before he died. Wanted to bring the real killer to justice once and for all."

"Well, what do you know…" Jack's voice trailed off on the last word. If Boone Shaw and his wife were telling the truth, Shaw and Jack had wanted the same thing all these years.

Jack wasn't buying a word.

"Does she know where he is?" he asked.

"No idea. Cell phone appears to be dead or disabled. He hasn't called her in over ten days, and he hasn't returned a single voice mail."

"Damn."

"But she knows where he was."

Another pause. Jack clenched his fist, wishing he . a drink right about now, something he hadn't thought in long time.

"Where, Max?"

"Elkton, Maryland. Said he'd found his man and was set to make contact the next day."

Elkton, Maryland. Less than forty minutes to the south of Wilmington. Too close to be coincidence.

"Nothing since?"

"Nothing."

"What about hotel possibilities?"

"Nothing on credit, but I'm working through the list."

"How many?"

"Not bad. Less than twenty."

Jack let out a long whistle. "That's a nice break. You'll let me know if you find anything?"

"The second I find it."

"Thanks, Max."

"I've got a package waiting for you, Jack."

"On a Sunday?"

Max laughed. "Hey, when you're good, you're good. I happen to be very good."

"So you keep telling me." Jack smiled, glad for the light moment in what had quickly become a very heavy day.

Jack fumbled in the nightstand drawer for pen and paper as Max rattled off the address and phone number for a local business center and shipping outlet.

Jack repeated the information, double-checking accuracy, then thanked Max for calling. He flipped to the map in the front of the phonebook, located the general vicinity of the shipping outlet address and noted the direction he'd need to take from the inn to hit the correct shopping center.

He found Abby standing in the suite's kitchen, staring out the small window over the sink.

Deep thoughts?"

She spoke without turning to look at him, frustration evident in her tone and stance. "You're a real jerk, Grant."

"I've been called worse."

When she did turn to face him, one corner of her mouth lifted into a crooked grin. "Good."

The woman was like no one—male or female—Jack had met before. Stubborn, beautiful and sharp as a tack. Abby Conroy was a force to be reckoned with, a force he hadn't anticipated or expected, and a force that was slowly eating away at his resolve to do nothing more than use her for information then turn and walk away.

Jack did something then that he rarely did. He apologized. "Sorry about before."

She closed the space between them, standing so near he could feel the heat of her body. "You asked me whether I started the site to assuage my guilt or to help others," she said, her eyes never leaving his, heating his insides with the depth of her scrutiny.

"I asked you about Emma because I genuinely wanted the answer. I wanted to know if I could help you somehow. I've been standing here ever since wondering why in the hell I care. Any ideas?"

Jack shook his head, but even as he did so, he lowered his mouth to hers, tasting tentatively at first before he took her mouth with his, covering her lips, easing them apart with his tongue to kiss her so deeply, passionately, that he thought some unseen force had taken over his every instinct.

Jack pulled her into his arms, reveling in the feel of her fingertips as they found the nape of his neck. The lush curves of her breasts pressed into his chest and he hardened instantly, unable to control his body's reaction to holding her, tasting her, wanting her.

Abby pulled away, bright color staining her chee
"And I had you pegged as emotionally distant."

Jack scrubbed a hand across his face, remorse flooding
his every nerve and muscle, even as his body screamed for
a deeper joining with Abby. "Mistake. Big mistake."

He brushed past her, headed for the door.

"Jack?"

He ignored her, not willing to risk what he might do
next if he stayed in the suite. "I'll be back. Do not leave
this room."

But as he drove away from the inn, Jack realized it
wasn't kissing Abby he regretted, it was walking away.
And that thought scared Jack almost as much as the realization that more than forty-eight hours into his investigation, he was no closer to the truth than he'd been the
moment he'd taken Herb Simmons's call.

Only now, one critical element had shifted.

Abby Conroy had become far more than a means to an
end. She'd become a target.

Jack needed to regain his control, his focus. He needed
to be at the top of his game to keep her safe, and suddenly,
keeping her safe had become priority number one.

Caving to a physical hunger was a risk he couldn't take,
a distraction he couldn't afford.

No matter how much he wanted to.

Chapter Ten

Abby seethed with anger and frustration. She didn't need Jack Grant, his so-called protection or his mind-numbing kiss.

She winced, remembering the way she'd eagerly pressed her body to his, the way she'd raked her fingers up through his hair, the way she'd come alive at the contact of their bodies—skin to skin, lip to lip, heat to heat.

She shook her head, muttering to herself as she headed back toward her bedroom.

She couldn't stay here. She couldn't sleep under the same roof as the man. He couldn't be trusted. For all she knew, he'd jump her in the middle of the night.

She could only hope.

Abby groaned, unable to believe her mind had become consumed by thoughts of being with Jack instead of thoughts of the threatening postcard bearing her photograph.

A solid dose of reality washed through her, grounding her, dimming the memory of being in Jack's arms, albeit briefly.

Thank God she'd insisted on bringing her car, the car she planned to drive straight back to her apartment. She'd call Gina and ask her to come over. That way, Abby wouldn't be alone and Jack couldn't accuse her of being foolish.

Conflicting thoughts and urges battled for space inside her brain and she shook her head. She'd figure it all out once she got home…to her apartment, her space, her things.

She had a right to be there. A right to stake her claim and refuse to be driven out of her own apartment.

Abby left her overnight bag and clothing behind. Right now she needed out of this suite and away from all thoughts of Jack Grant.

She slammed the door to the suite shut behind her, held her head high and headed for her car. The crisp winter air cleared her senses instantly, infusing her with a renewed alertness and determination.

She needed time to regroup emotionally and physically, then she'd be ready to face Jack and the case again.

For now, she planned to leave all thoughts of postcards, killers and frustratingly stubborn detectives behind. And as the image of Jack's face and the memory of his kiss took position first and foremost in her mind, she groaned, realizing that no matter what she told herself, Jack Grant wasn't going anywhere anytime soon.

She was stuck with the man and his case, whether she liked it or not.

THE EXPRESS PACKAGE sat waiting for Jack behind the counter at the nearby Package Plus, just as Max had promised. Not wanting to open the envelope in front of an audience, he headed to the bagel shop next door, ordering a tall black coffee before he settled at a corner table.

Inside the envelope, Max had tucked proof of the claims he'd made over the phone. The transcript of his recorded conversation with Shaw's wife. A copy of the e-recorded conversation, should Jack want additional ackup.

He skimmed the transcript, his gaze settling on random words and phrases. Terminal. Stage four. Death sentence. No contact for the past ten days.

Apparently Shaw had telephoned his wife each evening as he traveled across the country, starting back in his former New Mexico haunts then driving east. The last phone call had been received ten days ago, transmitted through a cell tower in Elkton.

Had Shaw been headed to Wilmington? Had he found the person he sought? And if so, why had he failed to check in with his wife from that point on?

Apparently, the wife had been unable to get anything but voice mail on Shaw's cell phone ever since, leading Jack to believe Shaw had met with either bad luck or foul play. Jack's gut would put money on the latter.

Chances were Boone Shaw had found exactly the person he'd been after, and that person had not been happy about the contact.

Jack flipped through the rest of the documentation. Medical records. Doctor's summaries. The disability paperwork completed once his condition had been deemed terminal.

The logo at the top of a piece of letterhead from Shaw's former studio snagged Jack's attention, tugging at his memory. He skimmed the sheet of paper and the handwritten list. Clients.

Jack recognized the names from his days on the case. Five names in particular—the victims—hit him like a knife to the heart.

What was Shaw after? And why would a gravely ill man leave his home and wife to travel cross-country if he already faced the killer each day in the mirror?

Short answer. He wouldn't.

What if the investigators and prosecutors had zeroed in on the wrong suspect all along? Yet all of the evidence had pointed to Shaw. If Shaw had any idea at all of the real killer's identity, why wouldn't he have provided that information eleven years earlier?

Had he been protecting someone?

Jack flipped open his cell and redialed Max's number. He spoke as soon as the line connected. "Did you find records on children or siblings for Shaw?"

"Nothing. He and his wife never had kids and Shaw was an only child. He came from a small family and he's the last remaining survivor, according to my search."

Another dead end.

Jack pressed a fist to the table, thanked Max for the information and the package, then stared at the evidence.

Don't let him get away again. Herb Simmons's words played in Jack's brain like a broken record.

The original investigation had settled on Shaw for good reason. The man had had the means and the opportunity. The investigation had assigned the motive—sexual predator.

But if the investigation had been focused on the wrong man all along, the trail of the real killer would be colder than cold by now.

Eleven years virtually eliminated the chance a second suspect would be found and convicted...not unless Shaw led Jack to the guilty party.

Jack took another long drink of his coffee and shook the envelope, wanting to be sure he hadn't missed anything.

A black-and-white photo fluttered to the floor, igniting memories of unwanted images from the case file. The victims in life. The victims in death.

Yet the face that greeted Jack when he plucked the

...ped photo from the floor didn't belong to a victim. It ...onged to Boone Shaw.

The man was but a shadow of his former self. Gaunt, older and wasted, Shaw's physical appearance left no room for doubt about the man's health.

Jack replayed Max's words in his mind.

He wanted to clear his name before he died.

Based on Shaw's photo, death wasn't too far off. Maybe Shaw hadn't met with foul play at all. Maybe he'd fallen out of contact with his wife because he'd met with fate. Perhaps his time had simply run out.

The ramifications of the evidence spread across the coffee shop table hit Jack like a dead weight between the eyes. Had he been focused on the wrong man from day one?

Maybe Boone Shaw hadn't gotten away with murder. Maybe he'd gotten away with his life after being falsely accused. And now that death held the man in a stare-down contest, Shaw had decided he didn't want to die without clearing his name.

Or was it that Shaw didn't want to die without tying up any loose ends?

What if Shaw hadn't been tracking the killer? What if he'd been tracking the one person with the power to condemn him once and for all?

Jack shook his head. His investigative brain was working overtime, and he wasn't being logical.

A man as ill as Shaw would not travel cross-country to open old wounds. He might, however, do so in order to leave his name and legacy clear, a goodbye gift to his wife, so to speak.

As loath as Jack was to admit it, the simplest theory made the most sense.

Boone Shaw hadn't committed the murderous Christmas killing spree. He hadn't raped and killed five young women. He hadn't killed Emma.

Jack had been after the wrong man for eleven years.

His sense of reality tipped sideways momentarily, then Jack righted himself, regaining control of his thoughts and focus.

His mission hadn't changed: to find the killer by working backward from the postcards.

The only thing that had changed was the target—or rather his opinion of the target.

Jack still needed Shaw. He needed to know exactly who the man was after and why.

Jack gathered the documentation and the photograph, tucking them back into the folder. Then he drained his coffee, pushed out of his chair and headed for the door.

Shaw had been coming this way when he went silent. The time had come to circle the wagons. After all, Jack had zero idea from which direction an attack might come, but he felt it coming.

He had to consider every possibility, and he had to prepare for any feasible development.

A misstep now might cost Abby her safety…or her life, and that was a misstep Jack had no intention of taking.

ABBY REALIZED AS soon as she set foot inside her apartment that she'd made a mistake.

Jack had been correct. She had no business being here. The sofa was still askew from where Jack had slept the night before. Her remaining furniture had been rearranged to accommodate the influx of investigative personnel who had responded to last night's call.

This wasn't her apartment any longer.

This was a crime scene.

She pivoted on her heel, intending to beat a fast path back to the inn with the hope of reaching the suite before Jack returned. With any luck at all, he'd never be the wiser about her excursion, and she'd be spared another lecture about her personal security shortcomings.

Dwayne Franklin stood in the doorway, his slightly overweight frame taking up every available inch of space.

"Dwayne." Abby's voice jumped as sharply as her heart. She hadn't heard so much as a footfall at the threshold behind her.

"I needed to see you." Dwayne's eyes appeared unfocused as he moved toward her.

Abby stood her ground, not wanting to back any farther into her apartment. There was only one exit door, and right now Dwayne Franklin loomed between Abby and her goal.

"Did you see what happened last night, Dwayne?"

He shook his head, taking another step toward her. He stood close enough now to touch her and did so, caressing a lock of her hair between his thumb and forefinger.

Adrenaline pumped to life in Abby's veins, momentarily leaving her unsteady.

"You're making me uncomfortable, Dwayne."

He'd never touched her this way before, never stood this close, and if she wasn't mistaken she could smell alcohol on his breath.

"Have you been drinking?"

The moment she uttered the question, Dwayne spun away from her, slamming his fist against the wall. "I've been cooking. For you. For us."

His sudden, violent outburst left Abby reeling. She had to get out of her apartment and away from Dwayne as quickly as possible.

Something had shifted inside the man. His tone of voice

and the look in his eyes bordered on unstable, flood Abby with trepidation and dread.

"You're scaring me, Dwayne. I need you to leave."

What if Jack had been right? What if Dwayne had left the postcard? What if he were somehow involved in all of the postcards as a way to get Abby's attention?

"I would never hurt you, Abby. You're my friend."

"I know you're my friend, Dwayne." She struggled to keep her voice calm, soothing, wanting only to reassure Dwayne and get him the hell out of her apartment. "I'm your friend, too."

Dwayne's features darkened, like a storm brewing just beneath the surface of his tentative control. "You're a liar."

Abby took a backward step, as if the force of Dwayne's words had physically pushed her.

"You forgot about our dinner tonight."

Dinner.

Dwayne was right. Abby had completely forgotten. Dwayne had been planning tonight for weeks. He'd wanted to make her dinner, and she'd agreed, thinking the gesture harmless.

How wrong she'd been.

"I'll have to reschedule, Dwayne. I'm sorry."

His voice dropped low and flat, detached. "Why? Because you're going to be with that cop?"

"Yes." Abby nodded, formulating her story even as she spoke it. "Detective Grant is on his way here, now. We have to work tonight. I'm sorry."

Dwayne's stern facade began to crumble and he turned toward the door. "You're not sorry at all. You're just like all the rest."

Before Abby could say another word, Dwayne was gone. The irrational part of her wanted to go after him, wanted to remind him that she'd been his friend when

...yone else had steered clear. But the rational part of her
on the battle.

She gathered up her purse and keys and raced for her
car, doing her best to ignore the window next door, yet
unable to miss the swish of the curtains and the bulky
figure watching her as she ran away.

Chapter Eleven

Jack was so angry with Abby he couldn't see straight.

Which part of *do not leave this room* had the woman failed to understand?

Abby recounted the incident with Franklin, repeating their conversation word for word, describing Franklin's actions and demeanor. Jack's gut tightened.

He said nothing for several long moments after she stopped talking, wanting to choose his words carefully. Tact was not the usual response for Jack, but as much as he hated to admit it, he cared about what he said to Abby and how he said it. In addition, the fact Franklin had given Abby the scare of her life was evident in the bright fear still shimmering in her eyes.

"You have to promise me you'll be more careful."

She opened her mouth to say something, but Jack held up a hand to stop her.

"First things first. I want to apologize for what happened between us earlier. I was out of line and I wasn't thinking. It won't happen again."

Jack reached for the express envelope he'd received from Max and pulled Shaw's photo from inside. "This is what I received from my private investigator today. A recent photo of Boone Shaw."

e waited while Abby studied the black-and-white photograph, her eyes going wide.

"I thought you said he was big and brawny?"

"He was. He's dying. And his wife hasn't heard from him in over ten days."

"You don't think he sent the cards?" Abby handed him back the photo and blew out a frustrated breath. "What's going on, Jack?"

"I wish I knew." He filled her in on the intel Max had provided and Shaw's last known location, Elkton.

"We should go." Abby hugged herself, pacing a tight pattern in the living room. Back and forth. Back and forth. "Maybe he's sick somewhere. In the hospital. Still in his room."

"Or dead."

Jack's harsh statement stopped Abby in her tracks and she turned to him, her expression one of surprise.

"We have to be realistic."

"Dead as in sick and died?" she asked. "Or dead as in he found whoever he was looking for and they weren't happy to see him?"

"Don't know." He saw his own frustration mirrored in Abby's expression. "For all we know, Shaw's visit was the trigger that inspired the postcards."

Abby sat at the dining table and lowered her face to her hands. Jack longed to reach out to her, to pull her into his arms, to tell her everything would be all right, but truth was, he couldn't make that promise when he didn't know what was going on. Plus, he didn't trust himself to touch her.

Not now.

"Abby."

She raised her gaze to his, confusion palpable in her pale eyes.

"We don't know what or who we're up against," he

continued. "We've got a lot of theories, but no proof. I need you to trust me."

"I do trust you—"

"Let me finish."

His chest squeezed as he spoke, and Jack realized he couldn't deny how much Abby had come to mean to him, no matter how he tried.

"Maybe Franklin's actions have something to do with this case, or maybe they don't. Maybe the guy is simply obsessed with you. Not a great option, but a step above having a serial killer on your trail.

"But in order for me to keep you safe, I need to know you're where you tell me you're going to be. I need to know you're safe, because if anything happened to you…"

Jack hesitated, not ready to tell Abby Conroy just how far she'd gotten under his skin. "That's it. I need to know where you are at all times."

Shock edged the frustration and confusion tangling for position in Abby's face. The unspoken part of Jack's words hadn't been lost on her, even in her current state of distress.

She moved toward him, taking his hands in hers.

The contact sent a jolt of heat through Jack's system, but he made no move to shift away—part refusal to show her proximity had any effect on him and part desire to be as close to her as possible.

ABBY FOUND HERSELF blown away by Jack's admission, even though he'd caught himself before he'd fully let down his guard.

Her encounter with Dwayne had set the detective on edge. She could see it in his eyes, hear it in his voice, sense it in the tension radiating from his touch.

"I'm sorry." She meant the words as she said them, fully and completely.

She'd screwed up and she knew it. She'd also been damned lucky Dwayne had backed down.

"I'd like to see the case files again, please."

Jack pulled his fingers free from her touch, reaching for his briefcase. "Some of this is fairly graphic."

"I'm a big girl, Jack. I know you want to protect me, but I need you to let me in a bit more. Let me help."

And so he did, pulling the folder from his briefcase and handing it to her, setting the carefully collected reports, notes and photos in her hands, then turning away, trusting her with his work.

He gave her space as she looked through the pages. He remained silent as she studied the photos, processed the available information, the horror of the killings, the loss of bright lives so young.

When she'd finished her review, she turned her focus on Jack, watching him as he watched her, reading the unspoken heartache in his eyes, measuring the weight he carried on his shoulders.

"It wasn't your fault," she said softly.

He narrowed his eyes, frowning. "Big brothers keep little sisters safe. Especially when the big brother is a law enforcement officer. I failed her, Abby, just like I failed each of those families by focusing on the wrong man."

"You didn't act alone. The entire team focused on the wrong man. Obviously the evidence pointed to Boone Shaw. Either you're wrong about his innocence or someone set him up."

"If Max can locate the hotel where he stayed, we'll have a place to start digging."

"What about our local victim?" Abby studied a close up of the eye branded into one of the victim's thighs. "Was she branded like this?"

"Bricken?" Jack nodded. "Similar method apparently, but a completely different mark."

"Like what?"

"A pair of lips."

Abby tipped her head from side to side. "I don't think a pair of lips is that far off from an eye, do you?"

Seeing. Talking. Ignoring.

She replayed Dwayne Franklin's statement in her mind. *You're just like all the rest.*

"Maybe the killer felt ignored. He used the images of an eye and a pair of lips to make his victims pay attention, to make them talk to him."

Jack studied her, visibly impressed. "I hadn't thought about it that way, but a killer's signature rarely changes."

"But the Bricken murder was six years after the others. Wouldn't it make sense that the killer might have changed in that time?"

"Anything's possible."

"Is that why you'd never heard of this case? He branded her with lips instead of an eye?"

Jack nodded. "I'd entered our cases to have the system send up a flag if a similar case hit. Meantime, the local case was coded as a cutting or engraving."

"Not a branding?"

He shook his head. "The database never picked up the similarity."

Genuine frustration pulled at Abby's gut. "Sounds like a lot of room for error."

"You have no idea."

"Do you think Bricken's murder is unrelated? Or a copycat?"

"Could be either." Faint lines bracketed Jack's dark eyes. He'd barely slept since he arrived on the east coast and the stress and exhaustion had begun to take a visible toll. "Or maybe it is my guy somehow."

She needed to get this man a good solid meal and then make sure he rested. But first, she had to be honest about her opinion of the cases.

"I think it's the same guy, Jack. Something about the way she was posed for the modeling shot." Abby pictured the postcards of the two victims and then Bricken's. "Melinda, Emma and Bricken's poses are identical."

"You think so?" He moved to the table, then sat across from her.

She nodded. "A photographer composes his shot just like an artist composes her canvas. The first three pictures were taken by the same person. I'm sure of it."

"And how do we explain that if our theory about Devine planting the postcard holds true?" A light shone in his eyes as they spoke, and Abby realized he was enjoying their give and take, enjoying working through the logic of the case together.

"Maybe he had the photo in his possession ever since he worked the story. Or maybe he didn't plant the postcard at all."

Jack stretched his arms up over his head and let out a groan. "We need to pin Devine down on the source of the photo and locate the hotel used by Boone Shaw."

Abby blinked, surprised and pleased that Jack was treating her as an equal partner. "First things first."

His eyebrows lifted in question.

"Food."

JACK LEANED BACK against his chair, thinking Abby had read his mind. He was starving and he was exhausted, not that he'd admit the latter. Detectives did not admit fatigue. They wore it as a badge of honor.

He couldn't help but notice that Abby had avoided all talk of the most recent postcard. "You haven't mentioned your photo."

"We both know I didn't pose for it." The smile she forced didn't reach her eyes. Jack knew she was trying to hide the fact the threatening message had left her unnerved.

But she was right about one thing. The fourth card was different, more different than just the style of photograph.

"Hayes called," he said matter-of-factly. "The fourth photograph was printed on completely different paper from the first three shots."

The local detective had called Jack as he drove back from Package Plus. The lab had completed its initial analysis of the photo paper used in each card.

"The lab says the photo paper used in your card is completely different from the others—a specialty stock only sold locally and not meant for printing high-resolution photography."

Confusion flashed in Abby's eyes. "A professional wouldn't make that mistake."

"Exactly."

"And the other three?" she asked.

Jack moved toward the door. "Same manufacturer, though it's the most common on the market."

"So not necessarily from the same source?"

"Correct."

"Has anyone checked out the specialty paper?"

Jack nodded, wishing he had better news. "Hayes visited the shop himself. No one there recognized either Shaw or Devine from their photos. He didn't have a photo of Franklin."

Abby frowned. She'd never seen a photo of Dwayne, come to think of it, but that didn't mean she couldn't find a way to get one.

"If Dwayne left that card for me, would he be charged with a crime?"

Frustration flashed across Jack's face. "Strong possibility, but that would depend on you."

"What are my choices?"

"Loitering, stalking, harassment." Jack shrugged.

Before today Abby wouldn't have thought her neighbor capable of any crime, but now…now she wasn't so sure. Based on the violent outburst she'd witnessed, he might very well be a danger to himself, if not others.

"What do you know about his background?" Jack asked.

"I've asked him, but he always changes the subject." She realized how foolish the statement sounded as soon as she spoke.

"I'll have Max run a check." He pulled open the door and gestured for Abby to join him. "In the meantime, what do you say you and I enjoy the inn's restaurant and give ourselves some time off?"

A bright smile lit Abby's face as she moved to his side, and Jack realized he wouldn't mind seeing her smile every day from here on out. Part of him couldn't blame Dwayne Franklin for fixating on the woman. She was friendly, intelligent and breathtaking.

Then Franklin's cold, calculating eyes flashed through Jack's mind and a fresh wave of anger crested inside him. "Maybe Franklin thought he could scare you then step in and play the savior."

Abby's brows disappeared beneath her fringe of bangs. "Seems to me that role's already been spoken for."

Her words took Jack by surprise. Did Abby think that's what he'd done? Put himself in a position to play savior?

Her grin widened. "You don't have to look so stunned, Detective, I know you're only doing your job."

But as they headed across the grounds of the inn toward the main building, Jack couldn't seem to wrench his thoughts from her words.

Was he only doing his job?

Or had his concern for Abby's safety become something much more? He was physically attracted to her. Of that, there was no doubt. Jack was fairly certain the feeling was mutual.

He'd apologized for kissing her and had given Abby his word it wouldn't happen again. Jack was determined to keep that promise.

When this investigation concluded, Jack would return to Arizona, leaving Abby and Delaware far behind.

Yet the more time he spent with the woman, the more difficult he found the truth to deny.

His feelings for Abby had become personal. Very personal. And a big part of Jack's focus now would be keeping those feelings from interfering with what had rapidly become a very complicated investigation.

HE STOOD INSIDE Abby Conroy's home, moving slowly through her things—her furniture, her books, her belongings. He sensed her, felt her, smelled the clean scent of her cosmetics, lingering still as if she'd just stepped out of the shower.

But she wasn't here.

The detective had moved her to safer ground.

Smart, yet not impossible to overcome. After all, sooner or later, the woman would return to work. He'd find her there, wait until she was alone, then make his move.

Abby Conroy didn't strike him as a woman who would tolerate the limits the good detective had placed on her for long.

Anyone who read her blog or had read the *People*

profile would understand that her work at Don't Say a Word defined her.

She wouldn't let anything keep her away from the blog, the postcards, the confessors.

Abby Conroy was far too stubborn to let a menacing message on a postcard scare her off for good. He was counting on it.

Sure, the woman could write her blogs from afar, but she couldn't check her mail, touch the handmade cards, feel part of her readers' lives.

And so, he'd wait, and he'd plan his moves accordingly, allowing for the possible choices Abby Conroy might make.

She'd proven to be no better than the others had been. She hadn't made time for him, listened to him, talked to him.

She'd ignored him.

He hated to be ignored.

The man's blood boiled and he brought a fist down on a table. Hard.

A framed photograph toppled over, and he righted the frame, deciding to borrow the keepsake from the shelf.

So much for not leaving any trace of his visit.

With any luck at all, Abby Conroy wouldn't notice the picture missing. Hell, she didn't notice anything except her precious blog site as it was.

He stared down into the objects of the photo—Abby and two other young women. Friends for life, supposedly.

And then it hit him, a moment of clarity so strong and pure it nearly stole his breath away.

He knew exactly how to reach Abby Conroy, exactly how to pull her out of hiding and into his plan.

He'd go after those she held most dear.

And he knew exactly where to start.

Chapter Twelve

Abby's cell phone rang a little after six-thirty the next morning.

"Where in the hell are you?" Robert's voice dripped with anger.

"Did we have plans?"

"No, but I'm standing in the freezing cold at your front door with today's *News Journal* and you're apparently nowhere to be found. At least, that's what your nosy neighbor told me."

"Dwayne?"

"I'm telling you the guy's interest in you isn't natural." The fact Robert had the decency to drop his voice low when he voiced his opinion of Dwayne wasn't lost on Abby.

"That's funny, Robert. Jack says the same thing about you."

"Jack?" The anger returned, a sharp edge breaking through Robert's control. "We're on a first-name basis now?"

Based on the anger and jealousy in her partner's voice, Abby realized Jack might have been correct in his assessment of Robert. Did he have feelings for Abby? Feelings she'd never read properly?

"Where are you?" he repeated, this time in a growl.

"I can't tell you."

"You can't *tell* me? I'm not some masked murderer here, Abby."

This was Robert, for crying out loud, and she was being overly secretive. "The Inn at Brandywine Valley, just until Jack and the police figure out what's going on."

Silence beat across the line. When Robert spoke again, the control had returned to his tone, as if he'd taken the time to compose himself.

"I don't suppose you and your detective have seen today's paper yet?"

"Why?"

"You might want to pick up a copy. I think it's safe to say Sam Devine decided to take your little story and run with it."

Five minutes later, Abby had pulled on a thermal shirt, down vest and jeans and had tugged her knit cap over her head. There were no signs of life from Jack's room as she headed through the suite, then jogged over to the main building.

"Morning, Abby," Sharron Segroves called out.

"Morning," Abby answered, gathering up two cups of coffee and two bagels in her effort to look calm, cool and collected when all she really wanted to do was grab a copy of the paper and race back to the suite.

Harold Segroves walked briskly past, carrying a steaming tray of bacon. "Morning, Abby. Tucked a paper under the desk for you. Wanted to make sure you got a copy."

"Morning." Abby frowned. "And thanks, I think."

Harold slowed and turned, talking to Abby while walking backward. "Jack confided in us when you all first checked in. He asked us to keep an eye out for anything strange. Knew you'd want to see that article first thing."

Abby thanked the inn's owner again, then braced herself as she ducked her head behind the reception desk. She wasn't sure what she expected, but certainly not the monstrous front page headline that waited on the desk's center shelf.

Home for the Holidays. Has the Christmas Confessor Moved East?

Abby snapped the paper from the shelf, zeroing in on the byline. Sam Devine.

So much for trying to keep the media from turning recent events into a circus.

"Bastard."

"My thoughts exactly." The rich timbre of Jack's voice took the edge off of Abby's shock, but she stumbled trying to juggle the paper, the coffee and the bagels as she backed out of the small space.

Jack smiled warmly as he reached for her hands, then gripped her arm, helping her straighten away from the desk.

They'd turned the corner during the dinner they'd shared with the Segroves the night before. Instead of mulling possible suspects and motives, they'd conversed like adults out for a relaxing meal. And they'd enjoyed themselves.

Jack's smile was testament to the fact the comfort level between them had increased ten-fold at some point during the evening.

They'd both gone to their bedrooms after the meal, but Abby had tossed and turned most of the night, wondering whether the attraction she felt for Jack was due to their forced proximity, or whether it could be something more. Something real.

"I thought you were still asleep," Abby said.

Jack shook his head. "Met Tim Hayes for an early

breakfast. I wanted to update him on our end of the investigation."

"Anything new from him?" Abby asked, hope welling inside her.

"Not a thing. So we talked about this." He tapped the front of the paper.

"I just heard." Abby flipped open the paper, grimacing at the black-and-white images plastered across the page. Melinda Simmons. Emma. Beverly Bricken. "Sorry, Jack."

He waved off her comment. "Been there, done that. If Devine's lucky he'll get one follow-up assignment to this insubstantial mess. There's nothing here except the ruminations of a reporter who missed his boat years ago."

He pointed to an inset shot. "One tiny point of note."

Abby followed his gesture, her breath catching at the picture, a shot of the investigative team's response to the card taped to her window.

"So he was there that night?" she asked, unable to remember seeing anyone but officers and friends.

"Apparently so, though who knows how far away." Jack picked up the coffees and bagels and tipped his head toward the door. Abby followed. "Or, he hired a freelancer. Those guys are masters at pulling off a shot like that unnoticed."

"How about a shot through someone's kitchen window?" Abby took one of the coffees from Jack and swallowed big. "Needs whiskey."

"Now, now." Jack pushed the door open with his hip and made room for Abby to pass. "Let's not let a fame-hungry reporter drive us to drink. Let's stick to the plan."

"Which is?"

"You go to work as usual, with one exception."

Abby grinned. "I know this one. I have my own security detail."

"At your service, ma'am." Jack laughed, the sound genuine and spontaneous, warming Abby from the inside out. "Now then, let's get this show on the road."

"What about Devine?"

"Don't worry about him," Jack answered, a muscle in his jaw twitching. "Let's worry about how the *Confessor* plans to respond to Devine's article."

WITH THE EXCEPTION of Devine's feature story on the Christmas Confessor, the day was uneventful. Jack had touched base with Max, who had found no information on Dwayne Franklin. Even more discouraging, none of Max's calls to the Elkton hotels had turned up anyone who remembered Boone Shaw.

Instead of babysitting Abby all day, Jack should have been handling the hotel questioning the old-fashioned way. On foot and in person.

Yet, he didn't trust anyone else to keep Abby safe, so here he stayed, holed up in the Don't Say a Word office.

When his cell phone rang late in the day, Jack expected the caller ID window to show Max's number. Sam Devine's name appeared in the small display screen instead.

Perfect timing. Jack had planned to share his thoughts on Devine's article in person, just as soon as Abby wrapped up her work day. But Devine launched into conversation before Jack had a chance to voice his opinions on the man's reporting skills.

"I've got something you need to see." Devine's excitement bubbled through the phone.

Jack had no patience for more of the man's scams. "Another card you put together? Speaking of which, where did you get the photo? From an old case file?"

The silent pause on the other end of the line confirmed Jack's guess wasn't far from the truth.

Devine stuck to his original topic as if Jack hadn't said a word. "You need to meet me. Same place as before. Half hour."

Jack glanced at his watch then at the hustle and bustle of the busy office. There were enough bodies here to keep Abby safe while he met with Devine. "I'll be there in fifteen."

A short while later he spotted Devine at the same table inside the mall. This time, Devine had cleared all but two chairs away.

Jack stood, scowling down at Devine. "This had better be good."

Devine brushed a lock of his hair from his face. Jack made the man nervous. Good.

Something akin to euphoria danced in Devine's eyes. "The article drew out your guy."

"Assuming you're telling me the truth, you've got my attention."

"He liked the piece."

"The piece?" Jack couldn't help himself. "Your piece is nothing but supposition and make-believe. You're lucky I don't have Hayes arrest you for interfering in an ongoing investigation."

"Seems to me this guy's delivering postcards faster than you can come up with leads."

Jack straightened defensively. "What was so important that I had to rush down here? I have better places to be."

"This." Devine patted the cell phone in his pocket. "He contacted me."

"Who?" Jack narrowed his eyes, impatience simmering inside him. He gestured for Devine to give him the phone. "You have no idea who we like for this, do you?"

But instead of backing down as Jack had expected, Devine stood, eyeing Jack head-on. "I know you've got three faces tacked to the board at the precinct."

Maybe the reporter had better sources than Jack had given him credit for. "But?"

"But the only suspect you need is the Christmas Confessor."

"Seems to me I've heard this story before."

Devine lowered his voice. "This time he sent a text message."

Jack held out his palm, trying to contain his disbelief but failing miserably.

Devine opened his cell, tapped the appropriate keys to pull up a message and handed the phone to Jack.

It's better to give than to receive.

Jack laughed. "I'm not so sure he liked your story."

"He likes his name, though." Devine reached for the phone, scrolled to the bottom of the message and handed the phone back to Jack.

Jack read the signature out loud. "Christmas Confessor." He checked the incoming caller ID and the blocked number. Then Jack shot Devine a glare. "Based on your track record, I'd say you sent this to yourself from an unlisted number."

Yet something about Devine was different. The last time they'd met, Devine had given off nonverbal clues that suggested he was lying. This time the only nonverbal cue the man emitted was his palpable excitement.

Someone had sent this text to the reporter as the result of the story, but who? Jack found it difficult to believe the killer would have let his fingers do the talking to Devine.

With the right resources, however, Jack could unlock the originating phone number in no time flat.

He moved to tuck Devine's phone into his pocket, but the other man pursed his lips and held out his hand. "Not so fast. No warrant. No phone."

Jack muttered a string of expletives beneath his breath,

then pushed away from the table, calling back to Devine as he walked away. "Leave that phone on. I'll be calling you to hand it over once the warrant's in my hand."

"HEY, NATALIE. What's your first reaction to this card?"

Abby had decided to feature special holiday blogs in order to lighten the severe mood she'd created online by publishing Melinda and Emma's postcards.

Abby walked to the lobby, staring at the postcard in her hand. "Natalie?"

Yet, nothing and nobody greeted her but an empty desk.

The office had emptied out as if someone had pulled the plug. The local news stations were forecasting snow by Christmas Eve and the last-minute shopping crunch was on.

Based on the way she could hear a clock ticking somewhere deep in the building, Abby would have to say most everyone had gone home early.

'Twas the season for shopping, after all.

Abby couldn't help but wonder where Jack had gone. He'd left to meet Devine over ninety minutes ago. Surely he should be back by now.

Dread wrapped its icy fingers around Abby's neck and squeezed.

"Natalie?"

Still no answer.

Natalie's chair sat empty, facing the wrong direction, as if she'd rushed away from the desk quickly. Furthermore, her coat and purse sat to the side of her desk, as if she'd been preparing to leave for the night, but had forgotten them in her rush to go…where?

Natalie's computer screen remained powered on, the option box for shutting down the system still blinking from the middle of the monitor's screen.

"Natalie?" Abby yelled out as loudly as she could.

Perhaps the young woman had decided to run one last check of the kitchen, making sure the appliances were switched off for the evening.

Abby hurried toward the kitchen. Empty darkness greeted her, matching the hollow sensation building inside her chest.

She blew out a sigh, bolstered herself and stepped back to the hallway.

"Natalie?"

The young woman had to be inside the office somewhere. She had to be.

Silence.

Nothing but silence.

Abby returned to the main desk, staring down at Natalie's purse and coat, but it was something altogether different that captured her focus.

She blinked, shifting her gaze to the desk, to the pile of mail Abby had asked Natalie to pick up earlier that afternoon.

One shiny postcard stood out from the pile, as if Natalie had slid it free to study the black-and-white photograph pasted to one side.

Bile rose in Abby's throat and she clasped a hand across her mouth.

She recognized the postcard's subject instantly. The blunt-cut hair. The fair coloring. The laughing smile.

The shot had been taken while the subject worked, obviously without her being aware she was being watched and photographed.

Abby slid her hand into one of her gloves before she turned over the card, not wanting to leave any prints.

Just like the others, this one had been labeled with a single sentence. The message brief, but effective.

It's better to give than to receive.

Tears clouded Abby's vision as she turned the card back over and reached for the phone.

Jack answered his cell on the first ring, at the same moment the reality of what Abby had found hit her full force, stealing her breath.

She choked on a terrified sob, unable to speak momentarily.

"Abby?" Concern and urgency tinged Jack's voice. "Where are you?"

"Natalie."

She forced the word from a throat clogged by emotion and fear, touching a gloved finger to the image of the young woman she'd grown to consider a friend.

"I found a postcard," she repeated, as a lone tear slid down one cheek.

"With Natalie?" Jack's voice climbed with uncertainty, as if he hadn't quite heard Abby correctly.

"Of Natalie." Abby leaned heavily against the desk, squeezing her eyes shut against the threatening tears. "She's gone, Jack. Gone."

"Are you alone?"

"Hurry, Jack."

"Don't move, and don't touch a thing."

THE CHRISTMAS CONFESSOR watched Abby Conroy's reaction from where he sat in his parked car. He enjoyed the mix of uncertainty, shock and fear that played across her pretty, know-it-all features almost as much as he enjoyed the Christmas carolers winding their way through the street.

A young man tapped on his window and waved. The Confessor waved back, mouthing the words, "Merry Christmas."

After all, it *was* a merry Christmas.

A *very* merry Christmas.

As far as the Confessor was concerned, the giving season was only now about to begin. Little did Abby Conroy know this year's festivities had been planned especially with her in mind.

The Confessor laughed as he watched Abby reach for the phone. He cranked on the car's ignition, knowing he had to get moving.

The woman was smart enough to realize the receptionist had been abducted, and no doubt the police would be here in full force any moment.

Much as he'd love to stay for the light show and the play of red and blue against red and green, he had things to do.

He stole a peek at the plaid blanket covering the receptionist's unconscious form on the backseat before he eased the car from its parking space along the curb.

Inside the building's reception area, Abby Conroy stood illuminated by the overhead lighting, arms wrapped tightly around her waist as she waited.

"Ho, ho, ho," the Confessor said under his breath.

The receptionist moaned and he forced his attention away from Abby Conroy and back to his driving.

Tonight, he vowed to give his full, undivided attention to the beauty in the backseat, but come tomorrow, he'd refocus on his ultimate target, his ultimate Christmas present.

Abby Conroy.

He had a feeling this Christmas would be his merriest yet.

Chapter Thirteen

Hours later, Jack led Abby through the door to their suite and pulled her into his arms. The protectiveness growing inside him during the past days had taken over every inch of his body, his thoughts, his plans.

During the on-site investigation and the questioning Abby had endured down at the police station afterward, she'd held herself together, kept her chin up, never wavered physically or emotionally. At least not that anyone would notice—anyone but Jack.

Jack, on the other hand, spotted the anger, tears and frustration lurking just below the surface of her control.

And the only thing he'd wanted to do for hours was this. He'd wanted to hold her, comfort her, wrap her up and shield her from the horror of whatever fate had befallen Natalie.

For Jack knew in his gut and heart that Natalie hadn't simply left her desk and walked away. She'd been taken. She'd been taken by whomever it was that had been sending the postcards, and she wasn't coming back.

The dread and certainty were so strong they threatened to overwhelm Jack, but he held the emotions at bay, compartmentalizing them, knowing his phone would ring the instant Hayes and his team caught a break…or found Natalie's body.

In the meantime, he'd hold Abby.

He pressed a kiss to her forehead, then to each eyelid, realizing he'd never felt such tenderness for another human being, not even for his younger sister.

Abby Conroy had reached deep inside his heart and taken hold. Even though Jack knew nothing would come of whatever it was that had happened between them, he decided to ride it out for tonight, for tomorrow, for however many days they had left together.

"I think she's already dead."

Abby whispered the words against his shirt as the first tear slid over her lashes and down her cheek.

Jack cupped her chin, staring into her frightened eyes. "Don't give up yet." He had no plans to tell her he'd given up the moment he'd stepped into the reception area and assessed the scene.

Years of investigative work did that to a man—to anyone.

Sometimes your instincts were wrong, but for Jack, they were usually right. He could only pray the distraction of falling for Abby had thrown off his judgment. Perhaps Natalie was safe somewhere right now. Safe. Unharmed. Alive.

Jack's gut protested otherwise.

"Stay with me, Jack." Abby tightened her arms around Jack's waist, her body pressed to his.

Heaviness descended over Jack as if he'd taken on a measure of Abby's heartache. He held her, thinking not of how much he wanted her, but rather of how much he wanted to comfort her.

So he did.

He hoisted Abby into his arms as if he'd done so count-less times before. She anchored her arms around his neck and tucked her tear-streaked face against his chest, and he carried her through the suite and into her bedroom.

"I'll hold you until you fall asleep."

She shook her head then covered his mouth with hers, tenderly pressing her lips to his. "Stay."

Jack held her until she stopped crying, until her breathing went even and smooth and the tension slipped from the arm she'd tucked inside his arm, the legs she'd intertwined with his.

Then he reached for the blanket folded neatly at the bottom of the bed, tugging it up and over her sleeping form. He did so with every intention of slipping out of bed, planning to check on her periodically, listening in case she should call him during the night.

Instead, Jack did what Abby had asked him to do.

He stayed.

And although the reality of the danger lurking outside was as near as the door to the suite, Jack slept, deeply and soundly, tucked against Abby. Together.

He didn't move until his cell phone rang the next morning, jolting him awake. He squinted at the bedside clock then pushed away from Abby's still sleeping form.

"Rockford Park," Hayes said the instant Jack answered his phone.

"Natalie?" Jack stepped into the living area and pulled the bedroom door shut behind him.

"I've got two uniforms on their way to pick you up."

"How bad?"

"Let's just say you'll want to let Abby sit this one out."

JACK HAD WOKEN Abby, breaking the news to her gently. One uniformed officer had stayed at the inn, standing guard outside their suite. Sharron Segroves had agreed to sit with Abby, and had arrived bearing fresh coffee and a breakfast tray just as Jack and the second uniformed officer headed out.

Now Jack stood shoulder to shoulder with Tim Hayes, their shared resignation hanging heavy in the frigid winter air as they watched the investigative unit process the scene.

An early morning jogger had found Natalie's body, naked and wrapped in a fleece blanket bearing the imprint of a laughing Santa Claus. Still-intact store tags suggested the killer had purchased the blanket just for this use.

Jack knew what they'd find in the way of evidence. Nothing. Sure, they could question each and every cashier at the megastore from which the blanket had been bought, but assuming the killer had paid with cash, chances were slim anyone would remember a thing about him.

It was Christmas week, for crying out loud. Holiday shoppers didn't buy festive fleece blankets to wrap around murdered women, did they? Why would a cashier notice one person more than the next in the throng of frenzied shoppers?

It's better to give than to receive.

"Bastard." Jack's warm breath created a burst of steam, dissipating into the morning air.

The heavy, gray sky seemed to grow more menacing while he and Hayes stood their ground, waiting, watching.

"Got something." The technician processing Natalie's body waved and called out.

Jack and Hayes stood over him seconds later.

"Not sure what it is." The tech shook his head. "I've never seen anything like it."

But Jack had.

He flinched at the mutilated skin on Natalie's upper thigh.

"What do you think?" Hayes asked, his tone a mixture of anger and repulsion.

"Lips," Jack answered.

Their killer had escalated from sending snapshots of his old crimes to killing anew. Just in time for Christmas.

'Son of a bitch," Hayes said flatly. "Think this is your guy? Or my guy?"

"Looks like they're one and the same." Jack inhaled deeply of the frigid December air and shoved his hands deep inside his pocket. "Looks like his Christmas giving has begun."

"More like Christmas taking." Hayes turned to get out of the technician's way. "Damn shame."

Damn shame.

The words seemed too slight to sum up the tragic scene, the lifeless body of the young woman who just yesterday had chatted with Jack about her plans to travel north for the holidays to be with her family.

Damn shame.

For all of his years of experience, the overwhelming senselessness of murder still gripped Jack at every new crime scene. He pictured the case board back at Hayes's office and wondered how quickly they'd add Natalie's picture to the victim column.

Then Jack wondered who was waiting at home for the visit from Natalie that would never happen. Who had wrapped Christmas presents for the pretty, young blonde who would never open another present again?

Then Jack fell back on the tried and true, grimacing even as he repeated the too simple phrase, in full agreement with Hayes.

"Damn shame."

A HEAVY SILENCE hung in Jack's rental car as he and Abby headed south toward Elkton, Maryland.

Jack had returned to the inn expecting Abby to be inconsolable. Instead, he'd found her showered, dressed and armed with a mapped list of every hotel in the Elkton, Maryland, area.

Her reaction to the discovery of Natalie's body shouldn't

have surprised him. She was a woman of action—
mined to help Jack and stop a killer from striking aga.

"Another ten minutes should do it." Jack could se
nothing more of Abby than the line of her jaw. She'd turned
to look out her window at the start of their drive and she
hadn't shifted positions since.

He recognized the posture, recognized the visible manifestation of defeat, grief and guilt.

"Not your fault," he said softly.

"Don't start with me, Jack. Not now."

The edge to Abby's voice was sharper than he'd expected, yet he was glad to hear the heat of anger tossed into
her mix of emotions.

She'd survive. Of that, Jack had no doubt.

"When Emma died, I blamed myself for months."

His admission did the trick. Abby turned to face him,
pale brows drawn together, a slight frown marring her
beautiful features.

"You've blamed yourself for years, Jack. You're blam-
ing yourself right now, aren't you?"

Of course he was. How could he not?

Jack nodded. "I'd like to tell you that time heals all
wounds, but I've always found that line to be a load of crap."

He sneaked a glimpse at her, taking his eyes from the
road for a split second, long enough to see the shimmer of
moisture welling at the line of her lower lashes.

"Thanks." She tipped her head back against the seat,
then dropped her focus to the map she'd prepared. "No one
could ever accuse you of sugar-coating things." She
pointed to the exit sign looming ahead. "This is us."

Jack and Hayes had come to the joint conclusion that
every possible lead had to be pursued immediately. No
more wondering what if, or theorizing about what might
happen next.

hypothetical had become the unthinkable.

They had a new victim on their hands and a killer on the loose.

Hayes had sent an officer to snap a photo of Dwayne Franklin with express instructions to get an identification from the photography shop as soon as possible. Sam Devine had been pulled in for questioning and a warrant was in the works for his phone and text messages.

Abby and Jack had planned a face-to-face hotel tour, complete with a stop-by-stop showing of Boone Shaw's photograph they hoped might unearth the information Max's phone call had not.

Hours later, they were just about to give up when an unmapped location caught Abby's eye.

"Pull over."

Jack slowed the car. "I thought we had another three blocks before our next turn."

Abby had twisted to look out the window behind her. "Bed-and-breakfasts, Jack. We never thought of smaller inns."

Sonofagun. Talk about an amateur mistake.

He pulled a U-turn, then eased the car into a parking space across the street from a turn-of-the-century home, complete with wide front porch and Welcome sign.

"Oh, sure," the older gentleman working the counter said with a nod of his head, "I can even tell you the guy's name. Boone. Never forget an unusual name like that. I'm a student of language, I'll have you know."

Abby nodded politely, but Jack wasted no time on niceties. They were racing against a ticking time bomb, and if Jack had anything to do about it, they'd figure out exactly who Boone Shaw had been tracking before anyone else died.

"Did he leave a forwarding address?" Jack asked.

The older gentleman looked at Jack over the top of his reading glasses, his annoyance palpable. "He left more than that."

"How so?"

"Well, he left an unpaid bill and a room full of personal belongings I've got no use for."

Jack's pulse kicked up a notch.

"Went out one day and never came back." The manager shrugged. "I suppose you'll be wanting to see his things, right? Like one of those crime shows on television?"

Jack spotted the twinkle in the man's eyes and played into the role. "You'd be doing our investigation a great service, sir."

"Got everything boxed up in the back. Follow me."

But after an exhaustive review of the box contents, Abby and Jack hadn't learned anything other than the name of the painkillers Boone Shaw took to ease his suffering and his preferred sock color.

They found no camera, no film and worst of all, no notes.

The manager promised to call if he thought of anything else, and Jack and Abby headed back toward Wilmington, hoping one of the other search angles had borne more fruit.

A dark, raw night had settled thoroughly over the region by the time they began their drive back, the atmosphere outside perfectly matching the mood inside their car.

Jack's cell rang just minutes south of the city.

With any luck at all, they were about to catch a break.

Heaven knew they needed one.

THE CHRISTMAS CONFESSOR moved stealthily through the apartment as if he'd been there countless times before. He laughed to himself as he took in the decorations, the framed photographs, all perfectly placed, perfectly planned, with no consideration given to how easily they could all be taken away…or destroyed.

The sound of water drifted into the apartment from the end of a hallway and he decided to wait, lowering himself to an overstuffed chair upholstered in an annoying pink-and-white garden-print fabric. Too old for a woman so young. Or on the other hand—he laughed—perfectly appropriate for someone at the end of her life. Whether she knew it or not.

He reached for the remote, feeling a surge of power as he gripped the object in his gloved hand. He powered on the television and chose the late-night news, smiling as the talking heads mentioned the mysterious appearance of postcards from someone dubbed the Christmas Confessor and the body of a young woman found in Rockford Park.

"Idiots," he murmured under his breath.

The media might think themselves brilliant for adopting the season-appropriate nickname, but they'd never find him. He did enjoy the attention, he had to admit. And why not? He was good at what he did.

Very good.

After all, he'd had a lot of practice.

And he was about to get even more.

The sound of water in the back of the apartment stopped abruptly and he muted the volume on the television, watching mindlessly as a female anchor did her best to report the day's sports.

What would it be like to snuff out the life of someone so well-known? She fit the profile. Aloof. Holier-than-thou. Female.

A door creaked at the other end of the apartment and he powered off the television, pushing to his feet.

He moved quickly to the doorway, pulling the cor
from his pocket.

Then he waited, rewarded before long by the sound of the woman's off-key singing filtering down the hall as she approached.

In one swift motion he brought the cord over her head and around her throat as she moved past him. Her body tensed, her hands clawed at her throat, her fingers furiously dug at the cord now squeezing off her air supply.

And as he pushed her toward a large mirror on the wall, her terrified gaze found his, and he smiled.

The light of recognition and horror in her eyes filled him with a satisfaction even more deep and pure than his earlier murders had brought.

After all, Gina Grasso was about to take her last breath, live her last moment, think her last thought.

And the Christmas Confessor wanted to make sure his was the last face she saw.

Chapter Fourteen

"She's not answering either phone." Abby did her best to keep her fear and anxiety at bay, yet she couldn't deny the way her pulse rushed through her veins, kicked to a frenzy the moment Jack relayed the purpose of Devine's call.

They'd been less than five minutes south of Wilmington when the reporter had phoned Jack.

He'd gotten another message, this one on his hotel voice mail, leaving only a street address. A street address Abby knew as well as she knew her own.

Gina's.

"Do you think Devine's making this one up?" she asked, hope flickering then fading inside her.

Jack looked away momentarily, as if testing out the weight of her question. When he snapped his dark gaze back to Abby, he reached for her hand. "I'm calling Hayes. He can get there faster than we can."

"Do you still think Devine faked the third postcard?"

Jack nodded. "But I think the Confessor liked what Devine did. He's reaching out to him now. I believe he's telling the truth."

As much as Abby didn't want to give voice to her next thought, she felt compelled to do so. "What if we're already too late?"

Jack squeezed her hand, keeping her fingers firmly anchored inside his own. The kind gesture didn't go unnoticed or unappreciated. "We'll keep trying to reach her until we find her."

Yet the moment they reached Gina's apartment, Jack knew they were already too late.

The door to Gina's apartment sat slightly ajar, no more than an inch or two, but enough to let Jack know something was amiss. Once inside, reality pushed at the perimeter of his awareness.

Furniture visibly askew.

A mirror knocked from the wall and cracked.

The imperceptible presence of death, so familiar and yet so foreign each time he experienced the sensation. An eerie calm that was too still, too quiet, too devoid of life.

"Jack?" Abby moved to push past him, but he grabbed her arm, pulling her back and behind him.

They'd beaten the police somehow, and the last thing he wanted was for Abby to come face-to-face with her best friend's body...or the killer. "Stay here."

"Gina?" Abby's cry shattered the unnatural silence of the apartment.

Something creaked to the right and down the hallway and for a split second, Jack hoped they might not be too late.

Sam Devine emerged from a back bedroom, hand clasped over his mouth, face so pale he'd taken on a greenish hue.

Anger seethed inside Jack. "What in the hell are you doing here?"

But Devine never answered. He managed only to shake his head before he rushed into a small bathroom, the noise of his retching reaching them a moment later.

"Gina?" Abby cried out again just as footfalls pounded down the hall.

Tim Hayes's features shifted and tightened the moment he crossed the threshold, having no doubt taken the same visual inventory Jack had. His stare locked with Jack's. "How the hell did you two get here first?"

But Jack said nothing, reaching instead for Abby, wanting to protect her from this place, from whatever sight had evoked Devine's reaction, wanting to take her away forever.

"Bad?" Hayes asked.

Jack nodded. "We haven't gone back. Haven't touched anything, but Devine's in the bathroom."

"Devine?" Rage tangled with Hayes's disbelieving tone.

Jack nodded toward the bathroom door just as more retching sounded.

"So much for preserving the evidence trail," Hayes muttered.

Abby pulled against Jack, freeing her arm from his grasp. She broke free and raced down the hall ahead of the officers who had arrived on Hayes's heels.

"Abby!" Jack cried out, taking off in a sprint, wanting to spare her from the horror he knew waited at the end of the hall.

But by the time he reached her, he was too late.

Abby stood frozen in the doorway to Gina's bedroom. Gina lay sprawled naked across her bed, the cord still wrapped around her lifeless neck.

A card sat on her stomach, a black-and-white snapshot of Gina, laughing, a cruel juxtaposition of life to death.

The stench of burnt flesh registered just as Abby let loose with an eardrum splitting scream.

Jack pulled her into his arms, spinning her away from the sight of her best friend's body, murmuring soothing words of empty promises in her ears.

"He won't get away with this. We'll get him."

But would they? Would they ever stop the monste who'd come back to life here and now? In the days before Christmas? In the sleepy city of Wilmington, Delaware?

None of it made any sense. None of it.

The sound of Hayes telling one of the uniformed officers to hold Devine for questioning burst through the sense of numbness pervading Jack's every faculty. Hadn't he just seen Gina two days ago? Laughing. Alive.

In his arms, Abby sobbed, her screams now silent, her pain palpable. Another loss. Another tragic death. How many would she have to endure before Jack found this bastard and made him stop?

Devine.

Devine had known Gina was about to be murdered. He'd been here first. Had he wrung the life from her body himself? How far was the man willing to go to create a headline?

Jack broke away from Abby, slamming his full body weight into Devine as the reporter emerged from the bathroom, wiping his face with a washcloth. The force of Jack's assault knocked Devine backward into a shelving unit.

"You sonofabitch."

A crystal vase hit the floor and exploded. Then a frame slid sideways, also hitting the floor and shattering with a crash.

"I didn't kill her. I found her like this. I swear." Devine's voice was that of a scared, little boy. "I must have interrupted him. I never expected to find her here. He usually takes the bodies outside. To a park." He was babbling now, fear and shock tangling in his features.

"What did you expect to find?" Jack asked.

Devine shook his head. "I don't know. Maybe he was trying to set me up."

Jack couldn't care less. As far as he was concerned, Devine's article had kicked the killer into high gear. Two bodies in one day were two bodies too many. End of story.

Three faces stared back from the photo beneath the pulverized glass.

"You planted the Bricken postcard?" Jack asked.

Devine nodded. "I thought the cards were some sort of game. I wanted to build it into something more." He broke down sobbing.

"You expect us to believe that's all you did?" Hayes spoke from behind Jack.

"I never meant for anyone else to die." Devine hung his head, his body sagging beneath the weight of his confession.

Jack shoved the reporter aside, into the clutches of a uniformed officer.

Hayes reached for Jack's shoulder, offering a steadying support, locking stares until Jack reigned in his fury and got himself under control.

Jack's focus fell to the floor, landing on the shattered frame, the exposed photo.

Vicki. Gina. Abby.

The same shot Abby proudly displayed in her apartment.

Three friends for life. Alive. Happy. Together.

"And then there was one," the crime scene technician called out from the bedroom, where he'd begun processing the scene.

"Say again," Hayes called out.

"The card," the tech answered. "That's the message on the back. 'And then there was one.'"

Jack lifted his gaze from the photo of the three friends to Abby's frightened and shocked face.

And then there was one.

Jack Grant planned to do whatever it took to keep it that way.

ABBY SANK INTO her favorite chair and shut her eyes, w
ing away the shock and the horror, the loss and the eme
tional anguish of finding Gina brutally murdered, her body
stripped naked and branded like a slab of meat.

After they'd finished with the police, Abby had asked
Jack to take her home—home to her apartment, to the
familiar, to memories of happier times. Much to her
surprise, he'd agreed.

Yet nothing about the familiar of her apartment could
wash away the images of Gina's brutal murder.

She'd been strangled, sexually assaulted and posed.

And then there was the postcard.

"Drink this." Jack's deep voice eased into Abby's consciousness, grounding her momentarily with his unwaver-
ing strength.

She opened her eyes, studied the steaming cup of what
looked like tea in his hand and shook her head. "Can't."

He took one of her hands, tucked the warm cup inside
then positioned her other hand to cradle the mug. "Try."

He dropped to his knees in front of her, his eyes display-
ing a concern so genuine it stole Abby's breath.

"Is this because of me?" She voiced the question even
though she'd been doing her best to shove the thought
deep down inside her mind.

"None of this is your fault." Jack reached to brush a
strand of her hair behind her ear. He let his fingers linger
against her cheek, his touch intimate and unexpected.

Abby didn't fight the contact, didn't shift away. If anything, she leaned into his strength and his warmth, hungry
for his reassurance that everything would be all right.
Praying for him to tell her Gina was alive and well. That
today had been nothing more than a bad dream.

But she knew better.

Warm tears stung at the back of her eyelids.

Abby had fought against crying since the moment they'd stormed into Gina's apartment. Now she could no longer fight the need to cry, the need to release her pent-up grief and anger.

Her body went limp, as if she'd lost the will to fight against everything—her tears, the truth, the Christmas Confessor.

"Why?" She managed only a tired whisper, ashamed of the self-pity she heard in her voice, but speaking the words just the same. "Why Don't Say a Word? Why Natalie? Why Gina? What did I do to draw him to us?"

Jack brought his face close to hers, forcing her to meet his stare, to look at him as he answered her. "He's a madman, Abby. You can't force rationality on a madman."

"Was it the *People* feature?"

Robert had warned her against the publicity. He'd accused her of losing focus on what really mattered—their loyal readers, the loyal postcard senders.

He'd accused her of wanting the limelight, when nothing could have been further from the truth.

But now...now the limelight was so bright Abby felt blinded.

Jack frowned, the move creasing his forehead. "He might have seen an opportunity. Who knows?"

But Abby suddenly focused on a more frightening thought. "What if this had nothing to do with the article?"

Jack remained silent, studying her carefully, his brows drawing closer together.

"I think he knows me." Abby whispered the words and what little emotional control she had left broke.

Jack plucked the cup of tea from her hands, set it aside and pulled her into his arms in one motion. Sobs wracked

her body as he held her, cradling her in his lap, stro
her hair, murmuring soothing words against the top of
head.

When his mouth found hers, she didn't fight him,
relaxing into his kiss, into the sensation of his lips on hers,
his tongue tasting, exploring, igniting the simmering heat
inside her she could no longer ignore.

The need to lose herself with Jack pushed aside all of
her fears and doubts, her questions, her anxieties. For a
moment, she thought she might be able to hide from the
world with Jack, lost in his loving embrace.

Then he broke contact, standing and walking across the
room, leaving her colder than she'd been a few moments
before.

WHAT IN THE hell was he doing? What was he thinking?

Jack forced himself to pull away from Abby, the soft
curves of her body and the sweet taste of her mouth.

The woman had just lost her closest friend and was
more than likely next on the killer's hit list and here he was,
acting like a sex-crazed animal.

Sure, stress could do strange things to people, but Abby
deserved better. Abby deserved his strength and his
respect, not his sexual advances.

"Sorry." He spoke the apology gruffly as he moved
away, putting as much distance between them as Abby's
living room would allow.

Hot color marred Abby's fair cheeks.

Embarrassment? Desire?

He shook the question out of his mind.

The Christmas Confessor was moving closer and closer,
escalating with each murder, and yet Jack had no earthly
idea of who the man was.

There wasn't time to pursue the attraction between him

Abby. There wasn't time to seek comfort in each other's arms, to make love with abandon if only for the moments of escape and pleasure their joining would provide.

The scene inside Gina's home confirmed that Shaw had not been her killer. No man riddled and weakened by cancer was capable of the violence they'd witnessed tonight.

Whoever had killed Gina had left her posed inside her apartment, breaking the usual pattern of taking the body to a public park. Chances were better than good that Sam Devine had interrupted the killer's routine. But then, the killer himself had allegedly called Devine, luring him to the address.

Detective Hayes had confirmed the muffled message on Devine's hotel voice mail, the caller's voice unrecognizable.

Why draw Devine and the authorities to the scene of the crime so quickly? Why?

What the hell was going on?

Jack needed to know who Shaw had been tracking. Find that name and they might have a prayer of stopping the killer before he killed again.

If only Shaw's personal belongings had yielded a clue, a name, a face. Anything.

I think he knows me.

Abby's words teased at the base of Jack's brain even as they sent a fresh wave of urgency through him. He'd thought the same thing himself a time or two since this journey had begun.

Could the killer be someone Abby knew?

Was familiarity the unknown factor that had triggered the first postcard? And what had set off the new Christmas killing spree after eleven years?

Had it been planned all along? Or had Devine's feat— article pushed the Confessor to his breaking point?

The targets were growing more personal. Natalie. Gina.

But was that because what had started as a card sent to a random Web site for publicity had become a personal crusade in response to Abby's blogs? Or had the killer known Abby all along?

Jack ran the list of suspects through his mind once again and focused, shutting out the fact he'd just kissed Abby and longed to do so much more.

Boone Shaw. Sam Devine. Dwayne Franklin.

Each fit in some way and not in others.

What was Jack missing?

Abby murmured something incoherent and Jack turned to study her. She met his gaze with moist eyes, red-rimmed with grief and shock and fear.

"Say again?" He urged her, keeping his voice even, his tone gentle even as possible motives, next steps and scenarios spiraled through his brain.

"I made him mad," Abby said, her throat working and her features smoothing, recovering from her crying jag and the shock of his kiss.

"Mad?"

"I called him a crank." She pushed herself taller in the chair, sitting up straight as if new determination had infused her with strength. "I made him mad."

Jack thought back to the call from Melinda Simmons's father and the night Jack had first read Abby's blog. He hadn't read that first blog again, but probably should have.

What if Abby's words *had* triggered the killer to kill anew? What if he'd only meant to send the cards? To resurrect his notoriety?

Whoever the killer was, he was all about control. Of that, there was no doubt. Yet, Abby had called him a crank, believing him to be a murderer. In effect, she'd publicly humiliated the man.

Hell, Abby's first response had made Jack angry back when he'd read it. What sort of an effect would it have had on the postcard sender himself?

Had the killer interpreted Abby's words as a dare? Had he felt the need to prove himself? Again. And again.

Jack had to start over from the beginning. He had to make sure he hadn't missed anything. And he had to read everything Abby had written through the killer's eyes, looking for triggers. Searching for clues.

"Jack?"

Jack had been so deep into his line of thought he hadn't heard a thing Abby had said.

He closed the space between them and took Abby's hand. "Let's go."

"Where?"

"Back to the inn. I need to reread your blogs."

"I can pull them up on the computer here."

"No." Jack shook his head, steering her away from the chair and toward the door.

Suddenly, he needed Abby to be anywhere but here. He'd let himself become distracted by her emotions, by her pain. He shouldn't have let her come back to the apartment.

If the killer had zeroed in on Abby and her world, her apartment was just as familiar to him as it was to Abby. For all Jack knew, the killer was waiting and watching, even now.

Jack needed to move Abby back to the inn, back to safety, and he needed to make sure no one followed them.

"The picture's gone."

Jack followed the line of Abby's focus, noting the empty spot on the shelf where the photo of the three friends had sat. "Are you sure you didn't move it?"

She frowned, shaking her head.

If someone had been inside her apartment and had taken the print, that was all the more reason to get Abby out of here, now.

He pulled her toward the door. "Move."

"Jack…" Confusion swam in her stare.

"No arguments, Abby."

He rushed her out the door, down the sidewalk and into the car.

Jack needed Abby tucked away somewhere safe.

Now.

HE WATCHED THEM move toward the car. The detective, so far out of his territory it wasn't funny, reaching toward Abby's back, then hesitating, as if knowing he had no right to be there, no right to touch her.

Anger churned in the Confessor's stomach, sending heat pumping through his veins along with a renewed determination to see through every step of his plan, every piece of his puzzle.

He'd stayed ahead of the detective and his paltry investigative skills so far.

Why should finishing the work he'd set out to do be any different?

Hell, the media had given him so much coverage lately, he was more famous now than he'd ever been.

The Christmas Confessor.

He laughed.

He'd make Abby Conroy pay for ignoring him, just as he'd made the other women pay. Every last one of them.

By the time Christmas arrived this year, no one would ever ignore him again.

And Christmas *was* coming.

nere was nothing more the Confessor loved than the
y of giving…over and over and over again.

"Ho, ho, ho," he muttered into the cold night air seeping
in through the open driver's side window.

The taillights of the detective's rental car illuminated as
the sedan eased away from the curb and headed down the
street.

Then the Confessor cranked on the ignition of his own
car, pulled away from the curb, and followed.

Chapter Fifteen

Abby didn't ask Jack to stay with her that night. Instead, she paced the small bedroom, from end to end, back and forth and back again.

She'd racked her brain trying to remember what she'd done with the photo of Vicki and Gina and herself. Tears threatened again and she blinked them back. She was done crying.

Jack was right. They were out of time. The only thing Abby had time for now was thinking. She was missing something and she knew it. Somewhere buried in her brain was a memory, a face, a word that would snap all of the puzzle pieces together.

She knew the killer.

She'd never been more sure of anything.

Sure, the man might not be a good friend, but at some point, they'd met. The attacks were too personal for him to be a stranger angered because he'd sent a postcard and she'd called him a crank.

Could Dwayne be the Christmas Confessor?

She pictured his outburst, his rare display of violence, but shoved the idea out of her head. It wasn't possible. It couldn't be.

he knew her well enough, certainly, and he followed the
og, but a killer?

There had to be someone else.

"Think, Abby. Think."

When she grew weary of pacing, she sat down on the
bed. Fatigue pushed at the edges of her consciousness, but
she fought against it, not wanting to sleep, not wanting to
do anything but solve the puzzle.

No, that was a lie.

She'd wanted something far different from sleep earlier.

She'd wanted Jack, but he'd pushed her away. He'd
given her glimpses of the emotion lurking beneath his
tough shell and she'd thought perhaps she'd finally broken
through.

For a fleeting moment, she'd fantasized about loving
him and being loved in return. Then he'd caught himself,
shut down his heart and pushed her away.

His expression and body language had shifted so
abruptly from sensual and caring to the all-business,
intense detective who had first shown up at the office that
he'd left her speechless.

Part of her had wanted to pound her fists against his
chest. Part of her had wanted to dare him to feel something.
To be with her.

But instead, she'd had her own shut down, isolating
herself, in the bedroom. Alone.

Alone.

She hated the word, but it was her reality. Abby was
alone now. Robert was the only friend she had left.

She looked at the clock and decided it was too late to
call him, even though she knew he wouldn't mind the in-
trusion into his sleep. She wondered if he knew about Gina.

Then Abby let herself lean back against the pile of
pillows. She'd shut her eyes for just a minute, then she'd

be recharged, ready to figure out what in the hell was going on.

She blinked her eyes shut, amazed at how heavy her lids felt.

Then she drifted, telling herself she'd rest only for a minute.

A minute.

Then Abby slipped into a deep, exhausted sleep.

JACK SPENT THE next day fielding calls, working through the pieces of the puzzle, waiting for Abby to wake up.

He'd heard her pacing during the night, until the wee hours of the morning. He'd checked on her a bit after four-thirty in the morning and had found her sound asleep.

He'd tucked her under the covers, regretting his decision to push her away even as he let his hand linger along the soft curve of her cheek.

She'd lost a coworker and her best friend in one day.

Jack couldn't help but wonder how much more she'd be able to take before she broke.

The winter sun was already beginning to set, dinnertime was approaching and Abby still hadn't awakened. Jack had checked on her again, as had Sharron Segroves. She appeared fine, other than being completely exhausted emotionally and physically.

Sleep was what her body needed, what Abby needed, in order to face the long road of grief and recovery ahead.

Jack's cell rang and he grabbed it on the first ring, not wanting the shrill noise to wake Abby.

"Two things." Tim Hayes's voice traveled across the line. "Got the positive ID on your favorite guy."

"Franklin?"

"You bet. Shop owner recognized his photo instantly. There's just one problem. We can't seem to find Franklin."

"Did you search his place?"

"Don't want to compromise evidence. Waiting on a warrant."

Another damned warrant. Jack groaned inwardly.

"We did, however, get the warrant on Devine," Hayes said. "Thought you might like to ride along."

"Wouldn't miss it."

"I'm headed over to his hotel in about an hour."

"I'll meet you at the station. Can I get an officer over here for Abby?" He'd been worried for her safety before, but now that he knew Dwayne Franklin was in the wind, he wanted someone with Abby at all times.

"Consider it done."

Perfect. An hour would give Jack time to eat and head out. And with a uniformed officer in place with Abby, he would know she was safe.

With any luck at all, by the time Abby awoke from her slumber, Jack would be able to tell her they were one step closer to ending the nightmare.

HE WATCHED HIS target, letting his mind wander while he waited to make his move.

The Confessor knew his past and his present were beneficial to some people—people who prayed on the curiosity of the public. People who craved the written word, who expressed themselves at the expense of their subjects.

There were some people, like Abby Conroy, who felt words could heal, words could soothe.

The Confessor knew the only thing words were good for were leaving messages.

And he knew the content of his next message just as surely as he knew exactly how he was going to take the next victim's life.

Actions.

Those were the things that really mattered, the thr.
that could alter the path of a life…or end it.

There was nothing like watching the life drain out of a
victim's face. Nothing like watching the glow of living
leave their eyes, their flesh, their strength.

Similarly, there was nothing like the satisfaction of
knowing a job had been well done. Nothing like leaving
his mark, a message…yes…but also an action.

The Confessor prided himself on actions of control, of
power, a reminder to others to watch and listen and learn.

The truth was no one knew when the Confessor would
act next, kill next, mark next.

He patted his pocket, feeling the stiffness of the postcard.
This one's for you.

The card was ready to be delivered, complete with message and photograph.

There was just one detail to be taken care of first. One
life to be ended.

He watched the target move behind the window of the
hotel room, his next victim's silhouette clear and sharp
against the room's sheer curtains.

It never ceased to amaze the Confessor how surprised
each of his victims were to see him. As if they never
imagined someone might want them dead.

The Confessor pulled on his gloves and stepped forward, sure in his movement, his purpose.

Action.

Then words.

He was about to kill as he'd never killed before, yet he
had no second thoughts, no doubts.

After all, he was a man with a purpose. A man with a
message.

And the action he was about to take would surely drive
that message home.

 action.

Then words.

Life really was simple if only people would take the time to pay attention.

ABBY COULDN'T BELIEVE she'd slept all day, and once she'd found Jack's note she'd done two things.

Ask the officer to move to a more discreet post and then go eat.

Sharron and Harold had said they'd help keep an eye out for strangers, and Abby had returned to the room, waiting for Jack to check in.

The officer had assured Abby he could watch the entrance to her room as effectively from his cruiser as he could from the door. Abby had thanked him, happy to have the security of his presence, but not wanting to do anything to jeopardize the inn's holiday business. Surely an armed officer standing guard didn't do much to keep the Christmas spirit alive.

Abby felt safe, and safe was something she hadn't felt since she found the postcard of herself on her kitchen window.

A chill danced down her spine. Every other postcard coincided with a murder. Why not hers? Had Jack's presence in her home saved her life?

She groaned and shook her head. Her life had forever changed during the past few days. Natalie and Gina were gone, lost to the ruthlessness of a madman. Don't Say a Word was forever tainted. If she were smart, she'd shut down the site forever.

But what about the true confessors? The growing numbers of postcard senders for whom confession truly was good for the soul? The estranged siblings for whom it was too late to say goodbye. The parent and child who would

never be able to say they were sorry. The child who
cheated her way through college, deceiving everyone s
knew.

Abby wasn't saying that their secrets were excusable,
but for the most part, they were forgivable.

But not the Christmas Confessor.

His sins were neither excusable nor forgivable.

Anger swelled inside her and a sudden compulsion to
write overcame her. Words and phrases filled her mind and
she scrambled to get to her laptop, pressing the button to
bring the computer out of standby.

The moment her word processing screen blinked to life,
she began to type, words filling the screen, fingers flying
on the keyboard.

She wasn't about to let some faceless killer intimidate
her or shut down her site. She'd be damned if she'd sit idly
by and not fight back. Jack knew how to investigate, how
to track criminals, how to process facts and evidence.
Abby knew how to write, how to express herself, how to
blog.

And so she wrote, rereading the piece when she was
done and changing not a single word. Her anger and determination and grief were there for anyone and everyone
to read.

She went through the necessary steps to get online and
into the management area for her Web site, then she hit
Publish, hoping the words she'd written might convince a
madman to stop, but knowing they'd probably achieve
nothing at all, nothing but making herself feel heard. Right
now feeling heard was the first step to taking her life back.

Abby posted the blog, gave it one more read to make
sure she hadn't missed any typos, then sat back against the
desk's chair. Satisfaction filled her, the feeling fleeting.
Reality pushed at the edges of her sense of accomplish-

, a reminder that Natalie was gone, Gina had been ...rdered, and their killer walked free regardless of how ...oundly Abby had condemned his actions, his thinking, his right to go on breathing.

The sound of the suite's entrance door clicking shut startled her from her thoughts.

"Jack?"

No answer.

A floorboard creaked and Abby's chest constricted. She scanned the surfaces of her room, looking for her cell phone, but not spotting it anywhere. She lifted the desk's phone receiver very carefully, just as another floorboard creaked, this one much closer to the entryway to her room.

"Jack?" she asked again, her mind racing as she searched for the button for the front desk and pushed out of the chair, moving toward the wall and away from the door.

"Abby?"

The sound of her name startled her, but the voice which spoke left her speechless.

Dwayne.

He cleared the doorway in one step, one arm behind his back, hiding…what?

Bright color flushed his cheeks and his eyes shone like those of a man possessed.

Had Jack been right all along? Was her neighbor a monster? A killer capable of taking the lives of Gina and Natalie and countless others?

"I missed you," he said flatly, as if it were normal for him to have tracked her here and found his way into her locked hotel room.

Abby's pulse raced so quickly the blood rushed in her ears. "How did you get in?"

"Were you calling someone?" Dwayne ignored her

question, nodded to the receiver in her hand, still keepi.
his own hand behind his back.

Abby shook her head. "Detective Grant wanted to let
me know he'd be here in five minutes."

Dwayne's eyebrows lifted. "I didn't hear the phone
ring."

Abby shrugged, unable to counter that particular observation.

Dwayne's expression shifted from gentle to ice-cold in
the blink of an eye. "Hang up."

"He already hung up," Abby lied.

"Hang up," he repeated.

Abby replaced the receiver without looking, refusing to
take her eyes from Dwayne and whatever it was he held
behind his back.

"How did you find me, Dwayne?"

"I followed you."

Jack had been right. They never should have gone back
to her apartment after they left the scene of Gina's murder.
Yet that had been almost twenty-four hours ago.

"From where?" she asked, trying to keep her tone non-
threatening.

"Your house. Where you belong." Dwayne's features
darkened, and his tone dropped low and intent. "It's not
right for you to be here…with him."

"He's protecting me, Dwayne."

Dwayne patted his chest with his empty hand, taking
two steps toward Abby. "I protect you."

Abby backed away from him instinctively, stopping
only when her back hit the curtained window behind her.

"I know you do, Dwayne. And I appreciate that, but
Jack's a police officer. He's keeping me safe while he in-
vestigates the man who's sending the postcards."

Dwayne took another step toward her, and Abby

anned the room for any object she could use as weapon of defense. Nothing. The only possible weapon—a reading lamp—sat too far away to reach.

"You need to come home with me, Abby. Where you belong."

Dwayne moved closer, just as Abby's cell phone rang from the suite's sitting room.

Then Dwayne made his move, swinging his concealed arm out from behind his back.

JACK DIALED ABBY'S cell as he pulled into the parking lot. When she didn't answer his mind began to run the possibilities. She was taking a shower, on another call, or the unthinkable had happened.

Yet, the unthinkable had already happened once today, and Jack wanted to be the one to tell Abby.

He'd spent the last hour debriefing with Hayes and his department.

Sam Devine had been murdered. They'd found him in his hotel room, strangled in the same manner as Natalie and Gina, yet he'd been fully clothed and unbranded.

His murder had served a purpose, not a need.

The killer had left behind a card. A photo of Abby taken outside Gina's apartment building, as if the killer intended to use Devine exactly as Devine had used him.

To tell a story.

This one's for you.

Had the killer taken Devine's life as a favor to Abby? Or as a favor to the investigators on the case?

The local police hadn't had any luck as far as originating numbers went for both Devine's text and voice mail messages. Both calls traced back to city payphones, located at opposite ends of the city. Local? Yes. Helpful investigative information? Not exactly.

Devine's luck had run out. The guy would no doubt lo
the headline his murder would inspire, but Jack was sure
he'd rather be remembered for his name in the byline
instead of the subject line.

Jack scanned the parking lot. And frowned when he
spotted the officer's silhouette, sitting in the driver's seat
of the police cruiser.

Jack launched himself from his car and crossed the lot,
pounding on the officer's window.

"What the hell are you doing here instead of by her
door?"

"She insisted," the officer answered.

"And you listened?"

Unbelievable.

Jack hurried across the lot, dialing Abby's cell phone
as he moved.

Sharron Segroves stood searching one of her service
carts, unaware of Jack's approach.

"Evening," he said, startling her. "How is she?"

Sharron twisted up her face. "That is one stubborn
young woman. Harold and I have been keeping an eye on
her room. No one in or out."

Jack supposed that was some sort of comfort, but it
didn't mean something hadn't gone wrong, it didn't mean
the gnawing pit of dread at the base of Jack's stomach had
exploded to life for no reason.

Sharron Segroves returned her focus to her cart, flipping
through the fresh towels she delivered each evening.

"Something wrong?" Jack asked, shifting his own focus
to the windows of his suite. One silhouette moved against
the window. Abby was in her bedroom. But why was she
standing pressed to the window?

"I can't seem to find the master key," Segroves said dis-
tractedly. "I can't imagine where I put it."

But as a second silhouette moved into view inside Abby's room, Jack knew exactly what had happened to the key. He sprang into motion and tossed Sharron his phone. "Call 9-1-1. Now."

He never heard Sharron Segroves's response.

He heard nothing but Abby. Screaming.

DWAYNE SWUNG HIS concealed arm forward and Abby launched herself into motion, moving sideways. She was boxing herself into a corner, but had no other way of keeping space between her and the steadily approaching Dwayne Franklin.

Dwayne clutched a stack of papers in his fist. Envelopes. Abby blinked.

"You forgot your mail." He scowled. "There's no need to scream at me."

Abby's head spun with disbelief. "You followed me to give me my mail?"

Franklin's eyes went cold, void of expression. "It upsets me when you forget your mail. What if someone needs you?"

Abby's mouth went bone dry. She tried to swallow, but couldn't. Where in the hell was Jack?

As if on cue, the Arizona detective crashed into the suite, dipping his shoulder as he charged Dwayne, dropping the other man to the floor in one swift move.

"Get out," Jack barked at Abby. "Move to the other room. Now!"

She scrambled over the bed, not questioning, just doing as Jack wanted.

"I brought her mail," Dwayne mumbled as Jack pulled the big man's hands and feet up behind him, holding him immobile as sirens wailed in the distance, drawing steadily nearer.

"He brought my mail." Abby realized how inane words sounded, but suddenly every word sounded inane, every reality surreal. What in the hell had just happened?

"He taped the card to your window, Abby." Jack leaned close to snarl in Dwayne's ear. "I want to know why."

"Because I love her." Dwayne's voice had gone soft, the voice of a frightened child.

"Jack." Abby stayed on the other side of the doorway, wanting to stay out of Jack's way. "He's not the killer. I know he's not."

"No." Jack shook his head. "I think he'd just a stalker and you're his lucky victim." He looked at Abby, pinning her with a glare so angry she sucked in a breath. "Devine's been murdered, so it appears we're out of options."

Abby staggered backward. "Murdered?"

Jack nodded. "And the Confessor left another card."

"Who?" Abby regretted the question even as she asked it. Suddenly, she didn't want to know.

"You, Abby." Jack's anger morphed to concern. "You."

Chapter Sixteen

The search of Dwayne Franklin's apartment turned up nothing that tied him to the murders. No cord. No branding tool. Nothing but evidence of a stalker's obsession with his victim—over two hundred black-and-white photographs plastered across Franklin's bedroom walls and ceiling.

All printed on the telltale specialty paper.

All taken from Franklin's side window, a perfect view of Abby's apartment and kitchen.

Jack had refused Abby's request to see the room. Seeing it had left him with an ice-cold chill in his veins. As far as he was concerned, Abby was better off not knowing what kind of madness had lived next door to her.

During the intake process, Franklin had admitted to living next door to Abby under an assumed name, living off of cash provided by his wealthy Massachusetts family. Turned out his family abhorred scandal, and Franklin's obsession with a woman outside of Natick hadn't fit the family plan. They'd paid off the victim and sent the disturbed son out of state...where he'd fixated on Abby.

Lucky her.

Franklin had followed Jack and Abby to the inn, waiting until he could make his move, lifting Sharron Segroves's master key and slipping past the officer on duty unnoticed. The officer had been reprimanded and assigned his desk until further notice.

Who knew what might have happened had Jack not arrived when he did.

Jack was so angry he was of a mind to head north with the sole purpose of giving Franklin's family a lecture in ethics, but he had more pressing commitments. Like keeping Abby alive.

They sat inside the break room at the precinct with Hayes and two other officers, talking about exactly how they planned to do just that.

"You've got to move her," Hayes said. "The inn location is compromised."

Abby squeezed her eyes shut, the lines of fatigue and stress evident once again, bracketing her pale eyes. "Why don't you just lock me up?"

Her sarcasm wasn't lost on Jack, but Hayes actually nodded as though he might consider the idea.

"What I'd like to do now is go to my office." Abby pushed to her feet as she spoke. "I'm sure that if Jack stays with me or one of you kind officers sits beside me, I'll be safe. I need a change of scenery and I need to *work*."

The urgency in her voice reached inside Jack and twisted his gut.

Hayes shot Jack an incredulous glare. "Is she kidding?"

Jack held out a hand just as his phone rang.

He read the display panel on his phone and straightened. The Elkton bed-and-breakfast.

"Yes, sir?" Jack pushed away from the table and stepped outside the room.

"Found something inside a drawer that I missed before."

Jack's blood pumped a bit more quickly. "Such as?"

"Looks like a family photo to me, but the one man is definitely your Mr. Boone Shaw."

amily?

"How many people in the photo sir?"

"Three." The line fell silent while the manager apparently admired the shot.

"Sir?" Jack urged.

"Looks to be the Mr. and Mrs. and their son."

But the Shaws hadn't had any children. Could this be the mystery person for whom Boone Shaw had traveled cross-country?

"Thought you might like to come on down and take a look," the manager continued.

Much as Jack would love to, he needed to stay close to Abby. She had a reckless light in her eye that suggested she was close to her breaking point. In his experience a crime victim either shut down or fought back.

Abby Conroy was definitely a candidate for the latter, and if she fought back against the Confessor, chances were she'd lose.

For all Jack knew, that was the reason she'd developed the sudden urge to get back to work. Maybe Abby thought she could draw the Confessor out, expose him and end his killing spree.

She was probably right. But was Jack willing to take that risk in order to get his man once and for all?

He refocused on his phone call.

How could he get his hands on the photograph and stay close to Abby?

"Do you have a fax machine, sir?"

"Surely do." Another pause. "I also have one of those printers that can scan in a picture and e-mail it, want me to try that?"

Bingo. Jack nodded, then realized the gentleman had no way of seeing him.

"I'm at the local precinct sir, let me get an e-ma
address for you to use."

"How exciting."

Jack had to smile at the enthusiasm in the manager's
voice. He could only hope the newly found piece of evidence would be worth the wait.

ABBY FELT AS though she was about to crawl out of her skin.

Frustration and determination tangled inside her. If the
Confessor wanted her so badly, let him come after her. Let
him put himself out in the open where Jack and the local
police could take care of him once and for all.

She'd go to the office. She'd let an officer go along with
her, protecting her every step of the way.

And she'd call Robert.

She needed to know he was safe. Needed to let him
know just how quickly things had escalated.

They were the only two friends left now, as surreal as
it was to think about Gina being gone.

Abby thought quickly about her parents, thankful they
were out of the country on their annual holiday cruise, but
knowing how devastated they'd be when they arrived home
to news of all that had happened during their absence.

She refocused, more determined than ever to put an
end to this mess.

They needed answers. The victims needed justice. And
Jack needed peace.

As far as Abby was concerned, she was the key to all
three.

The nightmare had started at Don't Say a Word. With
any luck at all, it would end there. Then Jack and the other
families would have closure. They'd finally have the justice
they'd been awaiting for the past eleven years.

Jack popped his head inside the room and gestured to Hayes.

"E-mail address?" Jack asked.

Hayes scribbled something on a scrap of paper and handed it to Jack. A moment later, Jack was back at the table, a hopeful light in his eye.

He reached across the table and squeezed Abby's hand. "The bed-and-breakfast manager found a photo."

"Of Shaw?" Abby straightened, feeling hopeful for the first time all day.

Jack nodded. "Shaw, his wife and a young man. Now we just have to hope the manager can figure out how to scan the image and e-mail it. He said he's never tried before."

Abby reached for Jack, her fingers brushing against his sleeve. "Let me go to the office. Send protection and I promise—" she held up a hand "—I will let the officer stick to me like glue. No arguments."

He searched her face before he answered. "You can't catch him by yourself, Abby."

Jack understood her better than she understood herself, Abby realized. The warning in his look rang crystal clear.

"I'm done waiting." Emotion choked her voice as she spoke.

Jack scrubbed a hand across his face, visibly torn between going with Abby and waiting for the photograph.

Jack turned to Hayes. "All right if I borrow one of your guys to go with Abby?"

Hayes nodded, pointing to the younger of the two officers. "Jones will stay with you."

"Thanks."

Abby headed toward the door and Jack followed, squeezing her elbow as she passed. "If Jones tells you to ~~r~~ out for any reason, you clear out. Understood?"

She thought about telling him she didn't appreciate h̄ tone of voice, but Abby knew Jack barked out orders because he cared about her.

Theirs might be a relationship born out of the pressures of the investigation and a chemistry neither could deny, but what they shared *was* a relationship.

And Abby couldn't help but wonder where it would lead if given a chance.

She touched her fingers lightly to his cheek. "Thanks. Call me as soon as you know something?"

He nodded, the hard lines of his face softening. "Will do. And I'll be there as soon as I can."

OUT OF HABIT, Abby headed straight for the kitchen and the coffeemaker as soon as officer Jones gave the office a walk-through. She and Jack had spent the most of the afternoon at the police precinct and the office had emptied out for the day.

"Be right back," she called out over her shoulder to the young officer who now stood guard at the door.

She shivered as she passed Natalie's desk, unable to wrap her brain around the fact she'd never see the young woman again. So many lives had shifted forever during the past few days. She could only hope the Christmas terror would soon end with the killer behind bars.

"Hey."

Robert's voice startled her just as she powered on the machine.

"Were you in the office?" Abby had called him on her way over, but had only gotten his voice mail.

He nodded. "Heard you come in, but I was on the phone with Gina's mother. I wanted to see what I could do to help with arrangements."

Abby winced. She'd been so wrapped up in her own world she hadn't called Mrs. Grasso to offer condolences.

"How are you holding up?" Robert's tone was more abrupt than usual, but she found solace in the friendship reflected in his eyes.

He pulled her into a hug and Abby welcomed her old friend's embrace.

"I was just about to put on coffee, unless you picked up extra on your way in today."

He usually did. Robert was reliable that way.

When he pushed her out to arm's length, the look of detachment in his gaze was one Abby had never seen there before. "You all right?"

He ignored her question, saying only, "You'd like that, wouldn't you?"

"What?" Her pulse quickened inexplicably.

Too much pressure, too many recent shocks to the system, no doubt. For both of them. Robert looked as shell-shocked as Abby felt.

"Coffee," he answered, his gaze darkening. "You'd like that if I brought you coffee. But do you ever bring me coffee?"

Abby turned to face him head-on. "Robert?" What was he talking about? She'd brought him coffee on countless occasions.

"You never say thank-you. You never say much at all, not unless it suits you in some way. You and Gina and Vicki were always like that."

Abby moved toward him, reaching for her friend's arm, shock sliding through her when he turned sharply away from her attempted touch.

Grief. He was reeling from the horrific shock of Gina's murder, surely.

"Let's go sit down."

But Robert had already stepped out of the kitchen, heading for their workspace.

Abby followed, but even as she did so, her insides

churned. What was going on? Where was the calm, lected Robert she knew so well?

As they headed back through the reception area toward their office, Abby realized Officer Jones was nowhere to be found.

"Did you see the officer who came over with me?"

A tight smile crossed Robert's face. "I suppose we'll have to hire you a bodyguard soon, right?"

She shook her head. "With any luck at all, this will all be over soon."

"Hopefully you'll get your wish."

Something darkened in Robert's gaze and Abby realized she wasn't the only one who'd lost a friend and a coworker this week. She wasn't the only one whose business had been terrorized by the Christmas Confessor.

Robert took a backward step and pointed to the door. "I did meet Officer Jones. He ran next door for doughnuts."

"Oh." Surprise and shock filtered through Abby. Not exactly a move she would have expected the young officer to make. Jack and Hayes would have his head.

Abby was struggling between forcing a smile for Robert and trying to process his rapid mood swings when she spotted a photo of her with Gina and Vicki sitting on Robert's desk.

Her photo.

The photo missing from her apartment.

"You have my picture."

Robert frowned, his features turning severe, rage glimmering in his eyes. "You didn't even thank me for fixing the glass."

"You were in my house?" She swallowed down the sudden tightness in her throat.

"So many times I've lost count. Some nights I stop by just to watch you sleep."

A wave of dizziness and shock crashed through Abby

e looked at Robert with new eyes, listened to him as
hearing him for the first time, and realized Jack's gut
about Robert might have been correct from the start.

Dread seized her gut and twisted. "Where is Officer
Jones?"

Robert stepped close, his tone and demeanor threatening. "Exactly where he needs to be."

JACK HAD THOUGHT the e-mail image would never come
through. The manager and his wife had made three attempts and after twenty minutes spent on the phone with
the precinct's computer whiz, the third image appeared in
Hayes's inbox.

The image had obviously been scanned from a worn
photograph, cracked and faded with age. The shot had
captured three people, just as the manager had described.

Boone Shaw stood with his arm around a woman Jack
imagined to be his wife. A third person—a young man
probably in his late teens or early twenties—stood slightly
to the side of Shaw, as if he weren't entirely comfortable
being included in the shot.

Then Jack noticed the similarity. The defiant set of the
young man's jaw. The narrowed eyes Jack had seen
recently…here…in Wilmington.

"Sonofa—"

Jack placed his fingers around the young man's image
to block his hair, almost shoulder-length in the photo.

The likeness was uncanny. And suddenly Jack had every
reason to believe his gut dislike of the man had been spot-on.

The memory of Abby's words rang through his mind.

*We've been together since grade school with the excep-
tion of the year after Robert's father died.*

How old was Robert Walker in the picture with the
Shaws? Seventeen? Eighteen?

Had he been in New Mexico at the time of the mu...

He snapped open his phone and called the bed-a...
breakfast manager, thanking the man for his help and h...
time.

"One other question?" A haze of urgency gripped Jack, sharpening his senses, his awareness of the fact Abby might be in grave danger even as he spoke. "Was there a date on that photo?"

"No," the older man said. "But it's the darnedest thing, we had to take it off of the card in order to get the computer to give us a good scan."

Jack reached for a nearby desk and gripped the corner. "Card?"

"Christmas card. The photo was glued to the front. Didn't I mention that?"

A split second later, Jack was in motion, racing for the exit. "It's Walker. It has to be Walker. And I just let her head to the office."

What a fool he'd been. And now he'd failed to protect Abby just as he'd failed to protect Emma.

Hayes scowled, holding his phone to his ear as he scrambled to catch up to Jack. "No answer."

"Jones?" Jack's sense that Abby's time was running out ratcheted to the next level.

Hayes nodded. "Not good."

"How far from here to there?" Jack asked.

"Fifteen minutes. Ten if we fly."

"Then we fly."

Jack broke into a dead sprint at the same moment Hayes called for backup.

As far as Jack was concerned, none of them would be able to cover the ground between the precinct and Abby's office fast enough.

And he'd let her walk right into the killer's web.

ᴜʟʟᴇᴅ ʜᴇʀ phone from her pocket, dialing Jack's
ɴᴀᴇʀ from heart. She needed him here, and she needed
ᴍ now.

"What are you doing?" Robert spun on her, slapping
away the phone with a force that shot the small object from
her hands.

Fury shone in his eyes. Had he gone mad?

"I was calling Jack." Abby dropped to her knees and
scrambled toward Robert's desk, reaching beneath a partially opened desk drawer for her phone. She could barely
make out the tiny square of metallic red beneath the bulk
of Robert's desk.

"Don't move."

The unforgiving tone of Robert's voice froze Abby to
the spot.

"He's a good man, Robert. He can help you. Let me call
him."

Robert answered with a shove, slamming Abby's shoulder into the sharp edge of the open desk drawer.

"I'm a good man, Abby. Pay attention to me." He patted
his chest. "Have you once asked me how I feel about everything that's happened?"

Abby's mouth had gone so dry she wasn't sure she'd be
able to form words, but she did. "How do you feel, Robert?"

He leaned close, the anger in his eyes morphing to
amusement. "I'm having the time of my life. You were
right, you know. Confession is good for the soul."

Raw fear tore at her insides, sending a shudder through
her entire body as she looked at him. "What are you talking
about, Robert?"

He laughed, the sound sharp and bitter. "I'm talking
about the fact I haven't had this much fun since I went to
stay with my Uncle Boone in New Mexico."

Abby rocked back on her heels, barely able to si⸺ Mexico?" She'd known he'd gone out west somew⸺ during high school, but New Mexico?

Robert blew out a disgusted breath. "My mother couldn't wait to be rid of me once my dad died, and Boone Shaw supposedly owed my dad for once saving his life or some bull like that. As I remember it, you barely knew I was gone. You and the girls were so wrapped up with your little popularity contests."

His words stung, but he was right. She had been self-absorbed back in high school, and she hadn't kept in touch during the time he was gone. But Boone Shaw? Robert had known Boone Shaw?

"You worked with him?" Her head swam. "Did you know the victims? Why didn't you say anything?"

Robert clucked his tongue. "You're typically not this obtuse, Abby. Honestly, I'm a bit disappointed."

She tried to remember exactly what Jack had said about the photo found in Boone Shaw's room. *Shaw, his wife and a young man.*

Robert? Had Robert been the person Shaw had traveled cross-country to find?

"What did you do, Robert?"

"To whom?"

He towered over her, his expression menacing. Abby reached for his desktop to pull herself to her feet. One file drawer sat partially open and she wrapped her fingers around the top of the drawer, seeking leverage to pull herself up.

An object shoved down between the vertical files stopped her heart cold.

A tool. Wooden handle. Metal point.

She'd never seen the object in Robert's possession in all of the times she'd gone into his desk for records or billing statements.

trying to decide if you deserve an eye…or a pair
s. Maybe both."

Robert's voice dropped so low and cold, Abby's mouth
went dry. The quickened rhythm of her heartbeat vibrated
in her throat.

A branding tool. Something that could burn into
leather…or flesh.

"Robert?" Abby shook her head. There had to be a
mistake. There had to be.

He reached past her, but she didn't move, unable to do
anything but try to make sense of what was happening.

She lifted her gaze to his, ice sliding through her veins
as she pointed to the object. "That's yours?"

He smiled, the practiced, casual smile she'd always
thought telling of his good soul. The smile she now saw
only as the outer manifestation of his inner evil.

Robert shrugged, his eyebrows lifting ever so slightly
as if mocking her. "You want this to end? Here I am."

Disbelief flooded her system, her senses, numbing her
to the shock of what she'd found, of what Robert said.
"You?"

"That's the thing about you, Abby." He stepped close,
reaching into the drawer. "Even now, faced with the reality
of what I am, you still don't see me at all, do you?"

What the hell was he talking about?

A madman. Jack's words bounced through her brain.
You can't force rationality on a madman.

But she had to. Somehow. If she had any hope of sur-
viving.

She'd thought herself so smart, coming to the office like
this, wanting to lure the Christmas Confessor into the
open, never guessing her own partner, her lifelong friend
was harm personified—pure evil hidden behind a designer
shirt and a smiling face.

The pieces of the puzzle came together, n⸍ focus inside her mind's eye.

The year Robert had spent out west after his fa⸍ death. His access to the blog. To the post office box.

To Abby.

To Gina.

To Natalie.

To everyone who had trusted him.

Bile clawed at the back of Abby's throat but she bit it back.

She longed to scream, to fight, to pummel him with her fists, and yet she did nothing. Nothing but process the reality of what her friend had done. The reality of the killer Robert was.

The reality of her fate. Then she thought again of the young police officer, knowing there had been no trip to the doughnut shop.

"What did you do to Officer Jones?"

Robert laughed then, a brief burst of emotionless air. "Let's just say you don't need to worry about him, shall we?

"I'm not entirely evil, Abby. Once I strangle *you,* the good news is, you won't feel a thing." He moved behind her and Abby closed her eyes, her mind frantic to seize upon a way out.

He squeezed her shoulders and Abby shuddered, the move once so familiar and comforting, now nothing but bone-chilling.

"We're going to take a little walk. I want to make sure no one interrupts my Christmas message. My final confession." He gave her shoulders another squeeze. "You, of course."

"I'll get you help, Robert. Don't do this. Please." She barely managed the words before he hit her, knocking her from her knees and onto the carpeted floor.

uld have thought about being attentive when
didn't depend on your actions." He blew out a
gh. "*That* would have been more convincing."

tars swam in her vision and she reached for a stapler
at had fallen, hoping to use it as a weapon. She had to
stall Robert, had to keep him from killing her before Jack
and the others had a chance to race across town.

And Abby had to believe that's what Jack was doing right
now, she had to believe that the picture from Boone Shaw's
belongings would be of Robert, and that Jack would realize
the Christmas Confessor had been in their midst all along.

She had to believe Jack would reach her in time, had to
believe he'd save her. She had to believe he loved her and
would fight for her.

She had to.

She'd live to see Jack again, to feel his arms around her,
holding her, keeping her safe. She'd see Jack again—or
else she'd die trying.

Urgency filled her, renewing her strength. She reached
for the stapler and swung.

Robert's foot connected with her wrist, sending the
stapler flying from her grip and crashing to the floor.

Abby scrambled to her knees, fighting to gain her foot-
ing, to get to her feet, to move away from him. *Away from
the monster she'd known all her life.*

She could think of nothing else.

Robert's foot connected with her back, pinning her to
the floor and crushing her face to the carpet.

But then a noise sounded in the distance. Sirens.
Blessed sirens.

He yanked her to her feet and shoved her toward the
building's back exit.

His fingers cut into Abby's upper arm, his hold so tight
no amount of squirming or fighting loosened his grip.

And as he shoved her through the back ex swirled down from the December sky, spiraling or sidewalk illuminated by holiday lighting and lamppo.

Something glistened in Robert's hand and Abo realized what he'd reached for in the moment they'd moved away from his desk.

The branding tool.

And if she'd had any lingering hope before, reality crashed through her system now.

Robert Walker intended to make her his next victim.

His *Christmas message*.

Then he turned the corner, leading her down a street so familiar she could walk this route with her eyes shut. He was taking her to the one place no one expected her to be, the last place they'd look.

He was taking her home, to her home.

And Abby realized her only hope of survival now was a Christmas miracle…named Jack.

Chapter Seventeen

Something shimmered from beneath Robert Walker's desk.

Abby's cherry-red phone.

They were too late.

Jack's world spun momentarily. She wouldn't have gone anywhere with Robert voluntarily once she put the pieces together, as he had to believe she'd done.

Had Walker knocked the phone out of her hand? Or had she been trying to let Jack know there'd been a struggle.

Walker had her. But where?

"Every car in this city is looking for them, Jack." Hayes's voice sounded from just behind him. "I've got responders less than a minute from Walker's home address."

Less than a minute. If only.

Cold, raw fear sat in the pit of Jack's stomach. "We could already be too late."

"The bus is here, sir," a uniformed officer spoke from beside Hayes, his voice subdued.

They'd found Officer Jones upon their arrival, unconscious, but alive. Based on his recent killing spree, Robert Walker had showed mercy. Either that, or he hadn't had time to finish the job.

Tim Hayes's phone rang at the same moment Jack's

focus landed on a familiar object—the photo c
Vicki and Gina. The photo that had gone missing fr
apartment. Same frame, same faces.

"No one home at Walker's," Hayes said, stepping int
Jack's line of vision, his expression frantic. "Ideas."

Jack nodded, having to appreciate the beauty of what
Walker had done, of where he had taken Abby.

The man was smart, but Jack was smarter.

"I'll get the cars," Hayes said, stepping away.

Jack reached for him, grasping his elbow as he steered
the man toward the door, breaking into a run.

"We won't need cars."

Right now, all they needed was time.

BILE CLAWED AT the back of her throat as Robert shoved
her through her own front door. The one time she needed
Dwayne Franklin's over-attentiveness, the man was long
gone, behind bars and awaiting arraignment.

Robert shoved her against the wall, then bound her
wrists and ankles with plastic ties. She fought against him,
clawing, scratching, trying desperately to escape his hold,
to avoid the ties, but he was stronger, faster, and before she
knew it, she found herself fully bound and shoved to her
knees, facing the wall.

"Nice Christmas lights, by the way."

Robert's voice set her teeth on edge, sent fear sluicing
through her veins.

"You always did like the holidays, didn't you?" he
continued. "I guarantee this year's will be your most
memorable. Not that you'll remember it." He laughed,
the sound cold and emotionless. "The public will remember
though. Even more importantly, they'll remember
me."

Abby twisted to face him, sitting down with her back

...ll. She studied the face she'd thought she knew
...1. "I trusted you."

That was your first mistake." He pursed his lips.

"And my second?"

"Ignoring me."

"I never ignored you, Robert. You were my friend."

His laugh intensified, growing deeper, fuller, yet even colder. "You were never my friend. A friend doesn't call another friend a crank. A friend doesn't call another friend's life work and best photos self-serving attempts at sensationalism." Robert dropped to his knees, speaking so harshly he spit.

The image of Gina's lifeless body splayed across the bed filled Abby's mind. "Why Gina?"

He nodded, grinning. "Why not?"

Dread reached deep inside Abby and pulled tight. He kept talking without prompting, leaning close, so close the warmth of his breath brushed Abby's face, churning her insides.

"I killed Vicki."

Vicki.

Abby shook her head. "She killed herself. I saw her."

"How many women hang themselves, Abby? Grow up."

"Why?"

The word squeaked from Abby's throat, and a shudder ripped through her at the insanity of it all. The murders. The friendships. The lies.

Robert shrugged. "Oldest reason in the book. She figured me out."

Abby frowned, unable to speak or find her voice.

"You're scared." Robert nodded and licked his lips. "I like that. You deserve to be scared, Abby. You deserve to be very scared."

"What did she figure out?"

Abby wasn't sure how she formed the words, ̣
did. She had to if she wanted to survive. The longe
kept Robert talking, the greater the chance she'd get
of this alive. Somehow.

"She found my photos."

His photos. She'd forgotten somewhere along the way
that Robert had once loved photography. Back in school
they'd spend hours—she, Vicki and Gina—mugging for
Robert after school, posing like movie stars for black-and-
white shots that never went much further than the high
school yearbook.

"I thought you gave that up when you went to college."

He shook his head, anger shimmering in his pale eyes.
"Just another example of how little you pay attention."

He straightened, pacing a tight pattern in front of her.
"I know about the phone call, by the way."

"The phone call?" Confusion whirled through Abby's
brain.

"To you." He came to a stop, staring down into Abby's
eyes, no doubt enjoying the position of power. "From Vicki."

Abby's mouth went so dry it might as well have been
stuffed with cotton. No one knew about the call. She'd told
no one.

"I was there, inside her house, waiting to kill her when
she called you."

Abby said nothing.

"I'd just spoken to you, so I knew you were home,"
Robert continued. "I knew you'd ignored her, Abby." He
leaned close again. "That wasn't very nice."

She shook her head. "I know."

"You weren't the only one, you know."

Abby fell silent again, not understanding what he was
trying to say.

"She called Gina, too." He made a clucking sound with

gue. "Gina ignored her, too. So you see, you both
a your friend."

"But you killed her."

"But the guilt ate you alive. Not me." He laughed again,
the sound chilling Abby to her core. "And I let it. Why
not?" He shrugged. "You needed me after that, and you
listened to me."

"You were my friend, Robert." And he had been. Or at
least, so she'd thought. Abby's heart broke a bit more at
the very ideas he'd never known her *friend* at all.

"But then the Web site took off and you forgot about
me again." Robert's eyes narrowed, his features tensed.
"You refuse to take me seriously, even after all this time."

"So you sent the postcard of Melinda."

"And you blew it off."

"You were the one who said it was a crank." Her voice
climbed defensively and she hated herself for showing
weakness.

Robert's smile widened. "I was playing to your stubbornness. I knew you'd take it and run."

"But I didn't." Realization dawned, sobering and heavy.
She was to blame for setting everything into motion. She
hadn't given Robert's confession enough print space.

"No." He shook his head. "You gave me one small blog
and then you set me aside."

"Then Jack showed up."

Robert drew in a deep breath. "Detective Grant.
Emma's picture was always one of my favorites."

"So you sent the second card."

"Went home at lunchtime to paste it together then
tucked it inside your pocket."

"How did you know the mail was in my coat?"

He leaned so close his breath brushed her face and she
cringed. "I, unlike other people I know, pay attention."

Why hadn't Abby paid more attention? Why hadn't she suspected Robert's involvement?

Because he was her friend.

Her heart gave a sharp twist. What a fool she'd been.

"What about Beverly Bricken?"

Robert shook his head and whistled. "I never expected that one."

"You didn't kill her?"

"Oh, I killed her. She was my one slip during all of those years, but her rejection of me was so harsh, she got what she deserved."

"But you didn't send the card?"

"That was Devine."

Abby blinked. "Did you know him?"

Another shake of the head. Another denial. "I knew of him. I was impressed, actually, that he took me seriously enough to copy the card."

"And that worked for you?"

Another nod. "Beautifully. Not so well, however, for Sam Devine."

Abby's brain whirled, racing against time to figure out a way to stop Robert from what he was about to do. She had to keep him talking, no matter how painful his admissions were to hear.

"Did you kill Boone Shaw?"

Abby's wrists and ankles throbbed from being bound so tightly. Sooner or later, her strength and determination weren't going to be enough to hold Robert off any longer.

"Let's just say I eased his suffering." Robert pulled a length of cord from his pocket, the same type of cord he'd left wrapped around Gina's neck. "Anything you want to confess before you die?"

Abby froze, saying nothing.

"Last chance?" He stepped close and unwrapped the

cord, anchoring either end around his hands and pulling the length taut.

"I'm sorry I ever thought you were my friend."

"That, Abby Conroy, makes two of us."

Robert made his move, shoving Abby off balance, then wrapping the cord around her throat.

Abby choked against the pressure, against the pain.

"I always knew what you needed, Abby. Remember that."

Then something shifted in his expression and he eased off on the pressure. He leaned close, his breath brushing Abby's face as he spoke.

"I wonder what it would be like to hear you beg for mercy as I take your body? Your life?"

He lowered one hand to her neck, trailing his fingers down the length of her skin to her throat, dipping his fingertips beneath the edge of her shirt, gently at first, then brusquely, cupping her breast and squeezing hard.

Abby's insides turned liquid and she squirmed beneath him, unable to break his hold.

Robert lowered his mouth to the hollow at her throat, pressing his lips to her flesh, the move anything but sensual, igniting raw fear inside her at the thought of the horrors he was about to inflict.

"Don't do this." She forced the words through her terror. "Please."

"You're not in charge anymore, Abby." He pushed back onto his heels, lowering the cord to the floor, reaching for the waistband of her jeans. "I am. And I'm about to make sure you remember that. Forever."

JACK SNEAKED AROUND the side of Abby's house, following the sidewalk. Light shone from the open door to her living room and voices filtered into the air outside.

Abby's voice. Frightened, but alive.

Relief rushed Jack's senses, but he concentrated maintaining focus, on not letting his heart screw up head.

The rest of the team had positioned themselves near the windows, and backup maneuvered up the same path, a few feet off of Jack's heels.

Jack raised his weapon as he peered around the corner of the steps. Walker squatted over Abby, undoing the waistband of her jeans.

Abby's feet and hands were bound—and the urge to kill Walker swelled in Jack's chest.

He could aim now, pull the trigger, and the man would pay the ultimate price for the lives he'd taken, the families he'd destroyed.

Abby struggled beneath Walker's touch, frantically trying to break free of the madman's hold.

Jack moved with lightning speed, barreling into Walker and slamming the man to the hardwood floor.

Jack pressed the barrel of his gun to the space between Walker's eyes and snarled, fighting the urge to pull the trigger.

"What are you going to do Jack, shoot me?"

Jack pressed the gun so firmly into Walker's skin his flesh turned white from the pressure of the gun's barrel.

He thought about pulling the trigger, thought about ending the life that didn't deserve to live, but he didn't.

He wasn't God, and he wasn't judge and jury.

He was a brother who had lost a sister, a detective who wanted justice, and a man who wanted the woman he loved to live to see the years of life ahead of her.

"It's over, Walker." The voice that spoke was Hayes's.

Walker, Jack and Abby were fully surrounded.

And the Christmas Confessor was finished.

Once and for all.

Epilogue

Abby had thought about shutting down Don't Say a Word. After all, she was alone now. She'd learned her failure to answer Vicki's call had in no way brought about her death—a murder Robert had committed in order to keep his dark secrets just that…secret.

Ironic for someone who had become Abby's partner in the confession site, yet that had been a lie, as well, nothing more than a way for Robert to gain Abby's attention. Though in his mind, it had been Abby who had failed him.

Abby opened her word processing program and stared at the blank screen then at the calendar.

Valentine's Day.

A typical mid-February snowstorm swirled outside her apartment window. She'd been unable to go back to the office. The specter of Natalie and Gina and Robert lurked around every corner.

Yet Abby hadn't been able to shut down the site. She hadn't been able to take away the outlet for those who needed it. She could only pray she'd never receive another postcard like the one that had set her nightmare into motion.

I didn't mean to kill her.

Abby's nightmare had been Jack's salvation, she supposed. He'd gone back to Arizona after Robert's arrest,

after the evidence in Robert's apartment had all b
the fact he'd been the killer all along—the ma
Devine had dubbed the Christmas Confessor.

Amidst the evidence found in Robert's home had bee
a diagram of a location in a remote section of New Mexico
desert where he'd buried a trunk. In that trunk, the local
police had found Melinda Simmons's remains. Her father
had been given closure...at long last.

Abby knew that piece of the puzzle had haunted Jack,
just as she knew the final resolution had provided him
with satisfaction for a job well done.

Yet, he'd shut down that day. At the moment she'd expected his walls to crumble, they'd risen stronger than ever.

And then he'd walked out of her life.

Sam Devine's body had been shipped home for burial
in a family plot in upstate New York. The media barely
gave the reporter's murder notice. Even in death, Devine
hadn't been able to grab the headlines he so craved.

The crime lab had concluded Devine had sent the third
postcard himself, never realizing he'd feed into Robert
Walker's master plan and motivate the man to kill again.
Devine had also never figured he'd become one of
Walker's final victims.

Boone Shaw's body had been located in a vacant lot in
Elkton, Maryland. His widow had flown east to accompany her husband's body home.

While Shaw hadn't been able to expose the true killer's
identity before his death, his actions had set into motion
the chain of events that brought about Robert's downfall.

Robert had killed because he'd felt ignored. Ironically,
his crimes had made him famous. Abby found herself
haunted by the realization notoriety was what the man
she'd once called friend had wanted all along, no matter
the costs in human lives.

had been one point during the days immediately
ng her brush with Robert Walker and death that
y had thought Jack might stay in Delaware, or that he
ght ask her to go back to Arizona with him.

He'd done neither, leaving without so much as a glance
back over his shoulder.

He'd closed the case and put his sister's death behind
him just as easily as he'd put Abby behind him.

They'd spoken a few times since that day. About the
case. About the victims. About closure. Yet, they'd never
spoken about the intimacy they'd shared or about the possibility of a future together, much as Abby had hoped they
might. She still held on to the hope Jack might show up
on her doorstep one day, yet as the weeks passed, she
realized that particular dream was fading fast.

For Abby, Jack Grant had unlocked far more than a
case. He'd unlocked her heart.

What a fool she'd been.

The familiar ache squeezed at her chest, but Abby did
her best to ignore it, focusing instead on the blank screen
and the blog she needed to post.

She'd chosen a single postcard to feature this week. A
grainy black-and-white photo of two small children holding hands, the message simple. Lost love. Missed opportunity. A lifetime of regret suffered in silence, but now
shared for the world to see.

Abby supposed she could have confessed her feelings
for Jack. She could have taken countless actions to let him
know how she felt, and yet she'd done nothing.

She stared at the image on the postcard and thought of
how she'd felt inside the safety of Jack's arms, how she'd
felt to lay bare her soul to the man, how she'd felt to trust
him fully.

She'd thought she'd come home…to Jack.

How wrong she'd been.

Here she sat, ready to share the confession of a stranger with the world, when it was her own secret that needed to be confessed.

She loved Jack. So what was she going to do about it?

A knock sounded at the door to her apartment and she jumped, startled by the sharp noise.

A young couple had moved into Dwayne's apartment. Perhaps they needed to borrow something, or perhaps they had a question about the neighborhood.

Abby drew in a deep breath then pushed away from her desk, away from her computer screen. She was only a few feet from the door when she saw the edge of the postcard slide across the sill.

The room spun and she reached for a chair to steady herself. She dropped to a squatting position, reaching for the card even as she questioned whether or not she should touch it.

What if Robert hadn't been the Confessor after all? What if he hadn't been operating alone? What if the nightmare was about to begin again?

"Cool it, Conroy," she told herself.

Robert would remain behind bars until the day he died.

Abby's fingertips brushed the edge of the card and she pulled it from beneath the door, her pulse quickening when she saw the photograph—a single red rose in a bud vase.

Slowly she turned the card in her hand, recognizing the handwriting instantly.

Can you ever forgive me?

A sob caught in her throat and she pushed to her feet, pulling the door open as quickly as she could.

Jack sat on the top step, his body angled so that he could see her, the shoulders of his leather jacket dusted with snow. A crooked smile pulled at one corner of his mouth.

"I thought you didn't believe in confessions?" she asked, her heart pounding against her ribs.

He pushed to his feet, brushed the snow off of his shoulders and shrugged. "I also said I didn't like snow."

"So you're saying you lied?" she teased.

His grin widened. "I'm saying I changed."

Abby swallowed, unable to believe Jack was real.

He took Abby's hands, his gaze locking on hers. "I was wrong to leave. I'm sorry."

Abby said nothing, holding her breath, not wanting to break the moment's spell.

"I thought you wanted me to fix things, to save you—"

"You did save me, Jack," she interrupted, unable to keep quiet any longer.

But Jack shook his head, his features softening. "You're wrong. You saved me." He squeezed her hands. "I don't want to live without you, Abby. I can't promise that I'll always be able to keep you safe or be the man you deserve, but I'd like to try. If you'll have me."

Abby blinked against the tears welling in her vision, not wanting to spoil the moment by dissolving into a sobbing mess.

"So?" Jack asked. "Do you have an answer for me? Can you forgive me?"

Abby nodded, relief and love rushing through her.

Jack pulled her into his arms and backed her into the apartment.

"Thank goodness," he said, his rich laughter heating Abby from head to toe. "I thought I might freeze out there."

"I think you secretly like the snow," Abby teased.

Jack kissed her slow and deep, then pulled back just enough to whisper, his lips brushing against hers as he spoke. "I hate the snow, but you, Abby Conroy? You, I love."

"I love you, too, Jack."

He kissed her again and this time, Abby broke contact.

"Are you sure you don't want to go back outside? We could make a snowman."

He slid his hands down her arms, kicked the door shut, then steered Abby toward the bedroom. "Now you're just pushing your luck."

"I see." Abby's happy laughter mixed with Jack's as she studied his every feature, thinking she never wanted to be apart from the man again. "Maybe I should just welcome you home then."

And as they crossed the threshold into her bedroom and Jack hoisted her up onto the bed, he reached for the zipper on her sweatshirt drawing it slowly downward as he spoke, this time his voice husky and full of heat.

"Now that—" he pressed a kiss into the hollow of her throat then moved his mouth lower and lower still "—I could get used to."

* * * * *

2 FREE BOOKS
AND A SURPRISE GIFT

We would like to take this opportunity to thank you for reading a Mills & Boon® book by offering you the chance to take TWO more specially selected books from the Intrigue series absolutely FREE! We're also making this offer to introduce you to the benefits of the Mills & Boon® Book Club™—

- **FREE home delivery**
- **FREE gifts and competitions**
- **FREE monthly Newsletter**
- **Exclusive Mills & Boon Book Club offers**
- **Books available before they're in the shops**

Accepting these FREE books and gift places you under no obligation to buy, you may cancel at any time, even after receiving your free books. Simply complete your details below and return the entire page to the address below. You don't even need a stamp!

YES Please send me 2 free Intrigue books and a surprise gift. I understand that unless you hear from me, I will receive 5 superb new stories every month, including two 2-in-1 books priced at £4.99 each and a single book priced at £3.19, postage and packing free. I am under no obligation to purchase any books and may cancel my subscription at any time. The free books and gift will be mine to keep in any case.

Ms/Mrs/Miss/Mr _____ Initials _____

_____

Surname _____
Address _____

_____
_____ Postcode _____

Send this whole page to: Mills & Boon Book Club, Free Book Offer, FREEPOST NAT 10298, Richmond, TW9 1BR